THE GREEN-EYED QUEEN

MORGAN TEAL

Cover and illustrations by Morgan Teal.

Made with human intelligence.

CONTENTS

PRONUNCIATION GUIDE

COUNTRIES

Calgham - KAL-gum

Norhagan - NOR-hay-gan

Byonea - bYO-nyuh

PROLOGUE

Bomin - BO-men

Wondi - WAHN-dee

Rikr - RYE-kur

NORHAGAN

Vinya - VIN-yah

Jae - Jay

Alton - AL-tin

Miho - me-HO

Kuro - KU-row

BYONEA

Jinhee - JIN-hee

Sooni - SOO-nee

Zhan - ʒAHN (ʒ is the *zh* sound in vision, leisure, version)

Wonho - WAHN-ho

Joona - JOO-nuh

Yuwon - YOU-wahn

Woobin - OO-bin

Jun - JOON

Hyosung - hYO-sung

Alastor - AL-a-stir

Daeya - DAY-uh
Nagne - na-GUH-nay
<u>CALGHAM</u>
Moren - MORE-in

PROLOGUE

The blade pressed against King Bomin's throat trembled in Wondi's grip, and while King Bomin was not afraid of dying, he feared what would happen to his country, Calgham. They would lose more than territory by the end of the day; control would be traded for chaos under an inexperienced new king. The men who had King Bomin on his knees would use that to their advantage.

He had done his best to train the boy, but in all twenty-two years of his life, his foolish son only followed the whims of his heart. He chased after every pretty thing that caught his attention—whether reciprocated or not.

Look where his actions got them.

His son condemned Calgham the moment he ran into the throne room, face wet with tears and wails filled with '*murder*'. Bomin and his men spent weeks attempting to regain control, trying to atone for his son's failures, to no avail. Disappointment sat heavy in Bomin's chest. The boy would deal with the consequences of his own actions, resulting in a better lesson than Bomin could ever give.

One last, futile attempt at reconciliation on his son's behalf amidst the war turned sour, and Wondi's side of the battlefield transformed into an execution ground.

Bomin's son stood in terror across the field, surrounded by their army and trembling in his armor. A white flag flapped in the wind above him.

Wondi's hand shook—in vehemence and anticipation—causing blood to trickle down to the leathers strapped across Bomin's chest. This man who had stood by Bomin's side for decades knew what needed to be done... The single word that Bomin's son cried out in the throne room had completely shattered everything the men had worked toward, along with their friendship.

Murder.

This war would only end when the appropriate blood had spilled. Every soul who stood on the bloody field knew a trade was necessary: a life for a life.

Norhagan's king stepped to Wondi's side.

"Do it," King Rikr grunted, his words as rough as his appearance.

Wondi's breaths caught on the back of Bomin's sweaty neck.

"We surrender!" Bomin's son cried out, the crack in his voice carried away by the wind.

But it was not his choice to make.

Not yet.

"Do it, *now*," Rikr repeated. "Breaking the boy will end the war, and you have my word that the treaty between Norhagan and Byonea will be signed."

King Bomin did not move. He only watched his son raise the white flag higher, waving it about as if the Norhagan King and Byonea's soon-to-be leader had not seen it.

Wondi's breaths shortened; he readjusted his fingers on the hilt of the knife, gripping it tighter.

King Bomin set his jaw; the last thing he heard was his son's scream across the battlefield.

I
BYONEA BOUND
265 YEARS LATER

The dew-covered grass glistened as birds chirped in nearby trees, singing their sweet tunes from their nests to wake this side of the world.

Citizens in Asper took the days as they came—slow. They savored every moment, turning acre upon acre of the expansive countryside into farmland, far from the hustle of the larger, bustling cities in Norhagan.

Vinya sat on a sprawled quilt, soaking in every detail of the sunrise: the bright fresh growth on trees, the wildflowers dappled across the hillsides, and the cows gathered at the gate, ready for their morning feed. A rooster stood atop the barn, flapping his wings as he crowed.

A breeze made Nutmeg, Vinya's cat, nestle deeper in her crossed legs. He had followed Vinya up the hilltop, unwilling to lose sight of her. It was as if he knew she would be leaving soon for her annual visit with her grandmother in Byonea.

Nutmeg heaved a sigh.

Vinya chuckled, imagining her father's grumbles when Nutmeg inevitably tried to squeeze between her parents in bed during her month-long absence.

She scooped up the cat and quilt, and made the trek back to her house, pausing only to watch a large bird of prey fly in the distance.

The smell of fresh rolls and stew overtook her as she opened the back door to their home—her mother had just set the table for breakfast. Nutmeg jumped out of Vinya's arms and wound between her mother's legs, waving his fluffy tail and meowing with impatience. Vinya's mother stooped to give him a scratch behind the ears, but he ducked around it, his attention on the small platter of beef and veggies in her other hand. Her mother shook her head and placed the cat's breakfast on the floor near the door beside Vinya's bags. Vinya sat at the worn wooden table and idly stirred her soup as she watched Nutmeg gobble his food down.

Her father, having finished his morning tasks with the livestock and saddling the horses for their early morning journey, stepped through the back door and stomped the dirt off his boots.

"I don't think that cat chews at all," he grunted, scratching the scruff of his short beard.

Vinya's mother smiled, the corners of her eyes crinkling. "He reminds me of you."

Her father chuckled and gave her a kiss, then planted one on top of Vinya's head before washing his hands and sitting at the table himself across from her.

Vinya ran through the list of things she'd packed the night before. Letters from her parents, a small wooden hawk she had carved as a gift, clothes, quill and journal, and medicines she knew Gran would never use. The woman relied on nature to heal her aches and pains, though she had difficulty getting around the gardens last year. Vinya would have to sweet-talk the stubborn woman into taking the medicines.

Vinya dipped the roll into her stew, soaking up the vegetable broth. The warmth of the food hitting her belly eased some of her nerves. She finished her broth-soaked roll, closing her eyes as she savored the last bite.

"Who was hired this year to fill in for me on the farm?" she asked.

Her father shifted in his seat, "Alton. He did an excellent job last year, so your mother and I decided to bring him back this year."

"I'm sure this has nothing to do with him being unmarried?" Vinya lifted the bowl and finished the remaining broth.

Alton met her parents several years prior when his flock of sheep had gotten out, traveling miles to her family's own pastures. With one look at his broad shoulders and smile, her mother was determined to see him marry Vinya.

Her mother clicked her tongue. "He's a nice man, strong enough to keep up with your father."

Vinya met her father's eyes across the table, he sat straighter and puffed out his chest, making her huff a laugh. She stood, pushing up her linen sleeves to help her mother with the dishes.

"It's just... Alton. He cannot keep the schedule straight." She turned the bowl over to scrub the bottom. "Plus, last year, if you remember, you sent him to pick up a cow you purchased, and he brought back the wrong one."

"Hm." Her mother replied as she cleaned off the silverware.

Vinya rinsed the bowl and set it to the side. "A *cow*."

Nutmeg jumped on the counter and batted at the soapy water in the sink. Her mother scooped him up and placed him back on the floor, flicking water at the cat to make him run out of the kitchen. "He is kind and good. There aren't many eligible men in Asper."

"That aren't seventy-year-old widowers," Vinya mumbled, earning a laugh from her father. "If Alton can't take proper care of our animals, how can I expect him to take care of me?"

Her mother's lips tightened. She placed the last of the dishes in front of Vinya and crossed the kitchen to stand by her father.

"And I don't need someone to take care of me," Vinya added. "I do a good job of it myself. I have no desire for marriage and no desire to be tied down or whisked away to who-knows-where."

She winced. Her father had given up his life in Byonea to marry her mother. But she was not her father, and she would not leave her childhood home for someone she hardly knew—let alone someone unreliable, like Alton.

She dried and put the last of the dishes away and turned to her parents. Her father was giving a pointed look with raised brows at her mother. They apparently had this same conversation amongst themselves, with her father coming to the same conclusion.

"This family is determined to see me wed. Even Gran mentioned a man for me in her last letter." Vinya pulled the sleeves of her blouse back down to her wrists, and jabbed her finger at each of them, adding, "I'll be able to solely focus on taking care of the two of you when you're hobbling around the farm."

Her father raised an eyebrow at her. "You'll be taking care of us, *and* the farm?"

Vinya shrugged. "Maybe I'll hire Alton if he can get his act together by then."

Her father's booming laugh rattled the walls of their home. Her mother smiled and shook her head.

The sight of them made Vinya's heart ache. She would be without their love for the next few weeks. She didn't desire a man when their love filled her heart. But the yearly trip to Gran's across the water could not wait any longer.

Her father's thoughts traveled there as well; his face fell as his eyes landed on her bags by the door. Nutmeg had made his way back into the kitchen and rubbed his face on the corner of her smaller pack. The leather crinkled under his pressure, but the cat continued.

When she was little, she and her parents would take the trip together. By the time Vinya was thirteen, they added a new branch of livestock which required more of their time. Her parents stayed in Asper to oversee the farm, sending their love and letters to Gran through Vinya, who had made the journey on her own for just over a decade.

Her father crossed the room and picked up Vinya's bags. "We'd better get going. Gran will be disappointed if you miss the ship."

Vinya nodded, and he took her bags to the horses outside.

She fidgeted with the hem of her sleeve as she looked at her father's bowl on the table, still half-full with soup. The bowl caught her mother's eye as well, and a crease grew between her brows.

She gave Vinya a sad smile. "He misses his mother."

"And I'll miss you," Vinya replied. She crossed the room and wrapped her arms around her mother, squeezing tightly as she buried her face in her mother's hair.

"A month will fly by, Vinya. You'll be back home in the blink of an eye."

Vinya nodded a second time. She slid out of her mother's arms and knelt to plant a kiss on the fluffy ginger cat before heading out the door after her father.

Vinya spent the first two days at sea in her room, emerging only at breakfast and dinner to eat and watch small islands drift in and out of view. She wrote in her journal to pass the time, running the feather quill's edge along her cheek, and often checked and double-checked that all the medicines were secure in her bags.

On the third and final day of the voyage, she spent the morning on deck. The rolling hills of Norhagan's countryside, where every homestead was separated by expansive acreage and hours of walking, were far behind her. She now faced the high cliffs and low valleys of Byonea's home-packed villages. But, a piece of her heart felt at home here.

The language and appearance of the people also differed. The round, bright colored eyes and fair hair of her home was traded for dark, almond-shaped eyes and sleek, onyx hair. Vinya was often told she was a beautiful mixture of the two countries. Her father was half Byonean, and she inherited emerald-colored eyes from her mother.

Vinya slipped seamlessly between the two languages as well. *One must be fluent in the language of the motherland*, Gran had advised in Norhagan when she was young. From then on, she only spoke in the *motherland* tongue. Vinya took to the language like it was hers from the beginning.

She stood near the bow at the dew-slick rail, watching Byonea's foggy coastline in the distance. Her stomach ached from skipping the stale bread and cheese offered by the crew for breakfast. Her belly would soon be filled with Gran's homemade food. She would spend the next few weeks with a full stomach, laughing and helping with whatever craft or garden her grandmother was working on at the time.

Down the rail, Vinya noticed another young woman who eyed the coast of Byonea. She leaned against the rail, tapping a foot on the deck and biting one of her nails. Her chestnut hair whipped around her face in the ocean wind.

The woman didn't bother moving them, she instead focused on biting her nails down to the quick. Her brows knit together, and she moved her hand to her stomach.

"It should only be a few more hours before we reach shore," Vinya said, keeping a careful hand on the rail as she approached the woman. "There's a market near the docks, they have wonderful loaves that may help your stomach."

The woman turned to fully face Vinya, and Vinya's brows rose. The woman's wild unbound hair could do nothing to hide her stunning beauty. Her sharp, angular eyes—the same shade of green as Vinya's—hinted at her ancestry.

The stranger seemed to come to the same conclusion, and while the woman looked to be the same age as Vinya, there was something in her assessing gaze that made Vinya feel years younger.

The wind pulled some of Vinya's onyx hair out of the loose bun she had styled this morning, and she tucked it behind her ear.

The woman removed her hand from her stomach and almost returned it to her mouth but set it on the rail instead. She still didn't bother to tame her own wild locks. "Yinuo?"

It was the name many men in Norhagan took for themselves after the Great War between Byonea and Calgham. Their descendants carried the name and a physical mixture of Byonean and Norhagan features—a reminder of unity that would last a lifetime.

"Yes, my grandfather was a general from Norhagan. He caught my grandmother's attention during a summer trip." Vinya smiled, thinking of the stories she had heard as a child.

The wind whipped around them; the billowing fabric of Vinya's pants snapped at her legs. The woman still refused to calm the wild tendrils of her hair.

The woman picked at her fingernails. "My ancestors fought in the Great War."

"Did you grow up in Norhagan as well?" Vinya pried.

The woman nodded, but did not seem eager to give any more information.

Vinya continued, "What part of Norhagan are you from? My parents and I live on a farm in Asper. We work with livestock, mainly. Do you own any animals?"

The woman remained silent, watching the approaching shore with furrowed brows.

Vinya went on, "One of my favorite animals was an injured hawk. I found it in the middle of winter a decade ago. It had a horribly broken wing, and my parents and I couldn't tell when it ate its last meal."

She closed her eyes, remembering how calm the cream and brown bird had been. "I tended to and fed it every day until it healed. When it took flight for the last time, it aimed east. Day after day I would watch the horizon, hoping it would return, but deep down I knew it had gone home. It's silly, but every year

I come here, I still keep an eye out for it. One of the hawk's feathers had fallen out with its initial injury and never grew back. We kept the feather and turned it into a quill."

Vinya pulled the quill out of her pack and held it up for the woman to see, hoping the she would respond with a tale of her own.

The *tick, tick, tick* of the nail-biting was her only reply.

Vinya twirled the quill between her fingers before returning it to her bag, unwilling to risk losing it over the side of the ship.

They watched Byonea grow closer in silence for a while. The woman seemed content with the waves lapping against the side of the ship being the only sound.

Vinya twisted her mouth to the side. "It's an unwritten rule that my feet hit the floor of my Gran's house this time every year. I spend a month cooking and crafting, repairing what's broken, helping her when she needs it—not that she would ever admit it."

That pulled a smile from the seemingly apathetic woman.

"At the end of the month, we throw a celebration for my birthday. Even though it's just the two of us, we eat and drink and laugh our way through the night, and the following morning I get on this ship to go back home. This year will be my twenty-fifth. Age was slowing Gran down last year, though, so I'm anxious to get to her."

She turned to the woman again. "Where is your journey taking you?"

The woman pulled her fingernail from her mouth, looked a shade of green, and rubbed her stomach again. "Ungeong."

Vinya's own stomach rumbled—fresh food couldn't come quick enough. "Ungeong is near Calgham's border, right? My Gran's village, Taejim, is on the way there. We could travel together until then?"

The woman turned to face Vinya; brows further furrowed. Something had this woman on edge and mistrusting of other people.

Vinya went on, "Traveling the last leg alone has always been the worst part. I passed men from Norhagan's army on my way to the deck this morning, they whispered of Calgham men spotted at some borders of Byonea. I think it would be wiser—and safer—to travel together." She patted her stomach. "We can pick up snacks for the trip at the market. Our bodies will thank us for not eating the hard bread and cheese they call *breakfast* on this ship."

A passing crew member clicked his tongue at her, which made the woman huff a gentle laugh.

She extended her hand to the woman and gave her a small smile. "I'm Vinya. I promise to be a wonderful travel companion and will not force you to talk if you do not want to."

Her face relaxing, she took Vinya's hand and replied, "I am Miho."

Miho spent the next few hours in her cabin—resting before the last leg of her journey, while Vinya opted to remain on deck. The women had agreed to meet in front of a well-known market stall that sold hand carved wooden figurines before continuing on the road together.

It was midday when they docked. Vinya gathered her packs and disembarked at the port village. Passengers climbed on and off the ship, crates of goods were unloaded and distributed throughout the town, and new crates were loaded and packed on the ship to travel back to Norhagan. It was a well-oiled machine of trade between the two countries.

Vinya made her way down the ramp, engulfed by the sights and sounds of the bustling market. The smell of salt and fish hung in the air close to the water, and faded with each step that she took into the harbor town. Smiles greeted her from behind each stall she passed as she made her way to the appointed stall to meet Miho.

Not many children were seen in this town. It was filled with bargains, buyers, and travelers eager to get home—or away from home.

The workers called out, holding their wares towards the citizens of Norhagan, enticing them to *buy. One of a kind. These platters are stronger than any other. This ribbon brings out the blush in your cheeks. This blush is a great contrast to our eyes.* Oh, *your eyes!* It was the one comment Vinya heard daily when visiting Byonea. She had to slip out of a gathering crowd when the stall workers called their friends over to gaze into her emerald eyes.

Vinya spotted the cascade of chestnut hair down the road and quickened her steps. Miho kept her own gaze on the array of wares set on the tables, not quite looking into the workers eyes. Miho picked up a wooden statue, turning it over to admire the work.

There was a commotion behind Vinya as she made her way to the stall, a lull in the noises of the market, low gruff voices, and heavy footfalls.

Miho glanced her way and returned the wave Vinya gave, but stiffened. Her hand paused mid-air—eyes widening.

Vinya slowed to a stop and twisted around. A group of royal guards were going booth to booth, leaning in to ask questions. They arrived at the booth and crowd Vinya had just slipped away from, the guard leaned in to speak with the worker. The older woman at the stall inclined her head, pointing in the direction of Vinya. Pointed *to* Vinya.

Unease panged through Vinya's chest as the guard locked eyes with her. He straightened, nodded his thanks to the woman at the booth, and motioned for the other guards to follow him. Vinya gripped the handle of her pack tighter as they advanced—a few of his fellow guards branched off to her left and right.

The questioning guard pulled a scroll from his belt, opening it without taking his eyes from her. "Vinya Yinuo?"

Vinya blinked, "Yes?"

The guard glanced at the scroll. "Granddaughter of Antony and Hae Yinuo, child of Norhagan, twenty-four years of age?"

"Yes." Vinya repeated, taking a cautionary step back.

The guard noted the movement. He secured the scroll in his belt and held out his hand. "Travel papers?"

Not wanting to cause unnecessary trouble, Vinya set down her pack and fished them out. He opened them, checked and double checked that she was who she claimed to be.

Vinya reached for her paperwork when he was done. "Is there something I can help you with?"

Instead of returning them, the guard pocketed her papers. "We received word that you were on this ship and ask that you come with us, by order of His Majesty King Wonho."

A crowd gathered around them, whispers growing wild at the mention of the King. The guard turned to the onlookers, and they retreated a few steps under his stare.

Vinya took a half step back, raising a defensive hand.

"Whatever is going on, I am not sure that I have a part in it. I'm traveling with a new friend, I'm on my way to my grandmother's house—" She spun around to catch Miho's attention, but the guards and a large wooden box blocked her view.

A palanquin had been brought, its door open and waiting. For Vinya to enter, she realized. Men stood in the front and back to carry her to the Grand Palace, whether she wanted to or not. It didn't look like a cell—with its carvings and paintings, it was much too elegant for a prisoner, but something about it made Vinya uneasy.

Sweat beaded beneath her linen blouse. She twisted back towards the guard. "My grandmother will have a fit if I'm late."

The guard only motioned toward the palanquin.

"There is no need for this," Vinya said as she copied the guard's movement. "I'm capable of walking."

The guard took a deep breath, arm still outstretched, while his other hand rested on the hilt of his sword. He was only a civil servant following direct orders from the King of Byonea. It seemed like he usually had *his* orders followed as well.

She chewed on the inside of her lip. If she wanted her papers back, she would have to go along with the guards. Whatever this was would have to be handled quickly.

Vinya climbed into the palanquin, unable to spot Miho in the crowd as they closed the door and carried her off.

2

The Treaty of Trust

Vinya sat in the enclosed palanquin, one pack in her lap and the other crammed into the small space near her feet, as guards escorted her to the palace. Through the intricately carved windows, she could see people staring through the cracks. The prying eyes wondered who this person was that had been surrounded soon after she stepped foot on land.

The men were part of the palace guards. They dressed in the traditional black robes—the neck and sleeves lined with red. The red and black tassels dangling from the hilt of their swords and off their wide-brimmed hats swayed with each step.

The stoic guard who initially stopped her stayed to the right of the palanquin with unfaltering steps. His hand never left his sword, and his eyes never stopped moving, regularly scanning their surroundings. The man did not speak during the hours they traveled, but the other guards often glanced at him. It was clear he was in charge of this escort.

By the time they reached the palace, Vinya's body was aching from sitting in the small space for so long.

The cream-colored palace walls were tall—designs carved into the stones along the top. The entrance to the outer courtyard was taller than the rest, but that was not the only thing that set it apart. Two massive statues guarded the gate—the feathered Byonean dragons, carved from white stone with wings spread wide. The one on the right looked down, its gaping maw angled toward any impostor that may attempt to slip through the gates. The one on the left looked out to the surrounding city and the skies beyond, its face was stern.

The latter dragon reminded Vinya of the guard who had escorted her here, who was now speaking with the gatekeeper. The gatekeeper gave instructions to open the gate. Vinya's guard returned to the side of the palanquin, nodding to direct his men forward.

Vinya's entourage followed a wide stone pathway through the middle of a spacious courtyard. Some workers stopped their work and stepped off onto the flattened dirt floor to let them pass. Other workers gathered in small groups, whispering to each other. Some of them outright followed the palanquin, trying to catch a glimpse of whoever was inside before they went through another gate to the inner courtyard.

The inner courtyard was smaller, its floor covered in stones. Guards patrolled along the walls of the courtyard, dutifully staying on task, while even more workers were scattered about the area. They paused as well to watch them pass, some with questioning or furrowed brows. Vinya sat back to avoid their stares; it was obvious this was not an occurrence that happened often.

They entered the innermost court, the gate with numerous guards, and the men carrying the palanquin turned, setting it down so that when the door opened, she faced the courtyard.

Vinya resisted the urge to stretch as she stepped out and dipped her head in greeting to the handful of women in front of her. They stood in a line, some wearing maroon and emerald robes, a few wearing pink and jade robes. Every woman had their hair pulled back into low buns. No braids or jewelry adorned their heads. These were the ladies-in-waiting for the royal palace, then.

The women returned the greeting. A young girl, no older than fifteen, shifted from foot to foot. A middle-aged woman beside her reached out to touch the young girl's arm, a reminder to stay still.

Vinya's guard approached the older woman in the middle. As they spoke in hushed tones, Vinya took the opportunity to gather her surroundings.

This courtyard was the smallest of all, though it could easily hold a few hundred men. A covered walkway hugged the surrounding wall, a few smaller gates to the left and right led to the buildings that loomed over them. Trees stretched above the wall on the opposite side, and buds were on the verge of blooming along each branch. Though the courtyard was barren, the woodwork that covered the underpart of the walkway was intricate. Each piece was meticulously painted an array of colors. Behind the ladies-in-waiting, the innermost courtyard held the Grand Palace.

Unmoving guards stood at the top and bottom of the stairs leading to the entrance, their eyes trained on Vinya. A few guards walked the length of the palace behind great pillars, Vinya surveyed the colorful pillars that stretched to the roof. The black tiles of the roof mimicked the deepest sea, splaying out at the corners of the building. At the corners were small statues of the dragons standing on hind legs.

A door opened on the third level of the palace. From the shadows, a man in sky blue robes emerged—his eyes locked with her own. He stepped forward and rested his forearms on the rail of the balcony, a smile playing at his mouth. His large eyes and soft features gave him a youthful appearance. When Vinya did not look away, he smiled fully for her.

The man was more than handsome, he was beautiful, but something in his stare made Vinya's skin prickle.

She broke his gaze and turned to the women in front of her, fidgeting with the hem of her sleeve. None of the people in this courtyard saw the man; or they deliberately paid him no attention. The guard and the older woman came to her side, and the woman bowed her head again.

"I am Jinhee, head lady-in-waiting. My ladies and I will accompany you to the living quarters to freshen up."

Vinya tipped her head towards the guard. "Will he be joining us?"

The guard stood unmoving, but she felt his eyes slide to her.

The head lady-in-waiting smiled. "Zhan has been put in charge of your safety and will be near at all times, but guards do not enter the women's rooms unless necessary. He will stand outside of the door."

The guard, Zhan, remained silent.

Jinhee turned, calling the fidgeting girl to her side. "This is Sooni. She is our newly appointed lady-in-waiting and will serve you well, though we found her tongue to slip from time to time." She gave a pointed look at the girl, who stepped forward and took the bags from Vinya. "You must let me know if she gives you any trouble."

Vinya did not know how much trouble the young girl would be in the brief time she planned to be here before continuing to her grandmother's house. She smiled at Sooni, and decided she'd allow the girl have free rein for the duration of her visit.

"I will be instructing Sooni as this is her first official full-time position and will check in from time to time." Jinhee stepped to the side and motioned behind her towards the living quarters, an invitation to follow.

As they passed the palace to the living quarters beyond, Vinya glanced upward through her lashes. The man still smiled down at her. She felt his gaze follow her until the doors closed behind them and she was out of sight.

Vinya ran her fingers over the silky fabric of her robes as she knelt.

The ladies-in-waiting had bathed her, getting rid of every piece of dirt from the travels. Vinya's skin was a shade pink from the scrubbing. Layer upon colorful layer of skirts were placed over her head, a thick band of ribbon wrapped around her waist, and a short jacket was layered on top. They braided her hair, rolling it into a bun and securing it in place with a silver hairpin. The end of the pin formed a dragon's head; its jaws gently cradled a pearl in its mouth.

In some countries, women only pulled their hair into a bun when they wed. In others, people of any class could adorn their hair with a pin. But in Byonea, only the royals wore higher, more elaborate hairstyles—the bun held in place with a pin.

The one in Vinya's hair was a heavy nuisance; she was no royal.

The women must have been instructed not to speak, as Vinya's questions went unanswered. As they worked, she pleaded with them to understand that she must not be who they thought she was.

Now here she was, kneeling on the polished wooden floor at the foot of the steps. On the dais before her were five thrones, the center throne sat upon a platform a foot higher than the rest. Byonea's dragon emblem was painted in gold on the throne's dark wood, a crimson cushion in its seat. The message was clear: here sits the King, omniscient and omnipotent. It also served as a warning to not cross Byonea. A grand staircase rose behind the thrones and split left and right, leading to a second level high above them all. The center of the steps were painted red as a reminder of the blood that was spilled in order to have Byonean rule.

Surrounded by women and guards, Zhan on one side with Sooni off to the side behind her, they waited for the king.

Six lines of men trickled in from doors in the far corners of the throne room. The colors of their robes, with emblems and ranks to differentiate between them, showed which of the six ministries of Byonea they belonged to—Personnel, Taxation, Rites, Military Affairs, Punishments, and Public Works. They conversed amongst themselves as they took up their appointed spots on the ornate rugs on either side of Vinya.

Over one hundred people were in the massive throne room, all for her. Even though she kept her eyes to the ground, she sensed their stares and scrutiny.

It had been hours since they had arrived at the palace. Gran must be pacing her front lawn by now, looking for her. Waiting for her. She curled her hands into fists, crinkling the fabric of her skirts. The Palace was wasting her time.

Pastel robes and skirts lined the wall to the left. They were King Wonho's many sons and daughters through concubines: The Shade Princes and Shade Princesses. Half royals. Though they would never wear a crown, never have the Byonean emblem stitched on their clothes and never hold any special place in the official royal family, they were still deemed important. The power of the King was on display in the sheer number of children he sired.

Vinya had counted fifteen when a familiar sky-blue robe shifted. The beautiful man from the balcony stood in the middle of the group. He certainly didn't look like the strongest, nor was he the tallest—but the air around him, the way he held himself, and how haughtily unbothered he was by the surrounding situation, screamed that he was the oldest.

Vinya had heard whispers about the King's first son, Shade Prince Hyosung. He was born less than a year before the Crown Prince. He owned the finest horses, dressed in the richest silks, and it was said a different woman accompanied him every week to extravagant parties paid for by his own coin. Not a hair was out of place, he had not a wrinkle in his robe, and no blemish graced his smooth face.

Servants carrying trays of drinks made their way around the outskirts of the throne room, offering some to those in attendance who stood against the walls. Hyosung lifted a cynical eyebrow when a servant raised the tray towards him, turning his attention back to Vinya instead of taking the drink.

She could still feel the itch of his stare when she turned to plead yet again with the women and guards, but a man in bright crimson robes emerged from a door under the stairs, his steps unhurried. All attention shifted to him. The Byonean emblem stitched in gold spread across the front of his robes, his grey beard cut so that it did not cover the symbol. King Wonho.

Everyone in the room dropped to their knees, touching their foreheads on the floor.

Vinya imitated the movement of those around her. Though she had been visiting the country her entire life and was taught about the royal family by her Gran, she'd never once been in their presence, not even from afar. She'd never had an opportunity or reason. There was an annual spring festival that King Wonho attended in Kima, a town near Taejim, but the date varied from year to year and never occurred during her visits.

When the men and women rose, she returned to the submissive kneel. This meeting was about her and her alone—following the rules would allow her to leave sooner.

Vinya kept her gaze low. At the edge of her vision, many colored robes filled the thrones, save for one. The royal family had trickled in behind the king, sitting to his left and right.

"Rise."

Vinya stood, smoothing the creases she caused in her skirt before lifting her eyes.

The voice had not come from the king, whose jagged golden crown sat tilted on his head, but from the man standing beside him. His robes were cream with an ebony neckline, belt, and a short-brimmed hat. The emblem of a tiger's face was stitched below the shoulder on each arm—he was the head adviser to the king.

Zhan dipped his head before approaching the thrones and passed the scroll and her travel papers to the adviser. He returned to Vinya.

The adviser opened both. Minutes went by as the man scanned the documents, glancing over the paper at Vinya now and then with a crease between his brow and a twitch of his nose, checking that everything was in order.

The royal family did not stir, despite the shifting and curious whispers around the room.

An older woman sat to the king's right. Her robes were adorned with the golden emblem, and a matching gold and jade hairpin embellished the braids piled atop her head. This was Queen, Joona, with a fraction of her famed fortune on display. Vinya caught the smallest sigh of impatience as the Queen looked sidelong at the adviser.

The Princess Jun, to the Queen's right, had kind eyes and a gentle smile that left Vinya feeling at ease. Her robes were nearly identical to Vinya's attire. Unlike Vinya's, though, Jun's robes suited her serene aura.

Vinya returned the smile, smoothing out her skirts once more, but it faded as she looked to the dais' opposite end.

The Crown Prince Yuwon kept his gaze on the wall ahead of him. Though his face retained a timeless, boyish quality, there was a hardness in his jaw that spoke of someone who had learned too much about the world's burdens too soon. He was known to be a reclusive prince, spending most of his time in his rooms, with the scholars, or training with the guard. He had rarely made appearances outside of the palace walls in previous years.

Vinya shifted her attention to the empty throne at the end, which should be occupied by the second in line to the throne, Prince Woobin, but his absence left the dais looking off-kilter. It was said by citizens that he was his brother's extreme opposite. The upbeat, social butterfly was often rumored to be the Queen's favorite child.

Finally, the man re-rolled the scroll with a sigh and leveled her with a stare. "Vinya Yinuo."

"Yes," she answered. The grand room soaked up her voice, making it sound smaller than intended.

The man motioned to the wall behind him. "Are you aware of what this is?"

High above the throne, on the wall where the stairs split in two, was the Treaty of Trust, signed in blood by both the Byonean and Norhagan leaders after the Great War ended. It laid out the terms of the alliance and served as a reminder of what will happen to those who dare to overthrow the newer, smaller country of Byonea.

Vinya nodded.

The adviser raised a brow. "Are you also aware of the Calgham threat in the North?"

She nodded again. "I'd heard men talking on the ship."

The man folded his hands in front of him. Another twitch of his nose. "Our spies in Calgham have confirmed that it is not just whispers in the wind, but an absolute truth. The Emerald King Moren openly speaks of this in his Calgham court. Due to this threat, and on behalf of His Majesty King Wonho of Byonea, we are not only calling upon the aid of King Kuro and his Norhagan army once more—but also the promise of a blood tie."

Murmurs rang about the room.

"May I ask, what role do I carry in all of this?"

"To marry the Crown Prince, of course," the adviser replied.

Vinya blinked.

The Crown Prince Yuwon did not look in her direction. Under his midnight blue sleeves, Vinya caught a hint of white knuckles as his fingers curled in carefully clenched fists.

Vinya huffed a laugh. "Surely this is a mistake. I've not come to *marry* anyone. I promise I'm not the person you're looking for, this is my yearly trip to—"

"*You dare question the King?*" he yelled.

She winced. Vinya never once had a man raise his voice at her; her father certainly never yelled. Words failed her as tears pricked the corners of her eyes. With everyone now looking at her, she wished she could shrink into the floor.

The man composed himself, working his jaw as he opened the scroll once more. "Vinya Yinuo, daughter of Jae and Sarah Yinuo, granddaughter of the late Antony and Hae Yinuo of Byonea, twenty-four years of age, child of Norhagan. I am not *mistaken*, child. You are exactly who we need to further bond our great countries together. As a scion of both Norhagan and Byonea, you will obey your king and remain in the Palace."

Vinya kept her head down; she tried to keep her voice from shaking. "I apologize, but you are mistaken once again. Only my grandfather has passed. My grandmother—"

"Your grandmother." He interrupted a second time, extending the scroll and her travel papers. Zhan approached the thrones to retrieve it as the man continued. "Hae Yinuo was found deceased in her home in Taejim by her neighbor last week."

Zhan halted on the steps of the dais, hand on the scroll. A small inhale came from Sooni.

The adviser slowly turned his attention to the guard. A silent command. Zhan collected himself and the papers, and returned to Vinya's side once more.

Her heart had turned to stone and dropped into an endless pit in her stomach. Days. She had missed her Gran by mere days. The letter of her death would arrive home soon, if a messenger raven or hawk had not already gotten there while she was traveling.

Two sets of gentle hands held her arms as she slipped to her knees. The adviser spoke on, but she barely heard his words. Something about her guard, ladies-in-waiting, descendant of a great king, strength of the countries, and a message he sent to her parents.

Muted agreements and cheers rang around the room.

Nothing. His words meant nothing to her. A piece of her had been carved out, leaving a hollow ache in her chest.

Jinhee was patting her back, but it did not soothe. Sooni passed her a cloth to wipe her eyes, but she did not take it. The ladies-in-waiting now waited on her. *They* were now *hers.*

Vinya curled over her knees as her stomach twisted further. It may have looked like a submissive bow from the outside, but there was no acceptance of the adviser's proclamation in the movement.

Tears streamed down her face as she lifted her head. The adviser helped the King stand. The officials, guards, and women in the room bowed deeply once more as the King exited with the Queen and Princess following behind.

The Crown Prince Yuwon was the last to stand.

She could plead with him, convince him that there was a mistake, if only he would look her way. If only her throat had not closed.

He did not look in her direction. He turned—jaw clenched—and followed his family.

The officials, Shade Princes, and Shade Princesses went their own way. Only one sky-blue robe lingered to her far left before stepping out of sight.

Their work was finished, and Vinya was left with her ladies-in-waiting.

Left in Byonea without her Gran.

Left to marry the Crown Prince.

3

A Flutter in the Night

Vinya walked back to the women's quarters in a daze. Zhan was their silent escort a few steps behind, a lantern in one hand while his other rested on the hilt of his sword. Sooni kept an arm linked through Vinya's, guiding the way back and complaining under her breath the entire time.

"I can't stand that man. Only the King puts up with Alastor—the king's adviser. People say he's *so* good at his job though, negotiating impossible trade deals between His Majesty and other countries. I think it's the only reason he hasn't been run through with a sword by any of us."

"Sooni," Jinhee scolded.

Sooni's mouth twisted into a pout as she peered around Vinya to her superior, lowering her voice even more as she continued.

"You know he's tactless when it comes to other people's emotions. The man only thinks about himself, and what he can gain through the King. Alastor keeps him holed away in his rooms all to himself. I've also witnessed him making Jun cry on three separate occasions, which of course sent Hyosung into a rage—"

Jinhee clicked her tongue at the gossiping girl.

Sooni dipped her head.

"*Princess* Jun," the young girl corrected herself.

When they passed a group of guards, the ladies-in-waiting smiled courteously, but Vinya did not take her eyes off the path ahead.

Her body felt heavier than the stones beneath her feet.

There would be no happy ending here. No more holding Gran in her arms. No afternoon strolls through her village. No yearly trip across the water. This would be her last visit to Byonea.

Once they were out of earshot of the guards, Sooni leaned in closer. "Still, the King didn't fire him. Deemed him too important to Byonea to let him go." She rolled her eyes with a sigh and kicked a small rock off the path.

They walked a little longer in silence before arriving at the living quarters. The men's and women's rooms were in separate buildings, divided by a stone-paved courtyard. A maple tree grew in its center, its branches stretched out, reaching for both buildings but not quite touching. Worn wooden benches hugged its trunk, leaving enough room for a carriage to squeeze through if need be. Lanterns strung along the porches of each building illuminated the courtyard. These buildings were for the unwed nobility, and the courtyard between served as their public meeting place.

Vinya and the ladies-in-waiting climbed the steps of the building to her right, her feet cumbersome as they entered the women's quarters. Halfway down the hall, a handful of guards and maids exited the same room in which the women had cleaned and changed her earlier that day. *Her* room, she realized.

Vinya stopped walking as a wave of nausea rolled over her. Zhan's footsteps halted behind her. She gripped her stomach and exhaled heavily through her nose, trying to expel her anxiety.

Jinhee placed a hand on her elbow. "The kitchens were closed for the night. I had some leftover tea, rice, and soup delivered to your room. It may help."

It was exactly what she told Miho on the boat. Disappointment washed over her, and Vinya hoped Miho had understood that she did not abandon her by choice.

Vinya turned to the older woman. Wrinkles splayed from the corners of her eyes and creases hugged the sides of her mouth. Her face was the result of a joyous life, but the concern on her face now was sincere—it was a drop of warmth in the cold dread that filled her chest.

Vinya nodded, nearing her room once more. She would be grateful for that warmth, and thankful for the simple meal that would hold her over for the night.

She had not noticed how barren the room was earlier in the day. One simple clothing chest occupied the middle of one wall, and an empty display cabinet was on the opposing wall—their dark wood was stark against the cream walls. A plain paneled silk screen stretched along the back wall behind her floor mattress, and a small, low table that held her meal sat in the middle of the room.

Her larger travel pack was on the floor near the one and only door, and her cleaned, folded clothes sat atop. The smaller pack with her wooden trinkets, feather quill, journal, her parents' letters, and Gran's medicine was missing. She wouldn't need the pack now, but it bothered her that her quill was gone.

Staring at her plain linen clothes, Vinya felt severely overdressed. She'd been dolled up and turned into a flower for the royal family. She longed for the comfort of home. She slipped her shoes off inside the door and aimed for the food when Zhan cleared his throat behind her.

He had hung the lantern on a hook across the hall from her door, and now subtly fiddled with the tassel on his sword. He did not seem to be the nervous type, perhaps he just was unsocial, but he obviously had something he wanted to say.

"I—" he began. He dropped his eyes to the floor, lifting them again when he found his words. "We were not told of your grandmother. You have my condolences."

"We would have told you sooner if we'd known," Sooni added. "We were instructed to not speak while preparing you for the King, but I don't think there's a good reason to keep something like *that* from you." She shook her head, deep in thought as she and Jinhee pulled out the paneled screen and night clothes for Vinya to change into.

These people had been put in her charge—tasked with taking care of her. They hardly knew her, but their kindness was not feigned.

"Thank you," Vinya quietly responded to them both.

Zhan gave a curt nod. "My second in command will take the first post. He will be right outside the door if you need anything."

He slid the door closed. Not long after, footsteps approached. His replacement guard. The men spoke briefly before Zhan left to sleep in the guardhouse.

The ladies helped her out of her many-layered attire and into her nightclothes. Her royal hairpin sat alone on the display cabinet. Vinya ate her meal in silence. Jinhee left for the servant's quarters while Vinya ate, and Sooni exited with the small table and empty dishes after she was finished.

Vinya sat on her mattress. Alone. She was completely alone in this country. The weight of the day pressed down on her the longer she sat. An hour passed, possibly two, before exhaustion pulled her towards slumber.

She had just laid down when a commotion came from down the hall. The thudding of boots and the sound of shifting fabric neared her room, halting in front of her door.

Voices rumbled, and her door slid open. No knock. No warning.

Vinya stood as one man entered her room, three others stayed in the hall. Their black robes were standard, but the golden tassels hanging from their hats and swords set them apart from the rest. These were the King and Queen's personal guards.

"Her Majesty has requested your presence immediately," declared the guard who had stepped inside.

His words were flat, and his face was impassive, no was not an answer.

Vinya looked down at herself. Her nightgown was not immodest, but it wasn't a decent outfit to wear in front of the Queen.

"Just come in what you have," said the first guard.

She only had the clothes on her back and the clothes in her bag. Jinhee and Sooni had taken her skirt and top, and her clothing cabinet held no robe to cover her nightgown. Her ladies would be too late if she were to call on them. Empty-handed, she looked at the guards.

He jerked his head towards the hall, and Vinya stepped into the midst of the guards. None of them paid special attention to her, neither did they offer to cover her nightgown. They were here on business alone.

In the late hours of the night, they walked in darkness. Regardless of the night air that sent a chill sweeping over her body, her palms began to sweat. She and her four escorts finally crossed the threshold of the royal quarters. The men inside did not stop them, no questions were asked.

The interior of the building was far from modest. Golden statues of Byonean dragons wound their way around the hall's pillars that led to the bedrooms. The polished floor was so smooth that she could see her reflection in it; the guards' boots clacked on the surface as they crossed the entryway to a hall straight ahead.

Vinya kept her focus ahead as they passed two sets of doors—each directly across the hall from the other. No movement sounded from within the rooms, not even a whisper to indicate someone's presence inside. She tried not to think of the man to whom she was falsely promised. Tried not to imagine which door was Yuwon's, the room into which the King and Queen so desperately wanted to shove her. She tried not to think of what would go through his mind if he were to see her right now. Annoyance at her presence perhaps, given he would not look her way hours ago. She was a wayward arrow shot into his monotonous days, further securing him in the politics of their countries.

Vinya huffed a quiet laugh. He may like that, given what she had heard about the prince.

Her heart leapt when the third and final door on the right opened, but it wasn't the banal Crown Prince that stepped out to greet them; it was an older lady-in-waiting, faint chirping coming from the room behind her.

The Queen's lady-in-waiting stood poised, her motions so perfect she must have practiced for years. Decades, even.

She paid no attention to Vinya's gown as she ushered her in. The guards did not move from their spot in the hallway, so Vinya walked in alone. The lady-in-waiting positioned herself beside the door after it was closed.

There was no need for a guard in the Queen's room… not when Vinya was unarmed and unassuming, a stark contrast to the extravagant decorations that touched every surface. But even the staggering display of tapestries, paintings, and jeweled statues paled beside the Queen's overwhelming presence.

Vinya's knees bent of their own accord; she bowed so deeply that her forehead touched the floor.

Dozens of birds—both common and exotic—that lined the walls chittered, each of them in cages that were too small. Vinya had never seen some of them before, she didn't know so many colors could exist on a single creature.

She rose from her bow and kept her eyes on her own hands, knowing she could not maintain eye contact with the Queen for long.

Queen Joona had not changed a single piece of her attire since appearing in the throne room earlier that afternoon. Every golden hair adornment glistened in the lantern light. The dragon on her robe stared at Vinya across the low table; its mouth was permanently curved into a smile that bordered on sinister.

But as the Queen evaluated every inch of her, that wasn't what made Vinya want to run from the room; there was a sneer she couldn't quite understand. The Queen's tongue worked inside her mouth like there were many things she wanted to say, but didn't know where to start.

Vinya regretted not calling for Jinhee or Sooni. She should have grabbed a shawl to wrap around her shoulders—even the blanket from her bed would have sufficed. She felt laid bare under the Queen's eyes, smaller than the birds in their cages.

A chirp sounded from a covered cage on the table, which made Vinya jump. There was something familiar about the tune... something that reminded her of home.

The Queen smirked, "I didn't disrupt your sleep, did I?"

Insincerity lurked behind her seemingly innocent question.

Vinya shook her head, unable to find her voice.

"Did I?" the Queen repeated, her words dropping to a threatening tone.

"No, Your Majesty," Vinya squeaked.

A frantic fluttering came from within the cage between them. The bird inside sounded like it was trying to get out, as if it were unaccustomed to the small space it had been allotted.

The Queen picked up a folding fan and smacked the cage. The bird grew quiet.

"Your grandmother, she taught you our ways? Our rules and laws, and what happens to those who betray us?"

"Yes, Your Majesty."

This was a test. Vinya didn't want to know what would happen if she failed, or which of the punishments she would receive if she didn't give the answers the Queen expected. Banishment would be out of the question as they wanted her here. Byonea was a peaceful country that thrived on order and loyalty, but public shaming was not unheard of. Would the Queen subject her to flogging? Twist her legs or break her shins? Would they brand her wrist as a permanent reminder to listen and obey?

Vinya tried not to fidget, though every inch of her skin crawled as the Queen stared at her.

"Your cycles—are they regular? You are in good health?"

Vinya glanced at the Queen. "Yes, Your Majesty. I've never had any health problems."

Cycles. *Heirs.* A tingling sensation took over her head.

"Good." The Queen replied, tapping a nail on the table. "One would hope so. I will still send the physicians for a thorough check to be sure. I have the highest expectations for my son and his future."

Vinya couldn't help but squirm at the thought of strangers examining her from head to toe.

Queen Joona lowered her voice. "Calgham could be defeated by our men alone, but tying our countries together once more will make them think twice about doing it again in the next few centuries."

"You understand you will do nothing to disrupt this union," the Queen went on. "The defiance you displayed in the throne room will not occur again. My ladies have been working to hush the rumors that the promised princess my son is to wed has a rebellious spirit. You will do as you are told, and you will not fight it."

Vinya looked at the Queen through her brow. She owed this woman and this country nothing.

The Queen sucked air in through her teeth, her lip curled upward in disgust. "A few of my women were at the gate when you arrived, they came back whispering that you had the eyes of the enemy. Has no one told you they are the emerald shade of Calgham?"

The coloring she inherited from her mother. She'd never been ashamed of them before, and she was unsure why she felt a tinge of guilt at the words.

The Queen slowly tilted her head. "The physicians may come up with a remedy, something to darken the tone—I refuse to have any descendants of mine walk these halls with those eyes."

The bird in the cage chirped again and tore Vinya from the ever-growing pit in her stomach.

The Queen placed her hand at the top of the cage, the fabric curling under her fingers. "Curious? This is my newest acquisition."

Queen Joona pulled back the fabric, and Vinya stilled.

Inside was a Norhagan canary.

This was nothing but a show of power. The Queen had waited until Vinya settled in her room, waited until she was alone to call on her, to taunt and belittle her. To show who was in charge and to command obedience.

"It's beautiful," Vinya stated.

"Rather plain, I'm afraid," Queen Joona replied.

The Queen sighed and waved a hand, ordering her lady to take the bird and its cage. She turned on Vinya once more. "Where do you suggest we place it?"

Another test.

Vinya scanned the walls. There was not an inch to spare. She wondered how the Queen had so many birds and kept them hushed. What harsh treatment would it take for wild creatures to be so tamed?

She took a deep breath, choosing her words carefully. "The bird could stay here on the table until room is made among the others."

The Queen smiled—a twisted grin that did not touch her eyes.

"Yes."

The lady-in-waiting returned the cage. The Norhagan canary flew in a frenzy until Queen Joona replaced the fabric, and rested her hand on top of the cage.

"That is all," stated the Queen.

Vinya looked the Queen in the eye once more before bowing.

As the guards led Vinya back to her own room, she had an inkling that she had failed the queen's test. Vinya settled on the bed once more, trying and failing to keep the thoughts of her grandmother out of her mind.

What had happened? How long had it been before someone found Gran? She convinced herself it could not have been too long. Surely Gran's neighbors noticed her health declining and had been keeping a close eye on her.

Her stomach twisted in knots and rolled. She shouldn't have eaten.

She could not learn more about Gran's death here in the palace. The king's adviser—Alastor, Sooni had called him—certainly wouldn't give her any information. Sooni seemed to know the ins and outs of palace gossip, but if she learned of Gran's death in the same moment as Vinya, she wouldn't be able to pry anything new out of the young girl.

So, Vinya waited.

Waited until the guard sat down, hours into his shift. Waited until the lantern light showed his silhouetted head bob. Waited deep into the night for his breaths to turn heavy, to turn into a snore. Waited a little longer before she changed back into her plain clothes, hefted the only remaining pack over her shoulder, and slid the door open enough to squeeze through before disappearing into the darkness of the palace walls.

4

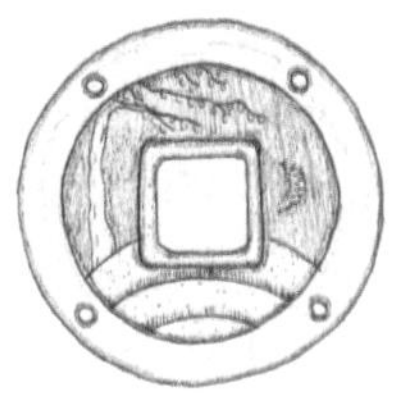

The Dragon's All-Seeing Eye

Vinya slipped a hat off the servant's wall as she strode by. The straw hat provided somewhat of a disguise as she wove her way through the buildings of sleeping residents. Something deep within her was screaming to *run,* telling her that someone was watching, but she kept her steps unhurried. Many people in the palace did not know exactly who she was except for those within the throne room, so she took precautions as her face might ring warning bells.

Lanterns lined the main paths and doorways, so Vinya chose a longer route, keeping to the darker alleys as she aimed for the outermost walls. She didn't know how far the grounds stretched back and to the sides, so the only logical choice was to go out the way she came in. Slipping past the guards would be difficult.

Vinya was halfway to the gate when a tingling sensation swept through her, raising the hairs on her arms. She was being watched. She flattened herself against a wall, scanning for any movement around her.

Nothing.

The crunch of gravel and the indistinct murmurs of men's voices grew near, and Vinya busied herself with a nearby rolling cart so she would not look suspicious. She wheeled it into the main path and almost collided with a guard who was making rounds with his partner. The man had quick reflexes, stopping the cart before it hit him.

"Careful," he said, scanning the contents of the cart.

His companion began shuffling through the cart's bundles, presumably searching for contraband.

"Only silks," the second guard grunted as he neatly stacked the bundles back into place.

Vinya kept her head down, watching them through the tiny openings in her hat.

The first guard raised a brow, opening the bundle closest to him. "Silk? Why would it be delivered in the night, oh—"

He raised the fabric with one finger to show his comrade. The smooth orchid silk shone in the lantern light before he put it back.

The second guard failed to hide the way his lip curled in disgust. He turned to Vinya, waving to the only building that was still lit within. "Take it to the concubines and go to sleep. They may work at night, but you still need rest."

"Be considerate of others while entering the main pathway," the first guard added with a grin.

Vinya hummed a laugh and pushed the cart around them, aiming for the small building. The guards spoke amongst themselves again, but they remained still, watching her every step. She could feel their stares creeping down her neck.

There would be no ditching of this crate—she would need to deliver it and head for the servants' quarters. Once she was out of sight, she would make a loop in the other direction.

Women's voices floated through the air inside. These women ate and slept in the building, waiting to be called upon. Still, it made Vinya uncomfortable.

A servant would not use the front door, so she went to the side and knocked before turning back to the guards, giving them a flat smile and a wave. Satisfied, the men waved back and resumed their patrol.

Vinya blew out a breath. This was taking too long. It had to be well past midnight already. There was no telling how close the sunrise was. Servants would wake soon to prepare for the new day, and she would have to avoid more people in order to get out. She might have to find somewhere to hide for an entire day when the alarm rose that she was missing.

Vinya chewed on the inside of her cheek. She went to knock a second time when the door slid open.

She blinked. The woman before her was stunning—one whose likeness could hang in art halls for people to admire the work or wish for her features.

"You won't find any scraps around here, girl. If you missed your last meal, that is your own fault." She said, clicking her tongue. The venom that poured out through her words was her downfall. The woman peered around Vinya, spying the cart.

"We were expecting those hours ago." She shook her head and called behind her for another woman to gather the bundles.

Vinya was more than willing to step back, leaving the cart of silks for the women to handle on their own. It wasn't her job, but a small part of her wanted to help as the other women seemed to tiptoe around the woman by the door—the one who snapped at any dropped bundles or crinkled silks.

The woman who opened the door had something the others did not: a golden circlet around her neck. Vinya wondered if it meant she was a high-ranking leman or if it had been an eternal gift of a lover; the band was unbroken, with no clasp or seam to be seen.

The women emptied the cart and retreated into their shared home, leaving the woman alone with Vinya once more. She dipped her head and turned, aiming for the servant's quarters, when the woman closed the door and approached Vinya.

"While you're out, go and fetch a meal for me. A *fresh* one. Make sure they know you're delivering it to the King's quarters." The concubine stopped so close to Vinya, she could smell the fine oils on the woman's skin. "Not sure why he needs the energy, the old man can barely get it up, anyway. No, his siring days are long over."

"And don't you dare take any food or I'll have you whipped," she added.

Vinya dipped her head in obedience. She aimed for the kitchens, but in the midst of being sent this way and that, her directions had scrambled. A thin hand wrapped around her jaw and yanked her back, causing the straw hat to slip off her head and hit the ground with a soft crunch. Wide-eyed, she was face to face with the woman.

"Other way, you impudent fool," the woman sneered, but she did not release Vinya's jaw.

Vinya cringed as the grip became tighter. The concubine's well-manicured fingernails stung as they dug into her cheeks.

She tilted her head to the side, scrutinizing Vinya's face. "I do not think I've seen you before."

Vinya tried to speak, but with her jaw locked in the hand of this woman, she could only choke out a garbled noise. The woman's eye landed on the strap across Vinya's chest and followed it around to her pack.

The woman eyed Vinya. "What is in your bag?"

The grip tightened, and Vinya cried out in pain. She pulled at the woman's hand, but it did not budge.

Her father had taught her a lot on the farm, but not much about fighting. Still, she figured a jab to the eye or kick to the shin would make this woman let go. She would risk the guards, risk being caught, just to take this pain away. A swing at her throat would stop the woman from calling for help.

Tighter. How this slender woman had so much strength baffled Vinya. She was about to execute her plan when a smooth voice called from a nearby building.

"I would advise you to let go, Daeya."

Daeya tensed ever so slightly before releasing Vinya's face. The woman turned toward the voice and dipped her head in a bow. Vinya rubbed her aching jaw, keeping silent as light footsteps approached.

The man stopped beside her, a lantern glowing in his hand. Vinya twisted to excuse herself and found herself eye level with Shade Prince Hyosung.

Daeya lifted her chin. The fierceness vanished from her face, replaced by an innocent, eye-batting concubine. "Your Highness."

Vinya braced herself, preparing to run. This man certainly knew who she was, and was no doubt going to raise an alarm.

But the Shade Prince did no such thing. His hand did not go to the slender blade at his side, he did not call out to the guards within view, he did not demand her to show respect as her superior. Instead, he studied Vinya's face.

She half expected a sly remark, but there was not an inkling of play as his eyes landed on the red marks from Daeya's grip.

His eyes darkened as he snapped at the concubine, "You may be with my father by night, but keep in mind that you are undeniably replaceable. Lay your hand on my servant again and you'll be out of the palace within the hour."

Daeya's eyes flickered, glancing at Vinya. "My apologies, Your Highness. It is late, and so dark, I was unaware of who she was."

The woman studied Vinya again and squinted. She brought a hand to her own mouth, feigning recognition as she turned her attention back to Hyosung. "Yes, yes, I see now. Forgive me, I did not know. What is one face out of a hundred servants? The fault is mine."

The woman bowed again, and Hyosung shook his head as she did. The corner of his mouth slightly curled into a sneer. It was apparent that the concubine disgusted the Shade Prince.

Vinya watched as the two locked eyes. The King's favorite versus the King's firstborn—one had absolute power over the other. Daeya raised her chin defiantly. Perhaps the concubine felt the same disgust towards Hyosung? It made Vinya wonder what had happened between them.

"If another servant crosses your path, you know where to send them," she sniveled at Vinya, retreating into her home to prepare for the king.

"Of course," the Shade Prince replied in her stead. He turned his attention to Vinya, motioning towards the series of courtyards and gates beyond. "Shall we?"

Vinya picked up the hat, brushing the dirt off before placing it back on her head, her disguise in place once more as she fell into step beside Hyosung.

Walking in the middle of the main path, Vinya kept her head bowed—unlike the prince, who greeted every guard they passed.

"You've been following me," she said once they were alone.

He dipped his head in response.

"Why?"

"Because, unlike everyone else within these walls, I believe that you *aren't* the promised princess."

Though the man sounded genuine, Vinya huffed an incredulous laugh. "Sure. That's why you stood by while I was in the claws of that snake."

It made sense, though. Why would he step in to help a commoner? If she was who the scroll claimed, the promised princess, he would have defended her from the concubine at the start—Daeya wouldn't have been allowed to touch her. She rubbed her jaw and winced; it would be sore for a few days at least.

"What makes you believe me?" she questioned.

The prince shrugged. "I have my reasons."

Out of the corner of her eye, she could see him looking at her as they walked. The lantern he held cast an angelic glow around his silhouette. A slight smile played on his lips. His free hand was in his pocket, his walk unhurried. Vinya sensed that he wanted something.

"If you think I would allow you to take advantage of me in return for your help, you are mistaken. Your position in the Palace holds no sway over me, and I have no interest in you," Vinya muttered under her breath.

Hyosung laughed, soft and lilting. "Contrary to widespread belief, I do not expect nor force women to do anything with me. Let the people think what they want. If a rumor finds its way into your mind, that doesn't make it true."

Vinya considered his words, touching her jaw once more. "What is the concubine's problem?"

His brow shot up. "Daeya? That *snake,* as you called her, climbed her way to the top of the kingdom and thinks everyone else is beneath her. Nothing but the best for the *King's leman*."

There was an unmistakable bite to his words.

They approached the first gate, and Vinya slowed her steps. "Are you not the same? I'm surprised you're walking the dirt streets in your ornate slippers."

She glanced at the shoes that peeked out from underneath his robes. Her jab did not fall; his slippers were as ordinary as her own.

Hyosung blocked her path. "Rumors. Unlike Daeya, I do not sell my body to get what I want. Nor do I pay for it."

His words struck something in her. As she glanced at the guards at the gate, Vinya's heartbeat quickened.

Hyosung tilted his head, a smile pulling at his lips. "I will not sell *your* body either."

The Shade Prince pulled a small wooden plaque from his pocket and presented it to the guards. The guards knew who he was, but the plaque was the official form of noble identity.

Vinya thought of the plaque that was no doubt being prepared for her. Her name and rank. She wondered what they would do with it once she disappeared back into the countryside of Norhagan. Burn it, hopefully. Forget her existence.

The gate door opened, and Hyosung waved Vinya through as she pressed her chin against her chest. "She is with me."

The guards dipped their heads in agreement, and she followed close as he strode into the inner courtyard. One gate down, three main gates left to go.

They passed by the Grand Palace where she'd first spied Hyosung on the balcony.

"What was your plan, exactly?" Hyosung asked. He looked at the Grand Palace, as if the answer would lie within.

Vinya chewed on the inside of her cheek. "There was a tree I noticed on the way in—"

"A tree?" he interrupted. A cheeky grin spread across his face. "Interesting. Perhaps we should have stayed with Daeya longer; she could have given you tips on climbing."

A scoff escaped her. "It was the only way out that I could think of."

"There are many ways in and out of the palace if you search hard enough."

Vinya looked sidelong at him.

"Though the easiest way is through the gates with the help of a friend," he added with a smirk.

"A friend," she said flatly.

"Mm."

Same as before, he showed his plaque, and the guards ushered them through the second gate, then the third.

Out of earshot of the guards, Hyosung clicked his tongue. He stepped back, grabbed the bottom of her pack, and gave it a shake.

Vinya spun out of reach. "What are you doing?"

The Shade Prince pointed to her pack, concern lined his face. "There truly isn't anything valuable in there. You took nothing to pay your way out of Byonea."

She shifted her pack. "I considered the silver and pearl hairpin. It would have covered the cost of whatever funeral my grandmother was given."

Hyosung did not move toward the next gate—waited for her to explain.

"Even though it would have helped, it would have been wrong. It belongs to someone else. The true promised princess, descendant of a great king, *uniter of countries*, all of that." She sighed. "I couldn't find it in me to steal something that held such importance to someone else."

Hyosung's brow furrowed, considering what she told him. "You're better than I am."

Without clarifying, he walked in silence to the next gate—the final gate. Freedom was moments away. They continued without speaking when an official called out to Hyosung from a side building, waving him over.

Hyosung glanced between the last gate, Vinya, and the official.

"Can a man not take a stroll with a woman in peace? Can business not wait until morning?" he called out.

Even at a distance, the official's impatience was clear as he moved towards them.

Hyosung waved him off with a smile, then turned to Vinya, his face serious. "Play along."

She could not do anything else as he pulled her in close by the arm. The official coughed, stopping in his tracks to turn and give them privacy. Hyosung was pretending to be the womanizer they believed him to be. His face was mere inches from her own. The spiced honey scent that hung in the air around him made it hard to breathe.

The Shade Prince spoke quickly. "There is a stack of crates against the side of the building on your left. Use those to climb to the roof. You'll have to jump to the wall, brace yourself for the drop, and *run* the moment your feet hit the ground. Go to your grandmother's house. I've seen your paperwork and know where it is, I'll come in a few days to check on you there."

Vinya could barely wrap her head around his rapid-fire instructions, yet found herself nodding.

Hyosung did not break eye contact as he tucked a loose strand of her hair behind her ear, his finger unintentionally ran down the edge.

"Smile so they believe it," he breathed.

Though his face was bright, there was no gleam to be found in his eyes.

She couldn't smile, couldn't move when the Shade Prince stood so close, not when every breath was shared.

Hyosung knew this, and grinned. He pressed a small piece of metal into her hand.

"A gift. From a friend."

Vinya didn't dare move as the prince followed the official, his beautiful smile stretched from ear to ear.

It took her a few moments to catch her breath. When she opened her fist, a shining gold coin sat in her palm. She snapped her hand shut again. The single coin was capable of not only buying her passage home, but an entire ship itself. Hyosung had no reason to help her that she could tell, yet he kept pushing her towards freedom.

Vinya shrugged off her pack and tucked the coin into a deep pocket before slinging the pack over her shoulder once more. As she made her way to the crates, Vinya counted the seconds between patrols.

Her heart pounded in her ears. She was so close to escaping.

A pair of guards strode by, and she busied herself with shifting some of the crates. The patrol paid no attention to her as they rounded a corner, and she started counting, hefting herself onto the first crate.

She had moments to climb the crates and reach the roof before the next patrol. Then, twenty more seconds to make the jump onto the wall.

Vinya was so close to the massive dragon statues. Eight wings splayed above her; the dragons ready for whatever intruder would come for them. She smiled to herself. Unfortunately for the dragons, they weren't looking *within* the walls.

Vinya had one foot planted on the next layer of crates when a pair of hands grabbed her waist, snatching her back to the ground. She whirled, swinging a fist at an enraged guard.

Zhan stopped her hand from colliding with his face. His jaw was clenched so tight she thought his teeth might crack. The guard's nightshirt had been hastily tucked into his pants, and he'd left it unbuttoned, giving Vinya a glimpse of his heaving chest. The man had run the entire distance. Fury radiated from him; sweat seeped from his pores. A hint of betrayal lay behind it all.

He was the one who guarded within.

"Zhan, *please*," she whispered.

The muscles in his jaw ticked as he twisted, half dragging her towards her room. Towards her cage. She tried to break free from his grasp, the straw hat fell to the ground in her fight, but his hold on her wrist never loosened. Maids, servants, and guards paused as the two of them passed. Zhan studied each of the guard's faces at the gates—they would no doubt receive an earful from him later.

She pleaded with him under her breath the entire way, but he ignored her.

The guard who had fallen asleep at her door was nowhere to be seen, and Zhan half dropped her onto the floor of her bedroom. Her hands stung as they slapped onto the wooden floor to catch herself. She glared at Zhan as he took up position, arms crossed, in the open doorway.

"I thought guards didn't come into the room," she snapped.

He remained silent; he wouldn't deign to give her a reply, or privacy.

Vinya huffed, peeled off her pack, and dropped it on the floor beside her. She didn't bother taking off her shoes as she slid under the blankets, facing away from Zhan and his unrelenting stare.

5

A Bird and a Cage

The soft sound of a window sliding open pulled Vinya from sleep.

She squinted against the rays of sunlight streaming into her room and rolled away from the light, pulling the thin blanket over her head to darken her view. Through a rumple in the blanket, she could barely make out a pair of dark boots close to her face.

Vinya folded the blanket down to see Zhan standing over her. His shirt had been properly buttoned and tidied, but his feet hadn't moved an inch. Vinya had tossed and turned so much that she'd worked her way off the mattress completely.

"The Princess Jun has requested a meal with you in a few hours. Your ladies are here to prepare you," he said down to her.

Zhan politely dipped his head in farewell to the ladies-in-waiting and instructed the guards at her bedroom door—all three of them—to remain vigilant while he rested.

He gave her one last stern look before he disappeared down the hall, one of the guards closing the door behind him.

She doubted there would be another chance to escape in the near future—not with Zhan's vigilant eyes.

Vinya sat up with a sigh, stomach rumbling as she turned to the women. She was about to suggest breakfast when Sooni gasped and ran across the room to her, dropping to her knees beside Vinya. Jinhee stood motionless at the window, shock on her face.

"What happened?" Sooni asked, her hands hovering over Vinya's jaw.

Vinya closed her eyes once more. The previous night's events had been kept quiet. She was a symbol of hope for the country and had tried to run; countless guards allowing it to happen. It would show great selfishness that the promised princess, no matter how false, left them behind to fend for themselves. How could she tell these women, who had shown her more kindness than anyone else in the past day, that she'd tried to leave?

She opened her eyes, trying to find the words, but failed.

Jinhee met her gaze. The older woman's face switched from concern to calm understanding; she knew from the way Vinya hesitated.

"Sooni," Jinhee said quietly, moving to her side.

Tears lined Sooni's eyes as she searched Vinya's face. "Who did this to you? Did someone enter your room last night? The marks are too thin to be a man, so it must have been a woman."

The girl's brows bunched together. Her mind at work putting the pieces together.

"Sooni," Jinhee repeated.

Sooni shook her head. "It couldn't have been a maid. We were all accounted for last night, and no servants work in living quarters after dark."

The girl chewed on a nail as she considered all other possibilities.

It reminded her of Miho. Vinya wondered if she had made it to her village safely.

Sooni's eyes went wide, and she leaned in closer to whisper. "Was it one of the Queen's women?"

Jinhee raised her voice. "*Sooni*."

The girl jumped and twisted to look at her superior.

Jinhee nodded towards the door. "Please fetch Her Highness breakfast."

Her Highness. It made Vinya's skin itch.

Sooni pouted, but obeyed. Vinya could still see the girl's mind at work, and fully believed Sooni would figure out who'd grabbed her jaw by noon at the latest.

Once alone, Jinhee knelt and took up Vinya's hand into her own. The softness of the woman's hands and gentleness of her smile stirred up memories of Gran. Vinya's chin quivered.

"Oh, no. No," Jinhee consoled her quietly. She ran her thumb over Vinya's hand. "I do not know what happened last night, I can only begin to guess. What I *do* know is that you are safe. Sooni and I will take care of you. Zhan will protect you."

"Zhan?" Vinya scoffed. "Zhan hauled me back here by my wrist last night."

She held up her arm, expecting it to be red from his grip, but there was no sign of his firm hold. The ache she felt must have been from her own pulling.

Jinhee nodded. "He may be stoic and strong willed, but every decision, every step forward, is with his heart, and with Prince Yuwon in mind. The two of them have been close since childhood. He is the only friend the Prince has ever had—he personally asked Zhan to look over you."

Vinya shook her head rapidly, cutting in. "I'm not who they think I am. I'm not the promised princess. I—I can't stay here."

Vinya reined in her emotions; she sounded like a babbling child.

Jinhee patted her arm. "I hear you. I hear you."

The corners of Jinhee's mouth pulled into a knowing grin. The older woman—full of life's experiences—understood.

But she could do nothing. She was in no position to help, held no power to prove or dispute Vinya's claims, and had no reason to believe her. She could only lend her ear and support where she was allowed.

Vinya decided she wouldn't place any unnecessary burdens on the woman, she didn't deserve the full weight of it all.

Vinya pulled her pack toward them, digging through the deep pockets. "I wonder if you could help me with something? I would like to have this on me at all times."

She pulled Hyosung's gold coin from her pack.

Jinhee's mouth opened slightly at the coin that was presented to her. She closed her mouth and gently lowered the coin and Vinya's hand. A silent question on her face.

"It was given to me, but I'd like to keep it hidden," Vinya stated.

A pause, then a nod.

Jinhee left the room. When she returned several minutes later, she pulled a thin, soft pink ribbon from her pocket. She took the gold, looping the ribbon through the hole in the middle of the coin and back around itself, making a necklace.

Vinya held up her hair as Jinhee adjusted the length, keeping the coin lower than any neckline would show. She knotted the ends of the ribbon and stood back, studying her work.

Satisfied, she nodded, giving Vinya one more smile before folding up the blankets and smoothing the fabric of the mattress.

Sooni came in carrying her tray of breakfast; a spread of greens, eggs, and noodles.

She thanked Sooni, but the girl did not acknowledge her words—her eyes were on the ribbon, and she looked to Jinhee, who shook her head. Sooni squinted before turning back to Vinya.

She answered in a merry tone, "You're welcome!" The young girl acted as if nothing was off.

Vinya pushed the food around on the plate as the women laid out her clothes for the day. They avoided pinks and red as to not draw attention to the marks. A high-waisted sea blue skirt flowed under a white top. A thick pale blue ribbon kept the top closed.

Vinya toyed with the edge of her sleeve as Jinhee left again and brought back a box of salves and makeup. The older lady-in-waiting did her best to conceal the marks on Vinya's jaw, and Sooni gave her own input here and there.

A knot twisted in Vinya's stomach as Jinhee placed the silver and pearl hairpin in her bun. The older woman patted her shoulder before gathering the breakfast dishes and passing a rested and freshly clothed Zhan on her way out. The crease in his brow had smoothed over since the morning.

He led Vinya deeper into the grounds. Sooni kept close to her side, speaking on and on about the upcoming Spring Festival and how she wished she could go this year. The further they walked, the buildings turned from practical to luxurious—the wealth of the royal family tucked away from the outskirts of the palace walls.

Zhan was silent, focusing solely on his job of escort and guard, but Vinya's questions gnawed in the back of her mind.

"What happened to the guard who was posted in my room last night?" she asked.

"Demoted. His duties are now outside of the palace grounds," Zhan grunted over his shoulder.

"The guards at the gates?" she pressed.

"Joined the first guard."

Vinya's head hung. "I didn't mean for anyone to lose their positions."

Zhan heaved an exasperated sigh, turning around to stop in her way. Vinya's slippers skid on the pebbles, stopping herself before running into him.

His voice dropped to a rumble. "Those who guard the palace and the royal family should be trustworthy. Anyone who isn't loyal will be relinquished of palace duties. *Especially* when they do not tell me who was helping you."

Vinya couldn't hold his stare. "Who said I was being helped?"

Zhan's face was incredulous. He began his escort again, with Vinya and Sooni quickening their pace to keep up.

"I'm not who you all think I am, Zhan," Vinya contended.

Zhan only shook his head as he prowled on.

They entered an expansive U-shaped hall, its inner walls open to a courtyard beyond. Noble men and women lounged about on all three sides, none of them paying any attention to Vinya's group.

A wide stream split the courtyard in two, flowing beneath the buildings that surrounded it. A cobblestone pathway wound through the gardens, leading to different stone benches and statues. Flowers on the brink of bloom spread underneath a gnarled willow tree, its branches swaying in the breeze.

A pair of canaries fluttered by, circling each other as they sang sweet songs. Untethered. They were a stark reminder of how Vinya herself had been chained to the Palace ground in the past twenty-four hours.

Vinya's gaze finally rested on a small gazebo that sat perched on a bridge over the stream. Gauze hung from the perimeter, obscuring the view from outside.

The wind picked up, and Vinya glimpsed Princess Jun within. She sat with such graceful poise; Vinya imagined her as one of the statues scattered around the courtyard's garden.

As they approached the gazebo, Zhan softly announced her presence to the Princess's guard, who moved aside for her to join Jun.

Sooni and Zhan took up positions at the base of the bridge, and Vinya stepped up and into the gazebo, hesitating when she got to the table. If she were promised to this family, if this woman was supposed to be her future sister, what were the honorifics?

Jun saved her from having to decide. She smiled, her high cheekbones rounding, and motioned for the cushion at Vinya's feet.

"Please, sit," she said, her voice airy and soothing.

Vinya did, noting another guard on the other side of the babbling stream. This was a wonderful meeting place for those who did not want to be overheard.

She met Princess Jun's eyes and quickly dropped them to the food spread across the table. Despite her growling stomach, the knot of nerves inside made the thought of eating unbearable. The two of them sat in awkward silence for a moment, neither one starting a conversation. Vinya idly picked at the hem of her sleeve when Jun spoke almost inaudibly.

"I hope I didn't cause any problems last night."

Vinya raised her head to find Jun picking at the food on her own plate. The princess chewed on the inside of her lip nervously.

"I'm not sure what you mean?" Vinya responded.

The news of her attempted escape had been contained, but loose lips were in every court. The building behind the princess had multiple floors. She could see scholars within, reading or carrying scrolls. Some men sat on balconies, some walked under the awnings. Their curious eyes wandered her way every so often, and Vinya wondered how much of their conversation the men were listening to.

"I came to check on you last night," Jun whispered, putting her utensils down and folding her hands in her lap, a genuine look of guilt on her face. "But... you weren't there, and the guard was asleep. I thought—I thought something cruel had happened to you and sent my guards to wake Zhan."

So that was how he had been alerted. "My guards later told me the events that transpired," she went on. "I wanted to say sorry."

Vinya was taken aback. The sister of the man she was betrothed to was apologizing for disrupting her late-night attempt at eluding the most powerful family in Byonea... the family that she was presumably a part of.

"Why come to my room in the middle of the night?" Vinya asked.

Jun's eyes skittered across the table of untouched food before she replied.

"My ladies told me that my mother called on you."

My mother. It was widely known the King and Queen had adopted Jun when her mother, the Queen's unwed sister, passed away before the Princess could even crawl.

Vinya nodded. She tried to ease the princess's nervousness by scooping food onto her plate. Jun may be able to give more information on the workings of the palace. One thing was becoming extremely clear—no movement here was unknown.

She hadn't noticed how tight Princess Jun was keeping her shoulders until she relaxed them, watching Vinya serve herself. The air around her lightened. It was working, then.

She met Vinya's eyes and gave a soft smile. "I cannot fathom the pain and confusion you've gone through in the past day. It must be difficult to have all of it thrown in your face at once. My father was told to keep it a secret from my brother for weeks because the high adviser Alastor was afraid that he would do something rash to prevent it. Yuwon was told only moments before you arrived."

Vinya took a bite out of her food, contemplating. That would explain the white knuckles, the refusal to look at her. It seemed not everyone in the royal family had been overjoyed at the union, and Vinya wondered what the Crown Prince would do now that he knew, if there was anything he was working on to prevent the marriage himself.

"My mother," Jun went on, picking up her utensils once more, "can be arduous. I've been called to her chambers many times over the last few years myself."

The princess pushed her food around her plate, still refusing to touch it. The queen seemed like a controlling and envious woman, but Vinya could not imagine why she would be jealous of her own daughter. Jun had gotten her beauty from her mother, so perhaps it was her youth that the queen envied?

Jun sighed. Food wasn't on her mind, either. Instead, she sipped from her tea. "I know firsthand what it's like to be used for political gain."

Vinya swallowed, the food catching on the sudden lump in her throat. No ring rested on the princess's finger.

"Are you betrothed?" she asked.

Jun shook her head, a secret smile tugged at the corners of her mouth. "No, I've been fortunate enough to avoid it so far."

But her smile slowly dropped, her voice barely audible above the stream. "My father isn't well. His health has been declining rapidly the past few years."

Jun ran her thumb along the rim of her cup and her eyes became distant, worried. Vinya knew that feeling. It was the reason she had brought new Norhagan medicines to help Gran's ailments, but she'd been too late.

Vinya set her utensils down, her mind wrapping around the situation. "They want their children wed before..."

She didn't finish her sentence—did not need to. Not when deep sorrow hung behind the sad smile of the princess, who nodded. The King did seem weak, slow to stand and needing help. Vinya realized that the King hadn't spoken a word, rather letting Alastor speak for him. The looming war would give an excuse to tie their children to other countries.

"What about your brother?" Vinya inquired.

Jun raised a brow, the other joined it soon after as she realized who Vinya asked about. She covered her mouth, a soft laugh wound its way through her fingers.

"Woobin? He has a spirit that cannot be contained. My mother and Alastor have tried many, *many* times to find a match for him," Jun shook her head. "He would be here but, he should be returning soon from celebrating yet another eluded marriage."

Vinya wanted to ask how she had averted marriage this far, maybe she could receive the same help. Before she could, Jun reached across the table and took Vinya's hands in her own.

"I hope we can be friends," she said earnestly. "The palace can be such a lonely place. Please call on me at any time, I would enjoy the company."

Light played in the princess's eyes, and Vinya couldn't help but find herself grinning in return.

Jun's face glowed as she squeezed her hand and stood. Vinya joined her as the princess gave quiet directions to her ladies-in-waiting, motioning to the table behind them.

"I'm afraid I requested more food than we were capable of eating. Please find someone to take what remains to the children in Nyrrem."

Nyrrem was the sprawling city outside of the palace walls. Its outskirts were known to be poor, and they survived solely off the generosity of others—people like Jun.

Vinya decided she would like to spend more time with the kind princess.

They exited the gazebo together. Jun released Vinya's hand, bidding her farewell, and walked towards the royal quarters with guards in tow as her ladies gathered the leftover food.

"Thank you, Zhan," she said to him as she passed.

The smallest of dimples pressed into his cheeks as he bowed. When Jun departed, he rose to find Vinya studying his face.

"Was that a smile?" she questioned.

The dimples disappeared, replaced with a cutting stare.

Sooni giggled beside her. "Everyone has a soft spot for the Princess, it can't be helped."

Zhan ignored them, focusing on someone approaching from behind. Sooni glanced back and closed her mouth. An odd behavior for someone who loved to talk. Vinya turned, and once again came face to face with the Shade Prince.

His eyes widened slightly before he replaced the surprise with a handsome smile.

Hyosung clasped his hands behind his back and swayed on his heels. "Ah, we finally meet. Vinya, isn't it? Rolls off the tongue nicely. *Vinya.*"

He knew how to put on a believable show. He spoke, feigning an air of submission towards Zhan—his voice as silvery as the pin in her hair. "Always a pleasure to run into you, Zhan. Mind if I take Vinya on a stroll in the gardens?"

Vinya looked to Zhan, but the guard locked eyes with Hyosung, his gaze sliding down to the hand outstretched to her. His hand was not one of a warrior. Not squared or hardened in any way. His slim features could pass as a woman's hand...

Sooni noted this and patted Zhan's arm, going up on tiptoes to whisper to him, "It wasn't him."

Zhan looked to Sooni for answers, but the girl only shook her head; she did not attempt to hide the sneer that pulled at her upper lip. She must have discovered who made the mark on Vinya's jaw.

Vinya smiled to herself; the girl would be helpful to keep around.

Not needing nor waiting for Zhan's approval, she slipped her hand into Hyosung's. The Shade Prince turned to wrap her arm through his and lead their small group through the winding pathway of the gardens.

"I've been curious about you since your arrival." His gaze dropped to her jaw for the slightest second. "You seem to be adjusting well."

With Zhan and Sooni close behind, they would have to speak in riddles.

"I took a bit of a tumble last night, nothing I cannot recover from," she replied.

He hummed as they leisurely walked past the gazebo. "Ah, *you're* the one who had lunch with Jun? I tried to get a better look, but her guards kept everyone from entering the garden."

"It's nice to have some privacy now and then." She looked over her shoulder at Zhan, who listened closely.

Hyosung's laughter chimed through the garden. Vinya had a hunch that he, too, had his wings clipped. An alluring bird forced to walk on the ground.

"Seclusion and secrets are difficult to maintain here," he added.

They crossed a separate, smaller bridge and began winding through the flower beds that were crowded and on the brink of bloom.

"I hear that Yuwon prefers seclusion."

Hand through his arm, she felt the Shade Prince stiffen.

"Mm, yes. Our darling Yuwon loves the company of books and swords rather than people."

"Did the two of you spend much time together growing up?" Vinya asked.

"No. We may be the same age, but his mother went great lengths to make sure we were kept separate as children. Perhaps that is why he prefers to be alone, it's all he knew as a child."

His mother, not *the Queen*.

Vinya wondered if that was the reason Zhan had been his only friend—Had Zhan's father been part of the guard, or had Zhan joined the guard at a young age to be close to the Crown Prince? Her heart stung imagining the tutors, the guards, the servants. How much did the Queen push him in his studies? Was he able to have a childhood at all?

"That must have been lonely."

"Mm, I believe—" Hyosung stopped both his words and steps.

Vinya followed his gaze, and a few yards away, in the midst of a small group of scholars, stood Yuwon.

She hadn't realized just how tall the prince was. He stood almost a head taller than the men around him. Like Jun, he had the ability to hold himself as still as stone. Only his eyes moved from Vinya's hand linked through Hyosung's arm, to Zhan, then settled on Hyosung.

Vinya felt the weight of his stare, the authority in the silence.

The group of men must have been on their way to another part of the building, but now the scholars around Yuwon respectfully waited, spoke amongst themselves, or moved so others could pass by. Even though the Crown Prince stood among them, he was distant; he was there out of obligation, not out of a desire for fellowship.

"*That* would be my cue to leave," Hyosung mumbled through his teeth.

Hyosung moved to walk past her, but leaned in close to her ear. Rocks crunched under Zhan's feet; the guard was prepared to interfere if Hyosung tried to pull anything over on her.

"This garden is the loveliest during the upcoming Spring Festival. I would love to walk with you again then," Hyosung whispered.

Guards would be divided, split between watching both the palace and the royals who journeyed to the Spring Festival in a few days. Hyosung was offering an invitation, an opportunity to escape once again.

"I would enjoy that very much," she responded.

His eyes dropped to her jaw once more, irritation flicked through his face. "I look forward to it."

Hyosung half-turned to Yuwon to nod farewell, and hummed a poignant tune as he retreated into the throng of people in the open hall; the nobility's reaction to him varied from sneers to smiles. Vinya watched him go, the pressure of Yuwon's stare from behind pushed into the skin on her back.

She turned back around to meet the Crown Prince's gaze for the first time. A strange flutter of nerves swept through her. Though he showed no emotion, there was a sadness in his eyes—maybe she only saw it because she had just been told of his somber childhood.

Yuwon's foot shifted in her direction, and she quickly turned to Zhan.

"I'm ready to go to my room, Zhan," she announced.

But Zhan did not answer, his focus was on Yuwon. His brows moved subtly, slight turns of his head and squints of his eyes. He was fully engaged in a silent conversation with his lifelong friend.

"Zhan," Vinya repeated.

At last, Zhan tore his attention from Yuwon and turned to her. A hint of concern lay behind his stoic mask. He was worried about his friend.

Vinya didn't care. She was finished playing dress-up, through with keeping up conversations. She needed to think and plan, and had no intention of wasting time.

Hyosung would not be able to get her straight through the gates a second time—he must have another way out. All Vinya needed to do was play along for the next few days.

With one last look in Yuwon's direction, Zhan nodded, "Alright."

Vinya did not bother saying goodbye to the Crown Prince. She walked past Zhan while Sooni hurried after her.

The three walked in silence back to her room, even chatty Sooni didn't speak, but Vinya's mind reeled. She was formulating a plan.

As soon as she was back in her room, she called upon the Palace Seamstresses. Vinya spent that evening and the entirety of the next day with the women, giving careful instructions on the details of a new robe. Jinhee and Sooni stayed close, bringing meals as the day went on.

Zhan's ever watching eye peeked through her door each time it opened.

She didn't mind now; he could watch all he wanted. The first step of a new disguise was underway, and in a couple of days, she would not have to see any of them ever again.

6

Scales Askew

One day.

One day is all it would have taken for her to be beyond this room. Beyond the walls. Liberated from her captors and running for Norhagan. For home.

Yet here she was, lying on the floor of the Queen's room, the robe she had commissioned sprawled beside her. She tried to breathe from the shock, tried to clear her clouded vision. Her cheek and eyes stung.

She'd entered the room and was slapped by the Queen of Byonea so suddenly and so violently that lights speckled before her eyes. Her plan to escape had been dissolved yet again, and she was left with nothing but despair.

Queen Joona stood above her; her rant was hushed yet full of fury. Vinya didn't need to hear her words to understand the trouble she was in. Spit flew from the Queen's mouth as ladies-in-waiting watched on. The scuffle outside of the door that had broken out after the slap had subsided.

The Queen's women smirked. Alastor failed to hide his sneer. Jinhee and Sooni covered their mouths in horror.

Though Vinya had tried to be careful, the seamstresses caught on. There was no way the promised princess would need a robe lined in orchid-colored silk.

She would have found a way out of her room the next night—some excuse to stray from her guards. She would have then flipped the robe inside out and played the part of a concubine walking through the gardens, waiting for her lover.

But the seamstresses whispered. Their hushed words were carried in the wind to the Queen's women, and the women delivered the news to their keeper, who was no fool.

Queen Joona was quick to let everyone know that the only fool was Vinya.

Was the Crown Prince down the hall? Had he heard the commotion and chose to stay away? She wouldn't have blamed him, if this is how his mother often treated others. Or had he been one of those in favor of her punishment? Was he, the one she was supposed to marry, the one who suggested this?

Perhaps it was his way of getting out of a marriage he did not want. She heard not one peep, did not receive one note from him, had no indication that he wanted a relationship with her at all.

The Queen spoke again, a command to rise, and Vinya pulled herself to her knees. Her collapse would have to take the place of a bow.

Vinya understood the birds now. Their chirps somewhat obscured the Queen's own squabbling, and they were especially riled by her outbursts. Prying ears would not be able to distinguish the words spoken within.

She looked for the Norhagan canary, but it was nowhere to be found. Vinya didn't doubt the Queen had managed to dull its coloring in the last few days, blending it in with the rest of the captive birds.

A hand smacked onto the table, and Vinya's eyes shot to the Queen as she spat at her from across the table.

"*I am speaking*," she hissed, but when she looked directly into Vinya's eyes, she recoiled a bit. "The King is... indisposed at the moment, and Yuwon will take his place at the Spring Festival in two days' time. As you were planning to use this time to scurry off, it's been decided that you will join him."

Vinya held her ground. She would not give the Queen the emotions she desired, she would not cry and beg at her feet. Getting out of the palace walls was what Vinya wanted, but it seemed impossible to slip through their fingers. The guards would now be tripled, quadrupled even.

Vinya would have to watch for the slightest opportunity to bolt. Though the Festival was near Taejim, they knew where her grandmother's house was, so she would have to seek shelter elsewhere or blend into the crowds until they gave up on her.

If they would give up.

The Queen continued. "You will bring one of your ladies with you—"

"Sooni," Vinya interrupted. The girl would be helpful for gathering information, and young enough to manipulate into letting her go.

She looked at the young girl, who still stood frozen from the blow Vinya had received. But, understanding sparked in Sooni's eyes.

Queen Joona's eyes flared as she continued, "One of my women will come along with you—to keep you company."

To keep her within sight.

Vinya blinked. The Queen said woman, not lady-in-waiting; it wouldn't be any of these poised peacocks in the room with them.

The Queen motioned towards the door, and it was opened. The gentle footsteps of her new companion approached.

Orchid-colored robes knelt, facing her, as the woman bowed with arms outstretched presenting a small box to Vinya.

Vinya glanced at the Queen, who tilted her head towards the box.

She reached and opened the box, her heart sinking further at its contents.

"A royal ring for the promised princess," the Queen said. Her ladies lightly clapped, feigning awe.

Jinhee and Sooni did not move.

The silver ring forked at the top, shaped into dainty florals and leaves, minuscule diamonds covered each of the branches. In the center sat a large cushion cut gemstone as red as Byonea's royal robes.

Vinya would have found it beautiful if she had not seen the ring as it was: a manacle in the form of a gift. A promise of blood if she were to step out of line again.

"Put it on, let us see if it fits," Queen Joona commanded.

Vinya complied and slipped the ring onto her third finger. She had to squeeze her fingers together so that it did not fall off.

The Queen's lip curled in satisfaction; she knew the ring would be loose.

She continued, "My choice of companion for you is a leman of the King." Turning to the woman with the orchid robes, she said, "Daeya, rise and greet Yuwon's future wife."

Not *future princess*.

What sort of reaction would the concubine have, once she realized who Vinya was?

Sooni's jaw was set. She knew without a doubt that Daeya was to blame for the first night's marks on Vinya's face and was being careful to not show it. Vinya assumed the Queen was now on whatever hate-list Sooni kept inside her mind.

She braced herself as Daeya rose, and shock rang through her when recognition did not pass over the woman's face.

Perhaps it was the lighting or the bright clothes the ladies had dressed her in today, but Daeya did not remember her.

The concubine's eyes lit up at the fresh mark on Vinya's face. The woman found joy in pain. Of course she would. She was obviously close to the jealous queen. Her like-mindedness and submission only gained her favor in the eyes of the royal family.

Daeya's speech dripped with sugar. "It is a pleasure to meet you. I look forward to our journey together and hope that we can become close over the next few days."

No amount of sweetness could cover the poison in her words. She was a spy for the Queen. Surely Joona understood that Vinya would see through the charade, but she had no choice except to comply.

Alastor spoke for the first time since Vinya entered the room. "Daeya has been in service for a few years, she knows Palace life well. The Queen and I agree that she will be an excellent tutor for you, to help you learn your place."

Daeya was a new piece in the Queen's game, another player to strategize around. Vinya needed to step carefully around the serpent placed in her path.

The first move was to acknowledge her new opponent. She dipped her head in a nod, which would look like an agreement to the others in the room. The others, Vinya realized, also wore the golden circlet around their necks. Not only were they ladies-in-waiting and concubines, but they were also the Queen's women.

"Daeya will meet you outside of your quarters tomorrow before noon. The road is long, so I advise you to rest well before your travels. You may now leave."

As Vinya stood, the Queen's ladies poured two cups of tea. One for the Queen, one for the concubine. Yet another insult rubbed in her face.

Vinya waited as the door was opened for her, and was met with a man her height standing on the other side.

Hyosung. His eyes did not move. They were trained over her shoulder and drilled into the Queen as if he could see through the door all along.

Though he did not move or speak, his wrath was apparent.

The Queen was silent behind her. Vinya turned to see the Queen staring right back at the King's firstborn. She was in between two people who had three decades' worth of untouched and unspoken disdain towards one another.

Even Alastor shifted on his feet at the sudden appearance of the Shade Prince.

Vinya had no words, no energy to move as Hyosung's eyes slid to hers.

He held an outstretched arm to her—an invitation. It was a welcome one that Vinya obliged while Jinhee and Sooni followed silently in their wake.

At the entrance of the hall, Zhan stood waiting on the opposite side and was being blocked by two guards. He was just outside of the Queen's door when Vinya entered her room. Had the royal guards removed him? He was commanded to protect her, and she had been left to fend for herself in this meeting.

Zhan shoved one of the guard's hands off as they approached and straightened his shirt as another guard handed him his sword. They'd taken it from him, Vinya realized.

She and Hyosung passed the guards, and Zhan's countenance turned to steel when he saw her face. Vinya could only assume that a red mark in the shape of a handprint covered her entire cheek.

As they exited the royal quarters, it dawned on Vinya that Hyosung walked on her left to block the view of the mark from onlookers; with it being the middle of the day, many nobles strolled about. Hyosung gave unforgiving glares to anyone who stared too long. She imagined Zhan did the same behind them.

These people did not matter to her. She was a point of interest, a topic of conversation held around dining tables. Poisoned gossip was being spread as the nobles walked through the beautiful gardens, but Vinya kept her focus ahead. She cared less and less about this country that offered nothing for her.

But no... that wasn't right either, she realized as she dropped her eyes to the arm holding her own. To the hand that offered to help her.

The red stone on the ring glistened in the sunlight and caught both of their eyes.

"It's too big," Hyosung stated.

The ring was physically loose, but she understood what the Shade Prince was saying. It was an unnecessary burden, far too great for someone in her place.

"The Queen will make it fit," she whispered.

Hyosung looked sidelong at her, genuine concern lining his face.

They were the only words Vinya spoke as he led her back to her room. Hyosung hesitated outside of the door as she dropped to her mattress and curled on her side.

Jinhee and Sooni moved around her, quietly preparing for the next day's journey. They brought in a trunk and packed clothes for the three days she would be gone. Vinya hadn't even noticed that the cabinet had been filled with clothes in her absence. The robes were too bright—too much like the birds that lined the Queen's walls.

Disgust twisted in her stomach. Vinya flipped over to turn her back to the robes, only to find Zhan watching her from the doorway. She wondered if he could see beneath the surface, that the Queen was draining her—molding her into one of her pets. Vinya hoped he saw it in her eyes. He closed the door, and Hyosung's uneasy voice carried through.

"She doesn't deserve this."

His words were resolute, there was no hint of pleading or anger, only pure truth.

Zhan did not agree, nor did he contradict the Shade Prince. The silence stretched on, only Hyosung's footsteps faded down the hall.

7

A Favorable Blow

Every bump in the road had solidified her decision. She'd go through the motions of the event, play the perfect princess-to-be during the Spring Festival in Kima, and sneak out the night before they had to leave. Her eyes slid to the window of the carriage and found Zhan already watching her from his horse. Vinya turned her attention to the opposing window.

Yuwon was alone in his own carriage at the front. A few officials, servants, and gifts for the festival were divided between the remaining three carriages. Two in front and one behind Vinya's own, with roughly ten guards surrounding each carriage.

The last small village they passed through quickly turned into a dense forest. Zhan would be the one person standing in her way—she would have to wait for or create some sort of distraction. She braced herself when their carriage hit a hole in the road.

Daeya smirked, having chosen the seat directly across from her, and turned to her companion, "Such a privilege, don't you think? The King so graciously allowed us to bring the carriage instead of individual palanquins." She stretched her feet forward, making Vinya pull her own back against the boards of her seat—a snake testing boundaries. "There's so much room, we can all travel so comfortably instead of being forced to rise on one of those dreadfully dirty creatures."

"A few things seem forced at the moment," Sooni piped from beside her.

Though small in stature, Vinya was glad to have her at her side. She had the heart of a warrior, never backing down from a potential threat.

Daeya's eyes popped open wide at the lady-in-waiting's comment, as if physically stricken that the girl would open her mouth to hint towards deception.

Another bump in the road shifted them in their seats, and gave Vinya just enough of a pause to step in before Daeya jumped the young girl again.

"On the contrary, the King's horses seem to be well fed and groomed, highly trained, and of solid countenance. They are far from dreadful or dirty." Vinya idly smoothed the creases in her skirt. "I'd heard in whispers just the other day that His Majesty would be gifting you with a mare of your choosing upon bearing a son for him. Should we send word to the King that his horses are not up to your standards?"

Daeya's mouth closed.

The whinnying of a horse gave Vinya an excuse to look out the window. Through it, Zhan watched the road again, but she could have sworn she saw a hint of a dimple push into his cheeks.

A cruel smile spread across Daeya's face. "How silly of me, I'd forgotten you were raised in the barns and fields of your own country."

Vinya tried to slide her hands out of reach as Daeya leaned forward, but the woman snatched one up anyway.

Daeya turned her hand over, inspecting the front and back. "We cannot expect our waters to cleanse the filth that has so *deeply* rooted itself in you, when you've slept with nothing but beasts."

Daeya held firm as Vinya tried to yank her hand free.

Despite the growing tension, Sooni barked a laugh. She lowered her voice, leveling a stare at the concubine, "As far as I see it, the only one sleeping with a beast is the King."

Daeya turned towards the young girl, her lips peeled into a sneer that sent shivers down Vinya's spine. Daeya's breath was slow and ragged as she dug her nails into Vinya's palm. The sting forced a yelp out of her.

Zhan called for the company to halt at the same time that Sooni swatted at Daeya's hands. Daeya refused to let go. Instead, she sank her sharpened nails deeper into Vinya's skin, breaking it and drawing blood.

This woman did not care that Vinya was promised to the Crown Prince. Her position did not matter, not when hatred dripped from her words.

Another cry came from Vinya as the carriage door swung open. Zhan had dismounted and wrapped his hand around Daeya's arm. His grip was so fierce that the woman's hold on Vinya faltered, allowing him to pull Daeya from the carriage and pin her between it and his mount.

Zhan's scolding was almost as satisfying as Daeya trying to step away from the *dreadfully dirty* horse. He'd placed her there on purpose.

Vinya kept her hand closed. Only one nail had broken the skin, but she did not want the blood to drip—didn't want to give Daeya the gratification of seeing it spilled. It was the second time Daeya had left her mark, even if she didn't remember the first time.

Sooni pulled a wooden box from a compartment in the carriage and opened it to an array of salves and bandages.

Outside, Daeya's whines of "*I didn't say anything*" and "*I did nothing to antagonize anyone*" were going unheard by the muscular guard. His jaw was clenched as tight as the hand by his side—he'd seen nothing but heard everything.

Sooni's work was quick and efficient, and Vinya watched in wonder as the girl wrapped up her hand, solely focused on the task. No wonder she'd risen in rank at such an early age.

Male laughter roared in the distance, and a playful male voice called out. "I can't recall a single time that your words *didn't start anything*. Your mouth was what helped you gain your current position."

So, her behavior was no secret.

Daeya's face tightened further and turned a deep red as nearby guards chuckled, but she kept silent.

Zhan did not laugh and gave a pointed look to his men, who turned away or rubbed their faces to hide their smiles.

He released Daeya's arm and motioned to the horse behind her. "You can ride my horse until we get to Kima."

A flash of disgust before she plastered a sweet smile, looking up at him through her lashes. "You will be riding with me?"

He stepped beside her and held out his hand, a gesture to help her onto the horse. "I will walk."

At Daeya's falling face, Vinya stifled her laugh with a cough.

Daeya's attention snapped to the carriage, her mouth opened once more with a retort, but was interrupted.

A ball of fire shot from the forest and buried itself into the side of the carriage, missing Vinya's window by mere inches. There was a single moment, a pause that stretched in the world as the flame from the arrow now licked and spread over the wooded door it had embedded.

"*Raid!*" was called out by many of the guards.

Women screamed. Swords were drawn. Guards aimed their bows toward the oncoming fight. They scanned the surrounding forest, which now came to life in the form of camouflaged men who had emerald green bands strapped across their foreheads.

Calgham men.

The men's shouts pierced the air just as the arrow had.

Vinya knew one thing was certain: their carriage would soon become a death trap if they did not move. Sooni had pressed herself against the opposing wall, blocking the way out. Daeya's companion shoved her out of the way to open the door and jumped out—leaving Vinya and Sooni to fend for themselves.

Vinya leapt onto the road and turned to help the wide-eyed Sooni out of the carriage as well, but the young lady-in-waiting had frozen in place and shaking, not taking her eyes off the fire that now spread inside the carriage.

The ambushing men reached the outskirts of their group, their fight echoing through the woods. More arrows, more fire.

"Sooni!" she yelled through the rumble of noise, but the girl still didn't move. Instead, Sooni covered her ears.

Vinya glanced towards Yuwon's carriage. Many guards surrounded it and were being pushed back. Closer, *closer*. Horses were cut from their ties, freeing them from the burning carriages. The charging Calgham men outnumbered the guards five to one. They may not be enough.

Zhan had drawn his sword, Daeya wailed as she clung to his free arm. His attention was solely on the carriage that held the Crown Prince.

Vinya could see his mind at work, counting men and debating his next moves. Too many men pressed too close to Yuwon. He met Vinya's gaze through the flames. She was his charge, but Yuwon was his Prince, his friend. He would have to choose, and soon.

They both understood who was more important. Zhan knew she would take advantage of the moment.

Vinya broke the stare. She held the door to the carriage open and yelled again for Sooni, to no avail. She pulled the terrified girl out onto the dirt road, away from the searing heat and the flames that lunged after their fleeing forms. The ambush grew more chaotic, a second swarm of men came in from the woods.

Having made his decision, Zhan's face crumbled in anger. He shook Daeya off, hiked her onto his horse and sent it running, with Daeya atop screaming, into the distance. He turned and ran in the direction of the Prince, leaving Vinya with the panicking girl on the ground.

Vinya turned on her heel at the battle cry of a Calgham warrior—his sword raised and ready to strike her down, but his assault was thwarted. A guard's sword protruded from the warrior's stomach, splattering blood onto her. The Calgham man fell to the ground, and the guard focused on the next attacker.

Out of her mind, Sooni tried crawling under the flaming carriage to hide. Vinya grabbed her ankle and used every ounce of strength she had to pull her several feet and into the tall bushes amid the trees that lined the road.

Whimpers broke from the girl as Vinya slid back out of the bushes to grab the short sword she had spotted on the dead Calgham warrior. She slid the sword through the thick belt at her waist and returned to the bushes.

Sooni's cries had turned into wails, and no amount of shushing would quiet her. Vinya clamped one hand over her mouth to muffle the noise, placing the other hand behind her head to hold her still. Sooni gasped as Vinya brought her face in close.

"I'm begging you to be quiet. You *need* to be *silent.* I don't know what exactly the goal of these men is, but I have a feeling that if they catch you, they will kill you."

Sooni's chest worked in shallow breaths, tears slipped down her cheeks and onto Vinya's hand.

Vinya whispered, "If I let go, will you be quiet?"

The girl's eyebrows knit together. Her eyes closed, and she took a deep breath that threatened to turn into another wail. Vinya gave her head a small but firm shake that snapped Sooni out of it.

Tears built in her own eyes. She would have to leave Sooni here. She would have to go alone, leaving this girl to fend for herself.

"Will you be silent?" she asked again.

Sooni dipped her head, and Vinya slowly released her grasp. She pulled the sword from her belt and passed it to the girl.

"Use this if you need to, but try not to be seen."

Another nod from the girl as her fingers tightened around the sword.

Vinya removed the silver and pearl hairpin from her bun, her braid falling free down her back. She slipped the ring off her finger and pressed both pieces of jewelry into Sooni's hands.

"Tell them I was taken." Vinya stood. She backed deeper into the woods, away from the road. Sooni turned from where she sat, her face twisting with realization.

Vinya's vision blurred. "I'm so sorry."

For a third time, Sooni nodded. "Go. If it's what you truly need to do, go."

She understood. Sooni's fingers tightened on the hilt of the short sword, and she turned back to watch the fight on the road. Vinya hoped that if it came to it, the girl would fight.

With the armed girl hidden in the bushes, and with more Calgham men than Byonean guards converging on Yuwon's carriage, Vinya gathered her skirts and ran.

8

Amber and Gold

The chaos hid her retreat, but even when the noise of the fight had faded, she did not slow. Vinya kept distance between herself and the road, backtracking their travels. It was safer than running straight through the unknown woods, safer than running into any more hidden Calgham men.

She ducked between shrubs with the sound of nearing horses. Men from the village rode by, likely summoned by a guard who escaped the initial attack.

Vinya noticed the Calgham warrior's blood splattered on her skirts when they caught on a branch of the shrubbery. She sighed, stripped the top layer of the skirt and outer shirt off and shoved them into the bush. This left her in a white top and dusty blue skirt that didn't exactly blend in with her surroundings. Those lavish outer layers could have been traded for plainclothes, food, and coins to spare. She would have to settle with trading her earrings for a change of clothes for now, and save her golden coin for later.

The village was her goal. After the mayhem died down, she would follow the road to Taejim—giving Kima a wide berth—and travel to Gran's house after a week or so. She had faith Sooni would spin a believable story about her disappearance, and they wouldn't continually search for her there.

After half an hour, Vinya reached the village. She tucked any loose strands of her hair into place and smoothed out her skirts before stepping from the tree line. The village was buzzing with the news of the raid. Women and children looked down the road as if they could see the small battle from this distance, while others peeked nervously from their windows. Vinya slipped between buildings and headed in the opposite direction of the gathering citizens, listening to their whispers as she passed.

"...attack on the royals..."

"...Calgham men? In Byonea?"

"...Prince took His Majesty's place, I wonder if..."

"...fire. More men than they could hold off..."

Vinya blocked out their words. She had finally freed herself from her captors, so why did a pit grow in her stomach? And why did she still feel the tingle of someone watching her? Vinya calmed her labored breaths and scanned the surrounding buildings. There were no faces she recognized, but she kept her guard up regardless.

Vinya passed the tea shop, apothecary, craft shop, and tavern, and made her way to the small marketplace off the main road. Here she could buy *and* sell. A few of the stalls had closed for the day, others did not have what she needed. Finally, she spotted the fabrics stall and the building it connected to.

She made her way inside and to the shop owner. She pulled off her earrings and requested a set of clothes. The owner took the jewelry and went to grab the plainclothes when another woman's voice called out from a corner of the building.

"Vinya?"

She spun and met familiar eyes, along with a cascade of chestnut hair.

"*Miho.*"

The woman crossed the room, her arm looped through a basket of herbs and tinctures. Her hair fell as free and wild as the day they docked. She took in Vinya's clothes with a face full of questions.

"I made a trip to Taejim yesterday, asked around to see if you had arrived. They told me..." Miho paused, unsure if the news of Gran's death had reached her.

Vinya nodded, a knot growing in her throat.

Miho placed a gentle hand on her arm. "I'm sorry. If there's anything I can do, will you tell me?"

The shop owner returned with Vinya's new bundle of clothes. The two women stepped aside so other customers could speak with the shop owner.

Vinya fiddled with the twine that held her bundle together. "I apologize about leaving you at the docks. It wasn't my choice."

Miho grinned. "I knew it was a mistake; even with our brief meeting, you didn't seem like the type of person to willingly break a promise. Whatever it was, you made it out unscathed?"

Vinya lifted her bandaged hand. "Somewhat. I'll be alright. I suppose you would know where I can change?"

Miho nodded. "I'm staying nearby."

She walked out of the door, her unbound hair flowing behind her, leaving Vinya to hurry after her.

The silence stretched between them as they walked—Miho was back to her quiet self. People milled about, still talking amongst themselves about the raid. She hoped Miho was not paying attention and wouldn't ask any questions.

"You were able to get here safely?" Vinya asked.

Miho nodded again, biting at her fingernails. She opened her mouth to say something, then closed it.

Vinya held up a hand. "You don't need to tell me anything you don't want to, remember?"

Miho sighed through her nose and moved her hand from her mouth to her stomach. "No. Yes, I recall, but no, I want someone to know."

Vinya's brow furrowed. Miho's stomach was acting up on the ship as well. It dawned on Vinya then—Miho hadn't been queasy with *seasickness*.

Miho beamed as Vinya understood, then her face fell.

"He's not from here," she whispered.

"He's back in Norhagan?" Vinya asked.

She shook her head.

Vinya saw it then, the fear. Her lover was from Calgham.

Miho nodded. "I stayed further East last year, in Ungeong near the border. I'm trying to get there, but I ran out of funds and... I don't know if I could make the walk on my own. He tried to defect so many times when he was younger, but they would catch him, take him back. I—I left last month to go home, not knowing..."

"What of your parents?" Vinya asked.

Miho's expression glazed over; her hand drifted to her mouth as she bit on her nails.

Vinya raised a hand. "I'm sorry, I shouldn't have assumed that they were alive—"

"Oh, they are!" Miho said, returning from whatever memory she'd fallen into. "I thought they would be over the moon, another descendant to add to the family history... but then came the questions. I should have known, really. An unmarried woman, having a child with a Calgham man during times of unrest? Instead of joy, I brought shame to them, and to Norhagan."

A second time, she pressed a hand to her stomach. "If I hadn't left, I fear they would have excommunicated me anyway. I would have left with only the clothes on my back if our maid hadn't stopped me with a bag of clothes and a handful of coins on my way out."

Vinya tried to comfort her by rubbing her arm. "It's okay, it'll be okay."

Would it, though? With the impending war, and with Calgham warriors already crossing the border, Vinya doubted the Queen would look favorably on a defector.

"Would he be able to give information that would be helpful to the royal family? Perhaps he could enlist in the Byonean army?" Vinya asked.

Miho shook her head. "He's not a warrior. He is a kind man, a good man. He doesn't want to harm anyone, he—he just wants out of that country."

Vinya understood why Miho had been so quiet. This woman wasn't shy, she was only keeping all of this to herself. Did she have no one to share it with? No one else to place her trust in?

They stopped in front of what looked like a hostel. Miho pulled out a key and opened the door with trembling hands.

"If he were found out, if *we* were found out..."

The woman was terrified.

"I will not tell a soul," Vinya assured her.

Miho's green eyes glistened, her gratitude shining through. "Thank you. I—"

She stopped, her focus on the other side of the road.

Vinya turned, and facing the building was a Calgham warrior. He stood unblinking with a wicked sneer. He must have been who Vinya sensed following her earlier—must have seen her run from the carriage attack and tracked her here. People scattered as he drew his sword, finding their way into the safety of the surrounding buildings.

Vinya stared at the man as she passed her bundle of clothes to Miho.

"Get inside," Vinya said. "Lock the door and hide."

Miho's brow pulled together. She grabbed Vinya's wrist and moved to step backward into the doorway.

Vinya shook her off and spoke quickly.

"He's here for me. I'm sorry I don't have time to explain. I'll lead him away; you *cannot* come after me. I'll try to see what I can do for your... situation, but you need to stay safe right now," she added.

The Calgham warrior began his approach and leisurely stepped onto the road. He took his time, savoring the panic.

Confusion crossed Miho's face, her eyes darting back and forth from the man to Vinya. "Wait. Vinya, wait, I need—"

"Forgive me," Vinya interrupted.

She grabbed Miho's shoulders and forced her into the building.

Heavy footfalls sped up behind her.

Vinya pulled the door closed, fear constricting her throat. She did not have time to wait for the lock to click. She didn't hear it over the sound of a second set of feet.

Lighter. Faster.

She whirled. The Calgham warrior was only a few yards away, sword raised and radiating fury. There was no feasible way she could escape his swift wrath.

A man in black robes crossed in front of her, blocking her from the warrior.

No, the robes weren't black—they were midnight blue.

Swords clashed mere feet away, halting the warrior's ambush.

Crown Prince Yuwon fought the Calgham warrior. He fought for *her*.

Yuwon moved with grace. He saw every move three steps ahead, dodged and blocked every stab. With each step and twirl, the sword was an extension of his arm. He showed no emotion, not out of boredom, but focus. There was no hint of anger or betrayal, no fear of the fight. Only a man in his element.

The whoosh of Yuwon's robes as he spun, his steady footing, and calculated moves made the clashing of swords secondary.

Vinya tensed as the Calgham man swung wide, aiming for Yuwon's neck, but the Crown Prince ducked and used the warrior's momentum against him, kicking him a few feet away. Yuwon used that moment to glance over his shoulder at her.

The concern that flickered across his features made her breath catch.

His glance cost him.

The man used that split-second glance to charge again, faster than before. He held his sword with both hands high above his head, as if he would chop the Crown Prince in half like a log.

"Yuwon!" she yelled, pointing at the warrior behind him.

He hadn't needed her warning. Yuwon blocked the oncoming blow with one arm, baring his teeth at the force, and slipped a long dagger out of his belt.

The Calgham warrior did not see that their dance was coming to an end.

One moment the men were poised, locked in a duel with their swords pushing against each other. The next moment Yuwon flipped his dagger and shoved upward through the man's ribs, straight into his heart.

The man's sword slipped from his fingers, and he fell on his knees, choking on blood until he slipped to the ground, lifeless.

Yuwon's jaw hung loose, his breaths ragged and shaking. He yanked the dagger out, wiping it and his hand on the man's shirt before he sheathed the blade in his belt, followed by his sword. He faced Vinya, scanning her. Sweat beads formed and dripped over his brow.

The sound of shouts and horses neared—people who had just stepped back out on the street scurried out of their way.

Yuwon nodded, satisfied with whatever check he had just performed on her. He took a wavering step closer and offered his hand to help her stand. The tremble in his hand was barely noticeable.

Vinya looked from Yuwon's hand to his eyes. The setting sun hit them from the side, bringing deep shades of amber within to light.

Some of their traveling party had made it to town; their shouts to Yuwon echoed down the street.

Vinya turned towards the noise, then glanced in the opposite direction. This could be her opportunity to flee again, but would the prince in front of her permit it?

Yuwon blinked. His fingers curled into themselves ever so slightly.

Before Vinya could get to her feet, she was tackled by a wailing girl.

"*My lady*!" Sooni cried.

The Crown Prince straightened and dropped his hand to his side, a princely stance once more. Zhan and other guards caught up to the lady-in-waiting, monitoring for any new threats.

Sooni put on quite the show. "Oh, my *lady*. I was so worried when you disappeared! It was terrifying to see those men drag you off."

She crawled off Vinya and sprawled herself on the ground. "Forgive me, my lady. I failed you miserably!"

Vinya looked to Yuwon, who observed the girl as Zhan questioned him through his teeth.

"Your carriage *burned to the ground*, which you were obviously not in. The reinforcements of this town helped squander the Calgham raid, but we were frantic looking for you." Zhan drilled his friend. His concern came out as anger that he had to keep in check in front of others.

"I was in the back carriage," Yuwon said.

Sooni's crying hitched. The young lady-in-waiting sat up and wiped the tears from her cheeks.

The four of them exchanged looks as Vinya stood and brought Sooni up with her.

Yuwon had watched her run. He'd watched, and followed her here. It didn't take long before Zhan pointed at Vinya—ready to give her an earful—when Yuwon forced his hand back down.

"No one will speak of this," Yuwon commanded.

Zhan's head whipped to his friend—a silent conversation ensued between the two of them.

Sooni nonchalantly backed towards Vinya, hands open behind her back. The royal ring rested in her fingers.

Vinya slipped the ring back on.

Zhan shook his head and turned to some of his fellow guards. "We lost some men, our brothers. Find someone to take their bodies back to the palace."

Exhausted and dirty from the fight, they nodded and obeyed. Zhan turned to another section of men.

"We will need replacement carriages and guards. See if we can borrow some from the town—open topped carriages will do. His and Her Highness will ride in one of the closed carriages that remain. Send a messenger hawk to the palace. Replacement guards should arrive in Taejim tonight."

The second group followed suit.

Zhan continued to give orders: To protect them. To put a plan in place to drop the bodies of the Calgham warriors at the border. To clear the burnt carriage debris from the road before they return. To have everything finished in an hour's time.

"We need to move you two to a more secure location until we're ready to depart," Zhan said, before he turned to his men one last time. "We also need a scout party to find Daeya."

"Do we *have* to?" mumbled Sooni, and sighed when Zhan gave her a flat stare.

Movement in the hostel's window caught Vinya's attention—Miho had flattened herself against a far wall, biting at her nails.

"Let's go," Zhan said.

When Miho took a step towards the door, Vinya subtly shook her head. Another time. She would explain everything the next time they met. If fate had pulled them together twice already, Vinya believed they would meet again. She didn't want to bring Miho into the tangle of her own situation, especially if her Calgham lover may come looking for her. The result would be catastrophic if the Byonean guards got to him first. Vinya offered her a grim smile, and Miho backed against the wall once more. Everyone moved towards the main part of the town, but Vinya hesitated.

"My lady?" Sooni questioned from Zhan's side as the two of them backtracked.

"I'll be right there," Vinya replied.

She slipped the coin necklace over her head and down her braid, keeping the gold coin hidden in her palm, and knelt by the hostel's door. She flicked the coin through the space between the door and worn wooden floor before Zhan stepped up to hover over her shoulder.

"What was that?" he asked.

Vinya stood and brushed the dirt from her skirts. She hoped Miho could hear her through the door. "I'm securing a dream."

"Is that some sort of Norhagan tradition?" Sooni asked, studying the bottom of the door.

"Something like that," Vinya said.

Zhan's sharp gaze caught more than she'd revealed. If she couldn't make her own dream a reality, she could help someone else with theirs.

He pressed on and reached for the door handle. "Who is in there?"

Vinya held her hand in his path, blocking him from grabbing the knob. Both of their hands hovered midair.

"A friend who will not be involved in any of this."

This one action would not hurt them. Leaving Miho alone would not bring Byonea tumbling to its knees.

The guard drilled Vinya with a stare.

She lowered her voice to a whisper. "This is my one request, Zhan. Leave her be, and I—I will not make any unnecessary trouble for you."

Zhan raised a brow and dropped his voice as well. "You will not run?"

Vinya swallowed. Was she really willing to give up her freedom for this woman she barely knew? She would have to find a way out of this pact.

"I—"

"Zhan," Yuwon called from the group of guards.

Zhan looked over his shoulder at Yuwon, and Vinya took the opportunity to step around him.

"We're coming!" she answered for him.

Vinya hurried towards the Crown Prince and guards with Sooni in tow, but did not miss the look Zhan gave her—one that said she was not out of this.

They were all given food and drink by the townspeople, and a hall was opened to host them until they were ready to leave.

Yuwon kept to himself, surrounded by guards in a corner of the room. He sat alone at the table, solemn and staring at his hands.

Daeya had been found and brought into the hall. When Vinya declined a local's invitation to freshen up, Daeya quickly asked to take her place. Her grass-stained skirt and scrapes of dirt on her hands and forearms suggested she'd taken a tumble off the horse that potentially saved her life.

Vinya wondered if she still considered them to be beasts, or if the snake would continue to nip at their heels.

With everyone rested and fed, wounds tended to, and reinforcements on their way, the traveling party climbed into the carriages once more.

Zhan opted to sit in with them, directly across from Vinya. Vinya did not let the discomfort of the close quarters, or Zhan's careful watch, show on her face.

The bandage around her hand had come loose, and Sooni rewrapped it as the carriage lurched forward. The young girl, though small, kept her knees tucked in while she meticulously tied the new bandage—as the Crown Prince Yuwon sat across from her, his long legs taking up most of the space between them.

Vinya sucked in air through her teeth when Sooni tied the bandage a bit too tight, and in the midst of the young girl's apologies, the Crown Prince shifted his gaze to Vinya's wrapped hand—his brow pulled together ever so slightly. He sighed. As if needing something mundane to occupy his mind, Yuwon slid the carriage window open and watched the trees pass by.

None of them spoke as the carriage picked up pace down the bumpy road. Yuwon continued his focus on the woods as the village faded into the distance, with what looked like a hint of regret.

9

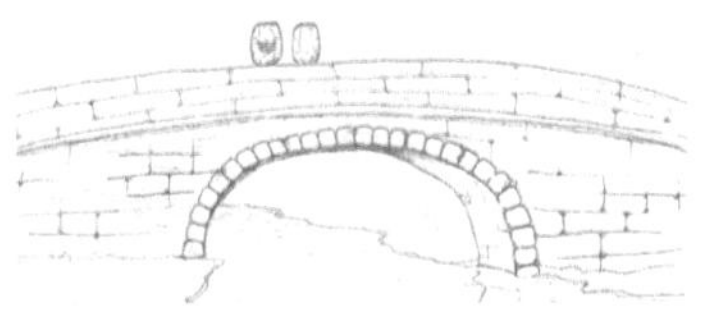

A Bridge Formed

They sent a messenger ahead to the owner of the building where they'd be staying, to let them know of their late arrival. After a broken wheel and a guard falling ill, it was well after dark by the time they arrived and unloaded.

Weary, they retired to their rooms, and a decent meal was served to them. Vinya and Sooni shared one room, Daeya and her companion were in the next bedroom, and the officials and servants spread out on the same floor. Guards escorted Yuwon to a room on the next level up. Half of the guards dropped their packs in the rooms surrounding him and fell asleep while the other half took the first shift.

Vinya felt guilty being able to sit and eat, while the men outside had to stand after such a long journey.

She and Sooni took turns taking sponge baths behind a screen and had just laid down for the night when a knock sounded on the door.

Sooni opened it to an exhausted Zhan—who lifted a finger.

"Do not fight me on this."

Zhan dropped his pack right inside the door. He stepped in, closed the door, and immediately laid down, head on his pack and body blocking the doorway.

"Excuse me?" Sooni exclaimed, hands on hips.

Zhan crossed his arms over his chest and closed his eyes. "I said *don't fight me*, did I not? His Highness commanded it. Believe me, I don't like it as much as you do."

Sooni huffed a laugh, her shock moving from one subject to the next. "Most men would *like* to sleep in the same room as two women."

Zhan stiffened and gave the girl a look that would send *most men* running.

"Oh, I think he breathed fire that time," the young girl said as she plopped down on her mat.

Zhan only shook his head, clearly over her antics, and shifted on the hard ground as he closed his eyes again.

He was only doing his job—but Vinya figured he did as he was commanded for more than just a job. More than just the blind obedience of a royal guard. He'd crossed the country, sprinted through the palace in the middle of the night, put up with Sooni's rants, and now laid at the threshold of her door. He did it out of love for his friend. And she'd caused much of that trouble for him.

Vinya pulled the top layer of padding off her mat.

"My lady?" Sooni yawned.

Vinya hauled the padding to Zhan. "Get up."

His brow bunched together.

"Please?" she asked.

He was skeptical as he stood. She folded the padding lengthwise and smoothed it onto the ground where he had been, careful not to put pressure on her still-wrapped hand.

Vinya motioned towards the mat she had made and was about to walk back to her own when she saw his face. All the steel had been wiped away as he stared at the padding.

"Well you watched me make it, so you know it isn't a trap," she said.

He met her gaze, "Thank you."

Vinya gave him the smallest grin before she folded what remained of her mat the same way. When she laid down and turned to check on the guard, Zhan hadn't moved—like the mat really would jump up and pull him through the floor.

Sooni whispered across the room to him, "Are you going to cry?"

In a blink, his steely gaze slid back in place. Zhan shot the girl a look and settled down on the mat.

Satisfied when his body relaxed, Vinya turned to face the opposite wall and didn't remember falling asleep.

They rose at daybreak. At some point in the night, Zhan had rolled his mat and left for his patrol shift without waking them, leaving his replacement guard outside of their door.

Sooni opened the trunks that had been packed for them, and pulled out combs, jewelry, and Vinya's attire for the day. It was the first official day of the Spring Festival, and Vinya needed to look the part of a royal representative, head to toe.

Layer after layer of bright green skirts, the white top tied high on her waist lined with salmon colored ribbon. Earrings, bracelets, and cosmetics. Sooni hummed as she combed, braided, and looped Vinya's hair into a bun. Metal flowers, with jade beads dangling from their centers, were placed all around her hair.

She was the epitome of spring, a goddess ushering in the floral landscape for the year.

It astonished her how efficient Sooni was on her own; she had Vinya finished and ready long before Zhan came to escort her to the festival.

A new bundle of nerves sparked in her stomach. Zhan assured her that she wouldn't have to speak, but the pressure of being in front of so many people all day had her fidgeting with the edge of her sleeve.

Daeya and her lady walked behind them in her usual attire, but the woman had gone the extra mile, adorning herself with a coronet of pink and purple flowers made from precious stones.

"She looks like a bush," Sooni had leaned in to whisper when Daeya first stepped out of her room.

Vinya bit her cheeks to try and hide her smile as she shushed the girl.

It didn't take long to hear the festival goers. Their joyful whoops and laughter echoed through the brightly decorated town. Streamers and banners had been strung across the roads. Children with pinwheels ran free, squealing at the top of their lungs as they passed.

A large white dragon costume wound its way through the streets; the performers inside kept the movements eerily lifelike, while others outside were in charge of moving the four feathered wings up and down with thin poles.

Townspeople adorned the white dragon with paper flowers in a multitude of colors as it went by—symbolic of flowers pushing through the winter snow, of the new year blooming before them.

Their small party made it to the main square, people bowing to Vinya as they passed. Entertainers set up in the middle and showed off their skills to the people who gathered around the outskirts. Sooni squealed and ducked when a man on stilts stepped clean over her.

The officials branched off to meet those in charge of the festival, while a handful of guards returned from making sure the area was secure. They led the group to a covered platform and motioned for Vinya and Sooni to take the chairs on one side, while Daeya and her companion took the others. The chair raised higher in the middle would be for Yuwon.

Zhan stood directly behind Vinya's chair and continuously scanned the crowd. His black guard's hat cast a shadow on his face, his vision to be unhindered by the sun.

Shouts arose down the street, and the people parted—bowing deeply at the waist—as their Crown Prince joined the festival. Though he was surrounded by guards, he scanned over the crowd. He sat in the middle chair, clenched fists peeking from underneath his robes, and gave a short nod for the merriment to start.

The Spring Festival began, and Vinya watched in awe as the performers danced. The dragon costume came swooping in from high stilts and pushed back the white fabrics of snow. It left in its wake the flowers that had been placed on it throughout the morning.

Hour after hour, they were entertained by the townspeople and their yearly rituals.

In contrast to spring burying the memories of the cold winter, the lively festivities couldn't bury the fact that this would've been the day that she and Gran would have walked behind her house—checking the new growths in her gardens. What used to be a journey filled with warmth and love was now only a memory, settled in her heart.

A bundle of white hair peeked through the crowd opposite of their platform. A hand weakly threw flower petal after flower petal into the circle of dancers.

Vinya grasped the armrest of her chair and halfway stood. There was no way that could be...

"Gran?" she whispered.

Vinya blinked and the old woman stepped out of the throng of people. A small child clung to the woman's other hand and passed the old woman the petals to throw. Her mind was playing tricks on her. Being this close to Taejim, Gran was all she could think about.

Vinya sat once more. Sooni had scooted her own chair closer to Vinya and passed her a handkerchief.

Vinya took a deep breath as the dancers faded into a blur. The colors of spring became a cascade of colorful rain swiped across her vision, just as her hopes of leaving Byonea were now dashed. There had to be a way. She dropped her head, and the tears fell straight to her lap.

A snicker came from the far right of the platform. From the corner of her eye, Vinya could see Daeya leaning forward. The concubine wasn't trying to make her movements inconspicuous. She only tried to gain attention as she shook her head at Vinya and laughed again. Her orchid-colored fan flapped in the wind as she glanced at the Crown Prince between them.

Sooni leaned around Vinya and stuck her tongue out at the concubine, who gasped dramatically and closed her fan with a snap.

Yuwon, in the midst of them all, sat unmoving. He wanted no part of the women's quarrels; he did not care to step in. Zhan did it for him, walking over and whispering something over Daeya's shoulder.

The concubine opened her fan once more and smiled sweetly up at Zhan. No amount of eye-batting would sway the guard, and he returned to his position behind Vinya.

Roars of excitement came from the crowd, jolting Vinya back to the present. She used the handkerchief to wipe away any remnant of tears and sat straight. She wouldn't let Daeya win whatever battle she had waged against her. It must be tiring to bicker with every person, every day, but perhaps that was the only way the concubine could entertain herself, given her nightly occupation. Vinya focused on the festival, even though, at times, she didn't quite see it.

They were served small meals as the hours crawled by. The townspeople put on performance after colorful performance. Children laid flowers at the foot of their platform. Daeya was sure to give too-loud compliments, pulling the attention to herself, to which Sooni rolled her eyes. The festivities lulled as the sun descended, and the people dispersed into the streets when glistening stars covered the sky.

Vinya stood to stretch her legs, leaning in to tell Sooni that she was ready for sleep. It was the absolute truth. She couldn't imagine how exhausted the performers were if she were this tired from sitting in one place all day.

Sooni shook her head. "The Festival isn't over yet. Everyone is just moving to the river."

"Why the river?" Vinya asked.

The young girl giggled. "Have you not been to a lantern lighting before?"

Vinya slowly blinked. She hadn't seen them before; she and Gran had always been inside after the sun had set.

Daeya stood soon after Yuwon and followed him down the steps of the platform. Sooni motioned for Vinya to follow as well.

Guards surrounded them as they walked to the nearby river. A large bridge stretched across, and on both sides paper lanterns lined the bank. Sparklers had been distributed throughout the people, but none of them were lit. They seemed to be waiting for something.

Two lanterns sat at the peak of the bridge. One plain, and one patterned with the four-winged feathered dragon.

The people had been waiting for them. She and Yuwon would start this ceremony. Vinya fidgeted with the sleeve of her robe. Sooni and Zhan would be with them as well, but to be the focus of so many people unnerved her.

Zhan searched the crowd, twice, three times. His surveillance did not stop moving as he approached them.

"Everyone is in place. If anything happens, get down and I'll come to you."

Vinya's heart cringed. They would be alone on the bridge.

Zhan's all-seeing gaze noted her hesitancy. "It will be fine. News of what happened yesterday should have reached Calgham by now, they would be fools to try again so soon."

He thought the threat of the enemy was what made her nervous. He was oblivious that being the center of attention, on the center of a bridge, alone with the Crown Prince the country was forcing her to be with, was what worried her.

Yuwon's arm moved, lifting as if he would offer it to her, but he returned it to his side. He took a shallow breath and began the ascent up the bridge.

It only took Vinya a split second to catch up to him. Side by side, they scaled the bridge. Her heart raced with each step that separated them from the crowd. With every step, the tension grew between them, and by the time they reached the middle, the air between them hung thick.

The Crown Prince's breaths seemed a little too controlled. He did not move. His arms hung at his sides, but that, too, was controlled. They weren't limp, but tense.

Yuwon was just as nervous as she was.

Murmurs from the crowded bank floated through the air. Impatient children tugged at their parents' pants.

Still, the Crown Prince did not move.

Vinya took a deep breath and reached for the sparkler that was placed between their lanterns. Yuwon followed the movement with his eyes. She pulled the sparkler from its holder and turned to Yuwon, who still had not budged. Vinya subtly nodded towards the larger decorated lantern. After a moment, Yuwon took hold of his lantern and lifted it so Vinya could light it from underneath. She took her own lantern and did the same before turning the sparkler upside down in its holder, putting out the flame.

Soon, the riverbank was alight. Hundreds upon hundreds of lanterns lit up, the water's reflection doubling it.

Vinya had never seen something so beautiful. It was as if hundreds of suns had awakened spring from its cold slumber.

The soft shifting of Yuwon's foot brought her attention back to him. Though he didn't look her way, his movement alerted her that it was time to release the lanterns. *His* turn to help *her*.

Together, their lanterns floated into the sky, followed by those of the townspeople. Cheers rang out from the crowd, and new tears pooled in Vinya's eyes—it was one of the most wondrous things she had ever seen. There was nothing like this in Norhagan. She had found something beautiful in Byonea.

Footsteps reverberated on the wooden planks of the bridge, grabbing their attention as Zhan approached from the side. His face was calm as he held out his hand low and subtly shook his head—there was no problem, he had only come to escort them back.

Yuwon sighed through his nose, and Vinya couldn't help but join him. She couldn't tell if his was one of relief from not being alone with her, not being the center of attention, or there not being a Calgham threat.

Perhaps it was a mixture of all three, just like she felt.

The crowd parted as they passed. Vinya was unused to people bowing to her—not the polite greeting of every day, but the deep bows at the waist reserved for the royal family. At first she thought they were only bowing to Yuwon, but they made direct eye contact before bowing to her as well.

It made her stomach flip over.

Daeya congratulated the Crown Prince on a job well done, but was interrupted by Sooni, who hopped around the concubine, holding her own sparkler.

"They said I could keep it!" she exclaimed as she waved the sparkler in circles.

The movement made her look childish, especially beside Zhan who stared at the sparkler like the fire hazard that it was.

Sooni gave the sparkler a few wiggles in Daeya's face—who swatted the girl away—before skipping to Vinya's side.

Yuwon had positioned himself in the middle of the guards as they walked back to their accommodations. Sooni linked arms with Vinya and spun the sparkler around until it burned out completely. She pouted the rest of the way back to the building, and Vinya hid her amusement between yawns.

They spent the night the same as before, with Zhan at the door and leaving in the small hours of the day before the women woke. Except this time, he came back.

He squatted beside Vinya's mat and carefully patted her shoulder until she woke. She sat up, confused, as he pressed a finger over his lips and pointed to a snoring Sooni.

Vinya understood, *don't wake the girl*, but why?

Zhan helped her stand and passed her a wrap-skirt and short robe to slip over her nightclothes. A makeshift outfit. He pointed to the clothes, then motioned up and down her body before he turned around, giving her a sense of privacy even though she kept her nightgown underneath the robe and skirt.

Vinya tapped him on the shoulder when she was done, and he pulled a scrolled note from his pocket. He motioned toward Sooni, waved the scroll, and placed it on Vinya's vacant pillow.

As soon as they got into the hall and the door closed behind them, Vinya turned to him.

"What is going on?" she whispered.

Zhan only walked down the hall, light on his heels as she hurried after him. Her braid swayed with the movement.

The shutters were still closed, which meant the sun was not yet up, but Zhan placed his guard's hat on as they neared the front door of the building. One guard who stood at the door gave Zhan a small straw hat—the same type she had worn during her escape attempt her first night in Byonea. He held it out to Vinya.

Vinya did not take it. "If this is some sort of test, some wild trap, I would rather go back to my room."

Zhan heaved a sigh.

"You will not run," he said.

There was no anger or trickery in his words. He did not raise his voice or lower it. It was a command, not a question. Vinya wasn't quite sure what made her agree.

"I will not run," she replied, as she took the hat and placed it upon her head.

Zhan searched her face, looking for any hint of rebellion. He nodded, and the guards opened the door for them to exit.

Before them, a guard sat at the reins of an open carriage. One of the horses huffed into the early morning air. The guard jumped down as they approached and bowed his head as he offered a hand to help her climb into the front seat.

Vinya looked at Zhan to ask where they were going, but he had already used the wheel to hop into the cargo area of the carriage. He still watched out of the corner of his eye.

The unknown bothered her. She'd been hauled across Byonea once before while her questions went unanswered. Had this country already taught her to keep her mouth shut? What was one more mysterious ride before her fate was absolutely sealed in stone?

She took the guard's hand and pulled herself up the first step.

"Vinya," the guard said.

She whipped her head to the one who spoke her name and was met with a familiar face. Someone whose eyes sparked with a mischievous gleam. Someone who had disguised himself as a guard.

10

A Crack in the Pottery

Yuwon lifted her hand higher, a reminder to keep climbing.

She was hyper-aware of the hand that gently held hers.

"The day will not wait for us here," Zhan stated from behind her. Although he focused on the piece of straw he twirled between his fingers, Vinya could see the dimples pressing into his cheeks.

She scaled the rest of the carriage and sat as stiff as the boards beneath her.

Yuwon settled beside her, gathered the reins, and with a gentle snap they started down the street.

Vinya's fingers drifted to her palm, still feeling the warmth of his touch.

Taejim.

They'd brought her to Taejim.

Morning birds sang them as they traveled. The dark sky turned the softest blue as the sun rose, morning dew settled on the foliage.

Silence stretched between them. An hour had passed since they left Kima. Yuwon helped her down from the carriage, neither of them able to meet the other's eye. As the three of them stood in front of her grandmother's home, Vinya knew this wasn't freedom being offered to her.

It was a moment to say goodbye.

She could not force her feet to move. She waited. Waited...

The door should open. Gran's arms open wide. The smell of flowers wafting from within the home. Questions of her journey, of home. Inquiries to see if her mother had finally decided to move to *the motherland*. Vinya's own questions of Gran's health would be waved away. The subject would be changed. She would fall asleep at the end of this initial reunion with a smile and a full stomach.

Instead, she was burdened with grief, and she could not move.

Yuwon and Zhan stood on either side of her, and they too waited. They would not push her to do anything until she was ready. It was her choice to enter the home or not.

A gravelly voice called from the next home over. "Vinya?"

Her head turned—the movement numb.

The old woman hobbled down her steps and made her way towards them. "We expected you days ago, sweetie. I told my husband to keep an eye out for you, but he *insisted* you'd received the news before you crossed the waters."

The old woman reached up and cradled Vinya's cheek, a sad smile on her face. "We are happy you're here, now."

Tears flowed down Vinya's cheeks, she could not stop her shoulders from shaking. "They said—they said she was found."

The woman's face twisted; her wrinkles deepened. "Found? No, sweetie, she was not alone. My husband and I were there with her, and a lovely young man from another village who checked in on her every so often. I held her hand as she passed."

The older woman recreated the moment, and Vinya looked at the wrinkled hands that wrapped around her own. She squeezed her eyes shut and tried to not imagine it being Gran holding her.

The old woman went on, "Your Gran knew it was time, and she wasn't afraid. She was at peace, Vinya."

Vinya blew out a shaky breath. Of course Gran had been alright—she wouldn't have let the dark thoughts take hold of her mind. Gran was more than likely waving off whatever being oversaw her in the afterlife, even as they spoke.

"She left everything to you," the old woman whispered. "The home, her trinkets, her jewelry. We couldn't find her wedding band, though. She must have taken it off and put it somewhere before..."

Vinya glanced at the home.

Gran would not be in there, but her memory was.

"You and your," the woman paused and raised a brow at the men by her side, "friends can go in if you'd like. We left it just as it was, just as she wanted."

Vinya nodded a second time, and the old woman hobbled off to sit on a bench in front of her own home.

"We will wait out here for you," Zhan murmured.

Vinya took a deep breath and approached the house.

The front door opened with a creak. The air was stale but still held the scent of Gran, of every spring, of her childhood, and of the tough yet tender love she received each year. Vinya entered, removing the straw hat from her head as she lingered just inside of the door. Everything was the same, but the home felt empty. Hollow.

Vinya looked over her shoulder and found Yuwon watching her from the side of the carriage. After a breath, he moved to close the space between them—leaving Zhan three steps behind and hurrying to catch up with the prince's sudden movements.

Yuwon understood. She didn't want to be alone.

Vinya went further into the home as Yuwon ducked under the low door frame. The Crown Prince of Byonea stepped into her grandmother's home. Her home. He looked out of place. A prince in a guard's uniform, standing in the house she'd spent every spring in.

He took in every detail around him.

The worn wooden floors, the table that took up the majority of the entry room covered in trinkets and paintings. The open shelves that lined the kitchen off to the right, the sparse cups, plates, and bowls spread across them. The tattered rug below the sink. The cobwebs in the corners of the ceiling that Gran never swept down. "*They help with the* bugs," she would say.

The hall off to the left led to the two bedrooms. One was Gran's, and the other was the spare where Vinya stayed.

Yuwon's brows lowered as he looked to the hallway, as if he knew that's where Gran spent her last moments.

Her childhood was here for him to glimpse into. Everything she'd known about Byonea was taught to her here. She felt small while the cracks in the walls of this home—her home—grew larger in her mind. She was aware of the creak in the floorboards if Yuwon were to move two steps to the right. The ceiling felt low, failing to swallow the presence of the Crown Prince.

She wanted to stay here, and yet she needed out.

The carved trinkets Vinya gifted Gran every year sat together on their own shelf. She wanted to cherish them, and something deep within her didn't want to look at them at all.

Zhan shifted on his feet—the stillness of the room overwhelmed him. "Let me know what you'd like to bring to the palace. I'll secure it in the back of the carriage."

Vinya dipped her head and paced the compact home. Her eyes ran over everything. Her hands opened every box and drawer that Gran's ring could be inside of, but there was no sign of the ring, and she could not choose anything to take.

A cream vase cracked with age sat in the middle of the table and was filled with early cherry blossom buds. They drooped from the lack of watering over the past several days. Vinya brushed her thumb over the buds, and one of them broke off between her fingers.

Her breath caught as Yuwon stepped up beside her. He tilted his head toward the vase.

"Is that what you would like?" he asked.

Vinya nodded. "My Gran... She would pick the early buds before I arrived. She never told me what she used, but somehow she'd make them bloom in the vase in time for my arrival."

She pulled the bouquet of dried buds out and placed them on the kitchen counter. "They were her favorite. The burst of color from something so plain, a new life after being contained for a short while..."

Vinya stared at the vase across the room. Yuwon looked from her to the vase. He grabbed it, scooting around Zhan who had reached out to take the vase from him.

Zhan glanced between the two of them, torn between following Yuwon to the carriage and making sure that Vinya didn't run.

Vinya crossed her arms and leaned back against the kitchen cabinets. She had nowhere to run to—this house had been her destination all along.

Zhan settled in the doorway to keep an eye on the Crown Prince, who placed the vase in the back of the carriage, and Vinya, who stared at the floor beneath her feet.

This is where she wanted to be, and yet there was nothing here for her. The contents of the rooms were not what made it feel like home, it was her Gran. Without her, it was nothing but a house of bittersweet memories. Perhaps she could breathe a bit of life into the vase, at least.

Zhan shifted again. "Is there anything else?"

The only thing she needed was air. Vinya shook her head and aimed for the door, grabbing the straw hat that she'd hung on the wall on her way out.

He moved out of her way and closed the door behind them as Gran's neighbor, made her way back to them.

“We scattered her ashes in the garden as she wanted, underneath the blossom tree.”

“Thank you.”

“You can visit us next door every day if you'd like.”

“Actually I—” Vinya paused. She fidgeted with the sleeve of her robe.

The old woman caught the movement.

“You know, you would pull on your Gran's sleeve just like that when you were nervous.” A knowing grin spread on her face. “You aren't staying.”

From the corner of Vinya's eye, she saw Zhan look in Yuwon's direction.

Vinya shook her head. “No. There are some things I need to do first, but I will come back. I promise.”

The old woman patted Vinya's cheek.

“I will see you then,” she said before she hobbled back to her home.

Yuwon once again helped her into the carriage, though she couldn't meet his gaze this time, then rounded the horse to climb into his own seat. Zhan jogged after the old woman and stopped her at her door.

Yuwon glanced over his shoulder to the vase. “That is all?” he asked.

“I would take my grandmother's ring, but I couldn't find it,” Vinya said.

The Crown Prince stayed silent, and she turned to watch Zhan.

Vinya didn't catch his words as he presented the old woman with a small bag. She tried to refuse, waving her hand between them, but he insisted with a grin.

Zhan's dimpled smile must have softened the old woman, because she took the bag and patted his cheek before she waved goodbye to Vinya.

Zhan returned to the cart and spoke to Vinya as he climbed in. "The home will be taken care of in your absence."

She twisted in her seat, and he held up a hand to stop her oncoming questions.

"Nothing will be changed, only maintained."

"Thank you Zhan," she told him.

Zhan nodded in answer and double checked to make sure everything—the singular vase—was secure in the back.

From her peripheral vision, she could see Yuwon watching her.

She turned to him, and for a moment they looked at each other in silence. The sadness that she hadn't been able to place in the palace gardens days ago had returned to his eyes.

"Thank you," she whispered.

His mouth twisted almost imperceptibly. Vinya couldn't tell if it was an attempt to not smile—or not cry.

Yuwon dipped his head and readied the reins.

The ride back to Kima was as quiet as before... but her heart felt a little lighter.

II

Fate's String

The ride back to the palace was uneventful. They purchased a few carriages to replace the ones that burned on their way in, and Daeya chose to spend the journey to the palace in a separate carriage than Vinya. Sooni was thrilled to have a seat to herself.

Once in the palace, Jinhee rushed them with questions about the raid. Satisfied, she urged Vinya to rest.

While Sooni went to her own room, Vinya refused. She needed to clear her head, stretch her legs, and had her own questions that needed answering.

A new guard stood outside her bedroom door, stating that Zhan had other business to attend to. He granted her request for a walk, and Jinhee joined them as the guard led the way to the royal offices.

The grand room was pretentious. Books and scrolls were stacked floor to ceiling along every wall—each shelf sorted into a controlled chaos. Empty tables were spread along walls for studying, their chairs tucked in tight. A faint musty smell hung in the stagnant air. The only movement came from a man sitting at the desk in the middle of the room.

His quill scratched along a small piece of parchment as he feverishly scribbled notes, then he rolled it into a scroll and sealed it with string. He moved on to another paper, rolling and sealing again.

Alastor was so preoccupied with his work that he jumped a bit when noticing their presence. He began shuffling the papers spread before him, folding and covering them with a few of the books that were piled high on his desk.

Vinya noticed a map of Byonea as they approached his desk—towns and trails had been marked and traced. Alastor slammed his hand on the map, covering what little was visible.

"You are not privy to the whereabouts of our encampments," he sneered.

His nose twitched, looking her up and down as if he suspected her to be some sort of spy. He motioned towards a corner of the room, and a young boy that Vinya hadn't noticed emerged from the shadows. The boy took Alastor's messages and exited into a side room. She suspected he was delivering them to the royal aviary they had passed on the way here.

Vinya fought the urge to remark on how she wanted nothing to do with this war, and instead focused on the task at hand.

"I was wondering—"

She paused. The two times she had met this man, he tried to make it fully clear that she was beneath him, that she would answer to him. But if Vinya was who he claimed her to be, then wouldn't *Alastor* be the one who would answer to *her*?

In a way, he reminded her of Daeya, vying for attention and recognition. Vinya decided she wouldn't give either to him. She would not cower.

She straightened her back. "I would like to see my family tree."

Alastor blinked, but did not move.

Vinya stood her ground, willing every ounce of authority to show. It wasn't a lot, but it seemed to work because the man stood.

His chair scraped on the wooden floor. He would do as she told, but he'd take his time as well. He made a show of searching for the book of lineages, glancing back now and then to see if he was dredging up impatience.

Vinya kept her face neutral, and it made Alastor's nose twitch yet again. He pulled the heavy tome from an eye-level shelf and dropped it onto one of the empty tables.

"The Norhagan accounts," he said. He half wiped dust off the chair before returning to his work.

Jinhee and the guard stayed near the door as Vinya sat. Her hands hovered over the cover. The answers she sought would lie within, the moment of truth at her fingertips, and yet, she hesitated. Alastor broke her trance.

"*Do not* rip or tear any of the pages," he ordered.

Vinya didn't know how that was possible. The book was ancient, several hundred years old at least. The binding had nearly come completely off, the edge of the pages tattered and yellowed with age. History was written here, sacred accounts of families and wars. If she managed to mutilate this tome...

Her eyes flicked to the High Adviser who was engulfed in his papers once more. Maybe she did fear Alastor a little bit.

With gentle hands, she opened the book. Each crinkle of the papers set her nerves on edge. She skipped the beginnings of Norhagan, its founding fathers, the wins and losses of wars, and went straight to the year 1261—when two hundred and sixty-five years ago, King Rikr Kaplin of Norhagan aided Byonea for the first time.

Vinya skimmed down the lineage with her finger following the last name Kaplin. Page after page of direct firstborn descendants. None of them rang a bell, and her name was nowhere to be found.

She sat back with a faint smile and shook her head. She truly was here by accident—a mistaken identity.

Vinya looked to the ceiling, as if she could see the sky above. She imagined the boat ride home, the grass on her feet, the comfortable clothes, her mom's warm stew in her belly, and Nutmeg keeping her feet warm at night.

She was ready to be back home, and no one would stop her now. She would show them this proof if needed. Vinya looked at Alastor, who was staring at her.

Slowly, Vinya stood. She left the open tome on the table for him to put away. Let him clean up his own mess. She was halfway to the door when Alastor's voice rang out.

"Second son."

Vinya's slippers stuck to the floor. The hope in her heart vanished.

She twisted, and Alastor's pompous demeanor and devilish grin had her dashing back to the tome. Her fingers trembled as she carefully turned back the pages.

Rikr's second son.

Alastor had waited until the last moment to throw it in her face. He had kept quiet long enough for Vinya to think that she was unbound from their rules and regulations.

Vinya followed the direct descendants of the second born son of King Rikr Kaplin.

Page after page she traced the names, until the last page… until the names began to sound familiar. Until one of the direct descendants of King Rikr's second son wed Jae Yinuo of Byonea.

Until Vinya's finger rested on her own name.

She sat in that position for what could have been seconds—could have been minutes.

Vinya's head spun. Her mother never mentioned any of this. Everyone knew the current King's lineage and all the possible heirs.

Alastor made his way to her side and clicked his tongue. "It looks like you'll be staying with us a while longer, your highness."

The book shut with a soft thud, and he returned it to its place on the shelf.

"If you don't mind, I *am* extremely busy and do not have time to play bookkeeper," Alastor sniped.

She stared at the empty table before her. "I want to write my parents."

"I'm afraid all of the messenger hawks are busy carrying important messages regarding the oncoming war with Calgham. They do not have the time to send sorrowful letters." He sighed. "Your parents were made aware of the situation in the same letter that contained news of your grandmother's death. Be grateful for this opportunity instead of trying to find a way out."

So the adviser knew about her escape attempts.

"Have they written to me?" she asked.

He leveled her with a stare. Any returning letters would not be deemed important enough to come before letters of war. If they did write, Vinya didn't trust that this man would even pass the letters on.

She took his dismissal as it was and left his office.

If she truly was a promised princess, did she have to accept this fate?

Vinya watched her slippers as they peeked from beneath her skirts. Her steps were slow, there was no reason to run anymore. The ring sliding around her finger felt even heavier.

She searched her memories for any hint of her mother's ancestry. She'd never spoken much about it, as her own parents had died when she was young. Her mother had no siblings, aunts, uncles, nieces, or nephews.

Is that why her mother chose to reside in the country, so far from the main cities of Norhagan? Did she want to be forgotten and left alone? There was only one way to find out.

Vinya stopped. Jinhee and the guard flanked her as she turned back to look at Alastor's office. She would not let the sniveling man stop her. Surely they could spare one bird, one message. She would walk it to the aviary herself even if Alastor breathed down her neck the entire time. He couldn't deny her this.

A large bird swooped high into the air from behind the building, leveling out to glide in Vinya's direction. She squinted as it got close. No scroll was attached to its beak or claw. Yes, one bird could be spared. As it flew above her, Vinya realized two things.

First: this was no ordinary messenger bird. It was a red-tailed hawk.

Second: it was missing a primary wing feather.

Vinya bolted so quickly that Jinhee and the guard were several paces behind her, with Jinhee yelling after her. A letter could wait, and Vinya wouldn't dare miss this opportunity. Not when the hawk—*the* hawk—may be in her presence.

Jinhee soon gave up and sat on the steps of a building, calling out that she would catch up later.

Vinya and the guard pressed on. It hadn't taken him long to realize that Vinya wasn't attempting to run away—but was running *towards* something. His commands for her to slow quickly turned into commands for officials and nobles to clear the path ahead of them.

The hawk continued—soaring over the aviary and beginning its slow descent over distant trees.

They wound their way through the business sector of the palace. Vinya had never been here before—she wasn't quite sure she'd be able to find her way back on her own. The guard grabbed Vinya's arm before she ran straight into the garden's vine-covered wall and directed her towards the entrance archway.

The hawk was now out of sight. It landed beyond the trees, beyond the lush garden that blocked their view.

Male laughter filled the air, coming from the same direction the hawk had flown. Guards were stationed throughout the garden, and her own guard waved them off as they passed.

Finally, the shrubbery cleared to a small field. Vinya and her guard slowed to a stop as they spotted three men in the middle of the field.

Zhan stood on the far left. His casual black outfit suggested that he had been given the day off, but his sword still hung at his side.

In the middle was a man slightly shorter than Zhan. While he wore fine, sapphire robes, it was his lively energy that Vinya first noticed. His brows shot high, and a broad smile spread across his face as he turned to the last remaining man.

Yuwon—her betrothed—watched her intently as she approached. On his gloved hand sat the red-tailed hawk.

Vinya didn't have time to ask about it before the unknown man in the middle swooped into a dramatic bow—his arm whipped out and nearly knocked Zhan. When he straightened, there was a wild spark in his eyes, brighter than the fine metals and jewels that adorned his ears.

It seemed to sparkle more when he spoke. "You must be Vinya. My brother hasn't stopped talking about you for the last few hours."

The man turned to Yuwon, who stared off into the distance—a flat look on his face. Yes, Vinya was sure that the *talkative* Crown Prince had been yapping away about their Spring Festival trip. Yuwon's younger brother must tease him often if he wasn't giving him any reaction.

The man placed a hand on his chest. "I am Woobin, your soon to be brother—and the most handsome of the royal sons, of course."

Vinya returned his bow, though not as extravagant. She couldn't place a finger on it, but there was something about him that pulled her in. She wasn't entirely sure the sweat on her brow was from her run here or the natural warmth of this man's personality.

Woobin had stronger features than his brother; a sharper jaw and eyes almost made him look older than Yuwon. But she found herself drawn to the Crown Prince's softer appearance, and didn't agree with the prince's claim.

The realization made her blink.

Woobin pulled a handkerchief from his pocket and passed it to Vinya. "Zhan, you didn't tell me it was a good day for a run. You could have tried to beat me."

Vinya patted her face with the handkerchief as Zhan shook his head.

"I have always beaten you in races, and *you* insisted on flying Nagne." Zhan motioned towards the hawk.

Nagne. *Traveler*.

The bird tilted its head to look at her. Vinya stepped towards it, pocketing the handkerchief. The hawk spread its wings as she raised her hand.

Woobin let out a small gasp.

"He doesn't do well with strangers," Yuwon warned, extending his free hand to stop her.

Zhan's own hand went to the hilt of his sword—a natural reaction to protect. Vinya wasn't sure he would use it on the Crown Prince's hawk, though.

Vinya whistled three notes. Two high, one low. It was the same tune she used when approaching the hawk after he crash landed at her home in Norhagan. Upon hearing the tune, the hawk's wings snapped shut. Vinya grinned and moved past Yuwon's hand to scratch Nagne on the side of his head.

"Around ten years ago, there was a red-tailed hawk that had tangled itself in some barbed wire fencing on our farm. The poor thing was exhausted and cold." Vinya moved to scratch the back of its head as she went on. "I took it in. He wouldn't let my parents anywhere near him, so I nursed him back to health myself. I admit I kept him a bit longer than needed after he had healed. I'd always wondered what place he had come from—where he went after flying off."

Vinya stepped back. Yuwon watched her—his face a mixture of realization and awe.

Woobin pressed his hands together in front of his wide smile.

"Yuwon cried so much when Nagne returned," Woobin said. He pulled on Zhan's sleeve. "Do you remember how swollen his eyes were?"

"Woobin," Yuwon warned, calm but stern.

Woobin bit his lips to flatten his smile.

Yuwon turned his attention back to Vinya, regret lining the tone of his words. "I pushed Nagne to see just how far he could go. It was a mistake I have not repeated since."

Vinya looked at Nagne's tail. "I'm sorry about his wing feather. I know they typically grow back, but in the month he was there, it never showed signs of growth."

"He flies fine without it," Yuwon replied.

Vinya nodded. "My parents found the feather at..." Home, she was going to say home. Was it still, though? If she truly was the promised princess, if her duty was to stay and create a new life here, would she now be expected to consider this her home?

"The farm," she finished.

Yuwon caught her hesitation. His gaze softened, and the sadness that she couldn't place returned deep within his eyes.

"Fate's string has tied you together!" Woobin exclaimed beside them, earning a pained expression from Zhan. He looped an arm through Vinya's and led her towards the dense garden path.

Yuwon stepped to the side to pass the hawk to the aviary keeper, and Zhan dismissed the guard who was with Vinya, taking on the duty himself.

Woobin rolled his eyes. "Zhan thinks he can protect more people than he's capable of on his own."

Zhan grunted behind them. "I'm sure we could find a small bush to hide you in, Your Highness."

Within earshot of the other guards, they were back to formalities—the friends would no longer be on a first name basis.

Woobin scrunched his nose as he studied the nearest shrub. "I would hold you accountable for every thorn cut, then."

Vinya smiled. "I think the Crown Prince would be able to hold his own in a brawl."

A mischievous grin grew on Woobin's face as he leaned in close. "Have the two of you taken a tumble already?"

"No, that's not what I meant!" Vinya exclaimed.

"Woobin," Zhan whispered through his teeth at the same moment.

Yuwon returned—his brow quirked together in curiosity. "What did you say now?"

Woobin stopped walking and whipped around to his brother, one of his earrings smacked his cheek with the movement.

"I said—" he started, but was cut off by Zhan, who changed the subject.

"There was a raid on our way to the Spring Festival."

Yuwon shot Zhan a warning glare, but it was Woobin's expression that caught her attention.

All play was erased from Woobin's face, replaced wholly with concern. This was a man who felt every emotion deeply, and Zhan and Yuwon had tried to spare him from this.

Tears pooled in Woobin's eyes as he held his brother's arms. "You didn't tell me."

Yuwon waved a hand. "Nothing to concern you with. It was small and over quickly."

Vinya glanced at Zhan behind Woobin's back. Small? He could tell that to the multiple burned carriages and numerous slain guards. Zhan shook his head once.

Yuwon patted his brother's head. "We're fine."

It seemed to convince Woobin, who nodded and wiped away stray tears from his cheeks.

Vinya linked their arms together once more and leaned in to the Prince. She pulled the handkerchief he had given her earlier from her pocket and waved it in the air. "I'd offer you a handkerchief, but mine is currently covered in sweat."

The laughter she'd heard earlier through the gardens now rang in her ear. Happy once more, Woobin asked her to tell them of her life across the ocean. As he led their group through the gardens, Vinya told them of Norhagan.

Of the home that was no longer hers.

12

A Flock of Birds

Children's laughter flitted down the street as they made their way to the royal library. The ship Vinya had travelled on brought in a new collection of Norhagan books, and Woobin, having learned all he could from Vinya, desperately wanted to get his hands on them.

Jinhee found them not long after they entered the business sector, and she now walked behind with Zhan.

The laughter grew louder, and soon the source rounded the corner of a building. They moved like a wave through the street—their smiles just as bright as their pastel robes.

Around a dozen young Shade Princes and Princesses passed out handmade floral crowns.

Vinya half expected the noble people and officials of Byonea to scoff at the gifts, but every one of them smiled and knelt so the children could crown them. One of the older officials with snow white hair shuffled off to show his coworkers his new crown.

One child caught sight of Vinya and the men and alerted their siblings.

"Woobin's home!" the girl exclaimed.

All of the children abandoned their crowning and ran to the prince. Woobin swept the first girl that reached him into his arms and planted a kiss on her cheek. She giggled and squeezed his neck. Yuwon and Zhan stayed a few steps away as the remainder of the children surrounded them with squeals of joy and questions of where he'd been the past week.

Woobin dropped to his knees to wrap each of them in an embrace.

"What are my little shadows doing today?" he asked in an effort to distract them from their own questions of *where have you been, why did you leave,* and *did you bring back gifts for us?*

His plan worked, and the children told him how they hand picked and crafted each crown.

"Everyone deserves a crown," one boy said. He couldn't have been older than five.

Vinya's heart ached. The Shade Princes and Princesses would never wear a crown of their own.

Woobin playfully poked the boy in his stomach. "You're absolutely right. Only stinky Yuwon gets a crown here."

Woobin squinted his eyes and feigned disgust as he turned to his older brother. Melodious giggles spread through the children.

Yuwon shifted on his feet, uneasy under the eyes of his many half-siblings.

Vinya had often wondered why the Byonean Shades weren't considered royalty as they were in the past, but after meeting Queen Joona, she understood.

Small fingers wrapped around Vinya's little finger and tugged. She looked down to find a toddler girl in a buttery yellow robe. Her full cheeks and two tiny hair buns jiggled as the girl hopped on her toes. Her other hand, holding a floral crown tied together with soft pink ribbons, reached towards Vinya's head.

Vinya knelt, and was crowned by the smallest of all the Shades. The toddler girl scrunched her face and huffed quick, excited breaths through her nose.

The girl's cuteness overwhelmed her, and Vinya couldn't help but smile.

"We'll go ahead," Zhan announced from behind.

As they turned to bid the men farewell, Yuwon's eyes dashed away from Vinya.

Woobin's raised brow seemed to say he caught the movement as well. He turned back to the children and waved a hand towards his older brother. "Say goodbye to Yuwon!"

In unison, the children dipped their heads to the Crown Prince. "Goodbye Yuwon!" they repeated.

The five-year-old boy copied Woobin's wave. "Bye stinky Yuwon!" he exclaimed.

Woobin clamped a hand to the boy's mouth, laughing as he shushed him.

Yuwon closed his eyes and shook his head. He leaned in to whisper something to Zhan, and they headed back into the business sector of the Palace.

"Where are you going?" Woobin asked them through his laughter.

Zhan called over his shoulder, "We'll meet you at the library."

Woobin rolled his eyes and tapped the five-year-old on the nose. "That was naughty."

"You said it first!"

"*I'm* allowed to!" Woobin retorted, tickling the boy.

The boy squealed and hopped out of reach. Woobin grabbed the next closest child and began tickling them when one of the Queen's guards appeared.

"Her Majesty has requested your immediate presence," the guard said to Vinya.

Woobin stood with her, patting invisible dust off his sapphire robes. "I'll come as well. I arrived not long ago and haven't seen my mother yet."

The guard opened his mouth to object but closed it—tapping the heels of his shoes together and dipping his head in a bow—and led the way to the royal quarters instead.

Side by side, they followed the guard and Jinhee. It was apparent that the bows the royal guards gave as they walked down the hall were to the Prince alone—they hardly glanced at Vinya at his side.

One of the Queen's ladies-in-waiting opened the door for them, her eyes widened at the sight of Woobin. She gave a quick glance inside as she bowed to the Prince, a warning to Queen Joona within. Whatever this was, whatever she had planned, the Queen's second-born son would complicate things.

When Vinya and Woobin rounded the doorway, Daeya stood beside the Queen.

Woobin didn't even greet his mother as he scoffed and pointed a finger at the concubine. "She can leave."

Queen Joona's face was pure shock and surprise—at her son's sudden appearance and his immediate demand.

"Daeya had many important things to say regarding her travels to the Spring Festival," the Queen said.

Woobin only stared at his mother. "I have many things to say about her that I'm sure she doesn't want to hear."

His disdain for Daeya was palpable.

Queen Joona dismissed the woman. "You may go, Daeya."

Daeya's mouth popped open. She had something up her sleeve and wanted to see it through.

"Your Majesty—"

The concubine shut her mouth because of the glare the Queen gave her. She bowed and left, but not before giving Vinya and Woobin a glare of her own.

Once the door closed, Woobin approached the Queen and brushed a light kiss on her cheek.

"Mother," he said flatly.

"Woobin. We weren't expecting you back for a few days, at least." The Queen pressed a hand to her perfectly groomed hair, taming invisible stray hairs. "But I'm glad you're home, it's becoming unwise to travel these days with Calgham warriors on the rise and pressing into our borders."

No doubt the Queen had heard about the raid. She did seem relieved that all of her children were within reach—though Vinya didn't know if that was for their safety or if she could control them better.

"Homesick," he explained as he sat, propping an elbow on his knee. He fiddled with the cup of tea that had been placed for Vinya.

Vinya joined him in sitting as the Prince went on.

"Though I don't miss *her*. She may be in Father's bed and *wants* to be in Yuwon's—she may be your little spy, but she does no actual good for the crown or Byonea."

Woobin was indirectly feeding her information, a heads up from a new friend.

The concubine's treatment towards her became clear. Daeya didn't want to be with the King, the true object of her desire was Yuwon. The jealous concubine was working for the jealous Queen, and through her, the Queen may have one more way to hold sway over the future of the country.

Queen Joona's smile was unnerving. "As I said, she had important things to say."

Woobin sighed, feigning disinterest. "Like?"

The Queen looked at Vinya. "The young lady-in-waiting that Vinya brought with her to the Spring Festival made quite a few remarks that aren't fitting for someone in the royal court."

The Prince's brow bunched together. "Who, Sooni? You know good and well I chose her to be my new sister's lady-in-waiting. If she went head to head against Daeya then I'd say Sooni is doing a phenomenal job already."

Woobin turned to Vinya and winked with the eye the Queen could not see. It made sense that he would choose someone who had no filter on their words, capable of standing up for themselves and others.

Sooni had been an unknown gift from someone Vinya hadn't met until today.

"The girl will be dismissed immediately," the Queen stated.

Woobin didn't miss a beat. "Sooni stays and I will personally pay her wages."

The Queen fumed, Woobin gave a curt nod, knowing he'd won that battle.

"Now, Mother, I think Vinya deserves a present as an apology for trying to take her lady away from her. Something that brings her joy. Hmmm..."

Woobin tapped his finger to his chin, his eyes resting on Vinya's over-sized ring.

He reached across and picked up Vinya's hand. "A new ring perhaps? This is humorously ill-fitting."

He gave a pointed look to his mother, who sucked her teeth with her tongue.

"I was unaware that Vinya was so..."

Small. Fragile. The Queen had to choose her words wisely with the look Woobin was giving her.

"Dainty," Queen Joona finished. "I planned to have it resized soon."

Woobin hummed and released Vinya's hand. "Jinhee will take care of it, then."

He stood and paced the room with his hands behind his back. He seemed to be deep in thought, but Vinya suspected he was up to something.

He proved her hunch correct when he stopped and lifted a finger. "I've got it! A bird."

The Queen blinked, stunned at her son's suggestion that she hand one of her birds to the woman in front of her. "A...bird? I suppose we can have a new one caught, or imported."

"No, Mother. One of these. Surely one can be spared," he said, sweeping his arm across the wall of colorful birds.

One bird could be spared.

Woobin smiled at Vinya from behind the Queen's back. Vinya had to bite the inside of her cheeks to keep a straight face.

Especially as Queen Joona's face turned a shade red. "Woobin darling, these are my prized possessions, my own personal collection. We can find a new—"

Woobin interrupted her, he was likely one of the few people in the world who could get away with it. "I think it's a wonderful idea, a gesture of good faith. Come, Vinya, choose whichever bird you'd like."

The Queen's chest heaved. She was about to retort again when Vinya pointed to the far wall.

"The Norhagan canary."

She'd spotted it as soon as they'd entered the room, like a veil had been lifted off her own eyes. It must have been there all along, but it caught her eye the moment the door first opened. Its colors hadn't dulled after all.

Woobin retrieved the bird's cage and passed it to Jinhee. His mouth twisted to the side.

"We'll have to see about getting a larger enclosure. For now, please deliver this to Vinya's room."

Jinhee nodded and left with the bird. Woobin extended a hand to Vinya to help her stand.

"A *Norhagan* canary. It's such a beautiful little bird, don't you think, Mother?"

The Queen sat unmoving. She refused to look at Vinya. "Yes. Very... bright."

Woobin chuckled. This is who he got his teasing from. Only he used it out of love, while Queen Joona used it out of jealousy.

Vinya bowed. "Thank you, Your Majesty, for the tea."

The tea that she did not touch.

The Queen slightly raised her brows. It was all she could do as she'd just been thoroughly defeated by her son.

As the two of them stepped out of the royal quarters, Woobin excitedly patted her hand. "Ah, that was good fun. Please send word any time she calls on you, and do *not* go into that room without me. She will push you so far that you'll fall over, but I'm not afraid to push back."

If he only knew his mother could do more than push.

Vinya studied his profile, his silver and sapphire earrings catching her eye. The far ear held an array of them. The longest had clusters of teardrop jewels that cascaded down to his shoulder. Above that was a coil that looped through his ear repeatedly, leading up to three single sapphire studs, each one slightly larger than the one below. The ear closest to her, however, held four small stones. The phases of the moon, Vinya realized, a full silver circle at the bottom and the slice of a crescent moon at the top.

Were the piercings a trait of collecting pretty things, like his mother and her birds? Or was it another form of rebellion on his part? Vinya couldn't determine which was correct.

He sighed. "I should join Yuwon and Zhan, but *you* should go enjoy your prize. I'll meet with metalworkers to have a new cage built soon."

He picked up her hand and swept the lightest of kisses over her knuckles. "I'm so happy you're here, Vinya. It'll be good for Yuwon to have someone, other than me and Zhan of course."

"Of course," she repeated, same as earlier.

He beamed and snatched the floral crown off Vinya's head—that she forgot she had been wearing. He placed it on his own head as he backed away, then tapped a finger to his chin. "Mmm, what color should the cage be... pink?"

Vinya scrunched her nose.

Woobin waved the color away, still deep in thought as he turned to the library. He made it halfway before turning again.

"Lavender?" he called out.

A few noblemen stopped in surprise at the Prince's yelling. Vinya made an "x" with her arms and smiled as he waved the color away a second time.

Vinya and the guard that had been appointed to her that morning aimed for her room. She looked forward to having something that was truly hers in this land. She tried to think of ways to make the canary more comfortable, when Woobin called out from the library's second balcony.

"Emerald!" he yelled.

She could see the surrounding scholars shushing him, but he was focused solely on her. He pointed to his eyes.

Emerald, a shade of green like her eyes. Emerald, the color of Calgham—the color the Queen despised. Vinya huffed a laugh and gave the Prince a nod.

He whooped triumphantly—shrinking a bit as he was hushed by those around him.

For the first time, Vinya didn't have a sense of dread while walking back to her room. She felt lighter, cared for. Woobin's mouth never seemed to stop, but she welcomed the change. She had a feeling they would become good friends.

Neither Jinhee nor Sooni were in her room when she arrived, nothing but the soft tweets of the canary filled the room that was once overwhelmed with silence.

Vinya asked the guards to send for her supper, then closed the door behind her. She placed her hand on the cage. Tomorrow. Tomorrow she would send a letter to her parents. Tomorrow she would continue her search for answers.

She pulled off the short outer shirt and went to put it in the clothing cabinet when something on her pillow caught her eye.

Vinya knelt to pick up the sprig of early blossom buds, along with one of Nagne's primary wing feathers and a note that had been attached.

"Thank you," was all that was written.

Vinya smiled and imagined the Crown Prince scouring the aviary for a naturally fallen feather—perhaps he'd gotten Zhan to do it.

She placed the items, along with her hairpin, on the display cabinet next to the canary's cage. Vinya slipped Yuwon's note, though, into a drawer for safe keeping.

13

Bittersweet Tea

It was the beginning of her seventh day in Byonea.

Vinya and Sooni stood at the hall leading to the royal quarters. Before the break of dawn, Vinya had received a summons from Princess Jun to join her for breakfast. Sooni had quickly gotten her dressed before they were escorted to the royal quarters, but they now faced a problem.

They hadn't been told which room belonged to the Princess.

The guard who escorted them that morning had not been granted clearance into the quarters, and the royal guards within did not answer Vinya's questions. Instead, they ignored her completely. The hall was empty, no extra guards stood outside any of the six doors, and no special markers indicated who occupied each room. A safety precaution, Vinya imagined.

Sooni chewed on her lips. The young girl had only been down this hall a handful of times, but still tried to be of help.

"We know for sure which room is the Queen's," Vinya whispered.

"And I have no plans to ever step foot in there again," the young girl replied as she eyed the door at the far-right end of the hall. The chorus of chirping birds could be heard from where they stood.

Vinya motioned to the door across from it. "I'm going to assume that one is the King's."

"Unless the Queen doesn't want to know when his *leman* comes to see him at night," Sooni muttered, her expression sour.

That was not something Vinya wanted to think about. She waved at the girl to shush her.

Sooni pointed to the next two closest rooms. "Perhaps it goes in order of succession? The King and Queen in the back, then Yuwon and Woobin in the rooms next to them. Leaving Jun in one of these two rooms near this end of the hall."

Vinya crossed her arms, thankful to have the royal ring off for the day. Jinhee had taken it to a jeweler to be resized, but now Vinya wished the older woman was with them to help solve this puzzle.

Sooni looked to Vinya. "Maybe we should knock?"

"If it's the wrong room, what then?"

"Say sorry?" The young girl's mouth curled into a pout as she twisted from side to side.

It was an effort to not roll her eyes at the cuteness of her lady-in-waiting. Vinya needed to think of a way to thank Woobin for choosing the girl for her.

Vinya pointed to the far doors. "King, Queen."

Sooni nodded.

"Yuwon, Woobin." Vinya pointed to the next set of doors.

The young girl's chin hesitated in the air before she nodded a second time.

Vinya motioned towards the door closest to her on the left. "Jun?"

Sooni lifted her arms in a slow shrug.

Vinya sighed and approached the door. There was only one way to find out. With a raised hand, she paused. If this were the wrong room—

The door before her slid open, and a pit opened in her stomach. Behind her, Sooni let out a gasp that was barely audible.

It was absolutely the wrong room.

Vinya was face-to-chest with a man—a thick book held by a large hand between them. Too tall to be the King, too tall to be Woobin... Which meant that when she lifted her chin, she would be staring at the Crown Prince.

Yuwon's eyes widened marginally as he searched her face. His lips parted, but no words came out. Even in the early hours, his robe was pristine. Not a wrinkle, not a fold out of place. One lock of his dark hair, though, fell over his brow.

The pit in Vinya's stomach transformed into something different, flipping over itself with a tingling sensation.

Sooni smothered her giggle behind her hand, but neither of them paid her any attention.

"Jun..." Vinya breathed. She pointed vaguely to the hall without breaking eye contact.

Yuwon's eyelids fluttered. He swallowed. "Ah."

He stepped forward, forcing Vinya to back out of his way, and outstretched his hand toward the door on his left.

Jun was in between the King and Crown Prince. Vinya kicked herself internally for not figuring it out. Though Jun was not next in line to the throne, she was the youngest, a woman, and would be seen as vulnerable. Naturally, she would be placed between the two men who held great power.

"Thank you," Vinya said, dipping her head in the slightest bow. She smiled softly, her words mirroring his note the day before, and as she raised her eyes, his gaze lifted from where it had been fixed on her lips.

Sooni's giggles only grew as she joined Vinya in the walk to Jun's door—which seemed much further than it should have been.

Vinya's body ached to be out of sight as soon as possible—each step itched to be faster. The sensation of someone watching her trickled up the back of her neck, leaving her feeling warm. She didn't face Jun's door as she gently knocked—and kept her back towards the nerve-wracking encounter.

A door slid behind her, and Vinya loosed a breath. Yuwon had gone back into his room. She turned to face Jun's door then, and out of the corner of her eye, she saw a half-awake Woobin blinking into the morning light of the hall. It was *Woobin's* door that slid open, not Yuwon's sliding closed; his room was directly across from his brother's.

Yuwon still watched her from his doorway, his expression unreadable.

Sooni's entire body shook, both hands now clamped over her mouth at the scene before her.

Mid-stretch, Woobin glanced between them all. A mischievous grin grew on his face as he stepped across the hall to Yuwon, Jun's door sliding open at the same moment.

"What is going—"

Woobin's question was cut off. Yuwon grabbed his brother by the scruff of his shirt and yanked him into his own room.

Vinya and Sooni hurried into a confused Jun's room, and Sooni shut the door behind them before she burst into laughter.

Vinya turned on her.

"Did you know?" she questioned in a forceful whisper.

The young girl waved both arms in front of her, her words coming out in the spaces of her laughs.

"No I—didn't—but I—I kind of—hoped." Sooni backed against a wall and slid down, giving in to her fit of giggles once more.

Vinya stooped to hold her hand over the girl's mouth. "*Hush.* If that's the King's room beside us, then I beg you to not wake him."

Sooni gave her a lazy nod and forced her giggles into silence, though her shoulders still shook.

Vinya turned to Jun. The Princess was bewildered as she stared at the two of them.

Vinya shook her head. "I am *so* sorry. We weren't told which room was yours and—"

She faced the wall that divided the two bedrooms. The low rumble of male voices came from the other side. Yuwon was doing the same thing as she, siblings giving explanations to siblings.

Vinya blinked. Her cheeks warmed again under the realization. Jun really would be her sister.

A soft hand rested on her shoulder. Jun had followed Vinya's gaze toward her brothers' voices.

"I see. Forgive my oversight." Her smile was as gentle as her touch, but it wavered.

It seemed something else was on Jun's mind as the three sat around a low table; something new plagued her thoughts. Jun served them all a modest meal, scooping bits of each food onto each plate. Vinya glanced at Sooni, who was studying Jun with a crease between her brows.

Vinya didn't dare start the conversation—she didn't want to push the Princess, who twisted her fingers together between each bite of breakfast.

After the noise of the men in the room next door had faded, after their plates were empty and Sooni was eyeing another roll, Jun lifted her head.

"Mother is sending me away."

The words took Sooni's focus off the extra rolls, her eyes popped wide. "What? Where?"

Jun set down her cup of tea. "To Haryn. Mother and Alastor think it's best that I meet the King's son there."

Vinya recalled the map of the continents, the country of Haryn rested North of Calgham, their borders touching. She also knew what the Queen meant by this command. *Meet* was the same as *marry*.

"She's creating a new alliance," Vinya muttered.

Sooni spoke in the same breath, the corner of her nose curled upward. "The Haryn Prince is well into his fifties. You'd be marrying someone who already has one foot in the *forever-box*."

Jun gave the girl a polite smile. "The Prince is in his mid-thirties at least."

"When do you leave?" Vinya asked.

"Tomorrow morning."

The Queen was spinning a new alliance with her daughter's hand. Would there be a cost?

Vinya's stomach curled once again. She had a feeling the Queen's sudden decision had to do with yesterday's meeting, metaphorically striking her once more. What stung more were the words that came out of Jun's mouth next.

"My personal ladies-in-waiting have fallen ill and will not be able to make the journey. My mother heard of it late last night and strongly suggested I take Sooni in their place."

There it was. The price to pay. A loophole around Woobin's refusal to fire the girl. The girl now looked at her with unasked questions—a hint of sorrow in her eyes. Vinya's gut told her that the ladies-in-waiting may not have fallen ill of their own accord.

Vinya shook her head, "Surely not forever?"

"Oh, no. Only until my ladies have recovered enough to make the journey to Haryn on their own," Jun explained.

Sooni's back straightened. "Is there any way to help them get better by tomorrow morning? Jinhee may have some remedy up her sleeve."

At Jun's raised brow, the young girl explained further. "I mean no offense, Princess, I don't mind going with you at all. But I want to come back to

Byonea as soon as possible. I wouldn't dream of missing out on Vinya's wedding ceremony preparations!"

Sooni beamed, but Vinya's heart skipped a beat.

She rubbed her thumb under her bare ring finger. A date for the wedding hadn't been announced. With more frequent news of Calgham warriors being spotted in Byonea's borders, Vinya assumed the marriage would take place soon—a month, maybe two.

Jun's pained smile was a poor guise. "I'm unsure. Mother told me the preparations for Yuwon and Vinya have already begun and she has moved their wedding day closer."

"When?" Vinya asked. The word broke from her mouth with inept decorum.

The Princess's smile waned, "Two weeks from now."

A dull thud sounded from the room next to them, like an empty teacup—or a book—slipped from someone's fingers and hit the ground. Vinya imagined the princes with their ears pressed against the wall between them.

"The journey to Haryn takes a few days, weather permitting. It's uncertain when my ladies will recover, but I will try to make it back for the wedding. If I cannot, know that my heart is with you." Jun's smile this time was genuine. "We will also have a travel companion appointed by my mother."

"Oh, please not Daeya," Sooni whined.

Jun shook her head, "No, Daeya chose to stay. The Queen won't be sending her as a travel companion any time soon."

Due to the last journey's events. The words seemed to float in the air between them.

Sooni let out a sigh of relief. "Good. If I had to sit in a carriage for days on end with that woman, I fear I'd elbow her in the eye."

Vinya shot the girl a look that told her to be quiet, but Sooni went on anyway.

"Well, *I* wouldn't fear. *Daeya* would have been the one shaking in her fancy orchid slippers."

Vinya failed to hide her smile as she audibly shushed her lady-in-waiting. Her smile soon faded knowing that Sooni would be leaving with Jun tomorrow.

Punishment straight from the Queen's hand.

"I'm afraid it's my fault. I—I haven't been the best—"

Jun held up a hand. "Don't say that."

"The Queen is more green-eyed than you are, my lady," Sooni blurted.

"*Sooni*," Vinya scolded under her breath.

Green-eyed. Envious and distrustful. The Queen doubted the strength of the alliance through Vinya and made strides to put another in place. The term Sooni had used suited the Queen well.

Sooni's attention snapped to Jun. The young girl's mouth clamped shut as she popped it a few times with her fingers, and dropped her head in a submissive pose. She'd slandered the Queen in front of her daughter, the Princess.

"Sooni is right, though a bit curt." Jun reached across the table to lay her hand on Vinya's own. "My mother can be a jealous woman, often leading with a heavy hand and harsh words, but I truly believe that this—these marriages and alliances—is what's best, what's right. We must do this for the good of our country."

Our country.

Vinya closed her eyes. Her country was of rolling fields and open sky, the distant sound of crashing waves hitting the cliff-side. Her country was the adoration of her loving parents. It was the great thunder of running horses, the cry of a newborn lamb, warm stew in her belly, a ginger cat keeping her feet warm at night, birds chirping in the trees—

No, Vinya realized as she opened her eyes, those faint chirps came from the Queen's room. It was the garbled coughs of the King—the rumble of servants and physicians' feet scurrying down the hall to attend to him.

This country was made of spiders and snakes, of stone walls and stone hearts. Those in power coiled their hands around the necks of those they ruled, tying a noose and using them as shields to protect their own country, their own selves. Byonea's politics felt like an ominous storm looming over them all.

But there was also light. There were these three siblings—loyal, passionate, and kind. There was Sooni and Jinhee and Zhan, Gran's neighbors, and Miho... Could she leave them all to face that darkness alone? Would she choose to leave them at all? Would she be able to make a difference in Byonea if she stayed?

"I empathize with you. I now understand your hesitancy," the Princess continued, and looked briefly at the wall separating them from Yuwon's room. "To marry a stranger, especially when so many rally behind the idea publicly is—"

"Terrifying," Vinya whispered.

The hand holding hers squeezed gently, and trembled. Vinya had a feeling Jun wasn't just sharing news during the meal—she was trying to convince herself of the duty and necessity in her mother's plan.

Jun dropped her voice as low as Vinya's. "Know that Yuwon was born into this role, a future leader, but he doesn't hold himself above the rest of us. He would put himself in front of you only to protect you."

Vinya had witnessed that firsthand before the Spring Festival. He had saved her, a woman he barely knew, from the Calgham warrior. How had that only been three days ago? How had she acquired so many warring emotions in such a brief period of time?

The Princess squeezed her hand one last time before letting go. "Promise me you'll spend more time with him while I'm gone."

Jun saw her unease and offered Vinya something to focus on.

"I promise."

14

The Sun

All women of nobility gathered in the open hall. Their friends and lovers passed through to watch the noblewomen show off their crafts and give compliments. The event was held with every change of season, a way for the royals to spend the day connecting with the citizens who lived within the palace walls.

Even though the thought of women being used—either as pawns in a game of war or for everyone else's entertainment—made Vinya's stomach twist; she chose stitch work, something she would have been doing at Gran's house, anyway. Something she didn't plan to make for anyone's entertainment other than herself. Sooni had procured the supplies soon after leaving breakfast with Jun and now scoured the hall for a place to sit.

Vinya stood in the entryway fidgeting with the edge of her sleeve, not ready to step into the throng of people before her.

Woobin flitted from one side of the hall to the other, leaving the people in his wake brighter. Jun sat before a large canvas. Many people stopped to watch her sweeping brush strokes, their words of Haryn and congratulations filled the hall over and over again. The Princess thanked them with a graceful dip of her head and a smile, but she kept her eyes on the painting in front of her.

"Vinya," Zhan said from beside her.

He motioned towards the right, where multiple royal guards surrounded a small dais that held five chairs. With Jun painting, the laughing Prince far across the hall, whispers of the King being too sick to attend, and the Queen holding a meeting with Alastor, only a statue occupied the last chair.

Yuwon sat nearly motionless—the Crown Prince barely blinked. But Vinya saw more—

How his eyes skimmed everyone's heads, not quite making eye contact.

How even through carefully clenched fists, his thumb was subtly picking at the chair's wooden armrest.

And how, when they approached the dais, Yuwon sucked in a breath a little deeper than previous ones.

A voice in the back of her mind whispered that he *would* make a perfect statue, with his high cheekbones and keen eyes that seemed to soak in every detail around him.

He stood as passing nobles offered their congratulations for the wedding ceremony date being chosen. Vinya had no idea how word had traveled through the Palace so quickly, but neither she nor Yuwon acknowledged them, especially when standing face to face, especially when so many eyes were on them.

Zhan broke the building tension around them. "If it's all right, Your Highness, I would like to remain by your side for the duration of today's events."

It was the most official way he could ask to keep his friend, the Crown Prince, company while alone on the dais.

Yuwon nodded, and Zhan took up position by his side.

Vinya pulled a scroll from her pocket and rolled it between her fingers.

She dropped her gaze to the scroll as she spoke to Yuwon. "I wondered if you'd be able to send this for me? It's a letter to my parents. Alastor didn't seem too keen on sparing a messenger hawk the other day, so I wanted to ask if—"

If she could use him. Use his authority over the nose-twitching adviser to send a simple letter across the waters, to ask her mother why her ancestry was kept from her.

Yuwon's hand came into view, palm up, to take the letter from her. The moment they locked eyes, Vinya realized she wouldn't need to voice her request—he would help her regardless. And when she passed him the letter, their fingertips skimmed across each other—slower than necessary.

Zhan stepped forward, holding out his own hand to take it from the Crown Prince. But Yuwon held on to it, his finger running against the grains of the parchment, and placed it in his own pocket.

Zhan's eyes sliced between them. When he confirmed that the letter contained no plea for rescue, he returned to his watchful stance.

"Thank you," Vinya whispered.

Yuwon gave her a small nod.

Silence enveloped them. Zhan's eyes once again slid between them, but he kept quiet as well, giving them the space he thought they needed. Vinya wondered what the guard saw that she, herself, couldn't.

She should ask Yuwon something. About the book he held this morning, about who taught him to wield a sword, more about his hawk. Anything other than the wedding...

"My lady!" Sooni called from nearby. She had cleared a small area for the two of them and was waving Vinya over.

Vinya jumped. She was thankful for the distraction, a reason to get off the dais, but there was another emotion within.

Zhan was already looking at her when she glanced his way, his dimples pressed in imperceptibly before he continued scanning the crowd.

Vinya quickly dipped her head to Yuwon in goodbye, grabbed her skirts to step off the dais, and joined her giggling lady-in-waiting for an afternoon of crafts.

Vinya barely made any progress. It had been hours of stitches, finger pricks, and tearing out the work only to start over again. Sooni had stitched a near perfect replica of Vinya's canary and now moved on to a second embroidery.

It had always been an enjoyable craft when she worked with Gran. Tea was brewed, and Gran worked on her own projects. There was no pomp, only calmness and contentment from being in each other's company. Vinya would hum the lullaby Gran put her to sleep with as a child.

Vinya hummed that tune now and listened to Sooni's nervous comments about the trip to Haryn. She stole a glance at the Crown Prince, and found his eyes already on her. Vinya's humming was cut short when she pricked her finger again. She was ready to call it quits when a hush flowed through the hall.

The nobles cast their eyes to the sky-blue bird in the entryway. While some of the women peered over their fans, batting their eyes at the Shade Prince, others were unable to hide their sneers or turned away from him completely. Hyosung ignored their disgust and smiled instead. It was the same wide, beautiful smile that sent a confusing chill down her spine.

His face felt like a snare—a facade he could hide behind. Vinya couldn't place her finger on what it was.

Hyosung scanned the hall, pausing on Vinya. His smile turned to a smirk as he dipped his head to her. She returned the greeting, half expecting him to come join them, but his eyes settled on Jun... and softened.

When Vinya looked to Sooni for answers, the young lady-in-waiting kept her eyes trained on the Shade Prince.

"Hyosung has always had a soft spot for Jun, some say more than one should when it comes to half siblings." The girl shivered.

Vinya whipped her head to Sooni, "He loves her?"

The girl nodded—her grimace swapped with contemplation. "Technically they would be cousins. Half cousins? No blood is shared between them, people tend to forget that. They say the two of them have been inseparable since childhood. I'm surprised you haven't heard of this—it's been quite the controversy since... forever."

Sooni dipped her head towards the Shade Prince, who made his way across the room to sit beside Jun.

The Princess smiled as she continued painting, and Hyosung watched intently, drawn to every stroke of her brush on the canvas. His face was one she had not seen before: calm. Content. This was where he wanted to be in the world, and nothing else around him mattered. It was a perplexing puzzle piece to the man Vinya thought he was, or who she *heard* he was before she stepped foot in the Palace.

Vinya chewed on the inside of her lip and hummed Gran's lullaby once more as sapphire robes moved across the corner of her vision.

Woobin stalked to the dais, his face hardly hiding his discomfort. On the dais, Yuwon stared straight ahead, ignoring the presence of Hyosung completely. Zhan muttered something under his breath to the Crown Prince, but Vinya was too far to make out what it was.

She glanced at the Shade Prince at Jun's side, and her humming was cut short yet again when she saw Hyosung watching her from beneath his brow. In a blink, he turned his attention back to the painting.

Servants paced the perimeter of the open hall, carrying trays of fruits and cheeses for those present. Jun graciously accepted what was offered to her. When the servant hesitantly turned to the Shade Prince, he ignored them completely, focusing solely on the painting before him.

Vinya, keeping her voice low as she leaned in to Sooni, asked, "Is this another reason she seemed hesitant to leave for Haryn?"

Sooni twisted her mouth to the side, watching Hyosung and Jun from across the room. Assessing. "I'm unsure. It seems like he doesn't know about her leaving—he's typically restless when the Queen puts forth a match, but he looks... normal?"

Distracted, Vinya sucked air in through her teeth as she pricked a finger on her needle.

"Does Jun reciprocate his feelings?" she asked.

Hyosung motioned to the painting, leaning in with a suggestion. Jun listened and nodded, giving him a sweet smile before making the change he had mentioned. Hyosung's eyes did not leave her face for a few moments. He was infatuated with her.

Sooni shook her head. "She has never seen him that way, and she's too kind to tell him to leave her be. It's like fate tied them together, and while Hyosung pulls at the string, Jun allows her end to hang loose. Some say she's using him as a barrier to ward off potential matches so she can stay in the palace with her brothers."

Vinya grinned. "You sure do *hear* a lot, Sooni."

The girl stopped her stitching. "When you're sent straight to the palace instead of school as a girl, your mind is empty enough to hold all of its secrets."

A sadness washed over Vinya. "I hope you're treated better here than wherever you were before."

Sooni's shoulders curled in. "Home. My parents sold me to pay their debts. They never sent letters—never inquired where I'd gone. I barely remember their faces."

The girl's eyes were distant, far into the past.

Vinya nudged her with an elbow. "Perhaps they should have sold themselves, I'm sure you're paid handsomely here."

Sooni blinked back into the present. "Oh *yes.* My head is filled with secrets, my pocket filled with coin." She stitched fervently now, a smile on her face. "And my days filled with you."

Vinya paused her own stitching. This girl had locked a grip around her warming heart.

Sooni smiled up at her. "I truly am happy you're here. It was so *boring* before as Daeya's lady-in-waiting. At least you let me talk—"

"Wait," Vinya interrupted. "You worked for *Daeya* before me?"

The concubine was on the opposite side of the room weaving an intricate bird's cage from delicate branches. The woman practically soared on the praises of the women around her.

The corner of Sooni's mouth curled in disgust. "It was the worst position I've held so far. That snake went on and on about things she's experienced—half of which I highly doubt are true...or even possible."

She seemed deep in thought before her face lit up, and Sooni scooted closer to Vinya, her voice barely a whisper. "Daeya twists stories and words as well as she's spinning those branches, creating a beautiful and believable story, though some can see right through it. She *did* speak poorly of Jun, often mentioning that Hyosung would write the Princess poetry but never deigned put ink to paper for her."

Vinya covered her mouth to stifle a laugh that burst from her. "Poetry?"

The room went silent for a breath. Her voice had risen above the murmurs of the room, and now Hyosung leveled her with a stare.

So that was the wedge between Daeya and Hyosung. She was jealous of Jun.

Vinya failed to hide her smile. To think of the lofty prince, sitting amongst his fortune, writing elaborate lines to prove his affection. Perhaps it was his personal form of riches: a small part of his soul. Vinya was oddly touched by it.

She tried biting the inside of her cheeks as he rose, his steps unhurried as he crossed the room to stop in front of them. Sooni scooted away and kept her head low, while Vinya lifted her chin to smile at the Shade Prince.

No humor graced his face as he looked down at her. His voice carried across the hall. "I sense I am the subject of whispers in this corner of the room."

"The talents of the people in this room are interesting topics, wouldn't you agree?" Vinya responded. "It *is* the reason we're all here."

"Hm." He hummed, oddly reminiscent of the song she had been humming moments before. Hyosung motioned towards the fabric in her hands. "Is stitch work a strong suit of yours?"

Vinya chuckled. "Not at all."

She lifted her work, showing the poorly done portrayal of a cherry blossom. "No matter how many times I thread the needle, change the color or angle, I can't seem to make this thread fit in the stitch work as a whole. Appropriate, don't you think?"

Hyosung raised a brow. "I would rank it in the same category as your climbing skill."

"Hm." Vinya copied him, dropping her hands and the fabric into her lap. "I would like to read this poetry of yours. If it's good enough to put in ink, it must be grand. I wonder if you would write a line or two for me?"

A challenge in front of an audience, it would be rude of him to turn her down as she would soon fall higher than him in rank. Two weeks from now, in fact.

Hyosung understood this as he raked his tongue across his pristine teeth, and a smile grew that didn't quite reach his eyes. "Very well, *Princess*. We'll see if my words live up to your standards instead of becoming the last line of a joke."

He gave a pointed look to Sooni, who still did not meet his gaze.

Vinya brought the attention back to her and stood. "Shall I expect it in say, one week?"

"With Jun leaving tomorrow, I may have some time to spare. You will have it in less than a week."

Vinya glanced at the Princess, whose focus on the painting before her was strained.

"So, you know?"

"Know?" he replied, a small smile playing at his mouth. "I was the one who suggested it to the Queen. Haryn may be geographically smaller, but their forces rival Calgham. This would be a great asset to the oncoming war. Jun will be kept safe, I'm sure of it."

Vinya watched him closely. The Shade Prince had gone to the Queen, the woman who obviously held a deep dislike for the man, and offered a solution that would send her daughter—the woman he apparently admired—away. Why would the Queen, who hated this man's existence, listen to him?

"You'll be staying here?" Sooni asked, a bit of a bite came through her tone.

A practiced calm washed over Hyosung's face—he understood the implication of her words. His eyes slid over to shoot Sooni another look that made the poor girl's shoulders curl inward.

"I will take that as a *yes*," Vinya said. She turned to leave when the tassel hanging from Hyosung's belt caught her eye. Moreover, the carved wooden hawk attached to it, knocking against the hilt of the slender blade at his side.

It was a trinket from her missing pack.

Hyosung followed her gaze and grinned. "Ah yes. I found your satchel while you were away for the Spring Festival. Rather, what was left of it. A few empty bottles and vials, Norhagan medicines that our physicians poured out I'm assuming, and this..."

He lifted the hawk, twisting the figure in the palm of his hand. He had drilled a hole straight down the center and threaded the tassel through, on the hawk's back rested an emerald bead—the same shade as her eyes.

"I don't know what it is about this that made me keep it, I couldn't force myself to give it back. You're better than I am, remember?"

Hyosung referred to her first night here, how she could not steal the silver and pearl hairpin that now rested heavily in her bun.

"Keep it," Vinya said. "It was for my grandmother, but you can have it."

Hyosung tilted his head. He let the hawk and tassel fall from his hand as he lifted a brow.

"You're not going to quarrel about it?"

Vinya shook her head.

The Shade Prince's head straightened. He lowered his voice to where only she and Sooni could hear.

"Have you changed your mind?"

His eyes flicked to the dais, then drilled into Vinya's. Hyosung wasn't just asking about the carved hawk. No, his words went deeper as he turned the conversation into something new.

Vinya sighed, dropping her stitch work onto the seat. Threads hung at every angle, some too loose, others stretched tight. She stared at the frayed work. "Sometimes a rest is necessary."

Hyosung nodded. A question hung in his eyes that she couldn't make out, a glimpse of warring thoughts flashed through. She was going to ask, but within a single blink, they were gone. Instead, Vinya changed tactics to let him know his offer to help her escape was not being rejected.

"I look forward to reading your eloquent words," she said with a smile.

Hyosung blinked again, his eyes dropped to her mouth for a fraction of a second. So fast she doubted even Sooni had seen it. He dipped his head and returned to Jun's side. Even though he looked at the painting, his eyes were far past Jun's depiction of the sun rising behind a blossom tree on the canvas.

As Vinya and Sooni walked back to her room, Sooni scratched her head.

"That was the strangest thing," was all she said the entire walk.

"Hm," replied Vinya, unable to find the right words herself.

15

The Moon

The guard at her door stood at attention, ready to switch shifts with Zhan. Even now, he refused to let anyone else on night shift. The thought made her smile. Vinya stepped out of her room just as he showed up, his brow quirked in question that she hadn't changed into her night clothes.

"I wanted to walk in the gardens tonight... if you'll join me? It's a full moon, and, well... my Gran and I made a tradition out of it."

Zhan glanced to her bedroom door, "Sooni?"

Vinya grabbed the lantern that hung across the hall from her door. "I dismissed her after supper. She seemed anxious about leaving tomorrow, so I sent her to her room to rest."

He nodded. "We shouldn't break tradition then."

As they wove through the palace gardens, Vinya told Zhan about her grandmother. Everything they did and worked on together. Though he didn't say much, his small nods and minute expressions showed that he intently listened to every word she spoke.

Moon beams bounced off rock lined streams, illuminating every flower petal along the swirling pathways. The night was so bright that Vinya wondered why she brought the lantern in the first place.

Vinya twirled a small cherry blossom she had plucked as she told Zhan about her life in Norhagan. The farm. Her parents. More details than she'd shared the other day when they returned from the Spring Festival. She didn't know why she felt this need to tell him about herself, and he never questioned her about it. He politely lent his ear to her as he continuously scanned their surroundings.

Vinya paused.

Zhan stopped in the same heartbeat, hand on his sword, "Is something wrong?" There was a hint of confusion on his face, wondering how she had noticed something before he did.

She shook her head, "I'm only realizing that this is what Sooni feels like, babbling on about whatever goes through my head. It's kind of nice to have someone listen. I hope it's not bothering you."

Zhan smirked, his dimples pressing in, "I don't mind. If you ever need to *babble on*, I'll be here."

His offer seemed genuine, and she believed him.

They began walking again when a jovial laugh filled the air, followed by a lower chuckle. The sounds pealed together—a melody that drew her in.

Vinya turned towards the noise. "Where does that trail lead?"

Zhan grunted, "The pavilion. Perhaps we should go this way?"

He motioned towards another path, one leading away from the pavilion. The sense of urgency in his tone only spiked her curiosity more. Vinya gave him a flat stare as she sidestepped and aimed down the path, giving him no choice but to sigh and follow.

The garden opened to a vast lake—its water so calm that it reflected the moonlight. A bridge led to the pavilion on a small island in the center of the lake. The circular pavilion had been built around an ancient cherry blossom tree in full bloom—its branches stretched far above the roof in the center. Guards stood at both ends of the bridge and the steps to the pavilion; a handful of guards were spread out across the pond that surrounded it. Vinya heard about this place, but she'd never ventured this far into the gardens.

It was not the intricate woodwork that caught her eye. It wasn't the lanterns scattered about that cast the area in a warm glow. It wasn't Woobin, who danced around the pavilion like it was his personal stage. It wasn't Zhan, who seemingly knew of Woobin's antics and wanted to avoid it. It wasn't even that the Crown Prince sat straight on the wooden floorboards, no chair or pillow for his own comfort. Nor was it the dark bottle tipped over beside him—which Vinya assumed was the cause of Yuwon's flushed cheeks.

It was his smile.

Ear to ear, Yuwon beamed as he watched his brother's reveling. It was like a ray of sun, as if the entire pavilion was illuminated by it and not by the lanterns. His laugh rumbled soft and low, and when he ran out of air, Yuwon tipped his head back and clutched his chest—shoulders still heaving with silent laughter.

Only when Zhan cleared his throat did the brothers notice their presence.

Woobin made a spinning stop. Yuwon stood—albeit a bit wobbly—and dipped his head in her direction. His brows scrunched together, and he blinked to clear his vision.

Vinya bit the inside of her cheeks to keep from laughing. There must have been more than one bottle if the future ruler of the country just made the smallest bow to her. Zhan caught the slight as well and pinched the bridge of his nose.

"Vinya!" Woobin exclaimed, his voice carried over the pond and echoed into the night. He held himself steady on the pavilion's rails.

She set down the lantern and fiddled with the cherry blossom, "I'm a bit nervous to ask what you're doing."

Woobin snorted. He crossed the space and led her to Yuwon, "Sit! Sit."

She remained standing as he pressed on, not wanting to cease his balter.

Yuwon made fleeting eye contact. He shifted on his feet before clasping his hands behind his back, trying to retain somewhat of a regal appearance.

"He thinks the moon is his friend," Zhan clarified, coming to her side.

Vinya whipped her head to him, "The... *what*?"

Woobin came to a full stop, unbothered as one of his many earrings smacked him on the cheek. He zeroed in on Zhan and jabbed a finger in his direction. "The moon *is* my friend. It sings to me, and I dance to its music."

Eyes wide and full of unspoken questions, Vinya turned to Zhan a second time, who looked exasperated. He'd clearly witnessed this month after month and had been glad to have another post tonight—sparing Vinya and himself from the Princes' foolery. But the night had cast a net, the Princes' laughter was the bait, and the inquisitiveness that swam inside her caused them both to be caught in the silly trap.

Woobin danced on, oblivious to the world. His robes flapped in the wind he created as he spun, his earrings ticking against each other as he slid this way and that.

It warmed her heart to see that they held their own full moon traditions. She soon found herself grinning at Woobin's dance, her heart dancing along as well. Vinya wondered if she could hear the moon's supposed song. She closed her eyes.

Crickets and frogs made their own melodies in the lake. Brief winds whistled through the trees, rustling the leaves and branches. A nocturnal bird sang far away. She needed to search higher, to reach into the sky and allow the moon to call to her. Vinya tilted her ear upward, but the sound of slippers scuffing toward her brought her back down.

Woobin fell into an exaggerated bow, his arm extended to Vinya. A playful grin spread across his face, "May I?"

Vinya looked at Yuwon. Not for permission to dance with his brother, but for a way out. She wouldn't be able to keep up with him. The man was practically bounding from one end of the pavilion to the other without so much as a labored breath.

Woobin didn't wait for an answer as he took her hand and kept a respectful distance as he pulled her into his dance. With each bound, her heart eased. With every duck under his arm, her worries were wiped away. Joy built up inside her with each one of his infectious laughs. Somewhere in it all, she dropped the blossom branch.

Vinya understood. She heard the moon's song.

It sounded like freedom.

Yuwon watched with rosy cheeks—hands still clasped behind his back.

Vinya wondered if he, too, had once been pulled into his brother's arms.

His knowing grin was her answer. He wanted Vinya to have this thrill, for her to experience the pure gaiety of Woobin's monthly escapade.

After what felt like too long, yet not enough, Vinya broke free, a bit dizzy and out of breath as she returned to Yuwon's side. How Woobin was still standing was a mystery if he, too, drank whatever liquid had been in those empty bottles she now spied in a basket off to the side.

Woobin turned his attention to Zhan. The guard immediately stiffened and held out an arm to block the Prince's approach.

"No."

Woobin slid forward regardless, a mischievous gleam in his eye.

It was now Zhan's turn to look to Yuwon for help, but the Crown Prince intently studied the pavilion's rafters above them.

Woobin didn't listen. He took the arm anyway, lifting it high to spin in circles underneath before plucking Zhan's other hand off his sword.

Zhan's face flattened in annoyance. It was apparent that when Woobin's mind had been made, there was no changing it.

Zhan would not add to the Prince's charade and kept his arms loose, they reminded Vinya of cooked noodles. The same thought must have gone through Woobin's mind, because he giggled between notes of his humming.

The Prince tried and failed to spin Zhan in his own circle. The combination of Zhan's stoic face and floppy arms at odds with Woobin's merry tune stirred something deep within her. A laugh burst forth as she watched the odd couple.

Vinya realized that she hadn't laughed, *truly* laughed, a single time since she stepped foot in this country. It created a crack in the wall she'd built inside herself—each wave of laughter chipped off a bit more. *A bit more*. She sensed someone's stare, and from the corner of her own eye, Yuwon looked at her, his face a mix of slight shock and awe.

She turned to him with a smile still spread across her face. The lantern light flickered in his eyes, a fire of life burning bright in a dim world.

But was it actually as dim as she'd thought? She'd spent the past week yearning for a taste of home, but anywhere in the world would have its own flavor of dark places. The farm back home was her peace, yet all of Norhagan wasn't perfect. There were people fueled by love and life but also those who would scorch the earth out of hate.

Byonea could be no different. Was it her own situation that blanketed her view? She could see the bonds people had with each other; the love Yuwon had for his friend and brother could no doubt spread to his citizens. Vinya believed that if he opened his heart to the people, they would love him in return.

These would be the men leading the country one day, and she was beginning to see the men they could be. Leading not with legalities and conquering in mind, but with their hearts. That is what the country needed. This is the king they needed... not the coughing King kept holed away and led around by a sneering adviser. Who knew what whispers Alastor was feeding the weak king?

Perhaps she could help shape Byonea into a beautiful country. Perhaps she could let the walls she'd built come down completely...

The sound of crickets began anew while the distant bird still sang its song. In their merry tune, Vinya realized that Woobin's own humming had stopped.

Together, Yuwon and Vinya turned.

The dancing pair of men had frozen in place. Zhan's face was a mixture of concern regarding the dance and a hint of amusement, as if he could visibly see a string of fate tightening around them. Woobin's eyebrows had shot so high they were nearly hidden by the hair that fell across his brow. His mouth was agape, a smile tugging at the corners.

The rafters in the pavilion were suddenly interesting to the Crown Prince again, and Zhan seized the opportunity to shake free from Woobin's grasp.

"I think it's time to go back to your room," Zhan said as he straightened his sleeves and retrieved their lantern.

Vinya nodded, knowing the guard was using it as an escape from Woobin. "I need to wake up early to see Sooni off."

Yuwon stopped them before they got to the bridge, idly twirling her blossom branch in his hand. Vinya wondered when he'd picked it up.

"Your letter, I personally saw it off with the last round of messenger hawks for the day."

"I'm sure Alastor wasn't too happy with your request," Vinya replied.

The Crown Prince grinned and shook his head, as giddy as a child pulling a prank.

Vinya hummed a laugh through her nose, she could imagine the twitches that had taken over Alastor's own nose when he'd realized who wrote the letter. She dipped her head in thanks and made her way across the bridge.

As Zhan walked her back to her room, she could hear Yuwon's laugh ringing through the Palace. Or perhaps they were only echoes that had embedded themselves into her mind...

16

A Portion Shared

Three days passed.

The wedding ceremony preparations entailed several meetings with the Queen, and Alastor had been present for every single one—though his twitching nose and shifting eyes showed he'd rather be elsewhere. Vinya couldn't wrap her mind around why there were so many things a Princess must learn. What to say, how to act, when to move, and *how* to move. So many lessons were shoved into her head, there was no way to retain it all. Even though she'd grown tired of the Queen and her heavy hand, there was a small part of her that feared the woman, so Vinya continued to play the part.

She had only caught glimpses of the Crown Prince over the past few days. Alastor had been trailing slightly behind him, feeding his own advice to Yuwon. The King had still been too weak to leave his room, so Yuwon took his place in war councils. With whispers of the King's health circulating around the Palace, Vinya couldn't help but think Yuwon was stepping into a position he would fully take over soon.

More frequent than the whispers of the King was the talk of Calgham sightings within Byonea's borders. It seemed a new town was named every few hours as they spread along the border, slowly drawing closer to the Palace. As the sightings became more prevalent, Vinya didn't know whether to believe them all.

And yet, there was still no sign of King Kuro and his Norhagan army.

The grumblings of the noblemen and women began the day Jun left and had only grown worse. The noblewomen looked down at her as they passed, clicking their tongues in disappointment at the *Promised Princess*; instead, their conversations turned to Jun, the Haryn Prince, and the men Haryn was already sending.

How could it be her own fault that they hadn't heard from Norhagan? Did the marriage need to take place before the Norhagan King sent reinforcements? Did she herself need to send a messenger hawk to him, and would he listen to her?

Was the Treaty of Trust even reliable anymore?

Vinya ventured into the Throne Room numerous times over the past few days. She climbed the crimson painted stairs—the Byonean dragon statues on the newel posts seemed to drill their eyes into her each time she passed between them—and stared at the Treaty of Trust mounted high on the wall: the scroll she laid eyes upon her first day here, marked with the blood of Yuwon's ancestors, and her own. It was a promise to unify the countries, and yet, there was no unity to be found.

A thought inched its way into her mind—it slowly consumed every move she made, each moment before she fell asleep... What was the purpose of staying if her presence made no difference? Was she only a bird being displayed by the Queen?

Vinya found herself scanning her surroundings, a chill raking down her back. She imagined glimpses of a sky-blue robe in the corner of her eye. When she closed her eyes, a beautiful smile and carved hawk flashed before them. Yet Hyosung was nowhere to be found.

Had he holed himself away, regretting his part in sending Jun to Haryn? Had he followed her without telling anyone? As a Shade Prince, he wouldn't be required to stay under guard during this time of a looming war. But as the King's eldest son—regardless that he wasn't royal—Vinya suspected he held some status among the rest of the King's children.

Jinhee had been by her side the entire time, taking Sooni's place while she was gone with Jun. The older lady-in-waiting gave her own advice during those days. *Womanly* advice. Though ladies-in-waiting could not be married, she herself had once been wed. After a terrible accident left her a widow, she needed something to keep her mind busy. Someone to take care of. So, she trained to be a lady-in-waiting.

Vinya was incredibly thankful for it. She was even more thankful when Woobin swept into their path on the fourth day and whisked her away, declaring they were going into town together for lunch and a surprise afterward. Jinhee would be given other duties at the Palace, and Woobin assured Zhan that his personal guards would be enough for the two of them, so Zhan would stay by Yuwon's side for the afternoon.

Woobin looped her arm through his own and led her through ornate halls and down stone-laden paths to the stables where they would take his carriage. The Prince either didn't see the side-eyes of the nobility or kept their arms linked in spite of the looks.

The social butterfly must have seen the stress his mother was putting her under and heard the nobles doubting her importance in Byonea, so he took it upon himself to cheer her up.

They took a slight detour to the kitchens to grab covered baskets—Woobin ordered his guards to carry a few, picked up his own, and passed the last one to Vinya. The smell of fresh bread wafted through the weaves of the basket—it pulled memories of home to the forefront of her mind. She could almost imagine her mother's own rolls and the warm, sweet notes of spiced honey floated through the air.

Vinya's heart skipped as the energy around them shifted. Woobin had gone silent, and his guards shifted on their feet. Those weren't the warm notes of her mother's bread she was imagining—it was the scent of the man in sky blue robes before her.

Woobin's disdain was almost palpable as he watched the Shade Prince approach.

Vinya wondered what Hyosung would say if she told him she gave his gift of a gold coin away. Her stomach turned. Surely it wasn't regret that twisted it. She was only hungry and the breadbasket in her hand fueled it. No, it couldn't be the way Hyosung did not take his eyes off of her, his face clear of jest or pride—and she did not take her eyes off of him. He was her way out of Byonea, if need be.

Hyosung stopped a few feet from her, and said nothing as he lifted his hand, revealing a small scroll between his fingers.

Vinya followed his lead as she took the note without saying a word.

He bowed, then left.

Woobin's brows were deeply furrowed—his gaze on the scroll when she turned to him. The Prince blinked, then looked away and offered his arm to her, plastering a smile across his face once more.

Vinya pocketed the note and took his arm as they continued to the stables, to lunch, and to whatever surprise the Prince had for her.

The four-winged dragon statues that guarded the Palace's main gate were barely visible by the time the carriage stopped.

Woobin hadn't asked about Hyosung's note, though she caught the Prince glancing at her pocket every few minutes, the crease between his brow reappearing each time. When the carriage pulled into Nyrrem, his concern turned to the dozens upon dozens of filthy children gathering around the carriage—their eyes wide in anticipation.

His eyes softened at the sight of them. He wiped the look from his face and burst from the carriage. The children turned to him, like flowers ready to soak in the warmth of the sun's rays.

Woobin scooped up the nearest child, a toddler no older than three, and spun her in circles. With arms wrapped tight around his neck, the small girl giggled and soon became distracted by Woobin's shining earrings.

Vinya would have expected a child her age to have plump little fingers, but the fingers that grasped Woobin's raindrop earring were alarmingly thin. Frail.

All the children were. And if Vinya looked closely enough, she could see their ribs through tattered shirts. These were the children Jun helped—the ones who received the meal she and Vinya didn't touch that day in the gazebo.

Vinya alighted from the carriage with one of the baskets, and the children turned to her as if she were the new sun. As if the fun-loving Prince before them was no more and the basket in her hands was the center of gravity. Vinya blinked back the tears from the hunger in the children's eyes as they formed multiple queues.

"Remember the rule," Woobin said as he sat on the rock and dirt road beside the carriage. The toddler refused to let go of him, and Woobin didn't seem adamant on making her get up; instead, he showered the little girl with praises and compliments.

As murmurs of agreement spread through the children, Vinya and the guards began passing out the bread.

'Only one loaf per child' was the rule Woobin referred to. All the children were poor, yet none of them tried to grab a second. None of them compared loaves with the child beside them, nor was anyone greedy for more. Each child thanked Woobin before running down the streets, going home to split the food with their families.

One of the little girls held a ginger cat reminiscent of Nutmeg back in Norhagan. Except this one was scrawny—its fur matted. A pang of guilt ran through Vinya for leaving Nutmeg at the farm; she would have to ship him over at some point. The cat didn't mind as the child shifted it over her shoulder and held the bread with the other arm. As the girl ran back into town, the ginger cat slowly blinked and rubbed its head on the girl's neck. The cat was loved and loved in return.

Vinya tried to memorize the children's faces as they stepped up to her; she tried to remember each word of thanks and every smile when the bread was placed in their hands. By the time sixty loaves had been distributed, Vinya's stomach no longer growled with her own hunger—it twisted into guilt.

The toddler in Woobin's lap was the last to receive a loaf. She leaned in to plant a kiss on the Prince's cheek as he smoothed the wisps of her hair in place. Holding her bread with both hands, she bounced down the road to her family's home.

Woobin stood and tried to discreetly wipe away the tear that had fallen as he watched the little girl go. He took Vinya's hand to help her back into the carriage, stepping in and sitting opposite of her. The driver cracked the reins, and the carriage started toward their next destination.

The Prince stared at the hands that rested on his silky sapphire robes and rubbed off some of the dirt on his palm with his thumb. "There's only so much that we can do. So much more that we *should* do, but my mother's eyes are focused elsewhere. She refuses to acknowledge the poverty at our doorstep."

Woobin lifted his face. "It's up to *us* to care for them, to make a change that my mother and Alastor have refused to take any real action on—even before the threat of Calgham came about. The bread is all that they allot. When we were in our early youth, Jun often found herself too full to eat her private meals. Only when Jun became too thin and weak, did her ladies tell Yuwon and myself. We had been blind to it all; the starvation happening within reach. Somehow, Jun knew, and took it upon herself to quietly right a wrong."

The prince closed his eyes. "After finding out, Yuwon and I took on some of the burden. Soon after, Zhan talked some of his men into sending off a meal every now and then. Even—even..."

"Hyosung," Vinya finished for him. No doubt the Shade Prince would have been worried for Jun, and if she shared the same affection for him, she would have kept it hidden so he wouldn't fret.

Woobin's eyes slipped to Vinya's pocket, to the scroll tucked within, as he nodded. "When Hyosung was told, he began sitting in with Jun's meals to make sure she ate. He used his own money to cover the meals that the people in Nyrrem weren't receiving—the meals that should have been provided by my parents to begin with. He would sneak out at night under the guise of being a womanizer, delivering the goods to Nyrrem himself. I hate to admit it, but that was the only time I actually admired him. I believe it was Hyosung's own rebellion against my mother. Once she learned what we were doing, she quickly put a stop to it, allotting loaves to be sent once a week. It drove the rift between us deeper, especially Hyosung's view of my mother."

Woobin sighed and closed his eyes once more, "My mother hated Hyosung before he was even born, knowing that she wasn't the one to bear my father's first child. She had called upon the greatest shamans in Byonea, prayed in the most extravagant ceremonies to bless her own womb... and yet the King's firstborn was through a concubine. Hyosung's mother—my father's first leman who is said to have been the greatest beauty of the land—was found dead only weeks after giving birth to Hyosung. Physicians could never pinpoint what happened to her."

Across the carriage, their gazes clashed. There was a darkness in Woobin's eyes that he didn't attempt to hide. It was a portion of the darkness that lingered over Byonea—its secrets and faults, and the pressure to keep them quiet.

But Vinya opened her mouth regardless, her words rose just above a whisper. "*The Queen had her killed.*"

Woobin's nod was barely perceptible. He glanced towards the door of the carriage before leaning forward. "My mother only began tolerating Hyosung when she saw how protective he was of Jun. She only tolerates the people around her if they are useful."

Vinya felt her cheeks warm, a stark contrast to the chill creeping down her arms and legs.

Woobin took her hand in his own. "You're safe with us. Me, Yuwon, and Zhan. We will keep you safe. She won't be able to touch you; we'll make sure she never has a reason to."

Vinya nodded, and didn't quite feel Woobin's hand slide out of hers.

The lid to Byonea's dark secrets had been opened, and Vinya was afraid of what she would see if she peered too deeply. And if she looked a little too far, knew a little too much, would she find herself at the bottom of that dark well... pushed in by the Queen's own hands?

17

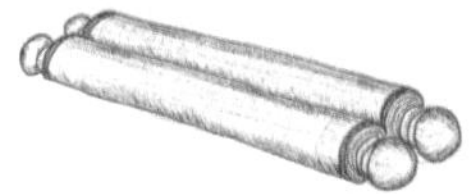

A Startling Note

They traveled an hour North of the Palace, to a large city called Chirdong—known for its exquisite craftsmanship. Passing by the shops, Vinya recognized some of the colorful banners that had been delivered to the Palace. They wrapped around the columns and were strung across the walkways in preparation for the upcoming wedding ceremony.

A canal sliced through the city. Bridges arched over it, which allowed people to cross and shop in the multi-story buildings—and goods to be delivered by small boats underneath.

Wind chimes rang out along the main road, catching the attention of shoppers. Children squealed as they wove through the adults and chased each other with wooden swords. Their parents sucked in a breath each time a child would trip, afraid that the children would tear or soil their pristine robes.

The stone paths on either side of the canal were wide enough for two carriages, but people scooted out of the way nonetheless, giving a wide berth and deep bows to the Prince within.

Wherever Woobin was taking her, whatever they were here to do, it was going to be extravagant and expensive. A knot formed in her stomach with Nyrrem fresh on her mind.

Woobin chose a modest place for lunch and made sure that his guards were served before sitting down to eat. While he was taking care of his men, Vinya pulled Hyosung's note from her pocket.

Elegant handwriting sprawled down the length of the parchment—it was the poem she asked for. He had delivered the haiku in less than a week, as promised.

Whispers in the night,
Reach for the elusive light,
Chasing shadows dark.
Heart divided, torn,
Between two roads, I sojourn,
Mournful, singing lark.
Madman's heart unfolds,
Calmness engulfs frenzy's hold,
Silent storms subside.
Temptations beseech,
Fair flower hangs within reach,
Path clear, I decide.

Vinya read it three times, then a fourth time for good measure. She rolled Hyosung's note and returned it to her pocket before Woobin sat down. Woobin spoke to his men and laughed at a joke a nearby guard told, but Vinya's mind was elsewhere.

Who was the subject of Hyosung's poem? Was it himself? If so, surely he didn't mean to suggest that his two paths were between Jun—and herself? Vinya had given the man no indication of being interested in him in that way; and if what Sooni said was correct, neither had Jun. Perhaps it was a personal struggle? He had helped Jun during their youth and apparently found ways to keep her potential suitors at bay... He'd also helped Vinya try to escape Byonea her first night here. But why would he help someone he just met?

Or had he truly been in the corner of her eye *and* mind the past few days, picking up on Vinya's own warring thoughts?

The ornate ceiling reflected on the surface of her soup acted as a lovely cover to hide all of the chunks that had settled in the bottom of the bowl. Vinya swirled the soup with her spoon, breaking the illusion and bringing the hidden ingredients to light.

The Palace had always been the place of dreams—a refuge and stronghold for those who could not provide for themselves. As a child, Vinya wished to be a part of palace life and was quickly humbled by Gran who forced her to be a servant; by the end of the day, she had changed her mind.

But being within the Palace walls, seeing a glimpse of the rotten skeletons Byonea's rulers kept hidden, Vinya wondered how they kept up the facade—wondered if Yuwon's seclusive tendencies were his way of keeping himself far from the dark parts of the Palace.

Perhaps this was why Hyosung helped her, so no more innocent lives would be tangled in the Queen's web.

She could hear him whisper her name.

Vinya.

The hand he offered was only to help, right?

Vinya.

If she were to take it, if she were to escape Byonea, would the Queen be able to find her at home in Norhagan?

"Vinya."

She jolted. Woobin had asked her a question, and she'd been staring at the honey-colored soup before her.

"Are you alright?" he asked.

"Y-yes, I..." Vinya stuttered. She scanned the table before her, her mind reeling for an explanation to give him.

His eyes dipped to her robes, to the pocket that held Hyosung's note. He had been within earshot when she challenged the Shade Prince with the poem, but she wasn't sure about sharing its contents.

Woobin followed her gaze to the food before her, to the bowl before him.

"Oh," he said. "Vinya—"

He was cut off by a distant scream.

The guards abandoned their meals and took up positions around their table. Some pulled their swords free from their scabbards, and a pair of them stepped out of the building to see what was causing the commotion.

Through the open window of the dining hall, a crowd surged and ran down the road. Frantic faces flew by, children were swept up and carried off, their fading wails replaced by new cries approaching.

There was no indicator of the cause. Nothing could be seen as Vinya looked for the source of the screams. Workers and civilians alike trampled down the road, confusion and fear pushing them forward. Then they heard it—amid the crowd, one word sliced through the air.

"*...Calgham...*"

The rest of the guards drew their swords. They followed close behind as Woobin grabbed Vinya's wrist and hurried to the back corner of the building, weaving around tables, chairs, and customers who were trying to get out of the shop.

Away from all windows and doors, the guards surrounded them, ready for a fight. Keeping watch on the front door, Woobin swept his arm around to pull her behind him, cramming her into the corner.

Stuck between two walls and Woobin, Vinya's mind raced.

How was it possible that Calgham warriors made it this close to the Palace? How is it possible that the second time she had ventured outside the walls, she was encountering the enemy?

Every time she blinked, flashes of the Calgham warrior haunted her mind.

Each blink, closer.

Each blink, his smile grew.

Vinya shook the image from her thoughts and forced herself to look over Woobin's shoulder — to the door that could open at any moment.

Woobin's royal carriage was just around the corner...

A balefire to the enemy.

Vinya's breaths came faster. Shorter.

The Prince's glance over his shoulder was strained, as if he too could not take his eyes off the door. He reached behind with his left hand, open for Vinya to take hold.

Something for her to focus on, just as Jun had done.

He held tight as she took it. A promise to keep her safe.

She was not supposed to be here—wasn't supposed to be thrown into the midst of chaos between countries. Her life shouldn't be put on the line every time she stepped beyond the Palace walls. Those walls were both her security and her cage...

Vinya had never been in trouble in Norhagan. She had never even witnessed two men fighting her entire life until she stepped foot in Byonea.

Between two roads, I sojourn

Hyosung's words, though written, echoed in her mind. Surely he spoke of his struggles, not her own. The nobility in the Palace were right to look down their noses at her. The Treaty of Trust had not helped them. *She* had not helped them.

The commotion outside began to subside, and the door to the building swung open.

Woobin's feet shifted, they locked in and became one with the floor beneath them. He would not be moved. But it was only the guards who had stepped out earlier. Their swords had been put away, a calm over their faces.

"Nothing but a common thief creating chaos so he could take what he wanted. No sign of any actual Calgham men. The thief has been handed over to local authorities to deal with."

The guards around them sheathed their swords. Vinya released Woobin's hand and dropped her chin in a sigh of relief—a glint of silver protruding from Woobin's right sleeve caught her eye.

He clutched a large dagger. Whorls and moons were carved into its hilt, a small red tassel hung from its end. Just as quickly as it appeared, it vanished beneath his robes.

Woobin turned to her and clapped his hands together. Every trace of distress had disappeared from his face.

"Well, that certainly ruined our appetites. Your surprise eagerly awaits!"

His robes rippled around him as he headed for the door, yet Vinya could find no trace of the dagger—no hint of a pocket or outline of the weapon revealed itself as she followed him to the carriage. A secret dagger... Vinya wondered what else the whimsical prince could be hiding.

A cabinet shop.

It wasn't what Vinya had been expecting when Woobin burst through the door, greeting the owner with a bright smile and warm embrace. The owner beamed and bowed to the Prince, who waved him off.

"Huang's shop creates the most beautiful woodwork in all of Byonea, and he personally makes the custom cabinetry for every member of our family."

Our family.

Woobin hummed his way through the shop, praising the owner on his recent designs and crooning over the vast shades of wood displayed along one wall.

Vinya wandered over to the case of jewels, stones, and precious metals. She ran a finger along their surfaces and stopped at a small sapphire. Its deep blue color drew her in, and the shop owner came up beside her as she picked it up.

"Mmm, interesting choice. That stone is often overlooked due to its size, forgotten and drowned out by the brightly colored stones around it. It's been sitting here for a while. Perhaps we could incorporate it in your cabinet? Do you have an idea for a design?"

The man plucked up a handful of stones and presented them to her. Pinks, purples, and greens glistened within his palm. "We could create a beautiful flower garden, overlooked by an intricate window. We could paint clouds above and carve a tree off to the side to give some depth. We could—"

"A hawk," Vinya interrupted, placing the deep blue sapphire on top of the colorful jewels in the man's hand.

Huang's mouth hung open as he stuttered. "A—a hawk?"

Vinya gave the man a close-lipped smile. "A red-tailed hawk, please."

Across the case of jewels, Woobin beamed and threw his hands in the air. "Perfect! A hawk it is! Excellent choice."

At Huang's raised eyebrow, Woobin pulled a money pouch from his robes and placed it in the shop owner's empty hand.

Huang weighed the pouch and dropped the jewels back into the case. "Very well, let us go over the details."

After much discussion, Vinya decided on tiger's eye and mother-of-pearl for the hawk's body, a deep amber stone for its eye, all set in a deep grey wood that reminded Vinya of the wind-worn fence posts of her home in Norhagan.

Woobin wanted to speak with the shop owner for a moment before leaving, and Vinya couldn't help but feel a pang of guilt as she climbed into the carriage.

Creating this piece of furniture made her place here feel permanent, a declaration of choosing to become part of this family.

Woobin bound from the shop, guards in tow, and waved goodbye to Huang at the door. The carriage door was closed behind him, and he sat on the seat opposite of Vinya with a satisfied sigh.

"It doesn't feel right," Vinya said, picking at the hem of her sleeve.

Woobin tilted his head, earrings clicking together with the movement, and pointed towards the shop. "We can go back in and make any changes, start over completely if you'd like to!"

Woobin was out of his seat in a second, but Vinya shook her head to stop him.

"No. I mean... it doesn't feel right to have something so extravagant when there are those who could benefit greatly from the money it took to build a *cabinet*."

A string came loose on her hem, and she twirled it back into itself.

Woobin gave her a flat smile. "Every member of the family receives a cabinet. This is my wedding gift to you. I hope you will accept it."

The word *wedding* rang through her. In a little over a week and a half, she would marry Yuwon. She would officially become a Princess of Byonea and could try to make a difference in the lives of those who lived beyond the Palace walls.

Vinya smoothed out her hem and nodded. "Alright."

When Woobin clasped his hands together and smiled. "Wonderful! Because I don't think Huang would willingly give that money back. I can't help but wonder what Yuwon will think of your design choice."

Vinya pressed her fingers against her warming cheek and yearned to be within the Palace walls.

The side gates of the Palace swung wide, and the horses and carriage were returned to the stables.

Vinya expected the stiffness from the ride as she stepped from the carriage, but what she didn't expect were the four men who stood near the stables.

Yuwon and Zhan were side by side, facing Hyosung and Alastor—the latter shifted from foot to foot, uncomfortable with whatever conversation was being held.

Yuwon turned—his strained expression wiped away when he saw Vinya. A hint of a grin pulled at the corners of his mouth.

Her heart skipped a beat, and Vinya couldn't help but return the smile.

Past Yuwon, Hyosung watched them closely.

Yuwon made it so easy to want to stay at the palace. Hyosung could see that—a muscle in his jaw ticked.

Her path was becoming clear.

Zhan did not turn to greet them. He kept his gaze on the men ahead, his hand hovered ever so discreetly near his sword.

As they neared, the air around them was tense, thinned.

Woobin's brow shot high, and he opened his mouth, presumably to ask what was being discussed, when a royal messenger interrupted—running towards them and calling for the Crown Prince. The frenzied messenger came to a halt and heaved to catch his breath as his eyes darted between them all. The man bowed to Yuwon and dug through the bag slung across his body.

"What is the meaning of this?" Alastor snipped. The adviser stepped forward to take the scroll the messenger procured from his bag, but the man refused to give it to him. He stepped around Alastor and passed the note directly to Yuwon.

As Yuwon read, he paled. He stopped reading, his eyes drifted far beyond the parchment in his hands.

Vinya's stomach twisted. Whatever news had just been received, whatever was on that note... was far from good.

Woobin snatched the scroll from his brother. "What is it? What's happened?"

With the note delivered to whom it was intended, the messenger relayed it to the rest of them aloud.

"A message from the Haryn border. When Princess Jun and her entourage did not arrive at Haryn on time early this morning, a group of scouts were sent out to see if they needed any assistance on the road. After a few hours of travel, they came across her carriage."

Woobin's chest rose and fell heavily as he finished what was written, his mouth hung open as he looked to his older brother. The crease between his brows deepened with each passing second.

The messenger went on, "The carriage was empty, the murdered guards left to rot at the scene, and the Princess is believed to be captured by Calgham warriors."

"No," Woobin breathed. "No, no, this isn't right. This—this is falsified. We sent some of our best men with her. There is no way... no way."

The messenger shook his head. "I personally know the man who sent the message. I believe it to be true."

Yuwon continued his distant stare ahead, unmoving.

Hyosung had frozen, his face turned to ice. He watched the messenger carefully, as if any wrong movement or word and he would send the man off a mountainside cliff.

Vinya ran a nervous hand along her throat. "The women that were with Jun, the Queen's woman and the lady-in-waiting, Sooni... what of them? They were taken as well?"

The messenger, awaiting Yuwon's orders, gave her a sweeping glance as he answered. "The bodies will be brought back swiftly for proper burials."

18

A Wilted Crown

Vinya's knees hit the gravel with a numbing crunch.

Woobin's voice broke through the ringing in her ears, asking the messenger for confirmation, asking for proof.

The messenger motioned to the scroll in the Prince's hands, quoting what was written. "A woman of the Queen, wearing her signature circle necklace, and a young lady-in-waiting, no older than fifteen, were found quite far from the abandoned carriage. The scuff marks on the ground indicate that they were forced out, dragged from the carriage, and slaughtered like—"

Vinya didn't hear any more. She did not *want* to hear any more. The ringing in her ears grew and smothered the remainder of his words. She braced herself with hands on her knees as everything around her began to spin.

How terrifying it must have been. Did Sooni fight as much as she could, struggling in the hands of those monsters? Or did she freeze, as she sat frozen during their attack on the way to the Spring Festival?

The girl who was so quick with her words would speak no more.

Vinya's stomach flipped over and over. The little breakfast she had early that morning unsettled and tried shoving its way up her throat.

Questions faded in, of Calgham warrior sightings, of where to begin the search for the missing Princess. Woobin passed the note to Alastor, who skimmed the parchment before he gave it to Hyosung and turned his attention to Yuwon.

"His Majesty will not survive a week if he leads the men into war. Your father would lead us straight into doom. This task must be yours."

War.

Woobin nodded. "I will come as well. It'll be better to have more eyes looking for Jun."

"Absolutely not," Alastor snapped. "To send an heir into war is one thing, but sending a second in search of the third? Ridiculous. Who would be the future of Byonea?"

Woobin looked to his older brother—who carefully watched the Shade Prince read the note.

Hyosung lifted his head, his large eyes rimmed red. "You cannot expect me to sit idly by while Jun is out there. Alone. Afraid."

The parchment crinkled in the Shade Prince's fist. "There is no order you can make that I will follow, you cannot tell me to stay within these walls. I will go. I will take Woobin's place in the search."

His clear path.

The half-brothers locked eyes, Yuwon no doubt weighed his options. Hyosung was no heir, and the man cared greatly about Jun. The answer was obvious to them all.

Yuwon nodded.

Hyosung returned the gesture and passed the note back to Alastor before he stalked off to gather supplies.

"I will alert Their Majesties," Alastor said. He bowed to the Princes, and with a twitch of his nose, the adviser scurried off towards the royal quarters.

Zhan twisted towards the barracks. "I'll get my gear."

"You will stay." Yuwon's voice was hoarse and raw.

Zhan halted. "Yu—Your Highness, I will—"

The Crown Prince cut him off. His voice rose, echoing off the walls of the stables as he pointed to the ground at his feet. "You will *stay!*"

Everyone quieted under the authority in his command. Zhan stood in shocked silence. Even Woobin paused as he helped Vinya stand.

Yuwon's jaw worked. He went to his friend and laid a shaking hand on Zhan's shoulder.

"Stay. Please." His voice cracked. Yuwon was breaking. A glimpse beyond his calm exterior.

Zhan studied Yuwon's face, and seeing beyond what was said, his eyes slid to the two of them—to Woobin who wrapped an arm around Vinya's waist, keeping her steady as she swayed; he needed the closeness of another person in this moment as much as she did.

Zhan dropped his head.

I can't choose. He seemed to say. *Don't make me choose.* But he couldn't. His Prince had given him an order, and with a reluctant sigh, Zhan nodded. He would stay in the Palace to protect them.

Yuwon took a deep breath as his hand slid off his friend's shoulder. "Ready the forces."

Zhan dipped his head in a bow, unable to look his friend in the eye, and Yuwon left to prepare.

Controlled chaos built around them as Zhan barked orders. Word spread. The battle bell rang. Men gathered and set off past the gates. Horses whinnied and stomped, sensing the change in the atmosphere, the urgency of the men hurrying around them.

It all blurred together.

The sun that beat down on them did not matter anymore, the light had been plucked from the sky.

Memories of the Princess and the young lady-in-waiting washed through Vinya's mind:

A painted sunrise.

A stitched canary.

A gentle hand holding her own.

A quipping remark.

A delicate smile.

A giggle from her side.

The bright peace that the two women gave.

One taken captive by an enemy.

One wiped from the world forever.

A familiar hand slipped into hers, Vinya didn't need to look to know that it was Woobin. Like his brother, his hand trembled.

They were all shaken.

Byonea had taken the first blow of war, the first death of thousands to come. There was no more waiting for the Norhagan army to arrive. Byonea would have to fight Calgham's massive army with the help of Haryn alone. They could win. They *had* to win.

Woobin's hand jolted, and Vinya lifted her eyes to see the cause.

Yuwon had reemerged, dressed in full battle gear. His midnight blue robes traded for midnight blue leathers—silver scaled armor had been strapped onto him. While a part of the men wore similar attire, other men—including Hyosung—wore solid black leather armor.

Yuwon would be a shining target in the middle of a battlefield. The image pierced Vinya's chest like the arrows that would soon rain down on the Byonean army.

Hyosung didn't acknowledge them as he lifted himself onto the horse. The solemn tune he hummed drifted between the clattering of metal and stomps of boots and hooves. The Shade Prince checked and double checked his gear—solely focused on the task ahead. Satisfied, he rested his hands on the horn of the saddle and watched as the Crown Prince moved through the gathering army.

Yuwon approached them, his gaze trained on her.

Jun's words echoed through her mind. *Promise me you'll spend more time with him while I'm gone.*

With each of Yuwon's steps, Vinya willed time to slow—to halt completely.

Each step closer brought the wall she'd built inside herself crumbling down.

This man who preferred books and seclusion day by day and drunken theatrics every full moon was about to ride among thousands of men into a war. For his sister. For his country.

Tears pooled and slipped down her cheeks, but she did not wipe them. She would not look away from the eyes that burned with fiery determination. Yuwon would stop at nothing to save Jun; she believed that with as much faith as knowing the sun would rise tomorrow.

His hand rose and hesitated near her face. Vinya could almost feel it—his hand cupping her cheek—but his fingers curled, and he dropped his arm.

"Take care of her."

Yuwon didn't need to look at Zhan and Woobin, they knew who the order was directed to. His lips opened once more as he searched her face, almost memorizing it, but nothing came out. Only unspoken words passed between them.

Don't go, she seemed to say.

I will come back to you, he seemed to reply.

He wouldn't say goodbye.

She couldn't tell him she would wait for him; her throat had closed and all Vinya could do was watch as Yuwon turned away.

This was it. The beginning of the war that had hovered over Byonea for weeks.

Yuwon mounted his horse and flew through the gates with hundreds of other riders and Hyosung—who held onto the saddle as he dipped into a low bow in Vinya's direction before joining the other men.

The Crown Prince rounded the corner and turned toward his lost sister. When the trail of dust settled, and she, Woobin, and Zhan were the last ones watching the empty road...

Vinya knew a piece of her heart left with him.

Standing before the empty throne, Vinya stared at the Treaty of Trust high on the wall, signed with the blood of the old Norhagan King, Rikr, and the first King of Byonea, Wondi. The Emerald King, the *jewel of the land*, had caused nothing but destruction hundreds of years ago. Now his descendant Moren followed in his footsteps. Her eyes trailed down the crimson painted stairs, the reminder of the blood that was spilled to bring the Byonean royal family here. It ran straight to the thrones, spreading to cover the entire dais and the chairs that sat upon it.

After Yuwon left, Woobin retired to his room, and Vinya wandered the Palace grounds aimlessly with Jinhee and Zhan, ending up in the throne room. In a haze, she approached the dais and with a soft gasp from Jinhee, Vinya stepped onto the King's platform. She ran her finger over the wooden armrest of the center throne—its dark wood had been polished smooth, not a crack or splinter to be found—and lifted her eyes to meet those of the gold Byonean dragon painted on the backrest. Its maw hung open in a smile... or a snarl.

Vinya wondered if it thirsted for blood, power, or justice. She wondered if the King and Queen satisfied its cravings in the form of death.

"I'd like to see Sooni's room." Vinya's voice rattled and scratched its way up her throat—it was a thought that struggled to be heard, refusing to lay dormant in her mind. They were the first words she had spoken in hours.

Jinhee shifted on her feet beside Vinya. The older woman opened her mouth, but closed it with a nod, offering a hand to help Vinya step off the King's platform. With one last glance at the Byonean dragon, Vinya turned her back and walked away from the throne. Blood would never be the answer, and she would be sure to never participate in feeding the ravenous beast.

Vinya would let it starve.

They wound their way through the Palace grounds, the paths vaguely familiar. They passed the wall she took the straw hat from on her first night here; the hat she had used as a disguise to slip through the alleys and escape the Palace. Her attempt to break free from the Byonean royals had been thwarted. Now, everything around her was at risk. Everyone within the walls was on edge.

Vinya, Jinhee, and Zhan rounded the servant's quarters and were met with dozens of quizzical eyes as they climbed the steps to its entrance. Men and women scooted back or shifted out of sight as the three of them made their way across the main level.

The older lady-in-waiting led them up three flights of stairs and through several halls. Vinya couldn't help but peek through the open doors as they passed. She also couldn't help but notice how those occupying the rooms would smile at Jinhee... their deep, genuine joy fading into a practiced doll-like smile when Vinya came into view. They bowed at the waist until she was out of their sight.

Maids and servants alike shared the sprawling building. There were no decorations placed about like the royal quarters—nothing was painted or sanded smooth like the women's quarters. No hall or floor separated men from women, young from old, servant or cook or lady-in-waiting. The building provided a resting place for those who served the royal family. Nothing more.

Vinya's chest squeezed tighter when Jinhee stopped at the top of the last flight of stairs and motioned toward the small bed in front of her—one out of six beds along a single wall in the room.

The lack of sunlight was suffocating, the stuffy air even more so. No walls separated the beds—only two folding screens in opposing corners of the room provided privacy for changing. A single candle rested on a table, casting the room in a faint glow. Traces of melted wax surrounded its base, having been scraped off the table and reformed into *new* candles.

The handful of servants scattered around the room paid Vinya no attention as she neared the bed, the floor beneath her feet groaning with each step. Her shadow shrunk on the rumpled blankets and the lumpy mattress underneath. Vinya's slippers hit a box that had been haphazardly shoved beneath the bed, and she stooped to pull it out, taking off its lid. The pink and jade robe of a lower-ranking lady-in-waiting sat neatly folded inside, along with a set of plainclothes.

Vinya rubbed at her chest in an attempt to quell the ache within and began to close the lid when something bright in the box caught her eye. Tucked along the side of the box, nearly covered by the clothes, was Sooni's yellow canary embroidery. Vinya stood and passed the embroidery to Jinhee, who had come to her side.

"Is this all that she had?" Vinya asked in a whisper.

"It's all we're allowed, my lady," Jinhee answered in an equally hushed tone. "I'm surprised she was able to keep this hidden."

The older woman flipped the embroidery over in her hands, inspecting it as if it had appeared by magic. The people in this building were allowed to keep a few pairs of clothes and the blankets for their beds. Nothing more.

Someone coughed behind them. A middle-aged man with a satchel hanging from his shoulder stood beside Zhan. He'd been sent to take up the bed Sooni left behind. No wasting time or space.

Vinya turned to Jinhee. "Would I be able to take her pink and jade robes?"

The lady-in-waiting shook her head, her lips flattening into a line. "Those robes will be reworked into new ones when..."

Jinhee's words trailed off, there was no need to say them. Another young girl would come to take Sooni's place, just as the man behind them came to take up her bed.

Vinya shook her head, not quite looking Jinhee in the eye.

"I understand, my lady," Jinhee interrupted, touching Vinya's arm, and motioned for them to leave. But the older woman stopped, and with a creased brow she walked to the head of Sooni's bed.

There was a whisper of paper against wood, sliding up the bedpost. A few light *ticks* on the floor as a few pieces of parchment broke off and hit the floor. Jinhee turned back to Vinya, raising her findings. Not paper. Flowers. Dried and drained of the color they had once been filled with. It was petals that had broken off and hit the floor, another dropped as Jinhee presented it to Vinya.

The circlet of flowers became all too familiar when Vinya wrapped her fingers around the base, where soft pink ribbons were tied into a dainty bow. It was the flower crown the little Shade Princess had placed on her head the day they came back from the Spring Festival. The crown she had worn when summoned by the Queen, that Woobin scooped off her head... and had given to Sooni, who kept it on her bed.

The stems of the flowers crunched beneath Vinya's unintentional fist, and she loosened her grip; taking deep breaths to calm the waters that rushed toward her heart, threatening to overtake and flood it.

A gentle hand touched Vinya's elbow.

"It's time to go, my lady."

"Mm," was all Vinya could manage.

She closed her eyes. She couldn't look at the bed. She imagined Sooni there, hanging the fresh floral crown on the bedpost, beaming and giggling. Even this stuffy room had not dampened the young girl's spirit. She was a light that had burned brighter than the candle in this room... and had been snuffed out.

The scaled Calgham dragon had eaten her, and the feathered Byonean dragon called for revenge, taking to the air with its four wings in repercussion for stealing its treasures.

"Mm," Vinya repeated, and allowed Jinhee to lead her from the room.

She ran her fingers over the delicate flowers as they descended flights of stairs, didn't take her eyes off the crown of flowers as they passed door after door. Person after person. Building after building. She followed the paths out of habit, her feet moving on their own. Jinhee and Zhan greeted those that were lighting the nighttime lanterns along porches and main paths, but Vinya didn't look away from the crown.

She wondered how people still moved, how they continued in their day as if nothing had changed? Byonea was off to war, Yuwon at its helm, Hyosung by his side. Jun was in their enemy's grasp. Sooni was gone. *Gone*. Vinya's stomach twisted into knots, and she heaved a sigh through her nose as they climbed the steps of the women's quarters.

Zhan announced he was leaving his second in command to guard Vinya's room for the night and was going to check in with Woobin. Jinhee nodded with a smile that was meant to soothe—but it did not reach her eyes. The lady-in-waiting leaned Sooni's stitched canary on the display table, against the wall and near the bird cage. Vinya followed suit with the crown of flowers, setting it reverently in front of the embroidery.

She stepped back and ran her hands down the sides of her skirts—then paused. Vinya slipped a hand into her pocket, and her fingers ran across the paper that contained Hyosung's haiku.

She took a deep breath... Hyosung would find Jun. Yuwon would lead and win the war. No one would ever take Sooni's place.

Her exhale did not quell the unease in her heart, and when she turned to her mat, a small satchel on the pillow only added to the torrent of emotions inside her. She retrieved the satchel, pulled loose its drawstrings, and dropped its contents into the palm of her hand.

Vinya's brows furrowed at the golden band that warmed against her skin, then upon closer inspection, she froze. It wasn't just a ring, it was *Gran's* ring—the wedding band that her neighbor could not find after Vinya's grandmother had passed away. In silence, she held the ring up to show Jinhee—tilting her head in question.

The lady-in-waiting blinked her tears away to see clearly what Vinya held, and shook her head. "I do not know that ring. Is there a note with it?"

Vinya stuck a finger inside of the satchel, but it was empty. No note, no indication of who dropped it off.

"It's my grandmother's ring, but I'm unsure how it came to be here. We thought it was lost." Something swirled in the back of Vinya's mind, pieces of a puzzle yearning to fit together, but she couldn't make sense of it through the fog of the day's events.

"Hm," Jinhee said. "I'll ask around and see if anyone knows anything."

Vinya slipped the band onto her right hand's ring finger, and stared at it deep into the night—wishing it would reveal its secrets.

19

An Arrow Awry

Vinya found herself eating the same bland meals. Wearing the same clothes. Walking the same halls and having the same conversations. The decorations that had been strung for the royal wedding were neglected. They slipped from their holds, and no one bothered to put them back except for Vinya—as if fixing them would end the war and bring Yuwon home, Jun and Hyosung with him.

The royal wedding ring had been resized and returned to her—no longer did it remind her of a chain. Its presence only served as a reminder of what was missing. She twisted Gran's ring on the opposite hand. It was a mystery that remained unsolved—no one seemed to know how or when the ring showed up in her room. Vinya chewed on the inside of her lip. She kept coming back to the same conclusion: Yuwon had someone go back to Taejim, locate the ring, and deliver it to her as a surprise. But she would have to wait for Yuwon to return to ask.

The royal wedding was not a topic of conversation among the nobles, but it crossed her own mind often. Gifts that had been arriving came to a halt as the transportation was needed for sending supplies to the Byonean and Haryn armies. Still, there was no sign of the Norhagan army. No whisper of their aid coming.

Vinya lost all faith in the Treaty of Trust that hung above the King's throne. It was no help... There was no help.

On the second day, Vinya went to Jun's room. The royal guards stationed without and within did not stop her. She paused in front of Yuwon's door for a moment and rested her hand on the smooth wood.

Zhan said nothing, a constant silent companion. He saw, he knew. Vinya often wondered what went through the guard's mind, what words and thoughts were left unsaid. Though every once in a while, he would sigh.

He did it again as Vinya's hand fell to her side and she continued into Jun's room. Zhan slid the door closed behind them, and Vinya sat at the low table where she and the women shared their last meal together. The cabinet beside Jun's bed caught her eye, a shining sun stark against the dark wood that surrounded it.

Of course the Princess would choose the sun. A symbol of the warmth and light she herself brought into the world. Vinya saw them now, the subtle sun designs spread throughout the room... Wooden beams flared from the round window behind the bed, suns were stitched into the bedding and carved along the edge of the table before her. Jun's rising sun painting leaned against the wall to her right—the wall Sooni had slid down, giggling over the room mix-up.

Vinya whipped her head away and squeezed her eyes shut in an attempt to force the vision from her mind.

When the door behind her slid open once more, she peeked to see Zhan offering a hand to help her stand. They walked down the hall, but Vinya paused and knocked on Woobin's door.

The lively Prince hadn't stepped foot outside of his room since the night Yuwon left, and Vinya was determined to get fresh air into his lungs. Woobin's door cracked open—a weary eye peered through. His disheveled hair waved across his forehead.

"I'm going to fly Nagne and would like your company," Vinya said.

Woobin's eyes fluttered then closed, he rested his head against the door with a soft thud. "Give me a moment."

The sound of drawers opening and fabrics shifting came from within. Vinya and Zhan stepped away from the still-cracked door to give the Prince privacy. He emerged in a simple cream robe and black pants. Vinya was stunned to see him in anything other than the bright sapphire blue. And there, attached to the belt at his side, was his moon-carved dagger. The small red tassel hanging off the end almost made him look like part of the guard.

The Prince gave them a small smile that didn't reach his eyes. "Alright, let's go."

Zhan's eyes dipped to the dagger, then led them to the aviary.

In silence, they flew Nagne—the only sound being Vinya calling the hawk back with her three-toned whistle. After the flight, they walked through the gardens. Woobin gathered flowers along the way while Vinya frequently looked at the ring on her finger. They ate supper with Woobin's bouquet displayed in the middle of the table. Zhan would glance at Woobin, the guard seeing more than was visible, as the Prince barely touched his food. In the quiet of the night, they returned to their respective rooms.

And thus began their daily routine.

The entire Palace had slowed to a hush. A dread had fallen over them all, the unknown haunting every moment. Hundreds of messages came to the Palace every day. Messages of victories and losses, captures and deaths. The scrolls piled up in stacks around Alastor's office, and he stayed there most days trying to keep on top of messages. The adviser would send out boys with letters to the families of those who had fallen, only leaving the office himself when there was any news he deemed important enough to alert the King and Queen.

On the third day, while on her way to Jun's room, Vinya stopped by Alastor's office to ask if her parents had responded to her message. She was met with condescending comments—how there were more important matters at hand than looking through the stacks of scrolls for personal letters. When Vinya offered to look for herself, she had promptly been kicked out of Alastor's office and, with a twitch of his nose, asked not to return.

While she sat in Jun's room—forcing herself to face her grief and discomfort—she heard the King's coughs from the next room. They sounded worse than before.

On the fourth day, in the middle of Nagne's flight, Zhan broke their day's pattern by mentioning training—a few self-defense and evasive maneuvers for Vinya to learn. Woobin was quick to agree, briefly touching the dagger at his side. Zhan noted the movement, brows knit together in an expression Vinya couldn't decipher.

Woobin still had not donned the traditional colors of a prince, keeping his attire bland—his eyes darkened with each passing hour.

Day and night, Yuwon was at war.

Day and night, there was no news of Jun.

On the fifth day, instead of walking through the gardens, Zhan took them to a small, private dirt clearing near the barracks to begin training. He and Woobin went through a series of slow steps, blocks, and jabs, instructing Vinya to copy Woobin's movements off to the side. They repeated the steps until Vinya had them memorized and sweat dripped down all three of them.

Jinhee passed out small towels and cups of water for a break. Zhan dabbed the towel across his neck while watching Woobin chug his water, the Prince's face expressionless.

Zhan grunted.

"Let's go full speed," he said. Zhan hung the towel on a nearby post and stepped back into the clearing.

Woobin's eyes snapped to the guard. He set down his cup and took up a stance across from Zhan, arms loose at his sides.

Without warning, the pair of men lost themselves to the movements. But Woobin... He moved like an arrow. Focused. *Fast.* All of Woobin's energy was redirected to this spar. Vinya had never seen someone capable of reversing their motions in a split second, with strikes and steps that doubled back on themselves in the blink of an eye. It was clear that the two had trained together hundreds of times over their lives. It was even clearer when the Prince began to add steps that weren't a part of their original routine—weaving and parrying to catch Zhan off guard.

None of his new strikes landed. Zhan always saw what was coming, and Vinya saw the smirk on Zhan's face right before he swooped Woobin's legs out from underneath him. The guard was on top of the Prince in a second, pinning Woobin's arms to the ground near his head.

"You're a bit distracted," Zhan huffed, dimples pressing in.

Woobin cocked his head to the side.

"Am I?" He replied with his own smile, and brought his knee up between Zhan's legs.

The guard went down with a groan beside Woobin, who patted his friend's cheek and laughed.

"Drinks are on you tonight!" he chirped as he sprung to his feet.

Zhan gave a weak gesture of agreement from the dirt covered ground, though they all knew Woobin would provide the drinks—and that he couldn't be charged for them either.

Woobin brushed the dirt off his own clothes and laughed again. The air around them felt lighter.

The spar was not only to teach Vinya to defend herself, but a distraction the Prince needed.

The lifted moods carried into the sixth day, when Vinya was paired with Zhan during training. Woobin gave his suggestions from the sidelines, and stepped in to correct Vinya's form when needed. The Prince's laughter and cheeky flirting with Jinhee often made Vinya lose focus while sparring, and her many layered skirts hindered her movements. No matter how many times she tried, she could not rush and pivot to sidestep around Zhan—her skirts flared and slapped against his legs. His hand always grabbed her arm before she could pass.

Zhan promised they would keep practicing.

On the seventh day, the King began to cry out. Vinya could hear his labored breaths through the walls of Jun's room—the greatest physicians in the land could not help him. Vinya couldn't help but overhear their concerns and Alastor's whispers when he visited the King.

Another sigh from Zhan. Another hand offered to help Vinya stand. Another trip to the barracks to practice, skipping the aviary completely.

She was given a stick the size of a dagger, its ends rounded and dull. Zhan and Woobin taught her vital points to stab if necessary. How to get to the heart and a vital artery at the base of the jaw. The men praised her efforts. Vinya cursed at the skirts that slowed her down, earning a smothered laugh from Woobin and a creased brow from Zhan. He understood it wasn't just the skirts that bothered her.

The Queen had insisted that the women in the Palace keep up appearances to lift the spirits of the men and guards who stayed behind to protect them. Vinya shook her head in disgust; she was nothing but a tool dressed in the finest silks for the Queen's charade. But she would continue to do so until Yuwon came home.

Vinya jolted at her trail of thoughts.

Zhan dropped his defensive stance, his eyes not leaving her face.

Did she, in less than a month, genuinely think of this as her *home*?

Zhan carefully took the stick from her limp hand.

"I think we're done for today," he murmured. Woobin hummed his agreement.

Later on the seventh day, Sooni's ashes were returned. The delivery was cold and unceremonious. Daeya stood off to the side and received the ashes of the Queen's woman. Her face was a practiced calm, but Vinya heard Daeya whisper "*they shouldn't have burned her*" to the woman with her as they carried the urn to the royal quarters. With Calgham invading Byonea, it would have taken too long to bring the bodies back.

With no indication of where Sooni's parents lived, Vinya and Jinhee received Sooni's urn.

It was too small. Too plain for the young girl who had been so *alive*. Vinya cupped the urn in both hands, running her thumb back and forth against the rough stone.

Woobin suggested spreading her ashes in the garden of a nearby village, but when they tried to leave, they found that the Queen banned them from exiting the Palace walls.

They weren't even allowed to deliver loaves to the children in Nyrrem. Instead, a handful of villagers walked to the Palace gates with their own baskets to collect the bread. Vinya noted that there were several less loaves than there were the previous week. Woobin's jaw tightened at the realization.

So, Sooni's urn was placed in Vinya's room on the display cabinet, in the middle of the dried flower crown between Gran's vase and the canary cage. Yet another reminder of someone she had lost.

Just like the past several days, Vinya paused by Yuwon's door. Unlike the past several days, Woobin stood in his own doorway across the hall, arms casually crossed and head resting against the frame.

"Go in," he said with a grin.

She wanted to refuse, she didn't want to break the privacy Yuwon's room held, but another part of her was curious.

Woobin huffed a laugh. "I've been listening to you stop by his room every day for the past week. It's fine, go in."

Zhan reached around her and slid the door open.

She closed her eyes. The last time that door opened, she was face to chest with Yuwon. The faint scent of parchment and ink, of leather and wood, and another smell she couldn't place a finger on... Vinya knew Yuwon would not be there when she opened her eyes, but when she did, he *was.*

He was in the shelves of books that lined the wall adjacent to the hall. There was everything from histories, to other countries, to the art of different fighting styles; some books were in languages that she'd never seen before. He was in the extra-long bed to her left, in the bow and arrows hung on the wall above it. He was in the woven rug covering most of the floor—a comfort in a hard place. He was in the desk that sat facing a massive window overlooking the gardens below, in the dried wax that hung down the side of a mostly burnt candle, in the stacks of parchment that rested on the desk's surface. A red-tailed hawk quill sat in a silver stand, the feather frayed from many uses.

The parchment on the desk weren't of politics or letters, but were covered instead by drawings. Vinya sifted through them. A sketch of his hawk. One of a fish swimming just below the surface of the water. One incomplete drawing of Zhan from the waist down—Vinya knew the hand that hovered near the sword in the likeness. One parchment was face down in the center of the desk, the ink soaking through from the front. She turned it over to reveal a sketch of a lantern sitting on wooden boards, a blossom branch wrapped around its base.

Vinya smiled. It was from the night of the full moon. She wondered how the Crown Prince had remembered such details while under the influence of whatever had been in those bottles. She lifted the drawing and turned to show Woobin and Zhan when the cabinet to the left of the door caught her eye.

Woobin's knowing smile grew.

Vinya laid the drawing down and approached the cabinet. A sprawling cherry blossom tree stretched from the bottom to the top. The blooms were crafted from a mixture of pink pearls and mother-of-pearl, its trunk and widespread branches were made with tiger's eye, and dotted throughout were tiny jade blossom buds.

She ran her hand along the wood and looked at Woobin. "Is this...?"

His brow rose. "The same *exact* wood that you chose? Mmhmm."

Woobin stepped into the room and looped an arm through hers. "We made so much fun of him when he chose this design, but Yuwon would take his books and read under its shade before the pavilion was even built. The pavilion is still one of his favorite places to go for solitude."

"Or for full moon escapades," Vinya added.

Zhan grunted.

Woobin laughed and patted her arm. "Yes, yes, and that."

The three of them fell into silence, their smiles slowly dropped as they stared at the cabinet.

Something reached within and encompassed Vinya's heart. She stepped out of the room, hoping that the distance would ease the pain.

"Alright, let's go," Vinya said, tucking a loose hair behind her ear and straightening the already-level hairpin in her bun.

The men exchanged glances before falling in step behind her to the aviary.

They had only trained for an hour when a messenger made their way to the barracks, a note for Woobin in hand. The Prince leapt from his seat with a whoop of *perfect timing* and declared that training was finished. He grabbed Vinya's hand and pulled her towards her room, leaving a disgruntled Zhan to pick up their towels and cups and follow behind.

Jinhee opened Vinya's bedroom door when they arrived. The evening sunlight streamed into her room through the window and bounced off the precious stones of Vinya's new clothing cabinet.

The craftsmanship was exquisite. There was not the one hawk she requested, but two. One on each of the cabinet doors, in flight and swooping around each other. Both hawks' feathers were a mixture of mother-of-pearl and tiger's eye as requested, with thin lines of gold glinting around each feather. She neared the cabinet, tracing the outline of a hawk's back, and smiled at a missing wing feather.

Vinya was about to thank Woobin when she noticed the branches that the hawks grasped in their claws. Early cherry blossoms. The swelling buds crafted from the perfect shade of jade.

Woobin stepped up to her side. "Yuwon told me about them. The flowers, and your grandmother. I hope you don't mind that I suggested the additions."

He took Vinya's hand—his sad smile made her heart ache. "I wish I had the opportunity to meet her, she sounded like a lovely person."

Vinya grinned. His infectious smile and flamboyant personality would have entertained her grandmother for days. She imagined Woobin playfully flirting with Gran, making the old woman blush.

She squeezed his hand. "Gran would have adored you."

He smiled again, smaller this time. The light in his eyes had faded, a drastic change from the bright-eyed man he was the previous week. Dark circles hung beneath his eyes—the vibrancy in the air around him had faded to a lull.

She didn't know how he handled it all—could not imagine the pressure he was under. His sister, gone. His father, weak. His brother, leading a war. The man wasn't getting much sleep, and his sunken cheeks indicated he wasn't eating much, either. Yet somehow, he'd found reasons to laugh. His warmth couldn't fully be put out.

Vinya's brow pulled together, and she turned to face the Prince fully. If something happened to Yuwon, would she still be obligated to fulfill her duty of uniting the kingdoms? Even though they hadn't heard a whisper from Norhagan, would the Queen still force a union? Woobin would take Yuwon's place as heir, and this hand would be the one she held at the wedding ceremony. She began to pull her hand away.

Woobin studied her face, expression softened as he gently placed his other hand on top of hers, running his thumb back and forth.

"Yuwon will be fine," he whispered.

Vinya blew out a wavering breath. She wanted to believe him. He sounded as if he was trying to convince himself as well.

She slipped her hand from his and smoothed out a non-existent crease in her skirts. "Go with Jinhee to the kitchens and eat a proper meal."

Woobin raised a questioning brow, well aware that as her superior he didn't have to do as she told.

Vinya huffed a laugh. "Please? I'll be fine here, Jinhee." She added to her lady-in-waiting.

Woobin shook his head. A touch of playful light returned to his eyes as he sketched a bow. "Very well. Jinhee? Tell me what dish you desire, and it shall be ours."

The lady-in-waiting took Woobin's outstretched arm, and Vinya could hear the woman's comforting words as the two of them walked down the hall out of the women's quarters. If anyone could breathe some life back into the usually yapping prince, if anyone could be stubborn enough to force Woobin to eat, it would be Jinhee.

Vinya slid the door closed behind them and approached the cabinet once more. She placed both hands on its surface and sank to her knees, finally allowing the grief she'd suppressed to engulf her. Her mouth hung open, but her cries made no sound. Her heart expanded and cracked beneath the weight of a thousand stones. She missed Yuwon. *Truly* missed him.

20

Spider Silk

Vinya was shaken awake by Jinhee, her body sore from falling asleep at the foot of the cabinet. She rubbed at her face and squeezed her eyes to orient herself, unused to waking somewhere other than her bed.

Jinhee guided her to the side of the cabinet and pulled out clean clothes for Vinya to change into. Vinya stumbled to her feet and, in a daze, she untied and shook out of the previous day's outfit. She hadn't realized she'd fallen asleep soon after Jinhee and Woobin left the night before.

"We must hurry," Jinhee urged as she slipped the new outfit on Vinya. "The Queen has requested your immediate presence."

Vinya blinked and looked towards the window. The sun had yet to rise, her canary still slept on its perch. What did the Queen need this early in the morning?

"I don't suppose we could decline this *request*?" Vinya mumbled, yawning and pulling her hair into a new bun.

Jinhee paused to give Vinya a flat look and helped guide the slippers onto her feet. The night guards at her door dipped their heads and followed closely behind as they exited the women's quarters.

"Zhan will meet us there," Jinhee whispered, careful to not wake any of the other sleeping women in their rooms.

On light feet, they made their way to the royal quarters, passing by groups of younger Shade Princes and Princesses that played quietly on the porch of their residence with their own ladies-in-waiting. The little girl who had placed a flower crown on Vinya's head bounced on her toes and curled her chubby fingers in a wave. The lady-in-waiting near her wiped her hand across her forehead, exhausted, as if the little Shade Princess hadn't slept a wink all night.

Vinya returned the wave, making the little girl giggle and the lady-in-waiting shush her.

There was no sign of Zhan upon entering the royal quarters, the royal guards let them through and opened the Queen's door.

So the women sat and waited. And waited.

Vinya's stomach churned with more than hunger as the sun peeked over the horizon, and the Queen finally emerged from her bedchamber beyond the far wall. A handful of her women trailed behind her and took up positions on either side as the Queen sat opposite of the low table. Vinya and Jinhee bowed and rose to the Queen's sanguine smile.

"I've been made aware that you're keeping the girl's ashes in your room."

Her words practically oozed with venom. The pit in Vinya's stomach deepened.

"Yes, Your Majesty," Vinya replied.

The Queen's lip curled upward as she stirred the tea in her cup, waving her other hand in the air. "I myself received the urn of my lady. Or... what was left of her body. It was quickly discarded."

Vinya blinked. "W—wouldn't the urn go to her family?"

The Queen stopped stirring, and leveled Vinya with a stare. "When these women become mine, they are *mine*. Why would I send them to the home that they deserted for me?"

Vinya knew the question was not for her to answer, so she kept her mouth shut.

The Queen went on. "And when they cannot serve me, they are no longer of use. Why would I keep them around?" she scoffed. "Imagine the shelves I could line with the jars of failures."

Ashes in the wind, thrown away as if they were trash.

The Queen flattened her hands on the table between them, and Vinya found herself shrinking away.

Something was wrong. She should have woken Woobin... Vinya had forgotten his request of joining her in his mother's room. Moreover, where was *Zhan*?

Vinya glanced at Jinhee, whose fingers carefully curled into her skirts. She sensed it too; something was off.

The Queen's voice dropped to a whisper. "I made it clear you were to get rid of that girl."

One of her women snickered. The others didn't bother to hide their sneers.

"Your Majesty, I—I'm not sure I understand." How could she get rid of her? Sooni was already gone.

"Get rid of the urn," the Queen commanded.

What would happen if Vinya refused a second time? What punishment would she receive if she stood up for Sooni, just as the young girl did for her?

Vinya shook her head. "No. No, I will not."

The smile vanished from the Queen's face, and grew on the women around her. "I knew you would say that."

The snickering Queen's women outright laughed now; each wave sent jolts through Vinya's body.

She was on her feet in moments.

"What did you do?" Vinya breathed.

Jinhee held a hand over her gaping mouth.

The Queen did not answer. She would not answer. This was a battle that the Queen won before Vinya ever entered the room.

Without the Queen's permission, Vinya twisted and slid the door to the side, running through before it was fully open. She slammed into a disheveled Zhan, hair a mess and shirt half tucked in as if he'd only *just* been alerted to the situation.

For the first time, he hadn't seen Vinya coming—he had been distracted, his expression distant and concerned as he looked towards the entrance of the royal quarters.

But his head whipped to her on impact, and—"*Sooni*." —was all he needed to hear to fall into place beside her, running as she bolted from the hall. Her skirts made the run difficult and slowed her down, but Zhan matched her pace.

"Go!" she commanded.

Zhan glanced at her, but stayed by her side.

"Go, go, please *go,*" Vinya choked out. Her throat was closing, her breaths turned ragged.

She did not have to tell him a third time. He quickened his speed and rounded a corner; he was out of sight before Vinya had time to gather her skirts to try and keep up. Her eyes burned. Her legs burned. Her heart squeezed and squeezed and *squeezed*.

Vinya did not look towards the little Shade Princess in the corner of her eye, who waved again. She didn't turn around after hearing Woobin's shouts from the royal quarters far behind her.

The hall in the women's quarters seemed to stretch on, and Vinya came to a sliding stop in her doorway.

Zhan stood in front of the display cabinet, his sides expanded and contracted with each heavy breath. Zhan turned—his steely face melted away. Behind him, Sooni's urn was gone. The dried flower crown was left in tatters, crumpled and broken on the cabinet.

Vinya let go of the door frame, her fingernails dug into her palms as she backed down the hallway.

The guards had left with her this morning. As the morning hour passed, the women's quarters were empty—everyone attending to their own affairs. There had been no reason to keep an eye out for a slippery intruder.

Vinya shook her head. "No, no."

She hobbled halfway down the hall when Woobin appeared at its entrance, breathless from his own run.

"Stop her," Zhan called from her doorway.

Vinya tried to walk around Woobin, but his hand whipped out and wrapped around her wrist, sidestepping to block her path.

She pulled against his grip. "No!"

Jinhee made it to the women's quarters. Zhan's footsteps grew from behind. Confusion covered Woobin's face—the Prince didn't know what had occurred.

Vinya twisted her arm and yanked her wrist free from Woobin's hold, the force of the motion swung her arm into Zhan's reach. He wrapped his arms around her, locking Vinya's own arms across her chest.

"No, let *go*!" She tried to wriggle out of Zhan's grasp, but he held firm—backing up so that she didn't kick the Prince in her attempt to escape. "Let go of me!" she yelled. Her cries turned as frantic as her fight against Zhan.

Jinhee whisked past them to see what had transpired in Vinya's room.

"*She* did this. The Queen!" Vinya didn't care to lower her voice. She allowed the rage seep out through her tears and words as she spoke to Woobin. "Your mother did this. She wanted us to get rid of Sooni, and we refused, so she did it herself. She sent her off with Jun to *die*."

Woobin inhaled with a startled blink, his eyes flitted across her face as he tried to fit the pieces together.

Vinya fought against the steel cage Zhan had become, a cage to keep her from going back to the Queen. Her will to break free weakened with the ever-building sorrow in her soul. There was no winning when it came to the Queen.

Woobin shook his head.

"No, Vinya, she wouldn't have done that," he murmured.

"Just like she *wouldn't have done* anything to Hyosung's mother?" she spit back.

Zhan tensed. A wordless conversation passed between the men.

Woobin let out a sigh through his nose. "I understand how you can see that, but... she wouldn't have put Jun's life at risk on purpose."

"What is Jun but another pawn in the Queen's game? Who are we all but people—*toys*—for her to play with? Could it be why she adopted Jun to begin with? A daughter to use for her own gain in the future? Who's to say that Jun's mother didn't die by the Queen's hand?"

Woobin swiped an arm across the space before him. "Vinya, that's *enough.*"

"It's *not*!" Vinya yelled, her voice cracking. A sob wound its way up her throat and broke free. "It will never be enough. We will never be enough for her and now... now I've lost Sooni. *Again.*"

Vinya ceased her fight and dropped her head backward onto Zhan's chest. Tears streamed down to her ears as she closed her eyes.

"She wasn't supposed to go," Vinya whispered. "I let her go."

Zhan's hold softened, though awkwardly as if he'd never held a woman before.

Jinhee came out of Vinya's room and tucked a loose strand of her hair in place. "It is not your fault, child. These things, though unfortunate, happen. Suddenly or... over time. The best path for us to take is to keep *living.* Keep the memory of those we loved and lost alive."

Zhan loosened his grip completely and dropped his arms to his sides.

Jinhee opened her arms, and Vinya fell into them. The lady-in-waiting folded her arm around her, patting and rubbing Vinya's back as she cried into the older woman's shoulder.

Feet shifted behind her, but the two men did not leave.

Jinhee addressed them. "I will take my lady into her room now, and will send word when she's ready to come back out."

Silence, then footsteps faded down the hall. Vinya allowed Jinhee to guide her back to her room.

Her bedroom felt as empty as her first night here, and Vinya's thoughts hollowed out as well. She was utterly powerless as long as the Queen was in control.

Breakfast felt trivial. The rice and egg held no flavor. Vinya chewed out of habit, staring at the far wall of her room. Jinhee moved around her, pulling out a simple robe for the remainder of the day. Changing her outfit once more felt like a poor use of time. It was an effort to keep her head upright as Jinhee slipped the shirt over her head, and she did not move from that spot as Jinhee cleared out Vinya's dishes; the food unfinished.

The walk to the aviary was sluggish. Her feet moved of their own accord, though gravity pulled harder with every step. She didn't hear the aviary keeper when he spoke and hardly felt the tough leathers of the falconry glove as she slipped her hand into it. Nagne had a difficult time flying against the brewing storm, the winds catching up wisps of Vinya's hair. She refused to tame the onyx strands, but kept her focus on the hawk instead—as if she lost sight of him for the briefest of moments, he, like his owner, would leave the Palace, too.

Zhan and Woobin met her in the field, standing to the side and conversing under their breath, giving Vinya the space she needed.

Thunder sounded in the distance.

Her ears perked up for another moment. Not thunder. Hooves.

Vinya recalled Nagne with the three-note whistle as the messenger—the same messenger who had delivered news of Jun's disappearance—slid off his horse and bowed deeply to the Prince.

"Your Highness," he said with a scroll in his extended hand.

The Prince stared at the man, then to the scroll, but did not take it.

Vinya wouldn't have taken it either. Not with how weighty the scroll looked, regardless of its compact size. Not when it seemed like the messenger holding it wanted it out of his possession as soon as possible—uneasy with the news it contained.

Zhan broke the tension. "Just tell us."

The messenger swallowed, eyes shifting between them all. When Woobin still did not speak, the messenger opened the scroll and cleared his throat.

Woobin grabbed Zhan's arm to keep steady.

The messenger took a deep breath. Another. "Byonean forces received a tip regarding Princess Jun's location. The Crown Prince stole into the night with a small force of men to scout the area. When His Highness and his men did not reach the designated checkpoint on time, another search party went out and returned with no indication of their whereabouts. The Crown Prince Yuwon is assumed to be physically lost in battle. Even without the Crown Prince in their midst, the war tipping in Byonea's favor. We will send immediate news if there are any changes."

Thunder sounded then, rumbling its way into Vinya and the wild beats of her heart.

The hawk landed on Vinya's gloved hand with a cry, tipping its head to look at the messenger. Vinya only looked at the glove, at the red string that had fallen out of place and floated in the breeze. At Nagne's large talons that unintentionally caused the string to come loose. At the feathers being ruffled by the wind. At the bright amber eye that looked back into her own.

Zhan took a controlled breath. "The King and Queen?" he asked.

"Being alerted as we speak," the messenger responded.

Zhan dismissed the man and turned his attention to Woobin—who tightened his grip on the guard's arm. "We've traveled this country many times together. You know as well as I do that he knows the roads; he'll find his way back."

Woobin watched the messenger ride away. A gust of wind pushed against his robes and his waving, unkempt hair. "That's exactly why it bothers me. He knows the roads."

And he was lost.

21

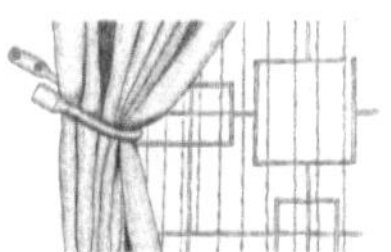

Shifting Walls

Live for those that you've lost.

Vinya refused to believe that something had happened to Yuwon. She tried her best to smother every dark thought that crept its way into her mind. She would know if something terrible happened to him—she was sure she would be able to sense it.

A muscle sporadically twitched in Zhan's jaw the following morning. No sound came from within Woobin's room, and when Zhan knocked, no one answered.

Zhan looked to the guards at the end of the hall, who nodded. The Prince had not left his room since the day before.

Zhan sighed and leaned toward the door. "Your Highness, we're coming in."

Vinya didn't remember Woobin's room being so dark every time he opened the door the previous days. She followed close behind Zhan into the dim interior and slid the door closed behind them.

The Prince's walls were covered in thick dark fabric. They pooled at the bottom like waves, touching the thick black woven rug that covered the entirety of the floor. Small lanterns hung in no particular pattern on the ceiling, though none of them were lit. Woobin had drawn the fabric across his window; the small holes cut into it scattered tiny beams of light into the room.

There was barely enough light to see where they walked. Zhan aimed for the window, but took one long step in the middle of the room. Vinya squinted at the floor and could see nothing that the guard could step over. She swept her foot along the rug, and bumping into nothing, she took a step. The board under her foot groaned.

"I'll get it fixed," a voice croaked from her right.

Zhan pulled back the curtains and tucked each one behind silver hooks. "He's been saying that for years."

Hundreds of sapphires hung on dainty silver chains in the window. Vinya could imagine how the morning sun would normally cast the room in a thousand blue sparkles, but storm clouds covered the sun today. The rain steadily beat on the roof.

Woobin's cabinet sat in the middle of the far-right wall, dark fabric draped around. Vinya couldn't help but huff a laugh at the design. She should have known it would be a moon.

His bed lay facing the window. Dozens of small silver weapons were displayed on the shelves above, a handful of unlit candles on every shelf.

Vinya pointed towards them—above the Prince who sat on the edge of his bed with arms resting on his knees.

"Don't you think those are a bit close to the fabric?" she asked.

Woobin gave her a weary smile, he must have heard the same concern from others. "I like to walk a fine line with fate."

Zhan stood with his arms akimbo. He shook his head at the candles—and the Prince. "Fate says you're coming with us."

Woobin shook his head. "I want to stay here."

Zhan approached the bed, stepping over the creaky board once more. "Worrying and waiting will not change anything with Yuwon. He will be back."

"I should be with him. I'm useless here." The Prince buried his face in his hands.

"Woobin, you are not useless. You're going to show Vinya the wall."

Woobin straightened, then stood.

"*The* wall?" he asked.

Zhan nodded. "A messenger came early this morning. A group of Calgham warriors have pushed their way across the land, less than a day's ride from the Palace. If something happens, if for some reason she is separated from us or feels threatened in any way..."

He paused. Glanced to his right—to the Queen's room at the other end of the hall.

Woobin followed Zhan's gaze. He took a deep breath and ran his fingers through his hair to swoop it out of his face. "Alright. We'll send word for Jinhee to meet us in the ceremony hall."

"What is so special about this... *wall*?" Vinya questioned.

"We won't talk about it here. You'll see soon," Woobin answered. He shifted a curtain to the side, revealing a small ledge built into the wall. He retrieved the moon-carved dagger from its stand on the ledge and strapped it to his waist.

The Queen's voice traveled down the hall as they exited Woobin's room, the three of them paused at her tone. Vicious. Livid.

Alastor backed out of her room, bent at the waist in a deep bow. When the Queen's door shut, Alastor's smile dropped, and the adviser nearly jumped back when he faced the hall. He dipped his head to the Prince and twisted to enter the King's room.

Physicians scurried around Alastor, in and out of the King's room. The King's wheezing muted every time the door closed.

Woobin's jaw worked. Vinya looped her arm through his. With a flat smile and pat on her hand, he led them under covered walkways to the ceremony hall.

Vinya had never been in the building before. Near the royal quarters, the ceremony hall was more of an enclosed room. Its high ceilings were held by deep red beams and the expansive floor gave lots of room for performances. It also served for large groups of people receiving official rewards, blessings, or praises from the King.

It would be their room to train for the day while the rain poured over the Palace.

A few ladies-in-waiting under Jinhee brought in baskets of items. Books, small crafts, small foods, a folding screen and change of clothes for Vinya. Zhan watched the other women with crossed arms—his feet unmoving on the polished white floor until they all bowed to Vinya and left, and only then did he follow to watch their retreat from the doorway.

Zhan pulled the massive door closed and slid a beam across, barring anyone from entering. He returned to their side, across the hall from the door, and rested his hand on the sword at his side.

"Can I trust you to keep a secret?" he asked the older woman, who gave him a small smile.

"There are many things I know about that I wouldn't dare to speak of without permission," Jinhee stated.

Woobin's brow twisted in question as he looked at Zhan, who stared at the lady-in-waiting through the slices of his eyes.

"If it doesn't hurt anyone, if it keeps Vinya safe, then you have my word."

A tense moment passed between the two. Satisfied with Jinhee's answer, Zhan dipped his head to Woobin.

The Prince's eyes darted between the two once again, then approached the paneled wall beside them. He laid both hands on one, the panel painted with the four-winged feathered dragon of Byonea—and pushed.

With a click barely louder than the rain, the panel snapped out of place. Woobin slid it to the side, a hidden pocket door. Beyond, a wood and dirt tunnel dipped into the darkness.

Woobin grabbed a lantern from inside the ceremony hall and descended into the shadows. He spoke as he led them deeper.

"This tunnel was discovered when the Palace was first built. No one knows its origins. Some speculate it was a trade route for the people who lived here, prior to Byonea breaking free from Calgham, but it was never confirmed. The workers who found and covered the entrance—as per my ancestors orders—were killed to keep the knowledge within the royal family and their few trusted guards, where its secret remains." Woobin stopped and held the lantern out. "It is our escape route if the Palace ever comes under attack. Thousands of men and women walk within the Palace walls, not knowing what's under their feet. The tunnel stretches east, half a day's walk past the Palace walls. Its exit is deep in the woods, hidden within large stones."

He turned to Vinya, a sense of purpose having fallen over his face. "It is now your escape, too."

Vinya twisted to Zhan; his expression unreadable. The man who stopped her on her first night here—who watched her every move for weeks—was showing her a way out.

"Thank you," Vinya whispered.

Zhan's dimples made an appearance, and he bowed his head to her.

Jinhee, staying true to her word, kept silent.

They exited the tunnel, and Woobin clicked the wall back into place behind them. Vinya's eyes ran along the edge of the panel. Even though she knew of its existence, it had been so well hidden that she couldn't see the seams. Zhan crossed the room and removed the beam from the ceremony hall's door. Training began shortly after. Though her skirts frustrated her, Vinya felt hope for the first time in weeks.

The rain fell harder as the day went on.

After training, Woobin had been called away by Alastor to meet about private matters. The Prince's skin turned a shade paler before he left.

Zhan walked a patrol around the outside of the ceremony hall, leaving Vinya and Jinhee alone to pass the time with crafts and books.

"The palace will fall apart at this rate," Jinhee muttered.

It wouldn't, of course. The wind pushed against the stone walls and rattled the reinforced paper windows, but the Palace was built to withstand the storms.

The lady-in-waiting wasn't satisfied with her embroidery and took it apart, careful not to snap any threads. Vinya was determined to complete her cherry blossom pattern in the hoop. Stitch after stitch, the art slowly came together. Each prick of the finger was a lesson in finding the correct placement. She blended the darker pinks into the lighter outline of the petals, Jinhee often gave compliments on how far she'd come.

The sun set. Zhan checked on them, gave them updates on the Calgham force near the Palace—which had not yet been defeated—and joined them in a simple dinner before resuming his patrol under the covered path around the building.

Jinhee pulled apart her stitchwork for the fourth time when a chill crept up Vinya's spine, and she set her embroidery hoop down. Something wasn't right. Something—someone—was coming.

"My lady?" Jinhee questioned. Her brow knit together as she scanned the empty room.

Vinya's only focus was on the door. The panel in the wall. The painted dragon's eyes that seemed to stare back.

Maybe it was her imagination, her own mind racing at the possibilities during this time of unrest. A secret door would be an awfully good passage if someone wanted to sneak *into* the Palace. Woobin said only the royals and a handful of guards knew about the passage. What if someone shared that knowledge with the wrong person? What if the wrong person squeezed that knowledge out of the few who knew?

As if she had willed it, the panel clicked.

Vinya stood, covering her heart with her hand. Surely her mind was playing tricks with her.

Jinhee followed her gaze as the wall shifted. The lady-in-waiting scurried off the floor and stood between Vinya and the wall, arms splayed wide.

The wall slid to the side, a handful of inches at a time. Vinya's voice was barely a whisper above the howling storm.

"Yuwon?"

The Crown Prince was haggard. His dark robe twisted oddly around his body, tattered and wrinkled.

"Get Zhan," she ordered Jinhee.

The older woman gathered her skirts and ran from the room.

Yuwon's eyes lifted and strained as he scanned the dim, lantern-lit room, following her voice. When their eyes locked, his shoulders sank, his face slackened.

This wasn't the man she'd come to know... His stance was off kilter, he couldn't hold his head upright as it lolled to one side—like he'd had one too many drinks. A voice in the back of her head told her that something was very, *very* wrong.

Yuwon took one sluggish step toward her, his foot not quite lifting off the floor, his hand slipping on the edge of the panel.

As he stepped closer, into the lantern-light, Vinya noticed the pallid tint to his face, drained of blood as if he'd seen a phantom—perhaps he was almost a ghost himself.

Yuwon's legs buckled and Vinya closed the distance between them, fumbling as she tried to catch him. His knees hit the ground, and there was no way she could keep him upright as his weight pulled her down too. She twisted, wrapping her arm around the back of his head to take the impact as he collapsed. Yuwon's eyes closed—his body tense as he sucked in air through his teeth.

Vinya searched his sweat-beaded face. The smell of metal hung in the air around him. Something had happened, and he needed help as soon as possible. His body was weakening and he drew in less and less air with each breath.

Vinya ran her hand along his face, wiping the sweat and calling his name. "Wake up. Yuwon, *stay awake.*"

Yuwon's eyes pulled open and fell on her face. The Crown Prince fought to stay conscious, like his eyelids were filled with lead.

"Yuwon, what happened?" Vinya pleaded. She needed to keep him awake long enough for help to arrive. She glanced toward the door, hoping that Jinhee would return soon.

He lifted his arm—the movement slow and cumbersome—to reach across his body.

Vinya saw it then. Her fingers shook as she pulled back the ripped fabric.

Yuwon was not only covered in drying rain and sweat, but blood. *His* blood. A slice the length of her finger had been hidden by the folds of his robes. His waist had been run through with a sword; she suspected there would be a matching wound on his back as well. The deep red liquid seeped into her skirts, the puddle beneath them growing by the second. His fall had moved the makeshift bandage on his wound—the bandage that kept him from bleeding out.

Zhan burst through the door in a full sprint and slid on his knees to their side. His hands landed in the blood on the floor and he snatched them back, accidentally splattering drops onto himself. They trembled as he turned his palms face-up, jaw hanging open at the sheer amount of blood on his hands. Zhan moved to wipe his hands on his own robes but stopped. Instead, the blood drip, drip, *dripped* onto the floor. The tremor in Zhan's hands spread through his body as he hovered over Yuwon, looking down on the Crown Prince—his friend—in horror.

"Yuwon—" Zhan whispered, but something shifted in the passage behind Vinya. Across from Yuwon, Zhan's eyes snapped to the dark tunnel, the guard's steely exterior sliding into place just as his hand flew to his sword—and paused. Zhan's jaw slackened.

Vinya twisted, and there was Jun.

Filthy. Ragged. Like she hadn't had a proper meal or bath since the day she left the Palace. Her hair hung like curtains on either side of her face, matted with small leaves scattered throughout. Gasps and murmurs filled the room as Jun hugged the wall, using it to stay standing as she too emerged from the shadowy tunnel.

Zhan stood to help her, but Jun sucked in a deep breath at his movement and wrapped her arms around herself, recoiling against the paneled wall. The Princess curled into a ball—the movement jerky—and only looked to the ground near her bare feet. Jun turned her head away when Zhan neared, and she scooted further when he closed the panel with bloody fingers.

The guard returned to Yuwon's side, eyes flicking between Jun and the fabric that had been used for his makeshift bandage. It was from Jun's dress.

"Jun..." Vinya started, but the Princess ignored her completely—her eyes not finding rest on any surface, or any face.

A stillness in Vinya's arms reclaimed her attention. Yuwon's eyes were half closed, and vacant.

Vinya shook her head.

"No," she said, defiant in the face of death. The Crown Prince inhaled slightly as she shook him awake.

Yuwon would live. He *had* to live. She would not lose anyone else.

Her chin quivered as hot tears flowed. "Stay with me, Yuwon... Stay. *Please,* don't leave me here."

Yuwon's arm moved again, reaching across his body and toward Vinya's face.

His fingertips grazed her cheek—touched the stream of tears. There was no more pain in his expression, only peace as he gave Vinya the smallest smile.

The Palace physicians and Jinhee entered the room and rushed towards the Crown Prince.

Yuwon's arm dropped. And when his eyes closed, they did not open again.

22

A Shadow in the Night

Thunder crashed around them. Vinya stayed without rest by Yuwon's side throughout the night and next day.

The storm never let up; Yuwon still did not wake.

The physicians continued to do everything in their power to repair the damage to Yuwon's abdomen. He was covered in numerous stitches in the front and on his back. Whoever struck him must have caught him by surprise. Vinya had seen firsthand that he could hold his own—he would have been able to defend himself if he knew it was coming.

Jun had locked herself in her room, only allowing her ladies-in-waiting to enter. No one had been able to pull an explanation from the Princess; she had not uttered a single word since returning to the Palace.

Vinya sat beside Yuwon's bed, dipping a towel in cool water to wipe across his sweating forehead. His fever was as unrelenting as the storm. Jinhee and Zhan pleaded with her to sleep, but she had refused. As long as Yuwon slept, she would stay by his side. Fatigue pulled at her. The pouring rain tried its best to lull her into slumber, but the cracks of thunder shocked her body into staying awake.

Hunger gnawed at her stomach, but her appetite was lost when she looked at Yuwon's bandaged torso.

Servants, physicians, guards, and royal family members moved in and out of the room at all hours of the day, checking on the Crown Prince. Jinhee and

Woobin were the most frequent, and Woobin often brought Yuwon's favorite books to read aloud.

Alastor had come with the King the first night, Daeya with them. The coughing King trembled so violently at the sight of his son that Alastor had him secluded to his rooms. He stated that no one needed to know their King was soft-hearted—no one needed to see a tear fall from the eye of this country's leader.

Every once in a while, she could hear the cries of the Queen. She'd called upon the country's greatest shamans—they burned offerings and pleaded to their gods to allow her son to live.

He was still so pale. No one knew exactly how far he had journeyed with the injury, but even with the makeshift bandage they'd found on him, he had lost too much blood. Everything that could be done was done. It was up to Yuwon's body to recover on its own... if he recovered at all.

Vinya heard the faint sliding of the door as Jinhee stepped in with a bowl of broth, one last attempt to get her to eat before retiring to her own room.

She knelt at Vinya's side and placed the bowl at her knees. Silence stretched between them. The wind howled against the outer walls of the room; rain beat down on the roof. Jinhee's voice barely rose above it all.

"You've been awake for so long."

"He's been asleep for so long," Vinya replied as she dipped a rag to wipe the gathering sweat off Yuwon's brow.

"He will be fine," Zhan said from the door, though Vinya didn't know if he was assuring himself more than her. Dark circles had formed under his eyes. He had insisted on staying guard in the room, only trading out with his second in command for a few hours at midnight and midday to sleep.

Jinhee placed a gentle hand on Vinya's forearm when she dipped the towel again. "He wouldn't want to wake to see you in this state."

Vinya had no doubt dark circles plagued her own eyes. She met Jinhee's gaze, the older woman looked drained as well. Weariness had blanketed the palace, leaving everyone sluggish and broken.

Every single person within the walls was worried about the Crown Prince. A handful of people were worried about Vinya.

Vinya sighed through her nose. She may not be able to heal Yuwon on her own, but she could help ease the worry in Jinhee.

She relented, and at her nod, relief washed over Jinhee's face. She plucked up the bowl of broth and exchanged it with the towel in Vinya's hand.

"I'd be satisfied if you only took two sips." She stood, and Vinya watched as she headed for the door. "I'll be back with blankets and a pillow, we'll make a pallet near the door, opposite of Zhan's chair."

"No," Vinya stated between sips.

Jinhee paused in the doorway.

"I'll sleep right here," Vinya said, and placed a hand on the wooden floor beneath her. Beside Yuwon's bed.

Jinhee exchanged a questionable glance with Zhan, who gave no indication of going against Vinya's wishes.

"Alright. As you say." The older woman dipped her head in a bow and went off to gather pallet supplies.

Vinya and Zhan stared at each other for a while, both exhausted and mentally worn down. Zhan's eyes dipped to the bowl in her hands as a silent reminder.

As Vinya finished the broth, a pallet was made on the floor beside Yuwon's bed. Jinhee helped Vinya take a sponge bath and change clothes in an adjacent room. Another set of clothes was brought in and placed beside her pillow, her silver hairpin resting atop the folded robes. She was so used to the weight, she'd forgotten it had been in her hair.

Vinya laid on her side as the storm continued on and was pulled into sleep as she watched Yuwon's chest rise and fall.

A strong gust of wind and a crack of thunder woke Vinya.

She must not have been asleep for long—Zhan's flat brimmed guard hat still sat upon his chair, so he hadn't yet traded his post with his second in command. Or perhaps she'd slept through the guard change, and he was already back? Either way, he had stepped out to speak with someone in the hall.

"None of the others have been found?" Zhan questioned the person with him.

Alastor's voice rose above the wind. "No reports have come in yet of anyone else's whereabouts, only the one guard who just arrived. He said Hyosung had been frantic and went off in search of Princess Jun on his own, despite Prince Yuwon's orders to stay together. The remaining men had gone after him when they were attacked, they were scattered in different directions. We can only hope that no harm has come to them and that they've found shelter. This weather has made the search... difficult. If Calgham men have used the storm as cover to attack once, I would assume they will try again. I sent more men out as soon as Yuwon arrived."

Through the blurred shadow being cast on the door, she watched Zhan raise a hand. "Send no further men, the palace needs the protection now more than ever."

The wind whistled through the rafters outside, covering the men's voices. A flash of lightning cast the silhouette of a guard stationed outside of the window—rumbles of thunder soon followed. Servants said the worst had passed, but they couldn't predict how long this storm would go on.

Vinya sat up to check on Yuwon. His breathing was steady, a fresh bandage had been wrapped around his wound, and a towel rested across his forehead. Someone had come in to tend to him while she was asleep. They must have had a difficult time getting to him, as his bed was against a wall and her pallet laid across the floor in front.

She suddenly felt like a nuisance, sleeping in their way.

Her eyelids drooped once again, and listening to the muffled conversation of the men in the hall, Vinya nestled back down on the pallet. She was about to close her eyes when there was movement at the window.

Lightning flashed again to reveal a new silhouette: the outline of two men, one holding a sword high above himself. Blood splattered onto the waxed paper window, the rain quickly washing it away. One of the men sank out of sight.

Her heart beat wildly as the remaining man sheathed his sword. A knife worked its way around the window's latch and popped it open. This person planned to escape the same way he came in, leaving no evidence of how he entered in the first place.

The man moved as fluid and silent as a shadow, slinking through the window and closing it behind him like a whisper. Another flash of lightning through the wall behind her illuminated the room—leaving Vinya in the shadow of the bed. The man slid against the wall opposite of her—his dark clothes gave no hint of his identity. Only his eyes were not covered in cloth, coal had been smeared around them, and they were trained on Yuwon's bed.

Vinya's fingertips touched the cool metal of her hairpin, and she used the next boom of thunder to cover the sound of her movement as she reached to grasp it tight.

While the men's voices continued in the hall, she could barely see the intruder glancing at the door before he took a step towards the bed. Rainwater dripped off his clothes onto the hardwood floor.

Calgham assassin, she should yell. *Come to kill the Crown Prince.*

Zhan and Alastor were just outside the door, yet she could not scream—fear had formed a knot in her throat. So, Vinya did the only thing her body would allow her to do...

She stood.

The assassin paused. He truly hadn't seen her in the shadows of the bed.

Flash. Boom.

He cocked his head ever so slightly to the side and moved away from the door.

An opportunity. An invitation. To not involve her—for her to run.

How fast his work must be since she only needed to get help by crossing the room.

A few steps. A single stab. A slip back out of the window.

A single stab.

Her breath quickened. This man had come to finish what he'd started a couple of days ago.

She took one step, but not towards the door. Vinya stepped forward and positioned herself between the assassin and Yuwon once more. She lifted the hairpin with a trembling hand and aimed it at the man, wielding it as if it were a dagger.

Fleeing was not an option.

There was no more running when it came to this life. Yuwon had protected her when she needed it most, he had left his best friend to guard her while he rode off into war, and now she would return the favor. Perhaps she could fend the man off long enough for Zhan to hear the commotion and come rescue them. Rescue Yuwon.

If the men outside of the door were too late, if she had to give up her own life to save his... So be it.

The assassin slowly dipped his head, accepting the fate she dared to choose.

He reached above his head; the slender sword whined as he pulled it from the scabbard down his back.

But the assassin hadn't latched the window behind himself—a burst of howling wind threw it wide open, amplifying the roar of the torrent outside. Lightning struck a blossom tree in the garden beyond almost simultaneously.

The man used the sudden crashing sounds to his advantage, rushing to move *past* Vinya. Toward the Crown Prince.

She was not his target—he would deal with her on his way out.

Vinya moved as well, her muscles calling upon the memory of Zhan's training. She sidestepped and brought the hairpin down with every ounce of her strength on top of the assassin's shoulder. A cry finally broke free from her throat. Not one of fear, but a battle cry.

The bedroom door burst open and light flooded in from the hallway lanterns, illuminating Yuwon's room.

The assassin yelped in agony as he dropped to one knee at her side.

Zhan shouted as he ran towards them.

Alastor stood in the doorway, mouth agape at the scene before him: at Vinya's hairpin protruding from the man's shoulder.

His sword thudded on her pallet, less than a foot from Yuwon's bed.

The assassin tilted his head to look at Vinya with large, hateful eyes. His gloved hand reached to cover her own, to try to pull the hairpin out.

Guards poured in from the hall.

Blood poured down her hand.

She released the hairpin as the guards shoved the assassin to the ground, his eyes filled with anger and pain.

Shouts and warning bells rang throughout the palace. *Intruder.*

The assassin thrashed against the guards as he tried to break free. His eyes darted in every direction, searching for a way out, and landed on Yuwon.

Vinya stared at her trembling hands—covered in the blood she promised herself she would not spill for this country.

The would-be murderer slipped out of the guards' grasps and lunged for the Crown Prince with wild eyes, grunting as the guards once again fought to bring him down.

Yuwon still slept. Even this turn of events did not tempt him awake.

The assassin did not take his eyes off the sleeping man.

His *eyes*.

Vinya must have whispered it aloud.

Zhan stopped cleaning the blood off her hand and looked at her with furrowed brows. "His, what? Eyes?"

He turned to the assassin.

The intruder stilled, as did the chaos of the room.

Zhan straightened, a muscle ticking in his jaw, seeing exactly what—*who*—was in their presence.

The assassin's thrashing began anew as Zhan approached, and he tried to back out of the guard's reach to no avail.

Zhan knelt to rip the tight hood off of Hyosung's head.

The Shade Prince ceased his fight. He tilted his head back to look at the ceiling and huffed a laugh of defeat, then slowly rolled his neck to stare at Vinya with a serpentine smile.

Her stomach threatened to empty itself.

Zhan stood, tossed the hood to the ground, and returned to her side as running footfalls grew closer in the hall.

Woobin used the frame of the door to come to a stop and took in the room.

Yuwon, peaceful and untouched. Zhan and Vinya by his side.

Woobin stepped into the room, relief washing over his face as he aimed for them, until he came before the kneeling assassin—and stiffened.

Hyosung shifted his gaze from Vinya to his half-brother in one slow blink.

Two steps and Woobin was upon him. The first punch stole the air from everyone's lungs.

Hyosung's smile only grew with the oncoming beating.

Words were unnecessary. Each punch Woobin threw, each crack of skin and bone, spoke for him. Knuckles and lips split open again, and again, and *again*. Tears pooled in Woobin's eyes.

All the while, Hyosung laughed manically on his knees, making no attempt to block the blows with his arms limp at his sides.

Some of the guards let go of Hyosung and shrank away—they surrendered the assassin's punishment to the second born Prince. Even the storm hushed in response.

Spit spewed between clenched teeth from Woobin's irate sobbing. Tears mixed with sweat. Blood flew from the Shade Prince's mouth, his neck snapped from one side to the other with each impact of Woobin's fists.

Only when Woobin's cries turned to a vengeful scream, only when Hyosung's face was nearly unrecognizable, did Zhan try to call him off.

The Prince did not slow. A fire had been lit within him and would not extinguish on its own.

Zhan stepped forward, "That's enough."

Woobin faltered, fist paused midair. His ragged breaths hitched with each sob.

There was a moment of complete silence before Hyosung mocked the sound. His mimicry transformed into a blood coated cackle.

Woobin had not yet gone over the edge. No, *this* was the tipping point.

Instead of bringing his hand down upon the Shade Prince's face, Woobin yanked the hairpin from Hyosung's shoulder, the dragon's head giving him grip, and held it above his own head, shaking in anger and poised to strike.

The Shade Prince dropped his swollen smile and grimaced.

"Do it," he ground out.

Woobin's lip trembled, arm still raised. Tears streamed down his face.

Hyosung breathed heavily, nose flaring.

"*Do it!*" he yelled, his voice guttural.

Woobin's cry broke in response, and he brought his arm down on the would-be assassin.

Zhan leapt. He grabbed Woobin's arm and halted the hairpin mere inches from Hyosung's eye.

All taunting had left Hyosung's face. Unblinking, he glared past the quivering hairpin to his weeping half-brother.

Zhan struggled to keep the pin from moving closer.

"That's what he wants, Your Highness. He doesn't want to face the consequences through law," Zhan grunted.

Woobin's entire body trembled, yet he still pushed against Zhan's grip.

Zhan dropped all formalities, not caring who was in the room to hear his insubordination. "*Woobin.*"

The Prince looked sidelong to his friend.

Zhan's stern face softened. "You cannot let him win this night."

After a breath that seemed to stretch into eternity, Woobin's face crumbled—his shoulders slumped. The hairpin clattered to the floor at their feet.

Zhan ordered Hyosung to be taken to the dungeon for questioning.

Woobin curled into the guard and wept, crinkling the front of Zhan's robes with bloody fists. Zhan patted the Prince's back in an attempt to console him, and gave orders to others in the room to triple the guards stationed around the physicians' hall.

Alastor and a handful of guards stayed in the room while everyone else followed commands, giving a wide berth as Hyosung was dragged out. The Shade Prince looked at the adviser, who tried his best to avoid eye contact. Alastor would be one of the men in the kingdom who held sway over what was to be done with him—Hyosung would no doubt try to get in his good graces.

Woobin calmed enough to release his grip on Zhan, and stumbled over Vinya's pallet before sitting on the edge of Yuwon's bed. He did not seem to care that his blood smeared on Yuwon's hand as he pulled it to his chest and rocked back and forth. His quick half breaths filled the room as the storm finally, *finally*, began to let off.

The stumble caught Alastor's eye. He pointed to the pallet, brows knit together in confusion. "What? Who?"

His eyes flicked from the pallet, to Zhan, to the seat where Zhan's brimmed hat still sat, to Vinya, then back to the pallet. He approached Zhan and spoke through clenched teeth, having put the pieces together.

"What is she doing *sleeping* in the same room as the Crown Prince?" Alastor's face was bloodshot, appalled at the notion of them being left alone. He went on, explaining that had he known she was in there, he would have never called Zhan out to speak. Alastor's rants turned static as the adrenaline wore off. Vinya and Woobin faced each other and exchanged small, exhausted smiles.

Yuwon was safe. They were safe.

Her body grew heavy, and Woobin's eyes widened slightly as his grin fell. There was a muffled call to Zhan. Vinya's head spun into darkness—her knees buckled and she collapsed. Silence and sleep engulfed her once more.

23

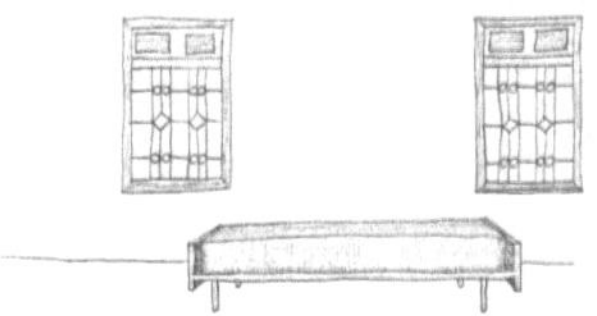

An Unbidden Toll

The canary's morning song broke out with the rising sun, its lilting tune at odds with the turmoil within Vinya's heart. Jinhee must have changed her attire during the night, the soft fabrics of her night clothes hung loose around her body.

Vinya did not move, and didn't want to open her eyes. She couldn't. Vinya hoped that if she stayed in this position, reality wouldn't hit her.

That Yuwon had never left and was never injured. That last night's events never occurred. That Sooni was still alive...

But that wasn't her reality. Her reality was full of shadows and secrets, promises that couldn't be kept, Kings and Queens who fought for crowns and land with malicious intent. What would she give to make things right? How could she make up for the wrongdoings of this country's leaders? Would she even be strong enough to do so?

Her bedroom door opened, and Vinya kept her breathing steady. The smell of breakfast made its way to her bed. Beef stew, fresh bread rolls. It smelled of Norhagan. Jinhee paused in the doorway before setting the tray on the low table, and knelt before Vinya's bed, placing her hands on her own knees.

"The war continues to shift in Byonea's favor, my lady. The Calgham warriors near the Palace have been eradicated. Haryn reinforcements have helped to defend the Byonean border and push Calgham forces back into their own land. They helped us, regardless of..."

Jun. The Princess that had been promised to them who never arrived. A bride in exchange for an army.

Vinya sighed and sat up.

"What of Jun?" she asked. "Has she said anything?"

Jinhee's pause was enough of a response. The lady-in-waiting opened her mouth to give a verbal answer when a bell rang. Its resonation was so low that it shook the walls—each new mournful peal rattled Vinya's soul. The sounds only meant one thing: death.

Vinya scrambled to her feet and was flying through her bedroom within seconds. She bolted past the guards, down the hall, and out into daylight. Her unbound hair whipped in the wind behind her as she sprinted through the Palace, her bare feet crossing over dirt and gravel and stone. No one looked her way, not when the death tolls interrupted their celebrations of small war victories. No one turned his or her attention to the woman in her nightclothes running towards the physician's hall.

To Yuwon.

Vinya nearly slammed into a young physician who was on her way out of the room Yuwon was occupying. The girl dropped the bundle of blankets she had been carrying.

His bed was empty, void of all blankets and pillows. The room was stripped bare of every indication that he'd ever been in it. A bucket with amber-hued water sat near the door, rags draped over the side—bristled brushes were near its base. It smelled of strong chemicals.

"Where is he?" Vinya pleaded.

The physician did not answer. She instead bent over to retrieve the blankets from the floor.

Vinya grabbed the girl by the arms and shook, repeating herself. "*Where is he?*"

The young physician blinked, and her face dropped as she recognized Vinya.

Vinya's heart sank, and sank.

The young girl pointed down the hall, which opened to a lush courtyard. "They took him—"

Vinya was already moving, unwilling to lose a single second. There was no way she would miss him, no way she would lose someone else. The hall seemed to stretch on forever, her feet did not move fast enough. It felt like a dream; the door forever just out of reach. But this was not a dream, and Vinya feared she was chasing after a ghost as she came to the open doorway, skidding to a stop on her bare feet.

Woobin and Zhan stood in the center of the grassy, shrub-lined courtyard—a handful of guards were scattered around the perimeter. Woobin's back was to her; shoulders slumped and bandaged hands at his sides. Zhan's head hung, eyes closed. For once, the watchful guard did not take in their surroundings.

Vinya held her breath as she stepped out onto the grass. She did not want to hear it, but she needed to know what the string of fate dealt her today.

She was halfway to them when Zhan's attention snapped to her as quickly as his hand snapped to the hilt of his sword. His rigid stance slackened, and he looked to the ground at his feet once more. The silence was overwhelming—even more so was the mournful, faraway look in the guard's eyes.

Woobin turned. In doing so, he revealed a chair that had been obscured by his robes.

A chair in which Yuwon sat.

Vinya rounded Woobin and dropped to her knees beside the chair, a small sob escaping her. No blood soaked through his robes, no pain lingered in his expression. Dark circles hung under his eyes, and each blink was strained—like he had to force them to stay open. He was alive. He was alright.

Yuwon wearily smiled down at her. A hint of color washed across his pale cheeks.

"I was so worried," she whispered through trembling lips.

Yuwon lifted his hand to cup her cheek and wiped her tears away with his thumb, but his smile wavered.

She covered his hand with her own. "Jun?"

His thumb stopped, and Yuwon's smile fell completely; his jaw tightened as tears lined his own eyes. He shook his head. The movement was jerky, as if his body wanted to reject what his mind already knew.

"Jun—" Zhan choked up. He coughed to clear his throat and started again. "Hyosung was interrogated into the early hours of the morning. When he broke, he—told us how he knew where to find Jun."

"*Find.*" Woobin gave a cynical laugh; ire coated his words. "You mean where he *knew* Jun was and who she was with the entire time."

Woobin clenched and unclenched his fists. He searched the sky with swollen eyes, looking for answers that weren't there. He blinked against the sun's rays.

"Hyosung planned it all, Vinya. The war, Jun's capture... He was their spy. Calgham's eyes, ears, and hands to tear our family apart from the inside. He couldn't be content in the life that was handed to him... his life of luxury at Jun's side. But he wanted her to himself. He didn't take into account that those Calgham warriors had their own minds, their own plans. He was on his way to meet them, to *save* her and look like a hero... but he was too late. She wasn't there. She had slipped away from the Calgham warriors just hours before, and it drove him insane. We were finally able to contact our Calgham spy this morning, who confirmed Hyosung's actions." Woobin rubbed his face with his hands.

"The bells?" Vinya asked.

A pause.

Yuwon's voice was hoarse. "Our father."

His thumb ran across her cheek one last time before he dropped it onto the arm of the chair. Yuwon's already shallow breaths slowed, his building tears fell as his eyes closed.

Woobin shook his head. "Mother claims her shamans pulled father's energy and gave it to Yuwon—not letting fate decide who lived, but mystics instead."

"Your father has been sick for a long time," Zhan corrected. "You're well aware that his health declined over the past year, no matter how much effort was put in by the physicians. Seeing Yuwon in that state was the final, devastating straw. No shaman has the power to transfer life energy from one person to another. Those old ways of thinking will only cause chaos among the weak minded—it's why it was so widely suppressed all those years ago."

Zhan referenced a history that Vinya did not know, one that she didn't care about. She only looked at the man before her, worn down inside and out—the weight of the country and his family's loss on his shoulders.

But there, in the shadows of his pain, a beautiful future waited quietly.

His mother would no longer be allowed to spin her webs. She couldn't use her selfishness to drive people to starvation or wars. Women in this country were not allowed to rule; the burden of running the country on her husband's behalf no longer rested in her hands, but in Yuwon's.

Yuwon's eyes rose, following Vinya as she stood. Careful. Questioning.

Jinhee appeared in the doorway of the physician's hall with a hand pressed against her ribs. The older lady-in-waiting approached them, but paused to bow deeply to Yuwon.

"Your High—Your Majesty."

Butterflies flitted in Vinya's stomach. The shawl Jinhee wrapped around her shoulders did not relieve the chill crawling up her back, but she did not look away from Yuwon.

Stay.

I will not leave you.

An answer to the question that hovered in the back of Vinya's mind.

An answer to the question that lingered in Yuwon's eyes.

Yuwon's chin quivered. He rested his head against the back of the chair.

Jinhee noted his movements and went back into the physicians' hall.

"When did he wake up?" Vinya asked Zhan.

"Before the sun, only hours after you were taken back to your room."

Vinya pulled the shawl tighter around herself. "Why didn't you wake me?"

Woobin huffed a small laugh through his nose and looped his arm through hers. "Yuwon was barely awake himself for a while. The physicians wanted him to get fresh air while they cleaned the room."

It had been washed clean of any hint of the break in and all traces of blood—Yuwon's from the bed and Hyosung's from the floor.

She imagined the blood that had coated her hand—the hand that stabbed him. There was something she still didn't understand... *Why.*

"Don't worry, I took up your position at his side the rest of the night," Woobin added upon seeing the crease between Vinya's brow. "Zhan personally took you to your room... I don't think I've ever seen him carry something so gently before."

Zhan's eyes slid to Woobin, who snickered and rubbed Vinya's arm; the motion meant to soothe. She didn't know how the man found a way to laugh. Perhaps he was sleep deprived and delirious—perhaps he saw no humor and only laughed out of habit or nerves.

Vinya only knew one thing for certain—that the bandages around his knuckles needed to be replaced. The clenching of his fists had undone and cracked open whatever scabs had formed over the night and morning.

Zhan changed the subject. "Once the news reaches Calgham, they'll launch their next rounds of attack."

A hush fell over them all.

One sick King in the Palace traded for an injured one. One Crown Prince leading the war traded—

Woobin nodded when Vinya turned in his direction. "I'm due to leave at noon. There's no way of knowing if I'll be back in time for the burial ceremony." Woobin cleared his throat. "I believe in our men, and have faith that we will come out victorious."

Zhan shifted on his feet. He subtly fiddled with the tassel on his sword, the red and black strings twirled between his fingers.

Jinhee reappeared. "The room has been cleaned if His Majesty is ready to return."

With a shallow sigh, Yuwon lifted his head in Zhan's direction.

The guard moved to his side, and so did Vinya.

"Let me help you," she said.

Yuwon searched her face. Zhan took half a step back.

Vinya slipped her hand beneath his arm, and Yuwon sucked in air through his teeth—wrapping his free arm around his bandaged torso as he stood. Zhan and Woobin hovered close behind in case she was not physically strong enough to brace him. She hoped she gave him the mental strength he needed.

Yuwon ground his teeth and took a few slow steps.

"I'm sorry about your father," Vinya said.

"He was gone long before last night," Yuwon replied between exhausted breaths.

A few more steps.

"I'm sorry about Jun," she whispered.

Yuwon's face threatened to crumble. He wove their fingers together and relied on her support as they walked to his room in the physicians' hall.

24

In the Wind and Hill

A somber hush fell over the Palace's inhabitants as the sun rose. The only sounds came from the shuffling of hundreds of feet down the roads and the bells attached to the King's casket. Three days had passed since the King's death, and the war had continued, but there were few reports coming in from the front.

As Jinhee dressed Vinya for the funerals—her attire completely white—she explained that the bells were to trap any evil spirits that would try to take over the King's body before he was buried. The ringing would drive the spirits into insanity, torturing them eternally for daring to seize the body of a royal. Once underground, the King would be safe—superstition from the old days that carried into the new ones.

Unable to make the long walk to the burial mound named King's Hill, Yuwon was carried in a small personal palanquin at the front of the procession. Zhan dutifully stayed by his side.

Vinya hadn't seen Yuwon all morning, nor the day before. She'd been told that Yuwon's side no longer bled when he moved, but internally he was still in pain. During that time, she had been kept busy having a new funeral robe fitted by the Queen's orders, who also insisted that her son needed to be alone to recover. It would take weeks for him to completely heal, but Vinya worried for his heart.

The Princess hadn't let the physicians into her room since the night she returned to the Palace with Yuwon—leaving the men scratching their heads as they exited the royal quarters. Her ladies-in-waiting had tended to her wounds—whatever they were—then stood as sentries at Jun's door.

No one dared whisper their conspiracies. No one was allowed to lament the King except for the Queen, and yet, there was silence.

The Queen followed behind the casket, showing no hint of emotion. King Wonho had died, and his wife did not shed a single tear.

A pit formed in Vinya's stomach while she tried to figure out why. Why would the Queen not mourn her husband? What motivation did she have for wanting her son to live, instead of the King? What web would the Queen spin now that he was gone?

Vinya walked in their wake. She tried to keep her focus on the ground before her, fearing that if she were to stare at the back of the Queen's elaborate robes, the woman would feel her gaze.

Following behind Vinya was a mass of people, trailing like the white body of a Byonean dragon through the roads: the sixty Byonean Officials including Alastor, the dozens of Shade Princes and Princesses, distant Byonean royals, the Queen's women, Noblemen and heads of prominent households from across the country, lemans, then the Palace's servants and commoners from surrounding villages.

Grief and tension flowed through them all. The loss of their King, the war ongoing and Woobin leading the front, and Jun secluding herself to her room.

Vinya knocked on her door early in the morning to see if the Princess had changed her mind about attending, but the ladies-in-waiting who opened the door shook their heads. Jun sat on her bed, arms wrapped around her legs, and looked out of the round window to the Palace beyond. The Princess had finally stopped crying, but was now hollow; a shell. Time would not heal the wounds that were forced on her, but time would ease the pain. That is what they would give Jun: time.

Except for the Queen, who demanded that Jun make an appearance. So Jun and her women were rushed to change and join the procession, keeping close to the Queen. Her ladies-in-waiting procured sheer fabric for a veil to cover the entirety of Jun's head. The Princess looked like a ghost, pale and nearly floating as they walked on. Her ladies-in-waiting surrounded her, keeping everyone else at a distance.

Vinya craned her neck around the Queen and walked on tiptoes to catch a glimpse of the palanquin. Zhan tucked his chin against his shoulder as he glanced behind—their eyes connected for the briefest of moments before he turned back to his watch.

Seeing Zhan in white was a stark contrast to his typical black. His and all of the other guards blended into the crowd as a stealth tactic; an outsider would hardly differentiate them from everyone else.

His skin seemed warmer, golden, but at the same time, it made the dark circles beneath his eyes more pronounced. Vinya didn't need to look into Zhan's all-seeing eyes to know that he was worried for his friends, both Yuwon and Woobin—one at his side and one leading a war.

They walked for hours, winding down the roads like a long singular ghost. They were only a whisper through the towns, the bells chiming on the casket along the way. People came out of their homes to bow as they passed.

It was when they passed through the fourth village that Vinya realized no one was shedding tears. They bowed out of respect, but nothing more.

Finally, when Vinya's feet blistered and ached from the new shoes the Queen had commanded her to wear, the King's Hill came into view.

A few men were at the top with crude shovels, a few more lingered at the bottom near a pile of rocks. They all backed away at the sight of the arriving group.

The sun was steadily rising in the sky when the procession stopped at the base of the hill, and the people spread out like a fan. Only the royals were allowed at the base. The sixty Byonean Officials surrounded them, and everyone else was held back to watch at a distance.

No eulogies would be uttered, no highlighting King Wonho's virtues or failures would be spoken at this sacred ground; there were only three things that happened at the burial of a king.

First, King Wonho's casket was carried up the steep hill and lowered into the freshly dug grave beside his ancestors. The men carrying the casket struggled through the climb, some losing their footing on grass that hadn't yet dried from the morning dew. The bell's songs grew dim until the casket hit the bottom. A short sigh came from the Queen in front of Vinya, the sound neither of irritation nor resolve.

Zhan shifted on his feet as Yuwon's palanquin was lowered, and when he stood in front of it, the sixty Officials moved, commencing the second step.

The Officials formed a line to pick up a stone from the nearby pile, returned to place it in Yuwon's arms—then one proceeded up the hill to take a shovel and drop a few scoops of earth onto the casket below until the grave was filled. Sixty men. Sixty stones.

For the third and final step, Yuwon began his climb. This was his weight to carry—his burden to bear alone. He struggled to keep solid footing while keeping the sixty stones balanced in his arms. The dew and his injury did not make the climb easy, and Vinya held her breath when Yuwon fell to one knee halfway up. If he dropped a stone, if he fell to both knees completely, it would be seen as ill fortune for the country's future during his reign.

The Queen still showed no concern. Jun stood beside her—hands wringing around themselves. Her veil fluttered against her face in a passing breeze.

But Yuwon did not allow a single stone to fall and pulled himself up on both feet, cresting the hill after a few more slips of his feet.

Only when he made it to the graveside was he allowed to drop to his knees—to bow before his father one last time—and build a cairn on top of the soil. The cairn would remain untouched by any other human; only the elements would shape the stones after Yuwon placed the last one at the peak.

Yuwon left his hand on the last stone long enough for the Queen to click her tongue.

Then Yuwon stood, holding his side, and descended the hill. He did not look at anyone as he climbed back into the palanquin.

The noblemen and everyone below them in rank dispersed, turning down the road to go back to their own homes—but the Queen kept Daeya and a handful of her other women with her. The royals, Sixty Officials, and guards still had one last task. The palanquin was lifted once more and the smaller group pressed on. Jun stayed far from the guards during the walk and stepped away if a man came too close—her ladies-in-waiting would shoo him away.

They went past King's Hill, beyond a second hill—large and rolling that was reserved for other royal family members, and aimed for a cliff on the far side. Another funeral, more intimate than the last.

The tree-lined cliff dropped to a gurgling stream, and Vinya chose to stand on the opposite side of the palanquin than the Queen—closer to the Officials and Zhan. She didn't care if anyone thought it odd, she wasn't going to risk an *accident* by the Queen or Daeya, whose eyes pierced Vinya's side.

Zhan placed a hand on her elbow, guiding Vinya closer to the cliff. Not to the edge, but just enough for the palanquin to fully block Daeya's view of her.

Again, Yuwon stood, albeit slower than the last time, and turned to the Queen's women. The women approached him and bowed, their gold circlet necklaces glinting in the sunlight. One carried a box, the second took off the lid, and the third retrieved an urn.

Yuwon's labored breaths were only noticeable by his expanding and contracting shoulders. He took the urn in both hands and ran his thumb across the portrayal of the Byonean dragon. His father's heart cradled in his hands. One last deep breath, and Yuwon drew near the cliff's edge.

The porcelain urn's lid and jar clinked against one another as he opened it. Yuwon did not speak, but from Vinya's angle she could see his mouth moving, his eyes closed. A whisper, a farewell, a secret that was his to keep. He turned over the jar, and ashes—the heart of the King—plunged down the cliffside to the water below. A gust of wind carried the ashes further down the stream. It reminded Vinya of how Jun's kindness spread like the rays of the sun—rays that now dissipated by whatever had occurred during her capture.

One of the Queen's women took the empty urn from Yuwon, and everyone dispersed. Whispers of Yuwon's official coronation arose from the Officials; their task for the day was done. They had already moved on to organizing their next task under their breaths.

The Queen did not look back to the cliff or her son as she, Jun, and their women retraced their steps. Daeya managed to shoot Vinya a grin before following behind the Queen, a handful of guards leaving with them.

Yuwon had not moved from the cliff's edge, his face tilted towards the sun. Most of the guards and the men who carried the palanquin were the only other ones who waited for him.

Vinya closed the distance and stood beside him—Zhan a few paces away. Even if Yuwon desired silence, she needed him to know that he was not alone, and he would never be.

The stream below them ever-trickling, the wind rustled leaves in the canopy above. A bird called out in the distance. It was strange to think that, during this time of war, there was a place of such peace; a haven tucked away from the arrows that flew across battlefields with hate.

Vinya jolted when Yuwon broke the silence. His voice was barely louder than a whisper, so no one further than Zhan could hear.

"I was going to let you go."

She looked up at him, his face still tilted toward the sun, eyes closed.

Yuwon continued. "On the way to the Spring Festival, when the Calgham warriors attacked and you ran... I was going to let you go." He met Vinya's eyes, a mixture of sorrow and clarity in his own.

"Why force someone to do something they didn't want to do? Why take someone's life away from them? I watched you run," Yuwon dropped his voice to a whisper, "and wished *I* could run as well."

Vinya placed a comforting hand on his arm as tears slipped down his cheeks.

"Then the warrior followed you, and I—I couldn't let someone else take your life, either. So, I did run. I watched you choose that woman's life over your own, shoving her into the building to save her from the warrior, and a selfish part of me was relieved when Zhan caught up. Because, if neither of us could run, I wanted to help you instead—I hoped to give you comforts in Byonea."

Yuwon took Vinya's hand off his arm and held it in his own. "Jun wanted to see Byonea brought back to its glory, how it was when we were children. A place of hopes and dreams, a place people want to be a part of."

Vinya's heart stung. *She* hadn't wanted to be a part of it when she first arrived. She wanted nothing but to get out, to go back to Norhagan.

Yuwon's chin quivered. "I promised Jun I would, even if I cannot say it to her face... I don't know that I can do it on my own."

Vinya wiped his cheek with her free hand and nodded.

"Together," she promised.

The wind carried her words down the stream, in the wake of the previous king's ashes.

25

Scales in the Woods

The walk back to the Palace under the spring sun was grueling.

Surrounded by guards, Zhan and Vinya flanked the palanquin that carried Yuwon. They were the last to return through the main entrance, the last to walk under the maws of the massive Byonean dragon statues who guarded the gate.

Three dragons had kept her from escaping the walls. Three dragons now kept her safe within—though Vinya only had faith in one. She glanced to her left, and through the palanquin's intricate woodwork, Zhan stared back at her. It was more than a job. More than obedience. A whisper in Vinya's mind told her that he guarded her out of something stronger than his friendship with Yuwon.

Zhan dipped his head in a nod, seeing what was unsaid. He would be there for them—both of them—just as she would be there for Yuwon until the end, whatever and whenever the end may be.

Yuwon rested his head on the back of the palanquin, rolling slightly from side to side with each step of the men that carried him. His eyes were closed, but he remained awake. Exhausted. His hand moved to his side—to the bandages that were covered by his white robes.

Zhan noted the movement as well and directed the men to carry Yuwon to the physician's hall. Jinhee met them there, and when Yuwon was settled and guards took up position in and around the room, Zhan escorted them to the women's quarters.

Few nobles roamed through the Palace paths, grief and uncertainty hung heavily over them all. No one graced the open hall or wandered in the gardens; the handful of people who walked by did not smile as they passed. They secluded themselves to their own houses or rooms, quiet in the wake of the funeral, unwilling to show face while looking forlorn.

Palace life was a heavy hand where facades gloved the filth. You must smile. You must dress in your best attire. You must follow the rules. You must flap about like an exquisite bird—impressing the one who ruled over them all as to not find yourself shoved into a cage. This day of all days, the inhabitants of the Palace utilized the mourning period in order to rest. Vinya couldn't blame them.

She was ready to get to her own room, her own small sanctuary. But when they climbed the stairs and entered the women's quarters, the air shifted. Tense.

Guards stood at the entrance of the women's quarters, uneasy. Two ladies-in-waiting stood outside of Vinya's door.

Zhan's brow drew into a hard line. He moved to step around Vinya and Jinhee, but the ladies at her door shifted. One held out a hand as they neared—a sign to stop. Zhan halted as his hand touched Vinya's door, raising a brow at the nearest lady-in-waiting.

A silent conversation. A slight shake of her head.

Zhan pulled the door open. After a quick look inside, he stepped back to take up position outside of her door. He turned and motioned for Vinya to go in.

His silence made sense as soon as Vinya and Jinhee rounded the doorway.

Princess Jun stood in Vinya's room—her hand rested on the canary's cage. An array of foods had been brought in; steam swirled from multiple bowls strewn across a low table. Jun's ladies-in-waiting closed the bedroom door as Vinya and Jinhee stepped inside.

"It doesn't deserve to be in a cage," the Princess muttered as she traced a delicate finger down the bar to the latch of the cage's door.

Vinya crossed the room—slowly, as if she would scare away the Princess like a wild, skittish animal—and came to Jun's side.

"I don't know how long the bird has been in a cage... its entire life, or only recently," Vinya said. "I'm unsure if it could survive on its own."

Jun's hand lifted off the cage, her fingers curling into themselves. "No. I do not think it would."

The Princess turned and moved on silent feet to the low table. Free of her veil, Jun's hair fell loosely past her elbows, the ends catching on invisible waves of air as she sat.

Jinhee eyed the Princess as she poured the women tea, catching Vinya's eye with a deep crease between her brows. Jun hadn't spoken to anyone other than her ladies, hadn't walked the halls or hosted a meal since her return. Yet here she was—but she wasn't *present*. The Princess looked like a spirit, eerie and lost.

For the third time since coming to Byonea, Vinya joined Jun at the table. The first, Jun had been helpful. The second, she had been hopeful. This time, the Princess seemed haunted. Her gaze passed through the table, far beneath the floor. Her shoulders slumped and her face was slack—a far cry from the poised statue in the garden's pavilion.

When Jinhee stood, the canary spooked—chirping and fluttering around the cage. Jun's eyes widened, her shoulders curved inward and she hugged herself—her delicate fingers digging into her arms through the white robe.

The older lady-in-waiting pulled a dark shawl from the clothes cabinet and covered the cage, effectively hushing the bird. But the Princess pulled her knees to her chest and began to rock back and forth.

"Jinhee, please give us a moment," Vinya said without looking away from Jun.

The lady-in-waiting exited the room and stood at its entrance with Jun's ladies-in-waiting.

"What happened?" Vinya asked. She reached across the table, hovering just beyond reach of the Princess. "Jun..."

The Princess gasped and jerked her hand away.

"Green. So green," the Princess whispered. Her eyes flicked between Vinya's own.

The color of her eyes had never felt like a curse until that moment. Vinya's chest squeezed, and she dropped her eyes to the table between them—pulling her hand back towards herself.

"I—I'm sorry. I didn't mean..." They were the first clear words Jun spoke. The Princess rubbed her own arms. "You did not choose that color. You aren't like those men who bore the green Calgham armor. You would never... never..."

The Princess squeezed her eyes closed and shook her head—as if trying to keep her memories from resurfacing.

Vinya spoke through clenched teeth, "*What did they do to you?*"

She tried to keep her voice even as her heart pounded. Something deep within her crawled to the surface—it slid through Vinya's veins and threatened to burn her from the inside out.

Jun wrung her hands together in her lap. Her eyes skittered around the table as if searching for the answers.

"It happened quickly," Jun started. "The journey had been an easy ride, especially with S—S—"

Vinya's eyes shifted to the empty spot on the display cabinet—where Sooni's urn should have been. Jinhee had tossed the crushed flower crown the night Sooni's urn went missing. Somehow, the space where the two items had sat took up more space than the rest of the items on the cabinet.

The Princess frantically wiped a tear from her high cheekbones and shook her head. "We had stopped near a stream to water the horses when we were approached by a group of men. There were so many of them—at least three Calgham warriors for every Byonean guard. Unremarkable, but there was a distinct coldness around them that caused our men to draw their swords. The attack was sudden and brutal—there was no time to run for cover. We were stuck in the carriage, utterly helpless as our guards fell."

"Our men fought for what seemed like an eternity. They tried their best to defend us, but there was no point. There were so many..." she repeated. Jun lifted her head, her breath shaking as she inhaled. "When the carriage door opened, Sooni shoved the Queen's woman towards them. The woman was snatched out by the warriors, screaming like a fox caught in a trap. And Sooni..."

Vinya buried her face in her hands. Her shoulders heaved with the oncoming sobs, unable to contain the torrent of emotions within her.

"She was fierce, Vinya. I've never witnessed someone fight so mightily to break free. She *clawed* at the ground—at the men's arms and eyes. They found not a girl in their grasp—but a tiger. The men put a cloth over my eyes, but I could still hear her battle with them until... until..."

Vinya doubled over herself, a moan slipped out of her unintentionally. She raised her hand and waved it in front of Jun.

"Yes," the Princess whispered, "let's not go over that part."

Jun stayed quiet as Vinya caught her breath. Only when Vinya composed herself did Jun continue.

"The men took turns carrying me through the woods—the blindfold and their backtracking succeeded in disorienting me. Every night, they set up camp in a dense part of the woods—far from any village. I'd always heard rumors of how Calgham men treat women, especially those that were unmarried, but I never knew..." The Princess paused, her eyes distant in memory. "No one could hear me when I screamed. No one came for me."

"I lost track of the days—of how many times they entered my tent. My eyes were kept covered, my hands tied behind my back. I often found myself far away from my body...floating in the trees among the birds—listening to them sing." Jun met Vinya's gaze. "I hate hearing my mother's birds."

As if in answer, the canary chirped and flew within the darkened cage. Jun jolted, her hands clenching and unclenching until the bird stopped. She let out a ragged breath before continuing.

"The only time I was allowed outside to relieve myself was during the day, and the cracks in my blindfold only showed the green of their Calgham leathers and the shrubbery, the brown of their scaled armor and the dirt. I wasn't allowed to clean myself if I couldn't hold anything in through the night."

The Princess ran a fingernail along her other nails, scraping at nonexistent grit in the grooves. "One day, a new voice sounded from outside of my tent. I was so tired, and struggled to move out of the new man's reach. My captors laughed when he touched me, but it was only to remove the fabric from my eyes. He shooed away the rodents that were eating the half-rotten meal left for me, dismissed the warriors that had followed him into the tent, and pulled a meager meal from his own pack. Bread and cheese. He told me his name as he cut the cheese with a small knife and fed it to me... Won, or Ren, or *Wen*. I didn't trust his niceties, but I wouldn't turn away his offering. I felt much like the children in Nyrrem, savoring the bread..."

Jun paused, and the two women looked to the grand meal before them that they hadn't touched—just as they hadn't touched the food during their first meeting in the gazebo. Back when spring had yet to come, when the wind brought promises of fresh growth and new life, and hope seemed like a tangible thing that you could reach out and grasp...

The Princess went on, words spilling out of her now that she'd chosen to open her mouth. "When the other warriors came in the tent to tell him off for feeding me, he sent them out—held some sort of authority over them that they begrudgingly followed. He sighed at their grumbles and told me he'd be back in a few hours with more food and a basin to wash in. He followed the other men out, but before my blindfold was replaced, he didn't notice that he'd dropped his knife."

Vinya met Jun's eyes across the table, and the Princess nodded. "I was able to grasp it with my toes. I sat on it for a long time and planned to cut the rope around my wrists once night fell. I waited for Wen to come back when he realized what he'd lost, but, he didn't return for hours—he and the men grew louder outside, their grand tales and grander laughter stretched on until their voices slurred."

"I thought he'd forgotten me, that he was off drinking with the other men, but footsteps came back in a rush. My heart sank. He pulled the blindfold off and asked me where the knife was, but didn't believe my lies—told me I needed to get better at it or to just stay silent. He said he couldn't believe that the men held me so close to a Byonean village, then he left." Jun ran thumb along her unbound wrists.

"After some time I was able to work the knife to my hands, twisting and cutting the rope that tied my wrists behind me. When I stepped out of the tent, he sat in the midst of the men and dipped his head to the woods—West. The men who were scattered around the camp were drunk, lying about as if it were the middle of the night."

Jun stared into the distant wall, mulling over unasked questions about the Calgham man—the apparent Byonean sympathizer.

"I kept thinking it was some cruel trick, that he would come and take me back, but he never did. I neared the village after an hour of walking in the rain, and realized it was near the Palace's tunnel exit. Or, for me, its entrance. A skirmish broke out in the nearby woods, so I hid in a bush while the men battled. The rain was cold. The thorns that crept into my skin were softer than the warrior's hands in the camp... but the men's cries of anger and pain were even more agonizing. I only moved when it had been quiet for a while... and there, leaning against a tree, was Yuwon."

"I thought my mind was playing tricks on me, that I was seeing a hallucination fueled by exhaustion or hunger. His head kept turning from east to west, back and forth—like an invisible string pulled at him from both directions. The relief on his face was fleeting when I came to him. The blood pouring from his side was too great, but I bandaged it the best I could before we set out for the village. It had been abandoned due to the nearby Calgham forces. I searched for some food—there was none left behind. We found the entrance to the tunnel and came home."

The pair had walked half a day in darkness, starved and battered.

Vinya ran a hand across her face. "After days of not speaking to anyone, why are you saying this now? Why tell *me*?"

"Because someone needs to know... someone who can make a difference."

"A difference that you can't make yourself?"

Jun shook her head, curling in on herself once more as the canary fluttered in the darkened cage behind her.

Vinya exhaled through her nose and stood. "I will be right back."

She left the Princess at the low table and stepped into the hall, closing the door behind her. Zhan raised a brow as Vinya placed a hand on his elbow, motioning for him to follow her down the hall. Even though they were out of earshot of her room, Vinya still dropped her voice to a whisper.

"Are there any female guards in the Palace?"

Zhan's remaining brow joined the first.

"No," he responded—his tone equally quiet.

"Outside of the Palace?"

Zhan sighed, shifting on his feet as he shook his head.

Vinya huffed an incredulous laugh and dropped her head. Of course. The Queen hadn't allowed women to fight or guard—the only female with any sort of power would be herself.

Vinya nodded towards Jun's ladies-in-waiting. "Train them."

Zhan blinked. Then blinked a second time. His eyes briefly shifted to the women who stood at the entrance of Vinya's room.

She stepped closer to the guard, gaining his full attention. "Train them as you trained me. Jun needs to be protected in more ways than one, and I believe it's in her best interests that those closest to her can be *fully* relied upon."

Zhan rubbed at his neck. "I'm unsure if Jun's mother would approve."

"Her wants and desires are no longer to be trusted," Vinya scoffed. "Speak with your men and set up a schedule. Perhaps training could be early in the morning or late at night—whenever the Princess doesn't require their assistance."

"And force them to stay awake longer than normal? What happens if they slack on their other duties?"

"It's for *Jun*. I'm sure they'll understand and will not fall behind, for the sake of their princess," Vinya said.

She looked at the ladies-in-waiting who guarded her bedroom door. Their jaws were set—their spines straight. A bold determination shone in their eyes, and they dipped their heads in a bow to Vinya.

"Train them to protect her, Zhan."

His eyes slid to her, something that bordered on pride flashed across his face. "Alright, I'll speak with them about setting up a schedule."

Vinya squeezed his arm and thanked him with a smile before returning to her room. Jun had not moved; she was still curled around herself as Vinya's canary fluttered in the shadows of the fabric.

"Perhaps the cage keeps the bird safe," Jun muttered.

"It doesn't deserve to be left in the dark, though," Vinya said as she crossed the room. She ripped the fabric off of the cage, standing nearby until the bird calmed. "Jun... there's something you need to know about Hyosung."

26

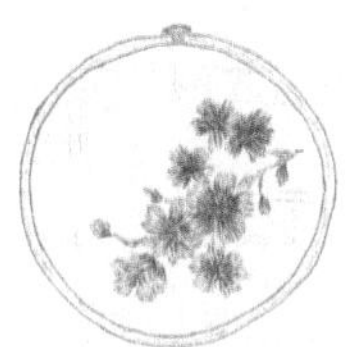

The Night and the Stream

Four days passed since the funeral of the King.

Yuwon had requested to be moved back to his own room in the royal quarters, and the Queen raged upon hearing it. She allowed her best physicians to move into the empty room between her own and Woobin's so they could keep a closer eye on Yuwon... Something she had not done for the late king.

By Alastor's orders, Vinya hadn't been allowed to visit Yuwon without an escort, but every time she and Jinhee went to Yuwon's room, he wasn't there. Yuwon refused to stay still. Vinya would find him leaning on Zhan to walk the Palace grounds—their conversations hushed. He went mainly to the library or scholar's building near the open hall, but sometimes she could not find him at all; he would hole himself away somewhere even she couldn't find.

But Vinya enjoyed the walks in the crisp spring air—she used them as an excuse to lure Jun out of her room, and little by little, the Princess calmed and pieced herself back together. Vinya and Jinhee kept Jun far from those living in the Palace. Not because they weren't to be trusted, but because the Princess panicked when large groups of people—men in particular—were present.

Jun's women were sent to train with select guards during those times so as to not disrupt their work for the Princess. The Queen's women caught wind of the training—but by the time the Queen showed up to put an end to it, the number of women being trained as Jun's personal guard had doubled. Jun's ladies-turned-guards giggled when they recounted how the Queen turned red upon seeing Yuwon standing to block her path—how the Queen nearly shook in anger when he said the women would continue being allowed to train.

The scent of florals and freshly cut wood was carried in the breeze around the Palace—the noblemen and women practically fluttered in a mixture of excitement over the upcoming wedding and nervousness over the war.

With the funeral over, preparations for their wedding and Yuwon's coronation were underway. Craftsmen and officials scurried around the Palace from daybreak to nightfall. The wedding of a prince was one thing... The wedding of a king was another.

The banners that had been put up weeks ago for their wedding had been destroyed in the storm the night Yuwon made it back to the Palace, and they'd been thrown away before the funeral. Replacements were in the process of being brought in.

No expense was spared by the Queen. Alastor would not listen and waved Vinya away when she brought up her concerns and suggestions to redirect some of that money to the villages that were recovering or still under the control of Calgham forces.

Vinya focused on working through the frustration by finishing her embroidery. She and Jun sat in Vinya's room late on the fourth day, admiring the work when it was complete. Vinya ran her fingers over the threads that had been so much work, the rendition of the cherry blossom petals were near perfect with Jinhee's tips and tricks.

"He'll like it," Jun murmured.

Vinya snapped her head to the Princess. "What?"

"Oh, I thought you made it for Yuwon."

Jinhee smoothed out the creases in her skirt with a smirk on her face and began cleaning the craft supplies, eyeing Vinya and the Princess. Jun knew that had not been the plan. She also knew that Vinya hadn't had a single decent conversation with Yuwon since the funeral.

Vinya huffed a laugh through her nose and stood. "Alright, let's go give it to him on the way back to your room."

The night air was as crisp as the gravel that crunched under their feet as they walked to the royal quarters, their ladies and a single guard in tow. The lantern light bobbed with each step that Jinhee took—casting the stone walls of the

Palace in a honeyed glow. But Vinya didn't like the way it enhanced the snarls on the Byonean dragon statues at the steps of the royal quarters.

The front door to the royal quarters swung open, and out stepped a woman in orchid-colored robes; the lantern-light danced in the golden circlet around her neck. Daeya's smile sent chills down her spine. The Queen's woman pulled a fan from a pocket in her robe and began to cool her reddened cheeks.

"Vinya. Princess." Daeya sneered in greeting as their group passed by.

None of them acknowledged the concubine. They kept their gazes ahead as Daeya scoffed; she turned on her heel and slithered into the darkness of the Palace grounds. Vinya wondered if Daeya could see in the dark, since the woman did not carry a lantern of her own.

The royal guards allowed them entry, and it wasn't long before they were standing at Yuwon's door. Vinya gave it a few soft knocks.

Heavy footsteps neared the door, and Vinya took a step back as it slid open; she could have sworn Zhan breathed smoke out his nose in fury. But the guard blinked, his anger gone in a flash.

Daeya must have come from Yuwon's room, not the Queen's. From Zhan's reaction, it had not been a welcomed visit, either.

"Vinya," Zhan said as he glanced behind himself. "Did you just arrive?"

"Yes," she replied, turning the embroidery over and over in her hands.

Yuwon strained to look around the guard from his chair at the desk across the room—his hair was a mess, ruffled as if he'd been running frustrated fingers through it. He rolled the scroll that had been spread in front of him. Nothing in his room had been changed while he was gone, but now that he was back, it seemed whole. Peaceful. Yuwon's presence seemed to soak up the room as he stood, holding his side as he slowly crossed the room.

Vinya's stomach twisted. Yuwon would be in pain for a while; his moving about did not help at all. Zhan stepped aside, and Yuwon took up position in the doorway.

It reminded Vinya of the room mix-up weeks ago—chest to face with a book between them, a single lock of hair falling across his brow, Jun waiting for her in the next room and King Wonho coughing in his room on the other side... the room on the end that was now vacant.

Vinya dropped her head to the embroidery in her hands, her stomach flipped into something different. Something that bordered regret. Yuwon had much on his mind, much on his figurative plate. It was such a simple and silly thing to bring him this hoop.

Yuwon removed his hand from his side and reached for the embroidery hoop, his fingers grazing hers as he took it.

"You've been working on this for a while," he muttered.

Vinya nodded, keeping her head down. She shouldn't have come. Shouldn't have allowed Daeya's venomous smile to eat at her. Shouldn't have interrupted his work, forcing him to get up from his chair. Shouldn't have thought he may want something as simple as stitch-work when he had a world of treasures at his fingertips.

"My lady wanted to give it to you," Jinhee said from her side.

Vinya lifted her head to tell him he didn't have to take it, but Yuwon was beaming. He passed the embroidery to Zhan with a secretive smile that only the guard understood.

"I know exactly where I'm going to put it. Thank you," Yuwon said. He ran his fingers through his hair to smooth it out. "I'm afraid I have some work to do. Paperwork, planning..."

The coronation. The wedding.

"I'll leave you to it," Vinya said with a dip of her chin, fidgeting with the sleeve of her robe.

Yuwon's eyes dropped to the movement, and scooped one of her hands in his. She had never noticed just how small her hands were compared to his.

"Goodnight, Vinya."

Jinhee, Jun, and Zhan turned away to give them some semblance of privacy.

"Goodnight, Yuwon," she whispered in return.

He lifted her hand and brushed a tender kiss on her knuckles. Whatever Yuwon saw in her eyes had him smiling against her fingers. She stepped back, and he closed the door with the same grin on his face.

Jun and her ladies retired into her room. The ladies-in-waiting clicked their tongues at the distant chirping of birds in the Queen's room, and quickly closed the door behind them in an attempt to block the sound.

Vinya was thankful for the dim lantern light on the walk back to the women's quarters—positive that if anyone were to look at her too closely, they would mock her for the crimson shade of her cheeks.

Determination filled Vinya as she and Jinhee made their way through the small garden near the scholar's building the next morning. The willow tree's branches shifted in the breeze that carried the sweetest scents throughout the area.

Vinya clipped a flower at the stream's edge and passed it to Jinhee, who bundled it into the growing bouquet in her arms.

She had received permission to clip flowers from any garden on Palace grounds for Gran's vase in her room, and she wanted flowers from the garden where she first met Jun.

Vinya stood and turned towards the small gazebo above the stream. The gauzy fabrics hanging from its sides danced along with the willow's branches. Jun sat at the low table, crafting a floral crown with one of the young Shade Princesses—Jun's women surrounding them both.

Something eased deep within Vinya. The Princess was being taken care of, she would never feel alone again. The young Shade Princess sitting with Jun lifted her own flower crown, and burst into laughter when it fell apart. The sound rang like bells through the garden, causing Jun to smile—and Vinya to freeze. The young girl's laugh sounded like Sooni's.

Jinhee placed a hand on her arm.

"I wish she were here too," she whispered.

Vinya closed her eyes and took deep breaths. She could do this. With Jinhee's support, she could do this.

A scoff sounded from the other side of the stream.

"If only we all had the spare time to stand around and pick flowers," Daeya called out. "Some of us have jobs to do."

She opened her eyes as Daeya crossed one of the small bridges, the concubine's companion in tow. Vinya scanned their surroundings. No scholars were at the windows or balconies, no nobles graced the open hall to her left. Only a handful of guards were scattered about, and their ears were deaf to Daeya's jabbering.

"Oh dear," Jinhee muttered under her breath, seeing that they were alone as well.

"I just came back from speaking with Her Majesty," Daeya said, waving a lazy hand in the air. "Alastor left early this morning, working through trade deals with countries in the West or something like that, so the Queen herself approved of some... changes that are in order."

Daeya came face to face with them, a smirk plastered on her face.

Vinya took a deep breath. If Zhan's attitude when opening the door last night was any indication, Vinya knew what was going to come out of Daeya's mouth next.

"I'm going to see about becoming the new King's leman. How would you like that?" Daeya scraped a well-manicured finger down Vinya's cheek. "We would practically be related."

Vinya swatted her hand away. "Yuwon wants nothing to do with you, Daeya. Even if the Queen has approved, he will refuse you."

Daeya rolled her eyes and tipped her head to the side. She brushed her thumb along her bottom lip, pure venom spilling from her eyes. "You seem so sure, but that's not what he said last night. You yourself saw how late I left the royal quarters last night."

Lies. Vinya shook her head. Nothing but lies came from this snake.

"You left, and they were glad of it, both he and Zhan."

It was Daeya's turn to shake her head. "You'll say anything to keep me from his bed."

"I will *do* anything to keep you from it, and I would dare to say that he himself told you that you are unwanted." Vinya's anger burned hot, rising to her face. Daeya would stop at nothing until she sank her fangs into whatever—*whoever*—she desired.

"Oh it's just a game that men play... They toy with you as a way to pull you in closer. You would know that if you'd ever been with one. The Queen has approved of the arrangement—and you will not get in my way." The concubine came in close enough that Vinya could feel her breath.

"He will be mine," Daeya whispered. "Are you even worthy enough to share his bed? Where is this *army* that was promised through the Treaty of Trust with your betrothal?"

"Worthy or not, a relationship that has to be begged for isn't a relationship at all."

Daeya straightened. The concubine's eyes dropped to the bouquet in Jin-hee's arms.

"Hm. I need to gather my own flowers. I recently came into possession of a new vase. Small, plain. A bit *dusty* on the inside, but I cleaned it out." The concubine feigned a gasp, waving her hand to the side. "In this very stream, right here!"

Vinya froze. Daeya hadn't been in the Queen's room the day Sooni's urn went missing.

"You will turn around and go back the way you came," Vinya fumed. She tried to force as much confidence and authority in her words, but her voice audibly shook.

Daeya huffed a defiant laugh and began to turn, to leave in the direction of the royal quarters. Before she could take a step, Vinya's hand shot out and wrapped around Daeya's jaw, wrenching the concubine's face back to her own.

Daeya tried frantically to pull away, but Vinya had had the advantage of surprise, and her grip was unrelenting.

Vinya would not allow the woman's antics to waste one more moment of her time. Heart pounding, she decided to jog Daeya's memory of the night they met—when their roles were reversed, and Daeya had been the one grasping at power.

Vinya lowered her voice and spoke through gritted teeth. "Other way, you impudent fool."

Daeya stopped her thrashing, her eyes went wide as she remembered those words. The words *she* had spoken during Vinya's first night in the Palace. She studied Vinya's face—the recognition Daeya had feigned to Hyosung that night was now real.

One hand still locked around the concubine's jaw, Vinya grabbed the front of Daeya's lilac robe with the other hand and shoved.

Daeya's limbs splayed as she went down, wailing as her body hit the stones that lined the bottom of the stream. Her cry and the splash echoed off the walls of the surrounding buildings. Daeya called out to her companion. The woman hesitated before stepping down the slippery stones to help Daeya up, but the woman's footing did not hold, and she slipped in as well. Daeya's dress was soaked, and now she'd need to change clothes in the concubine's building. Her hair had come undone and was waterlogged, pressed flat against her body like scales.

Vinya stood on the stream's edge and watched her writhe in the water. Jun and her women watched on with wide eyes from the gazebo. Jinhee's mouth hung open in shock, awe, and a hint of amusement. It must have been the largest tantrum Daeya had thrown, yet none of the guards moved from their positions to help her.

Daeya and her companion sloshed their way out of the stream and aimed for the concubine's building, spitting curses at Vinya the entire time. The trail of water in their wake looked an awful lot like the slime slugs leave behind.

Jinhee grinned behind her hand. "She will have large and unsightly bruises on her rear, and may have to sleep on her stomach for a few weeks."

The older woman tried to disguise her small laugh as a cough, but stopped short when her eyes landed on something across the garden.

Vinya followed her gaze to a bridge further down the stream, where a shocked Yuwon and Zhan stood—brows raised and wide eyed, having witnessed what occurred.

The women stilled. The men hadn't been there when Daeya arrived, and Vinya felt a bundle of nerves grow in her stomach.

The men approached, and Vinya struggled to find the right words to explain. She opened her mouth, then closed it. Open, closed again—like a fish held in air.

Zhan broke the silence by clearing his throat. "She deserved it."

Yuwon's neck snapped in surprise to his friend, who shrugged. The men continued to walk past them, and Yuwon clasped his hands behind his back.

"Deserved what?" he said, meeting Vinya's confused stare with a gleam in his eye. "I saw nothing."

Yuwon's cheekbones rose with his grin, and Zhan cleared his throat a second time to cover his chuckle.

She and Jinhee watched the men as they made their way toward the royal quarters. Vinya looked at the bouquet in Jinhee's arms and straightened.

"Let's go. We have an urn to recover."

27

A Rose-colored Heart

It had been one month since Vinya set foot in Byonea.

Even though the wind blew against the walls of her room and storm clouds threatened the distant horizon, the sun felt hopeful. Warmer. Her canary whistled its morning song on the display cabinet—next to Sooni's urn.

Daeya had shrieked when the women walked through the concubine's building, but put up no fight when she saw the fire burning in Vinya's eyes. The urn was recovered, and though Sooni's ashes had been washed down the stream, it was all Vinya had left of the young girl.

Jinhee brought in breakfast, and Vinya had finished and changed out her night clothes when a knock sounded on her door.

She was face to face with Zhan, whose dimples pressed in lightly with his small smile. He extended an exquisite bouquet of flowers to her.

"A very happy birthday to our Vinya," he said.

Vinya grinned. "Thank you, Zhan, and good morning."

She reached for the bouquet, but Zhan passed it to Jinhee.

"Please put these in a vase for us, Jinhee," he said. Zhan turned on his heel and held out an arm for Vinya to take. "We have somewhere to be."

The dimples appeared again.

Vinya linked her arm in his as they strode down the hall and into the morning air. "What is going on, Zhan? Where are we going?"

Zhan took his other hand off the hilt of his sword to shake it side to side in front of him. "Don't worry about it. You'll see soon."

They wound their way down the Palace roads, passing through gate after gate, and past workers tying down their wares and carts ahead of the oncoming storm. *It won't be bad like the last one*, an elderly woman said as they moved across her path. Vinya had an inkling to believe her.

When they stepped into the gardens, Vinya knew where they were going, though she kept it to herself. Zhan seemed to like the idea of keeping a surprise, so she kept her mouth shut.

The moment the lake and pavilion came into view, though, she truly was surprised. Vinya blinked against her vision, stumbling a bit as their feet hit the wooden bridge.

The pavilion was enclosed. Walls and wax paper windows—which were swung open on hinges—had been erected between the pavilion's beams. New additions branched out on the sides, and Vinya suspected on the back as well. Workers still occupied ladders, painting and weatherproofing the new walls. The steps led up to double doors, the outer corners curved at the top. Upon closer inspection, cherry blossom trees had been carved into the doors, and when they opened...

It took Vinya's breath away. The massive blossom tree in the center of the pavilion remained intact, the roof pressed as close to the tree as possible, but the trunk was open to the house. Because, Vinya realized, this *was* a house. Not the lavish wealth of the Palace, but an actual home.

To the left of the tree, a table and chairs. On the wall behind the table, a closed door. To the right of the tree, a quaint kitchen and wood burning stove. A few servants gave quick bows before scurrying out of the building that was half furnished, still under construction. Another closed door was at the edge of the cabinets, to her right. Vinya pulled her arm from Zhan's and rounded the blossom tree. On the far wall, a third door was open to reveal a study of sorts. Bookshelves filled top to bottom. A desk in the center of the room. A jar of ink, a quill in its stand, and an unlit candle sat upon its surface.

Behind the desk, leaning over and pressing a hand against his side as he studied the paper below him, stood Yuwon.

Vinya made it to the study's door before he noticed their presence, and when he lifted his head, Vinya stifled a laugh behind her hands.

Yuwon had a spring of cherry blossom tucked behind his ear, which he quickly snatched out.

"Zhan," he said. A hint of betrayal and embarrassment wound their way through the tones of his voice. To her, he said, "We had *planned* to bring you later, when everything had been brought in."

The guard shrugged at her side. "It's her birthday, allow her to enjoy the day, at its fullest."

Yuwon straightened. He studied Vinya and dropped the sprig onto the desk. "What do you think?"

So much detail had been put into this room. Hawk feathers were painstakingly painted onto the sides of the rafters. Windows overlooked the lake on the sides of the room. She stepped up to the desk and turned around. Jun's painting of the rising sun had been hung on one side, and on the other, Sooni's embroidered canary and her own cherry blossom stitch-work. She hadn't even noticed that Sooni's embroidery was missing from her room.

Vinya took a deep breath to stave off the burning tears. "I think... Woobin will have a fit."

Yuwon threw his head back in laughter, the sound easing the ache in her heart. Zhan pinched the bridge of his nose and shook his head.

Yuwon held his side again and blew a breath to slow his chuckles. "He still has room to dance around the tree, if you don't mind a guest every full moon."

"I—this is mine?"

"Ours."

She twisted. He was leaning over the desk once again. A fire burned in the deep amber eyes before her. The room felt smaller than before.

"Zhan," Yuwon muttered, not looking at the guard. "Go fetch a new jar of ink, I seem to have run out."

An eyebrow shot high as Zhan's gaze dropped to the very-full ink bottle with a knowing smile. He looked back at Yuwon, who waited patiently with his hands on the desk.

"Hm." Zhan pocketed the bottle as a hint of his dimples pressed into his now-rosy cheeks, and with a dip of his head, he left.

As soon as the front door closed behind Zhan, Yuwon straightened. His footsteps on the wooden floor as he stepped around the table were the only sound in the room. Vinya feared that if he came close enough, he would hear her pounding heart as well. She tried to keep her breath steady, but once she looked up into the eyes that burned with longing and a question, the air was pulled from her lungs.

Nothing existed, nothing *mattered*, but this moment.

Without looking away, Yuwon retrieved the sprig.

"I wanted the home, our home, to be a safe haven. Not across from Woobin or down the hall from my mother, but somewhere peaceful. The moment I heard you laugh here, I knew I would cherish this place forever."

"I don't deserve all of this," she whispered.

Yuwon shook his head in disagreement.

"Everything I have is yours," he whispered.

He placed her hand on his chest, over his heart.

"Everything I *am* is yours."

She didn't need rooms of treasures; she did not need servants or silks or the finest foods Byonea had to offer… All Vinya wanted was before her. Him.

Yuwon pulled her in closer. He tucked the sprig behind her ear, then traced her jawline with his fingers, lifting her chin towards his face.

Vinya could hear the muffled conversation of the workers outside of the pavilion, of their home.

Closer. Yuwon searched her eyes, shifting from one to the other. Vinya found herself lifting onto the tips of her toes.

A commotion from the bridge pulled at her attention.

Closer. Their breath mixed. Her heart beat faster, wilder. She closed her eyes. The scent of parchment and ink, of leather and wood, filled her senses—and the ocean. The notes that were missing from Yuwon's room while he was away. He smelled like the ocean breeze rolling up the hills of Norhagan.

The voices grew nearer.

Closer. Their lips brushed one another, she curled her fingers on his chest, crinkling the robe beneath. Hoping, hoping that the people outside would leave them be for a few moments more…

Zhan's voice rose outside as the front doors burst open against his permission. They broke apart. Yuwon's hand fell from her face as Vinya's uncurled from his chest, the sudden space between them feeling vast and cold.

The tree had blocked anyone's view of them. An older man in tan robes rounded the tree, Zhan close to his side with a hand on the man's arm. The man was flushed, clutching multiple papers in his hands. Some old, some new.

"I *must* speak with His Majesty." The man pulled up short upon seeing Vinya. "Alone. She needs to go."

Yuwon and Zhan protested, but Jinhee had come with the man, and she took Vinya's arm to lead her to the door.

"Come, my dear."

Something was wrong. It was in the air, in the sweat on the man's brow, in Jinhee's taut expression, in Zhan's eyes that were working to solve the problem before it was uttered.

Vinya turned back to Yuwon, but he was right behind her and followed her to the open door.

"This isn't necessary," he told the man. "Vinya can stay."

The man shook his head. "Apologies, Your Majesty, this matter must be handled privately. I insist that she leaves."

The older lady-in-waiting pulled Vinya onto the bridge, guiding her across as Vinya looked back at Yuwon and the man—who had not wasted a single moment and delved into the matter at hand.

"Jinhee, what is going on? Who is that man?" Vinya said as she faced the woman.

Jinhee patted her arm and took a few deep breaths. "That man is from the Office of Censors and Advisers. He's second in rank right after Alastor."

Vinya halted. "Woobin. Has something happened?"

"No, no. It isn't news from the front." Jinhee motioned for them to keep walking. "That man has been in charge since Alastor left yesterday morning, and in the lulls of letters of war, he's been sorting through the piles of *other* letters and scrolls... Ones that had been deemed unimportant and shoved into piles around his office."

They were nearing the end of the bridge now. Vinya felt they were almost to the point of the conversation as well.

"One of his men found a scroll from your mother—a response to the letter you sent her. Its contents prompted the adviser to gather more men to help search the office for a missing paper—a specific page in the old Norhagan accounts... Your family lineage."

Some old paper, and some new. Her mother's reply was in the hands of the adviser in the pavilion.

"They... found the page they were looking for. It had slipped between the shelves of the office—the original page replaced with an inaccurate copy. Someone made a mistake while righting their wrong, and, the outcome..."

The women stepped off the bridge, and Vinya turned to the lady-in-waiting. "Jinhee, tell me plainly, what is happening?"

The older woman wrung her hands in her skirts, avoiding eye contact. "I'm afraid that your letter to your mother was met with her own confusion and worry. She responded in great detail of your heritage, of your ancestry. Historians were brought in this morning to confirm and corroborate."

Through the front doors of the pavilion home, Vinya watched as Yuwon clutched not his side, but his chest. Zhan's face was of shock and disbelief. The adviser held out the papers for them both to see.

"Vinya, you have no royal ancestry, you descend from no great king of the past. Your being here, your betrothal to His Majesty, was all based on a mistake."

The world seemed to pause. The wind ceased, the cherry blossoms held tight to their petals, and Vinya forgot how to breathe.

There was nothing, absolutely nothing, but anguish in Yuwon's face as they held each other's gaze across the bridge.

Zhan glanced between them all and snatched the papers from the adviser's hands, earning an earful from the older man. Zhan shook the papers in the man's face like a creature of rage. As the adviser closed the doors to the pavilion, Yuwon wiped his own cheek.

Vinya's breath came back to her as Jinhee gently took her arm—broke her from her trance.

"I've been asked to see you off... To help you pack."

It was the truth Vinya knew, what she had told them from the beginning. But somewhere along the way, she had stopped wanting to leave.

Thunder rumbled as the Queen's guards surrounded her on the walk back to the women's quarters. They were not there for her protection, but for the Palace's.

A page torn and lost... And in the chaos of fixing it, the wrong lineage had been recalled and written. She had been a fraud. The mistaken lineage was the reason Norhagan's King Kuro had not sent aid. She was the reason the Queen spun another web—made another ally—by promising her daughter to Haryn. It resulted in Sooni's death. Jun's assault. Yuwon's attack. The King's demise.

If they had believed her from the beginning, if she had gotten the letter to her mother sooner, none of it would have happened. A single choice would have changed the trajectory of the last few weeks.

But the war still would have come. She would have been sheltering in Gran's home in Taejim during Calgham's siege on Byonea. Perhaps she would have stayed with Miho as they and Gran's neighbors would have sought shelter in the Palace walls...

No, the Queen wouldn't have allowed it. She wasn't permitting aid to the countless villages in Byonea. She only protected herself.

The Queen would have never protected the woman who stood in the door of what she called *her room* for the past month. The canary chirped, the bouquet of flowers Zhan brought flared out from Gran's vase, the clothing cabinet with the hawks sat ominously against the wall. The pack she brought with her to Byonea rested at the base of the door with her old clothes on top. She held her breath, not wanting to break down in front of the guards.

She would not let the Queen gain satisfaction from this catastrophe.

Leaving the Queen's guards in the hall, Jinhee closed the door behind them and helped Vinya undress. The silks rippled and whispered as they came off her skin. The linen slightly scratched her skin as she pulled it over her head. Her feet slipped effortlessly into her worn leather shoes. With the silver and pearl hairpin placed on the display cabinet, Jinhee twisted Vinya's hair into a singular braid down her back, tucking loose strands behind her ear one last time.

Vinya's stomach tumbled as Jinhee removed the ring from her finger and placed it next to the hairpin. She couldn't look away from it, even as she slung the pack across her shoulder.

She walked to the display cabinet as her canary fluttered around in the cage, and her hand hovered over the ring. She had grown to love all these, but could only take some items in the form of a memory.

Raindrops ticked on the roof of the building, and the guards knocked on the door before opening it.

"Time to go."

Vinya let out a heavy exhale and opened the display cabinet's drawer instead—where the feather, the dried-out blossom bud sprig, and Yuwon's note from the day they returned from the Spring Festival rested. She scooped up all three and presented them with open hands to the head of the Queen's guard.

"I'll be taking these, my grandmother's vase, and the bird."

The man raised a brow. He jerked his chin to the canary, and one of his men crossed the room, searching its base for any hidden compartments.

The head guard then studied the items in her hands. He picked up Yuwon's note and flipped it over to see what was written.

The guard's eyes flitted to the display cabinet where the hairpin and ring rested. He scoffed and shoved the paper back in Vinya's hand. "Keep your trash."

He didn't know the note was worth more to Vinya than a thousand rings.

The canary's cage was deemed clear, and the guards led her out of the room that was once her own cage. When they exited the women's quarters, an open carriage awaited at the bottom of the steps, giving Vinya pause.

"Am I not allowed to say goodbye?"

"To whom?"

Vinya faced the man. He knew exactly who, but showed no emotion. The canary and vase were loaded into the back of the carriage, a thin tarp thrown over the cage by the driver to block the sprinkling rain.

Jinhee stood in the door of the women's quarters, hand over her heart. Vinya backtracked as the guard yelled at her, and she pushed the dried blossom sprig into the older woman's hands.

"Please," Vinya whispered. "Please get this to him. Put it in his room... *something*."

The guard stomped after her. He grabbed Vinya by the arm and pulled her towards the carriage.

Jinhee nodded, cradling the sprig as the delicate treasure it was. "I understand, and I will."

The guard picked Vinya up by the waist and dropped her into the back of the carriage, her wrist stung as it smacked into the canary's cage.

"There's a thick blanket back there if the rain falls any harder," the carriage driver croaked. He snapped the reins, and they lurched down the path, towards the side gates that the merchants use.

Jinhee waved as they faded from view. Vinya couldn't find the strength to return it. She could not say goodbye. She took a deep breath, tucked the feather and note into her pack, and faced the road ahead.

To the freedom she longed for from the beginning.

28

A Head, Turned

The inn near the harbor was exactly where Vinya had hoped to be at the beginning of this month, now it was the last. It was a place for her to dry and change after the torrential rain slammed against the plain open carriage that brought her here. The thin tarp she had used to shield herself from the rain had been soaked through halfway to the harbor town. The driver had scoffed when she chose to cover her pack and canary cage with the thicker cloth.

It wasn't the loss of the exquisite lifestyle that had Vinya looking down her nose at Byonea, it was the treatment of the people they didn't deem important. She'd only been treated well because she was a pawn—a glue to bind their countries together.

She had hoped to repair the mistreatment of other citizens with the help of Yuwon, Woobin, and Jun.

Vinya shivered as she lugged her pack, vase, and bird cage up the stairs to the hall lined with bedrooms. She left drops of rainwater and muddy footprints in her wake. It was a much smaller, much dirtier version of the royal quarters in the Palace.

The inn was bustling with travelers, preparing to leave or return to their homeland. Vinya had to press against the wall in the tight hallway for others to pass by. She soon found her room for the night and placed her things on the floor.

Home. She was going home.

She stripped off her soaked clothes, hung them to dry in the washroom, and pulled on the only other outfit in her pack. The only window in her room overlooked the harbor. The rain beat against it; maybe the weather would delay the ship. Maybe she would have one more day in *the motherland*.

Vinya sighed. Perhaps she could send a letter to her parents instead, about settling into Gran's home—her home. The road to Taejim dipped south of the Palace, so she could avoid traveling near there. She wouldn't have to look upon the walls that were her temporary home.

Vinya closed her eyes and took a deep breath to stave off tears. She was losing them all. They would now turn their focus and care for the new princess, the *true* princess and soon-to-be Queen. One day, to them, she would only be a hazy memory. Jinhee's nurturing heart, Zhan's all-seeing eyes, Woobin's infectious aura that pulled everyone in, Jun's warm peace, and Yuwon...

She could almost imagine her hand in his, could almost feel his fingers lifting her chin. She would never see the fire in his eyes again, hear his voice, or watch him throw his head back in laughter. She thought she'd lost him when the sword had sliced through his body, but now he was really and truly gone. Pulled away not by death, but by force. It was *that* force that ripped open her soul. Fate's string had not come to tie the two of them together, but to tangle her thoughts.

Vinya clenched her fists, fighting to stop the onslaught of emotions, but the absence of her ring was made more apparent with the movement. She opened her palm to look at the small crescent-shaped scar fading from pink to white. Daeya had been right... she was a fool. And Sooni would still be alive if not for her.

She needed to find something to do, something to take her mind off the ever-swirling pit that sucked her in.

Vinya pocketed the small bag of coins she had been allotted for travels. Stew was being made downstairs when she first arrived, and the smell wafted into her room as she opened the door.

There was something nice about not being noticed—about blending in as she wove her way through the crowded upper hallway. No one stopped to move out of her way, no one cared enough to look her in the eye. It was the jarring feeling of being one of millions, and yet completely alone.

Vinya's growling stomach distracted her from thoughts of the Palace, though she could almost hear Daeya's venomous strikes, almost hear the silk threads of the Queen's controlling web being spun, almost hear Alastor's sniveling voice...

She stopped in the middle of the hall. No, that *was* Alastor's voice she'd filtered through the cacophony of the inn's noises. She wouldn't have cared if it had not been for the ecstatic tone to his voice—would have kept walking if not for a second male voice shushing him, telling him to keep quiet. But Alastor was not listening.

Vinya followed his voice to the door of his room and planted herself against the wall beside it as something deep within her gut told her to *listen*.

"...won't need any more delivered. It took much longer than expected, but the job is finally done, and I still have enough left over to—"

"*Keep it down*," the other man growled.

His voice had an edge to it, a sharpness that said this was more than just a trade deal for Byonea. What an odd place to meet for one, too.

"These fish people don't know anything other than nets and bait. Being this close to the ocean, I assume the saltwater had dulled their brains."

A passing woman, a worker at the inn, looked toward the cracked door, then met Vinya's gaze. The woman only shook her head and kept walking. These people were used to the slander and mistreatment—there was nothing they could do but keep their heads down and continue on. That was exactly what the woman did, taking her bucket of water and rags to clean up someone else's mess.

Alastor went on. "You said it would be faster."

"The *timing* is up to how much is used."

"Now I can't exactly shove an entire bottle of poi—"

"*HUSH.*"

Vinya's heart raced. Poison. She was sure the word was about to come out of his mouth. It would explain why the physicians couldn't identify his illness.

The head adviser dropped his voice just above a whisper. "Do you understand how *difficult* it is to administer when eyes are always on you? To dip a finger into a broth and test it yourself while dipping *it* in with another? The K—"

"*If you do not close your mouth—*"

A thud vibrated the floor, accompanied by the sound of a hand slamming onto a table. She brought shaking fingers to her lips. If there was about to be bloodshed, she didn't want to be anywhere near it. She had seen enough of it over the past few weeks.

Alastor went as silent as the grave, seeing his own could be dug at any moment.

"I am too far, and far too close. You will be the undoing of all our work if you do not keep your mouth *shut.*"

It was too late for that now.

"The... offspring?" the second man asked.

"Will be easily dealt with. The second will go faster than the first."

Woobin. *Yuwon.*

The King had not succumbed to an unidentifiable sickness—the final blow seeing his son gravely injured. He had been poisoned. Murdered. His sons were next on the chopping block, and Alastor was already preparing to take those steps.

She needed to get back to the Palace to warn them.

Vinya's mind reeled, she turned to walk past the door and slammed into another customer of the inn. She frantically apologized, the man's face turned red as his belongings were now scattered on the floor. They both stooped to gather his items. The man's arm bumped the door beside them, knocking it wide open.

She didn't mean to glance inside—she couldn't help but look.

To the man who sat facing the door, Vinya looked like just another passing commoner. His dark hair fell below his ears—framing the sleek, fox-like features of his face—almost covering the scar curved along his jaw. He subtly shifted the neckline of his robe, but not quick enough. Vinya had spotted what was underneath.

But to the man dressed in plain clothes whose back was toward her, the one who twisted in his seat to look at her—the rat who had brought disease into the Palace, whose nose twitched as his face drained of all color... He knew exactly who she was.

Alastor was not subtle in his move to grab the slim saber at his side.

Vinya was on her feet within seconds and shoved her way through the crowded hall. Shouts of alarm rose behind her at the armed man who chased her. Her feet missed the first step on the stairs, and she yelped as her elbow rammed into the handrail.

The slip cost her, and the sounds of Alastor's pursuit grew nearer. Vinya found her footing and flew down the rest of the stairs as she began to yell.

"Move! *Move!*" She switched between Norhagan and Byonean languages as she bolted through the main floor of the inn.

Her cry was not for *help*. It didn't seem like anyone would step in to help a commoner here, not in a harbor town where she may be an outsider. An outcast. Someone who didn't want or desire attention. Someone who could be a fraud. Wasn't she all of those things though?

Her body felt as if it were on fire as she raced for the door. Still, she yelled.

A figure stepped into Vinya's path and reached out to stop her—but she only saw the sword at the man's side and the broad hand hovering over its hilt.

The door was in view, and Vinya took no chances. With adrenaline pumping through her veins, she aimed for the man's left, then spun back to his right.

It was much easier to move in pants, without the layers of skirts weighing her down. Much easier to switch the forward motion into a side-step wearing proper shoes instead of the slippers of Byonea's Palace. She didn't have time to find gratification in the man's hand that—even as it followed her maneuver to his other side—grasped nothing but the wind in her wake.

The door of the inn was within reach. Confused patrons unintentionally blocked Alastor's path behind her. She burst through the front door, off the covered porch, and straight into the blinding torrent of rain.

Vinya's shoes squelched in the muddy road. She blinked hard against the rain pouring down her face. No amount of wiping could keep it out of her eyes.

She spun in circles out into the road. She had to find something to get word to the Palace. A horse. A carriage. A messenger boy. *Something*.

Disoriented with a sense of being trapped in the open road, gusts of wind turned the sky into waves above her. Vinya couldn't tell where the inn was anymore; she could only see a few feet in front of her.

A shadow appeared to her right. When the figure from the inn emerged, dread seeped into Vinya's skin deeper than the rain. There was nothing to use as a weapon to defend herself, so she stooped to grab a handful of mud and threw it at his head. The moment the man covered his face, she turned to run, but the ground did not hold the same traction as the floor of the inn, and onto the muddy road she fell. The man pursued her again.

She would go down fighting, no one was going to take her prisoner again. She twisted onto her back and brought her knees to her chest. She'd kick the man straight in the—

"Vinya!"

Her name shot through her like an arrow, effectively pausing her defense.

She'd been so focused on escaping that she had not studied the man's face—Zhan's face. Relief mixed with the fear that still loomed within her.

He took off his guard's hat and knelt to place it on her head, the brim shielding her eyes from the downpour. The rainwater washed away whatever remained of the mud on Zhan's face as he examined hers. He blinked against the rain and read every minute detail of her expression.

The moment of peace did not last. Another form stalked through the rain. Alastor approached from behind Zhan, his saber dragging alongside him as he came.

Zhan didn't need her warning. Whatever he saw in her face had him whipping around to his opponent, sword ready.

Vinya did not need to see his face to know that he balked.

Zhan's body jerked—frozen for a moment as he took Alastor in.

"Do you even know who she is?" Alastor called out. "That wench has been lying to us this entire time. She is no princess. No descendant of *any* great king. I had only just found out and was on my way to inform His Majesty Yuwon. Turn your blade not to me, but to the foul woman who dared to become royal under our noses."

Zhan did not move. "Vinya only spoke truth from the moment I met her. The Palace is well aware of the mistake, and she is being sent to Norhagan. I suggest sheathing your sword, Alastor, as I doubt the Dowager Queen would look favourably upon you for killing an innocent woman."

Alastor's eyes widened. Vinya could swear that, through the rain, she could see his nose twitch.

"Joona? You think that old *hag* cares at all for innocent life?" The high adviser scoffed and pointed his sword at Zhan, who stiffened. "*You have no idea what she does behind closed doors.*"

Alastor's face twisted with anger, angling the blade toward Vinya once more. "That prevaricator knows too much about the Palace, and doesn't deserve to draw another breath. Not in Byonea, not in Norhagan."

Vinya opened her mouth to tell Zhan about what she'd overheard, but Alastor stepped toward her—sword raised to silence her forever.

That single step was all Zhan allowed. He closed the space between them, taking the fight out of reach from her.

Vinya did not expect Alastor to move so quickly—she did not expect to see the older man dodge and parry each jab. The onslaught of rain eased enough to give a clearer view for them all.

Zhan moved exactly as she'd imagined. His was not the smooth fighting style of Yuwon, nor the swift strikes of Woobin. No, this was brutal. The force of a mighty beast thrown into each swing. A vicious roar accompanied each strike.

Alastor tried to hold his own, but he couldn't keep up for long. He was no match for the man half his age.

The King's guard.

Her friend.

The head adviser was one second too slow as Zhan feigned to the right, then swooped to the left. There was no time for Alastor to recover from his mistake. His head and body thudded onto the muddy road—separately.

Bile built in Vinya's throat. She clamped her mouth shut and swallowed to keep it down.

Zhan knelt beside her, sword still in hand—blood dripped and washed away in the rain. His mouth moved, but she didn't hear him. Vinya shook her head. She could not breathe, couldn't speak. Zhan placed a hand on her shoulder to comfort her, but it only felt like a weight that kept her here—that stopped her from running back to the palace to tell Yuwon.

"*Yuwon,*" she garbled through the rain.

Zhan's brow furrowed. It was now his turn to shake his head. He twisted to look back at Alastor—at what remained of Alastor—and tried to put the pieces together. He had come to her aid and slew the head adviser... without knowing why.

Of course he didn't. The dragon who had stayed within her shadow, breathing flames down her neck that first week to keep her in Byonea, had become a distant surveyor to watch her leave. He hadn't been in the hallway—had not heard what the adviser said.

A few of the harbor town's guards converged around them. They covered the body and awaited orders from the King's guard.

Vinya scrambled to her knees. She grabbed Zhan by his shoulders and shook. *She* shook.

"We have to tell Yuwon."

His words were audible once more. "Tell him what? What is going on?"

"The King—King Wonho—he didn't just die. Zhan, he was *murdered*. Alastor had been poisoning him for months, if not longer. He was in the inn bragging about it to—"

Vinya hadn't seen if the other man—who had been in the room with Alastor—had slipped out of the building's only entrance during the storm... The man who had subtly closed his outer robe in order to conceal a second robe underneath—one lined with green ribbon.

She released Zhan and pointed to the inn. "There's a Calgham informant inside. He was with Alastor, he looked to be about the same age as Yuwon and Hyosung. There's a large scar that curves across his jaw."

It made sense now. How uneasy Alastor had been while allowing Vinya to investigate her ancestry, telling her to be careful with the tome lest it fall apart. He had been cautious so that she wouldn't stumble upon the actual truth... That *he* had been the one to falsify the documents. Her ancestry. The scroll Zhan carried here himself to take her to the palace a month ago. It had been a false claim to fully disrupt and nullify the union brought about by the Treaty of Trust, making Byonea a laughingstock to the world—to make them crumble and fall to their knees before Calgham.

Only one other person would know what Alastor's end goal had been.

Zhan's eyes narrowed and darted across her face—seeing the unsaid. The pieces of a puzzle snapped together in his mind. "Hyosung wasn't the only one working with Calgham to bring Byonea down. He and Alastor were working *together*?"

"We have to tell Yuwon," Vinya repeated as he helped her stand.

Zhan sent a handful of the guards back into the inn to search for the Calgham informant when the sound of an approaching horse grew through the rain.

Zhan pulled her behind him. He picked up Alastor's sword and took up a battle stance—ready to take on whoever was coming their way—armed with two blades.

The dark horse halted in front of Zhan and Vinya, with a man in crimson robes upon its back—the same robes he'd been wearing early that morning.

Yuwon slid off his horse, slippers splashing into the mud as he solemnly looked at the decapitated man on the ground behind her. Both he and the horse were soaked to the bone, and the hand that gripped his torso was covered in fresh blood.

Zhan threw Alastor's blade to the ground and sheathed his own sword.

"*Are you insane*?" he roared at Yuwon.

Yuwon looked sidelong at his friend through the hair plastered across his brow and gave him half of a smile. He reached into his robes and retrieved something small.

Through the rain, Vinya couldn't make out the dried blossom bud until Yuwon stood directly in front of her. When she reached to take it, he slipped his fingers around her hand and pulled her close.

Zhan's dimples pressed in. He twisted to give orders to the town's guards nearby, scattering them between tasks to get rid of Alastor's body and finding a carriage for the King's return trip to the Palace.

Yuwon leaned in, under the brim of Zhan's hat still on her head. His lips brushed her ear.

"Don't go," he whispered.

Vinya let out a breath. "I was coming back to you."

He slipped his hand behind her neck and cradled her head as he closed the space between their lips.

Curse the Treaty. Curse the advisers. Curse the Queen and her bird-lined walls. This was her home. Yuwon was her home.

His tongue slipped between her lips as he deepened the kiss, and Vinya wrapped her arms around his waist. She would trade all the sunrises and sunsets of Norhagan to stay here.

Yuwon's fingers curled in her hair as he sucked a ragged breath in through his teeth.

Vinya almost forgot about the rain, almost forgot about...

"I'm so sorry!" She exclaimed, taking a step back and covering her mouth.

Yuwon struggled to stand straight. She'd pressed herself against his wound.

He huffed a small laugh through his nose and carefully clutched his torso. "I'll be fine."

But Yuwon's eyes remained closed as he shuddered. Vinya looked at Zhan.

Zhan—who had kept watch over them from the corner of his eye with a mask of indifference—rubbed his neck and shook his head.

He helped Yuwon to the inn, where other guards had apprehended the Calgham informant and were hauling the frantic man to the local authorities. Vinya suspected he would be transferred to the Palace for questioning soon.

If the people in the inn had been stirred over the arrest, they were in shock at the entry of the King. They cleared a room for him—the town's physician had been called upon to repair the stitches Yuwon had snapped during his ride. Vinya held his hand through it all.

After a stern word, the physician rewrapped Yuwon's torso and ordered Zhan to keep the King on bed rest until he had healed completely. While the physician worked, Zhan explained what had happened.

Yuwon listened without remark. He was eased into the carriage, and Vinya's belongings were brought from the inn.

Before Vinya stepped into the carriage, she turned to place the brimmed guard hat back on Zhan's head.

"Thank you."

For more than just the hat.

Zhan dipped his chin in a bow. "You're welcome."

She returned his smile and climbed into the carriage. He closed the door behind her. Mounting his own horse, Zhan rode beside the carriage as it set off down the muddy path.

Back to the Palace.

Back home.

29

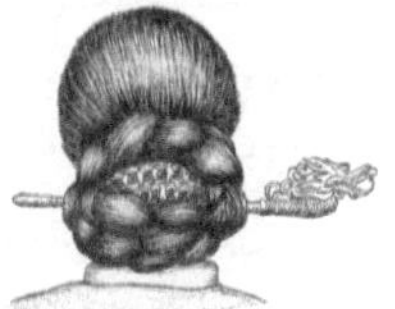

A Gift Returned

Weeks prior, Vinya had been dressed as a princess and ushered into the throne room. She had knelt before the King and was commanded to marry the Crown Prince—the man whose hand she now held as the doors to the throne room were opened wide. The setting sun shone through the waxed paper windows, casting the room in a honeyed orange hue.

Something was missing, and something was new.

The Queen sat upon the throne—the *King's* throne—and straightened at the unexpected appearance of her son. Jun sat in her appointed chair to the Queen's left, surrounded by her ladies-in-waiting. The Officials, thirty on each side of the throne room, standing in three lines of ten, dropped to their knees and touched their foreheads to the floor at the sight of Yuwon. When they rose, they murmured amongst themselves, glancing between Yuwon, Vinya, the Queen... and the woman who knelt before the throne.

Beside the woman, Jinhee glanced over her shoulder to see who had entered. The older woman had to look twice. Her jaw slackened and face lit up, but her eyes followed the same pattern as the Officials.

The woman, whose back was to Vinya, was dressed in the robes she herself had worn; she knelt in the same exact spot. She was likely given the same treatment. *Told* to do things, not *asked*. Vinya could imagine the heavy hand and harsh words that came from the Queen.

Yuwon and Vinya rounded the woman. Yuwon aimed for the throne, but Vinya couldn't take her eyes off the kneeling woman—whose chestnut hair had been twisted into a bun, bound with the silver and pearl hairpin.

"Miho?" Vinya breathed, halting her steps.

The kneeling woman lifted her head. The whites of Miho's eyes were red from tears, contrasting the green shade of her irises.

Even Yuwon paused, blinking as recognition flashed across his face.

Miho's eyes widened. "Vinya? I—"

The Queen cleared her throat, interrupting the woman. "Yuwon, this is Miho Yinuo, Princess and granddaughter of the current King Kuro of Norhagan, and your *true* betrothed. We were able to trace the lineage on the original Norhagan accounts to her, and my men tracked her down to a village just outside of Kima."

She hadn't left the village where they last met—had not made it to Ungeong to her Calgham partner. Perhaps it was for the best, with Calgham invading; Ungeong would have been one of the first towns overtaken by the warriors. She would have been one of the first to be captured—or killed. Miho looked up at Vinya with a crease between her brows. She brought a nervous hand to her mouth and began chewing on her nails. Jinhee reached over and gently brought the woman's hand down.

That was what Miho had been trying to tell her in the village. That was the authority she picked up on while they were on the ship to Byonea. That was why Miho's father—King Kuro's one and only son, the Crown Prince of Norhagan—had excommunicated her. She was carrying the child of a Calgham man...

Yuwon turned to his mother. "True or not, she is not who I will marry."

He slipped out of Vinya's hand and stepped up the dais to come face to face with his mother. He clutched his freshly wrapped side as he rose, rose, *rose* above her. The Queen shifted on the throne; her fingers curled around the dark wooden ends of the armrests.

The Queen's mouth pulled back into a careful sneer. "You are king in name alone. The official ceremony has yet to take place, pushed back on account of other... *plans*. You cannot sit here until then."

Yuwon had postponed the coronation in order to focus on the pavilion, a home prepared and ready for them, before he was proclaimed king in front of the masses.

"A dowager queen has never ruled in place of the king. You have no right to sit on the throne—nor do you still hold the power to make decisions on my behalf. That privilege was taken away the moment father took his last breath."

Even though the King's throne on a platform a foot higher than the rest of the chairs, Yuwon still towered over his mother.

"*Move.*"

The Queen—the Dowager Queen—subtly tilted her head. A shake, a refusal.

Yuwon straightened. "Zhan."

The guard stalked from Vinya's side to the throne with slow, calculated steps. He climbed the dais like a dragon that had found its prey.

Vinya fidgeted with the linen sleeve of her shirt, unable to see what the Dowager Queen faced; what did the older woman see in Zhan's eyes that made her own eyes widen? Joona shrank under his gaze and scurried out of the chair before Zhan was within reach.

The Dowager Queen composed herself, smoothing out her skirts and lowered herself in her regular chair.

She studied Yuwon as he stared at the empty seat before him. The sunbeams through the windows enhanced the golden four-winged dragon painting on the back of the throne; its eyes almost seemed to stare back at the man. Yuwon's fingers curled and uncurled at his sides, but he did not move.

Everyone waited with bated breath.

Even though the crown and throne were his by right, Yuwon had verbally made his claim and now needed to act on it. He turned around to face Vinya.

She nodded. Together... They would do this together. The Queen could no longer shut him in a room away from the world. He would never be alone. Vinya would make sure of it.

Yuwon closed the space between himself and the throne and sat, holding his newly bandaged side. Whispers began anew throughout the room. He observed the sixty grown men—the Officials in different ranks muttering amongst themselves like children during playtime.

Children.

Vinya glanced at the far-left wall, absent of any Shade Prince or Princess. That's what was missing. The Dowager Queen must have gotten rid of them all, sending them back to live with their own mothers. No trace of King Wonho's many children—other than Yuwon and Woobin, and Jun since he adopted her—would be allowed to reside in the Palace.

Zhan stayed at Yuwon's side. His fiery gaze slid over them all, challenging. A power exchange was taking place in front of their eyes. Just as Yuwon stepped into his new role as King, Zhan stepped in as the new head of the King's guard. To add to the changes, Yuwon directly addressed the woman kneeling before him, not using an adviser to speak on his behalf.

"You are the woman my Vinya saved near Kima."

My Vinya.

The Dowager Queen twisted in her chair and opened her mouth, but snapped it shut at Yuwon's raised hand.

"I apologize for your troubles and your unnecessary travels to the Palace. If there is anything you need, anything we can give you to atone for the Crown's error, name it and it will be yours."

Before Miho could reply, the Dowager Queen scoffed.

"Don't be absurd, Yuwon. The Treaty must be upheld in order to gain Norhagan's forces. The war is ongoing—your brother at its head. Tradition must be followed. No royal can marry some... commoner."

Vinya had enough and motioned to the woman at her feet. "The only absurdity would be marrying your son to someone who is—"

She stopped, shaking her head and pushing the thought from her mind. It was not her secret to tell, but it would save both herself and Miho.

Miho's voice barely rose above the quiet, "I am with child."

The gasps around the room not only came from the revelation, but also from the women's disregard for the Dowager Queen's commands.

In status, the older woman had been ranked just below the King, but now as Dowager she held no power. She was allowed to step in if something dire happened to Yuwon, and only if he remained unmarried. And Vinya was as she said, as she had been all along: a commoner. She held no sway in the throne room.

The Dowager Queen's eyes bore into the two women, but Vinya did not look away. She would no longer be pushed around or manipulated by the older woman. Vinya wouldn't be a pawn in Joona's games any longer. And yet, the older woman smiled.

"I see. You think my son's fondness for you gives you license to challenge me here. Your strength is nothing but insubordination. Delusion has wound its way into your head the last few weeks you've been in my Palace. Worn my clothes. Eaten my food..."

"Mother."

The Dowager Queen rolled her shoulders at her son's words.

"Even if the woman here is with child, surely she has a sister. A cousin. Some distant relative with a link and claim to the Norhagan throne." She turned to Zhan, waving a lazy hand in the air. "Go, retrieve the Norhagan accounts."

Zhan did not move. The guard acted as if she hadn't spoken at all.

The Dowager Queen turned icy. "*Guard.*"

Yuwon raised his voice, "If you utter one more word... if I so much as hear a sigh from your direction, I will have you removed from this room."

His mother's jaw worked, and she leaned back in her chair.

Yuwon turned his attention to the women and Officials in front of the dais. "My brother, Woobin, believes in powers that we cannot see. His heart and soul lean toward the Old Ways. The day he met Vinya, Woobin made mention of Fate's string. I thought the comment to be nonsensical, but over time, my heart saw the string as well. I felt its pull. Tradition may frown upon me, but destiny brought her here. I stand firm in my decision; our betrothal shall not be broken."

The Dowager Queen sprung from her chair. "Outrageous! What about the war? What of the Treaty and aid?"

Zhan had been ready for the outburst.

"Take her," he commanded his men.

The King's royal guards surrounded the Queen, her eyes flitted between them all as she took a step backwards, the back of her legs knocking into her chair. Jun shrunk in her own chair and covered her ears with her hands. The women around her comforted the Princess as the skirmish broke out. The Dowager Queen refused to allow the men to grab her; instead, she walked out the room on her own accord, making vicious comments the entire time.

Yuwon sat alone on the dais. Four chairs, two on each side, unoccupied save Jun.

Only when the Dowager Queen's snaps and remarks faded down the hall did Yuwon continue. "Our forces, with the help of Haryn, have been enough to hold off and push back the Calgham army. We've been offered help from those who ask for nothing in return, only justice. We do not need Norhagan's army. The Treaty still stands, and will continue to hold its value until the day comes when we truly need it."

He zeroed in on Miho as Vinya helped her to her feet. "The father, he's Byonean?"

Miho covered her stomach. "He—he's not from here."

Yuwon's brow creased. "What is his name?"

The Norhagan Princess shifted on her feet and began biting her nails once more. Jinhee lightly clicked her tongue, and Miho dropped her hand. "Wen Myang... of Calgham."

Gasps rose from the sixty Officials, their cries of "*treason*" and "*immorality*" thundered throughout the throne room. The men jabbed fingers in Miho's direction. Exaggerating their words with upraised arms or rubbing their faces, the Officials pleaded with Yuwon to send her away, *immediately.* Miho closed her eyes and wrapped both arms around her stomach in the midst of them all.

Yuwon and Zhan's gazes clashed, and Yuwon silenced the room with a raised hand. "That name, and what I'm about to say, does not leave this room. Does everyone understand?"

Questioning glances and mumbles of reluctant agreement fluttered around the throne room.

Yuwon took a breath as deep as his injury would allow. "Wen Myang... has been a vital key in this war. This man single-handedly tipped the scales, giving us information on Calgham. Battle camps. Formations. Dates and movements of their warriors. He played a vital part in my own sister's freedom." Yuwon paused to look at Jun—who stared with tear-filled eyes at the woman in front of the dais. Yuwon went on, "The country of Byonea is forever in his debt, and Wen Myang has already been granted full citizenship. I would like to extend that to both of you, if you'd like."

Miho's mouth hung open. "I had no idea. I mean, I *knew*, but not to that extent." She pulled off her necklace, the golden coin at its end, and presented it in the palm of her hand to Vinya.

"Please, take this as my gratitude and apology."

Vinya closed Miho's fingers around the coin. "It was a gift for you and your family. I will not take it back."

Miho shook her head, forcing the coin into Vinya's hand. "I feel I have deceived you, not telling you sooner who I am, who my father is. I will send a letter to him, to see if he'll send money for land or a home somewhere quiet."

The coin felt heavier, yet smaller than it had been in the past. A gift from Hyosung, for Vinya to get back to her family.

Her family...

Vinya looked at Yuwon, who was already grinning. He dipped his chin in a nod.

"Miho," Vinya said as she pocketed the coin. She took Miho's hand in her own. "There is a house in Taejim, my late grandmother's house that was left to me. It's small and quiet. I don't see myself visiting often enough to keep it maintained, so it will need a tenant. It isn't extravagant and may need a bit of work, but the neighbors are extremely kind and helpful. If you cannot take the coin, then please accept the house."

Miho's finger hesitated near her mouth. "Are you sure?"

"I wouldn't want anyone else living in it. I'll come visit throughout the year. It will be good to have a friend to spend some time with."

Miho returned Vinya's smile with a sparkle in her eye. She lifted onto the tips of her toes, readying to pull Vinya into a hug. "Yes, yes I accept! Oh—"

She stopped and slipped the royal ring off her finger—the ring Vinya had become so accustomed to wearing.

"I believe this is yours." Miho passed the ring to her, then pulled the silver and pearl hairpin out of her bun; her chestnut hair flowing freely down her back once more. "And this."

The Norhagan Princess nibbled at her nails. "I suppose this entire outfit is yours..."

Vinya held up a hand. "Feel free to keep those on for now."

Miho huffed a small laugh, and Jinhee stepped to Vinya's side.

"It's lovely to have you back, my lady."

The older woman went down on her knees and touched her forehead to the ground at Vinya's feet. Like a gentle wave, robes shifted. The Officials and Miho followed suit.

Vinya turned toward the dais. Zhan bowed deeply at the waist, his dimples pressing in deeper than she'd ever seen them.

Yuwon beamed. He stretched out his hand in invitation.

Up the steps, her world felt lighter. Up the steps, she could see the tears that lined Yuwon's eyes. Hand in his, they would change Byonea for the better.

His Vinya.

Her Yuwon.

30

A Clipped Wing

The dungeon was ill-lit and dank. Stomach-churning smells of bile and urine hung in the air that no mask or cloth could dispel. Men shifted in their cells, turning to watch Vinya and the prison guard who was escorting her as they passed by. A trickle of water echoed down a distant dark hallway—Vinya half expected a rat to scurry across her path at any moment.

The prison guard escorting her motioned towards a cell on her right, where a figure stood with one fist clenched behind his back as he gazed up through the sliver of a window high on the wall—soaking in every ray of sunshine that he could. Vinya nodded to the guard, who stepped away a few paces.

A cot occupied one corner of the man's cell, a small hole in the ground to relieve himself in the opposite corner. She supposed it didn't matter how far apart the two were since the smell of excretions permeated the walls of this place.

Her stomach threatened to empty itself, and Vinya blew out a long breath to quell it.

"You get used to it after a while." Hyosung's melodious voice rang out at odds with his dark surroundings and words. "I sometimes wonder if I, too, will fade into the stones. The eldest Shade Prince turned into nothing but a shadow himself, left to rot away alone."

He turned from the window, but did not approach the cell bars. He had been given plain clothes that seemed to be secondhand, passed down to him from a previous convict. His right arm was wrapped close to his body, a sling keeping it from moving.

A nasty red scab raked down from his mouth to his chin. It would leave a scar—a remnant of Woobin's rage, a horrid crack in his beautiful face. His once unmarked skin had been broken in a single, violent night.

Hyosung caught the glance, and approached the bars of his cell, resting his free forearm on a crossbeam. He lowered his voice. "I heard they found the page. The *genuine* one. How easy it was to produce a counterfeit—no one took the time to second guess it. No one looked into the lineage far enough to realize that the true promised princess, the descendant of the great King Rikr of Norhagan, wasn't some farm girl who took yearly trips across the water. It was far too easy to find a foreign woman the right age with such a predictable schedule."

Vinya's brows knit together, a chill spread throughout her body.

His smile widened. No, this man had not been broken. The dim cell did nothing to fade his beauty. His eyes were as bright as his pearly white teeth, it amused him to see her tormented.

"I've been watching you for *years,* Vinya. Every trip the same. Every long walk to your grandmother's house." He picked at the dirt under his nails as he continued. "You'd stop to buy the early blossoms from a market near Taejim, and while your grandmother would grumble about the money you spent on them, she adored them. Adored you." The look he gave her was unnerving. "I'm surprised she never mentioned the visits she'd receive from the young palace man throughout the year. The way she spoke about you... I almost couldn't go through with it."

Hyosung hummed Gran's lullaby, the same tune Vinya hummed in the open hall while Jun painted her sun. Here in the dungeons, a haunting edge wove its way into the song.

A chill wound around Vinya's finger. Gran's ring turned colder than the bars of Hyosung's cell. It hadn't been Yuwon that delivered the ring to her, but *Hyosung* who took it from Gran's house.

Hyosung—who had been at Gran's side when she passed.

Hyosung—the young man Gran wanted to introduce to Vinya.

Vinya's throat began to close. "What did you do to her?" she ground out through clenched teeth.

Hyosung backed away with an uplifted hand. "I didn't touch her. Nature took its toll, paving the way for destiny. For *this*."

He looked to the ceiling, so caught up in his own world that he'd forgotten where he was. He dropped his arm in defeat.

"I've never known such joy than to see my plan coming to fruition... That you'd been ordered to leave because the *true* descendant of Norhagan had been found." He exaggerated a frown. "So sad. Did you come all the way down here to say goodbye?"

The guards weren't allowed to speak to him, let alone tell him of the world outside his lonely cell. Vinya's confusion must have shown. He pointed to the window behind him.

"The citizens whisper. Not all the time, but enough. Even when they know they shouldn't. The citizens' words are like music to my ears." Hyosung took a deep breath, as if savoring the taste of the gossip he had overheard.

Vinya shook her head. "Alastor poured his own poison into the late King Wonho's food—mixing in a flavor he would enjoy," she responded with clipped words. "All that you hear through the little window may not be true... Or trusted."

Hyosung tilted his head. "So, he was found out. Alastor told me he would burn the true page, but the fool failed to follow through—too distracted with my father. I knew he would slip. I held out hope that he would find a way to free me."

"Why Alastor?" Vinya asked. "What motivation did he have?"

Hyosung rubbed the back of his neck. "He hasn't been questioned?"

Vinya's eyes dipped to the motion. "I didn't have time to ask before his head fell to the ground."

Their gazes locked. Hyosung slid his hand to graze the front of his neck, and failed to suppress a shiver.

"The man with him, the one with the scar," Vinya traced her finger along her jaw, "wouldn't answer any questions. It was odd... A message came directly from the Emerald King—requesting permission to imprison the man in Calgham under his own personal guard's watch—it was the only moment the scarred man showed emotion. Fear. The next time the guards checked his cell—"

Vinya allowed the silence to speak for her.

Hyosung's potential routes to freedom had vanished like wind in the night, the gravity hitting him so suddenly that he swayed and sat on his cot. He looked far beyond the stone walls of the dungeon as he answered her question in a whisper.

"Alastor had his reasons. So my sire was my savior?"

Vinya stepped closer to the bars. "Did you not hear of the King's death? *Yuwon* was your salvation. The rest of the palace called for your existence to cease. Immediately. But he granted you mercy because of your love for the only other person than yourself. Jun."

Hyosung's face turned sour.

Vinya went on. "Her suffering was obviously not a part of your schemes, a blind man could see as much."

Hyosung looked at the window, hiding his face from Vinya. She knew she was throwing knives at a downed man, someone who had lost everything except for his own life, but she went on.

"You are well aware that no one would have accepted her as your wife, if that was your intention. They would have overthrown you the moment you announced it to the world. What then? Claim the crown as your own? No one would have allowed a half-blooded tyrant to wear a crown."

Hyosung stilled. His hands curled into fists—tears glinted in the lantern light as he shook his head. "I wouldn't have made her my wife. You don't have to marry someone to show you love them, to care for them more than the air in your own lungs. She was so precious, the most beautiful soul. I would have protected her until our dying days."

His voice shook, and something cracked within her. He destroyed the royal family—the last thing Vinya wanted was to feel *sorry* for the man.

Hyosung wiped his face, still avoiding her eyes. "I assume I've been stripped of my title."

"Yes," Vinya replied.

"And my belongings?"

"Sold. The money divided to help the broken families of casualties."

Somber, he dropped his head. "It wasn't supposed to end this way."

"What did you expect? That Byonea wouldn't fight to keep their freedom? People would have died no matter what route you took in your rebellion."

"Not Jun. She was never supposed to get hurt. The plan was to take her to Calgham while the war waged on in Byonea. I would have retrieved her after Byonea surrendered and the dust had settled. The men went too far. Too far..." Hyosung rubbed at his chest. "When I went to the front with Yuwon, the men who took her weren't far from the tunnel's exit. Yes, I know of it. I used the cover of the storm to find them. It wasn't hard to get into the camp. The handful of warriors knew me, trusted me. But they hadn't believed the warning I gave when they first received the plans—no harm was to come to her. They told me what they did to her, that they...they..." A cry cut off his words.

Vinya couldn't breathe. She didn't want to rehash what those men had done to Jun, she didn't want to imagine.

He visibly shook now. "I slaughtered them. Moved so quickly they didn't see it coming, they were still so drunk in their own small *victory*."

He looked at her then. A brief softness flashed across his face, the way he would look at Jun. "When I came to her tent, it was empty—she was gone, and I had left no man alive to tell me what they did to her body."

It took Vinya a few moments to find her voice. "Her... body?"

Hyosung's chin quivered, running a shaking hand through his hair. "I should have checked the tent first—should have made sure she was okay, but they had been so *proud* of what they'd done to her—broken her—that they wouldn't let me past without boasting."

"Her *body*?" Vinya asked again.

"Stop it, Vinya," Hyosung interrupted, seething through clenched teeth. "Jun and I knew from a young age that she would be swept away to wed some foreign country, customarily rarely coming home afterwards. This palace is—was—her home. To be sent off to a country where she didn't know anyon e... I'm sure others assumed, but I was the only one who truly knew how much that frightened her. I made her a promise that I would take care of her."

His jaw worked, forcing his voice to remain steady. It cracked anyway. "We knew the time was near when she turned twenty. Her mother started searching for a suitor. We already had ties with Norhagan, so she searched beyond. Past Calgham. She saw Jun as nothing but a tool, a means to amass more riches. I would never be able to change the Queen's mind, so I had to change the system."

Vinya blinked. "You started the war to save her."

Hyosung's eyes were distant, not quite seeing the wall in front of him. "I would have done anything for her."

"It drove you down the path of insanity. You were willing to sacrifice your own family for her."

Hyosung's eyes snapped to Vinya. "You know *nothing* of sacrifice. You haven't a clue of what the Queen will do, who *she* will burn to keep her own life—her own world—safe."

"Your mother."

When the former Shade Prince grimaced, something snapped into place in Vinya's mind. The war wasn't only to save Jun from the Queen's webs—it was revenge.

"The Queen had nothing to do with the war, did she? She played no part in the King's death or Jun's capture? Did she not know of your or Alastor's schemes?" Vinya questioned.

Hyosung held her gaze, a shadow fell over his eyes. Somewhere deep down, Vinya knew she had unveiled a truth.

"And Yuwon?" she pressed.

He blew out a long breath. "A few Calgham scouts followed me back when I returned from my attempt to retrieve Jun. It was sooner than planned, but it would have happened anyway. Everyone scattered in the chaos. Yuwon saw that the Calgham men weren't fighting me—nor I them. I could see the wheels turning in his head, and I was the only one who could get close enough to him. I didn't know that when I drove my sword through him, I had missed all fatal points."

"I'm glad you missed." Vinya's voice was flat.

Hyosung huffed a laughed and motioned toward his wrapped arm and shoulder. "I won't be able to properly use this arm again thanks to *your* aim. Blood is on your hands as well."

"I'm unsure if I would have slept more peacefully had you died."

Hyosung tilted his head to the side, a hint of shock replacing the sorrow on his face. "You care?"

"Perhaps a little."

"Why?"

"You were strong-willed enough to reach for something that you wanted, brave enough to step forward and take it. I only wish you had used that power for the *good* of this country, even though it isn't yours to lead."

"Mm. For the country you are now leaving. Byonea shouldn't matter now that you're heading back to Norhagan," he scoffed.

Vinya turned the conversation, curiosity getting the better of her. "What of me? Would I have been put down with the rest of the family, knowing that I wasn't the actual *promised princess*? Why try to help me escape my first night here?"

Hyosung shrugged with his good shoulder. "A distraction. Byonea's eyes would have been looking for you. I would have found you one way or another after the war. I knew where your grandmother lived and just as easily could have found your home across the waters. Asper, am I correct? As King, having a Norhagan wife would have been beneficial for the trades to continue."

Vinya shook her head. It had all been a ploy to gain her trust—to get his foot in the door as the provider for Byonea after thoroughly destroying its royal family.

Looking back, she could see herself falling for him. He had stood up for her and tried to help her escape the first night, promising to visit her in Taejim. If the war had ended the way he'd hoped, she probably would have been hidden away—or captured and rescued along with Jun. Vinya knew her face reflected her thoughts, and a shiver snaked its way down her spine as Hyosung smiled, looking up at her through his brow.

He stood and rested his forehead on the cell door, his eyes level with her own. "You and I could have moved the mountains of *Calgham* together if we tried. It would have been a delight to have you as my wife, keeping me company night after night."

Vinya didn't take the bait, did not let him see just how badly his words made her skin crawl. She reached into her pocket, pulled out the item she'd brought and placed it on the crossbar of his cell door. Wood softly clicked against the cool metal.

It wasn't the carved hawk that made his eyes widen—that made him freeze as still as stone—it was the royal ring on Vinya's finger. Understanding flashed across his face and he backed away, his eyes not leaving the ring as it glinted in the small stream of light from the window.

"This is for you. A gift, from a friend. To keep you company night after night," she said—referring to the wooden hawk.

He rushed the cell door to grab at her hand, but Vinya stepped away—her gift clattering on the floor near her feet. As she did, she cleared Hyosung's line of vision, and his eyes landed on the woman who had been standing in the shadows behind Vinya the entire time.

Tears streaked down Jun's cheeks. She covered her mouth with both hands, horrified at the man before her.

With wide eyes and a slack jaw, Hyosung dropped to his knees. His brow pulled together and a fleeting, incredulous smile shot across his face.

"Jun?" he whispered.

He had not known—had not heard the whispers through the cell's window that the Princess had returned. He scanned her trembling body in search of any physical harm that may have befallen her.

He smacked his own face—taking a few deep breaths while staring at the cold stone beneath his knees, and he broke into sobs when his eyes met Jun's once more.

"You're truly here? You're *alive* and well? You... you..." Hyosung's joy faded when he noted Jun's movements, not to come to him—but to step further away. His gaze landed on Vinya, face twisting into hate as his breaths hitched. "*You tricked me*!" he spewed, gripping a bar to shake the cell door.

The pure and gentle Princess had not believed the tale Vinya had told—would not believe that the man she had known her entire life had turned his back on their family. Her soul was bright like the sun, radiating warmth. So Vinya brought her to the dungeon to learn the truth for herself—from the filth in the shadows.

Vinya ignored his rage and addressed the guards, wrapping an arm around the shaking Princess at her side. "We're ready to leave."

Hyosung stretched his arm through the bars, trying at first to reach the women, then pulled the wooden hawk toward him by his fingertips. He cradled it in his hand like it was worth a thousand pieces of gold. He lifted his chin, eyes lined with tears once more.

"Vinya, Jun, *please.*"

He begged. Just as she begged Zhan her first night in Byonea. For a moment, she pitied him. She truly wished she could help him. But unlike her, there was no returning from the trouble Hyosung caused for himself.

She turned, nodding to the guards that they really were leaving this time.

"No. No, no, *no, no, no*!" Hyosung's wails turned frantic. His voice began to break.

Each crack in his desolate cries etched itself into her memory. The wails of their names echoed down the frigid halls. With hurried steps and an aching heart, Vinya left the beautiful and broken bird in his cage—and knew the sound of his misery would haunt her forever.

31

A Crimson Sleeve

Jinhee slipped the singular skirt over Vinya's head and wrapped the crimson ribbon around her waist. Vinya brushed her fingers along the fabric. It was lined along the bottom with green and pink blossom buds. She refused to wear more than one layer of skirting, her lady-in-waiting gave no objection when Vinya made the announcement.

The canary sang happily from its cage on the display cabinet, surrounded by dozens upon dozens of gifts. Bolts of silk, newly crafted tea sets and tableware, and custom name seals—one for herself and one for Yuwon—were among the gifts. On top of the closest box sat Nutmeg. The cat kept a careful eye on the bird day and night.

Two months after Vinya left Norhagan, her parents made the trip across the ocean, leaving Alton and a few other neighbors in charge of the farm during their absence.

Yuwon had accompanied Vinya to pick them up at Byonea's harbor town. While Vinya and her mother hugged and cried, Vinya's father bent at the waist in a bow to Yuwon—which the King stopped with a handshake: the typical Norhagan greeting. He stumbled through an introduction with Vinya's mother in the Norhagan language before her mother took Yuwon into her arms like he was her own son. Formality had been thrown out the window, and they spent a week getting to know one another and sharing in great detail what had occurred over their time apart.

During that time, a short trip to Taejim had been made. Miho and Wen hosted Vinya's family as they gathered for an intimate ceremony to honor and remember Gran. Vinya's mother fawned over Miho's belly—which had begun to swell with child—while her father roamed the quaint home and yard. His steps were slow as his eyes followed the garden paths, across the stone bench, and up the limbs of a sprawling tree. He had returned to the home, wiping his nose on the back of his hand, right as the neighbors stopped by to greet the boy they watched grow up with deep-wrinkled smiles and hugs.

When the neighbors greeted Vinya and turned to Yuwon, the old woman's eyes flashed in recognition. She wagged a finger at him and laughed quietly to herself. "I knew you would come back with her," she said, patting Yuwon on the arm.

Now, the canary fluttered to the opposite side of the cage when Nutmeg swatted at it. Her father had been adamant about bringing the ginger cat to the Palace. He said it was to keep her company, but Vinya knew he didn't want the animal curling up on his bed every night.

Vinya shook her head and went to move the cat against Jinhee's wishes.

"You'll get fur all over your new robe!" the older woman said, sucking air in through her teeth.

Vinya sat Nutmeg on the ground and laughed, holding out her arms for her lady-in-waiting to search for ginger fur.

Jinhee clicked her tongue and pulled off a few hairs. She stood back and assessed her work, her lips pursing into a strained line. The older woman was holding back tears.

"You're beautiful. You always have been, but today—I can't even find the right words," she said as she dabbed her eyes with a handkerchief.

"Ravishing!" a warm voice called from the door.

The women turned to Woobin, who spun in a circle to show off his midnight blue robes.

The war had ended with Byonea as the victor with the help of Haryn, and Calgham was pushed back into their own territory. The sights and sounds of war did not take their toll on the man. He'd made it back to the Palace on the full moon, proclaiming the pavilion's transformation *brilliant*, and had danced the night away—breathing life back into them all.

Woobin sauntered into the room and swooped into a dramatic bow to Vinya, exactly how he bowed the first time they met. The fine jewelry in his ears clinked against one another with the movement. Woobin rose and closed the distance between them, spreading his arms wide.

"I figured I'd borrow Yuwon's robes until another heir came along."

He gave a playful poke to Vinya's stomach, and she swatted his hand away.

"There is a lot of time for that later, Woobin."

He sighed and scrunched up one side of his nose in disappointment. Vinya couldn't tell if it was genuine or feigned.

"I guess I'll still give you this."

Woobin waved a hand behind him, and a man came in holding a crimson pillow. On top of the pillow sat a circlet; delicate blossoms and buds sat amongst leaves—the gold shining in the sunlight that streamed through the pavilion's windows. A golden ring, identical to the silver one she had been given by the Queen, rested in the center of the pillow. Vinya rubbed a nervous thumb along Gran's ring on her right hand.

Woobin lifted the circlet off the pillow and turned to Vinya, dropping his eyes briefly to the ground at her feet.

Vinya huffed a laugh and knelt.

The air in the room shifted. Not only from the Crown Prince hovering above her, but the gravity of the moment. The royals of Byonea were not crowned by any of the Sixty Officials in front of a crowd, but by a loved one in private; witnessed by the head Official of Rites. The man watched from the door of the pavilion with his hands folded neatly in front of him.

Vinya fidgeted with the hem of her robe as Woobin placed the circlet on her head, securing it in place with small pins that Jinhee passed to him. Physically, the circlet was light, but the weight of what it stood for would be a daily reminder of her new life. Who she chose to be, and who she would promise to protect. When Vinya stood, both hers and Woobin's eyes glistened.

Woobin rested his hands on either side of her face.

"I'm so happy you're here," he whispered.

Vinya covered his hands with her own. "I wouldn't dream of ever leaving."

A sniffle came from the spare bedroom in the pavilion where Vinya's parents stood.

Her mother crossed the room and pulled Vinya into her arms. Her father scratched the scruff on his chin and held out an arm for her.

"Everyone needs to stop crying," Vinya said as she placed the new royal ring on her finger and looped an arm through her father's arm.

Her father threw his head back with a booming laugh, lightening the mood in the room. With renewed smiles on their faces, Vinya and her father led everyone out of the pavilion. Her mother, Woobin, Jinhee, the guards, and the head Official of Rites followed close behind. Over the bridge. Through the gardens. Her entourage slipped through the back of the throne room and climbed the crimson painted stairs to the room high above.

Vinya stifled her laughter when Woobin gathered his robes to climb the stairs—he hadn't gotten them resized to fit himself instead of Yuwon's tall frame. But the Crown Prince Woobin was quick to shove the sleeves back over his hands—covering the dark pink scars that lined his knuckles from the horrible, thunderous night weeks ago. He would likely have those scars forever.

She absently rubbed her fingers over her own scar. Unlike Woobin's, the white crescent-shaped scar on her own palm would continue to fade, one day disappearing completely. Vinya smirked to herself; the scar would leave just as the person who caused the scar had vanished. After hearing that Daeya—by his mother's orders—had been the one to steal Sooni's urn and ashes, Yuwon banished her from the Palace, barring the concubine from entering for the rest of her life.

Daeya's blind obedience as a Queen's woman was her own demise, and Vinya was thankful she would never have to lay eyes on the venomous woman ever again.

A group of women clad in black stood near the top of the stairs, dipping and raising their heads in a quick bow when Vinya and her entourage crested the landing. Much like the pink and jade tassels hanging from their swords, each one of them stood tall—a sharpness behind their eyes that Vinya believed could have only come from Zhan's personal training. Jun's women had come a long way, and continued to grow in their talents every day.

Jun emerged from their midst to hug Vinya, brushing a soft kiss on her sister's cheek. Her high cheekbones filled as she squeezed Vinya's arms, and she led her women to the far side of the room.

The women split, revealing large double doors that led to a balcony and the two men who stood before it. Zhan's jaw slackened for a fraction of a moment before his dimples pressed in. Without taking his eyes off of Vinya, Zhan tapped Yuwon's arm with the back of his hand to get his friend's attention.

Yuwon turned to her, his regal demeanor crumbling as the breath whooshed from his lungs. He dropped his face into his hands—shoulders shaking.

Vinya pulled his hands away from his face, lifting onto her toes to plant a kiss on his cheek—the weight of the traditional many-layered skirts now gone. She reached higher to straighten his golden crown. Fans of delicate leaves rose and fell across its circumference.

"Together," she said. Her eternal promise.

They waited for this moment. Waited for her parents to arrive in Byonea, so that they could support their daughter's decision in person.

Her path. Her home.

Yuwon composed himself with deep breaths. He twisted to stand at Vinya's side and nodded to Zhan when he was ready.

Two guards opened the double doors before them, and the roars of the crowd beyond streamed through—the cries of thousands upon thousands of civilians. She brushed his hand with her own, a comforting motion. With a wave of Zhan's hand, Yuwon and Vinya stepped into the sun.

The crowd stretched beyond Vinya's sight. Young and old, peasants and nobles, all cheering under the new colorful banners and flags decorating the Palace. Bright colors adorned every post, every doorway and windowsill, every robe, every pinwheel held by children. Fresh colors for a new beginning for this country.

They stepped to the balcony's railing, and the cheers increased. Courtyard after courtyard, the people of Byonea clapped and cried out their praises. For them. They cheered for them—all they represented, all they would bring to this beautiful country.

Many things had changed in Byonea over the last month. Princess Jun made sure that adequate food was being distributed to the poor—Jun's Basket, the people called it. Women were being treated more than just objects. Servants were paid fair wages and were no longer owned by the Crown, free to seek higher educations or leave the Palace altogether to start their own lives or families. The man who found Vinya's mother's letter and the Norhagan account's true page had been appointed as the new head adviser.

Yuwon and Vinya bowed at the waist, the one and only time they would do so to their people. A promise to fulfill all that was expected of them—to serve this country with humility and honor. A vow to lead them with fair hearts, minds, and hands.

When they rose, the crowd bowed in return, accepting their leadership. A promise to follow, to respect, and to serve with a loving heart for years to come.

She turned to Yuwon, who smiled brightly at the crowd, his thumb picking at the wooden rail. The man was still nervous in front of crowds—he always would be—and his crimson robes only enhanced his flushed cheeks.

Yuwon met her eyes, then dropped to her fingers that fidgeted with the hem of her robe. His smile softened, and he took her hand. Tears pooled in his eyes yet again, threatening to spill over. He cried with joy—with pride.

They would make the land prosperous once more, unite their countries, and would conquer any army that dared to rear its head against them. Together.

He, the new King of Byonea.

And she, the green-eyed Queen.

EPILOGUE

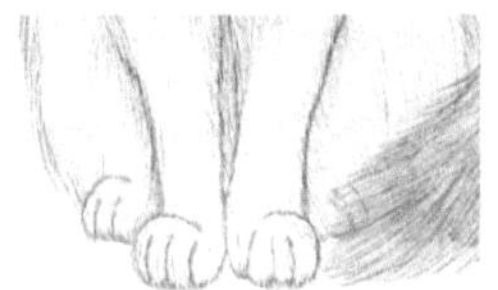

A decade had passed in Byonea since Calgham's attack, and not a whisper had come from the country to their east.

The Dowager Queen—stripped of her power and of her flock of women—gave Vinya a hard time for three years until their son Yoonjae was born. Then a second son, Jihoon, four years after that. The Dowager Queen quickly turned her scheming into doting on the boys. Woobin suggested that her age and slowly declining health played a part in her change of attitude.

Miho and her husband Wen had reconciled with her father, the Crown Prince of Norhagan, and her excommunication rescinded upon hearing what Wen had done for Byonea—though her inheritance would be skipped entirely. Miho and Wen's nine-year-old son would take her place in line for the throne. The women often tossed around the idea of arranging Miho's three-year-old daughter with one of Vinya's sons, which was always met with the pinching of noses and weary shakes of their husbands' heads, who had become close friends.

The annual trip to visit her family quickly became Vinya's favorite time of year—a break from the royal duties in Byonea. During the first trip, though, Zhan learned that he and his stomach did not do well at sea and spent the entire month dreading the voyage home. Woobin laughed upon hearing the news, claiming he didn't want Zhan to leave, anyway. From then on, Zhan was content to stay by Woobin's side in the Palace—even if it meant suffering through Woobin's full-moon antics alone.

The sun crested the trees in Asper, Norhagan. Sheep and cattle were scattered over a distant hill, grazing as the morning birds fluttered about.

Vinya's mother wrapped an arm around her waist as they watched Yuwon and Vinya's father play with the lively seven-year-old Yoonjae across a field, a wooden sword in each hand. The poor boy had been cooped up in the ship's cabin for three days, then the carriage ride for a couple of hours, so he desperately needed to release his pent-up energy. At least once a week, Jinhee made mention that the Palace walls weren't for safety, but to keep the rambunctious child contained—as the boy often tried to scale the walls.

The spring breeze wound around the women, carrying fresh floral scents across the farm. Three-year-old Jihoon sat on the grass not far from their feet, satisfied with petting the ancient and cranky Nutmeg curled in his lap. Jihoon took after his father, quiet and calm. He refused to leave his companion behind in Byonea, so year after year, the cat reluctantly climbed into a crate to be hauled across the waters.

With Vinya's absence, Alton moved onto the farm, building his own room in the barn's loft. The man still made mistakes, but Vinya was thankful that he was helping her parents.

Alton approached from the other side of the fence, having finished the morning chores that had kept him from greeting them upon their arrival. He rested his forearms on the fence between them and nodded at the bundle Vinya held. "What is this one's name?"

Vinya smiled down at the sleeping babe in her arms.

"Sooni."

THE EMERALD KING

What if the hero became the villain?
One flip of a coin, one simple choice can change everything.
In *The Emerald King*, return to Byonea... but now, Vinya isn't the promised princess that could rescue the kingdom. Instead, she's a weapon aimed at its heart. A spy. A betrayer. One sent with a match to burn it from within.
Same woman. Same princes. Same secrets lurking in the palace shadows.
Only this time, fate's string has snapped, and Vinya refuses to be pulled along by destiny's design.
Every alliance is a lie. Every truth is a weapon.

An alternative timeline to *The Green-Eyed Queen*
Coming 2026

ACKNOWLEDGEMENTS

I must give credit where credit is due.

To my alpha reader, Taylor Fancher: This book wouldn't be what it is today without you. You spent your precious time reading the *incredibly* rough draft, and I truly believe you'll be blessed for trudging through that mess! I will treasure the original manuscript with your notes and drawings for all eternity. Thank you for allowing me to bounce ideas off you, and an even bigger thanks for inadvertently giving me the best idea (sorry not sorry about Sooni's death).

To my beta readers, specifically Danny Raye, Taylor Voynova, and Noémi Russell: Every single question, comment, and bit of feedback on the book helped shape and round out the story. Thank you for pushing me to expand or drop specific sentences/scenes, and for reassuring me that the story is worth sharing. The vulnerability of handing over my manuscript was great, but y'all handled my firstborn-book-child with such care!

To my editor, Tanya Bosarge: Look, Ma, I did it! You may have seen a handful of grammatical errors on this page, but that is the exact reason my manuscript was placed in your hands. I greatly appreciate the hours you spent skimming over the book with a fine-tooth comb. With your help, my skills will (hopefully) improve with every book. Less work for you, yay!

To my friends and family: Your encouragement and support of this venture has not gone unseen, and has been my greatest motivation. You are the gas to my creative engine, the legs to the chair on which I sit, the caffeine inside my coffee. Your excitement spurred me on to finish and publish. Without y'all, I wouldn't have the courage to share my stories with the world.

To my sons: I know I say you aren't old enough to read the book right now, but one day you will. I sat for countless hours in front of my computer writing this book over the past year, and the patience and understanding you boys showed is beyond amazing. Thank you. You are my two favorite people in the entire world... love you love you!

The tools used to create this book: I am immensely thankful for Scrivener, Word, and Google Docs. Your programs and apps aided my writing and gave me the tools to share it with others. Atticus, thank you for making formatting so dang easy! And to the creators of Affinity Designer, thank you for having the tools available to people like me—to create my cover art. To my personal printer, I'm sorry for shoving so much paper through you, but you did your job well.

To my cat, Walnut: Why the heck is my desktop your favorite place to lay? You were a constant, silent companion as I wrote, and were the inspiration for Vinya's cat, Nutmeg. You obviously can't read this, so I'll have to thank you in the form of lovies, cuddles, and catnip.

Last but certainly not least, to my readers: This hermit of an author cannot express her gratitude enough. You read my debut novel, and now you're reading the acknowledgements? I'm deeply honored. I hope this book transported you into another universe where your heart was both shattered and healed. Your support means the world to me, and I aspire to satisfy your reading needs in the future—whether it be fiction or fantasy.

ABOUT THE AUTHOR

Morgan lives in Mobile, AL with her two children and three cats. She has been writing for the past 17 years, but has had her head in books for even longer. When she's not writing or reading, she's drawing or illustrating—or is elbow deep in crafts. She hopes to travel the world one day, with the ultimate goal of visiting South Korea when the cherry blossoms are blooming. For now, she's content exploring distant lands through her stories, one page (and one cat nap interruption) at a time.

www.ingramcontent.com/pod-product-compliance
Lightning Source LLC
Chambersburg PA
CBHW020930310726
48980CB00007B/705/J
* 9 7 9 8 9 9 3 8 1 1 2 1 5 *